Forevermore

A KWENTITAS ROMANCE ANTHOLOGY

AURORA PAIGE   ELLE CRUZ

JUNE GRAY   KAYE ROCKWELL

LIZ DURANO   MAAN GABRIEL

MAIDA MALBY   MIA HOPKINS

SARAH SMITH   TIF MARCELO

EOT Publications

Copyright

FOREVERMORE, A Kwentitas Romance Anthology

ISBN: 978-0-9995432-5-2

10 9 8 7 6 5 4 3 2

Foreword

Dear Readers,

Thank you so much for purchasing our anthology. We hope you enjoy our stories celebrating Filipino American heritage, history, and joy as much as we had fun writing them.

All the stories have an introductory page containing the story title, the author's name, a short summary, and the following:

Content Notes – Notice of any potentially sensitive content which may be distressing—to anyone, particularly those with related experiences—and/or triggering to those with PTSD or similar mental health conditions.

Tropes and Sub-genres – Romance categories and themes.

Heat Levels out of 🔥 🔥 🔥 🔥 🔥

🔥 - kiss only

🔥 🔥 - closed door (sex is implied)

🔥 🔥 🔥 - open door (euphemistic description)

◊ ◊ ◊ ◊ - explicit description

◊ ◊ ◊ ◊ ◊ - erotic (multiple partners, alternative lifestyles)

Happy reading and, we hope, happy reviewing too.

~ Kwentitas

Table of Contents

Copyright 3

Foreword 4

Table of Contents 7

Moonlight Serenade 9

The Memory of You 67

Maybe This Time 119

Someone's Always Saying Goodbye.................................173

Moments In The Vineyard.................................227

Double Exposure.................................289

Stay With Me 351

The Stand-In.................................413

Win Your Love.................................455

Now That I Have You.................................505

Acknowledgments.................................563

Moonlight Serenade

MIA HOPKINS

Moonlight Serenade

MIA HOPKINS

Blurb:

After surviving the war, Natividad Moore, her husband Robert and their three young children move from the Philippines to Robert's family home in Napa, California. There, instead of a peaceful refuge, they discover isolation, a failing vineyard and Robert's cold, disapproving mother. In the face of these obstacles, Naty yearns to reconnect with Robert. But has the war changed him, and their love, forever?

Content Notes: Mentions of wartime violence, Post-traumatic stress disorder

Tropes and Sub genres: Opposites attract, fish out of water, marriage in trouble; Historical Romance, Multicultural Romance

Heat Level: 🌢 🌢 🌢 🌢 (Explicit sex)

Prologue

Present

Sitting in her wheelchair near the dance floor, Naty Moore watched the newlyweds. Bathed in golden light and looking into each other's eyes, Rafa and Vida waltzed together surrounded by friends and family, young and old.

So many people. Naty knew them. Most of them, anyway—but what were their names? A blur of descendants, gathered here for another joyful wedding.

Naty had watched this dance many times before. She'd danced it once herself, years and years ago. Heavy rain had poured down on her wedding day, but she'd been so deeply in love, the sky itself could have fallen and she wouldn't have noticed.

Oh, how her granddaughter glowed tonight. What a lovely bride.

Rafa and Vida's dance ended in cheers and applause. Naty smiled to herself and said softly, "You were right, Robert. You were right. Everything is okay."

Chapter One

1945

Natividad Soriano Moore longed for rain.

For a darkening sky. For a flash of lightning, for that rolling grumble of thunder over bright green hills. For the percussive tapping of drops on her old red payong, soft and familiar.

Back home, the rainy season ruled over all. Whoever was in charge—Spanish, Americans, Japanese, the bayonet, the rifle, the sword—everyone had to bow to the mighty rainy season. Floods, landslides, typhoons—the smell of home rose in her memory, the scent of fertile soil soaked and salted with tears.

But here in Napa, Robert told her no rain would fall for months. The July heat felt dry and raw on her skin. Bouncing along the dirt road, the big Mercury Eight kicked up giant clouds of fine dust over endless rows of grapevines.

Robert sat up front with the driver his mother had sent to pick them up at the train station. Next to Naty in the back seat, the children chattered and squirmed. Naty had tried her best to make them presentable to meet their grandmother, but their clothes were wrinkled and Luz's hair was already a mess. Naty's hair was black and glossy. Luz's hair was black too, but it was coarse like her father's, and Naty had no idea how to tame it. Wind from the open car windows had blown it into a wild mane.

Smack!

Francisco hit his brother on the side of the head.

"Ouch!" said Armando. *Ouch*, not *aray*.

"Stop that now," Naty said sternly in Tagalog.

The boys stared at her blankly.

Naty frowned. Did they even remember the language? They settled down, but when she turned to look out the window again, the three of them giggled behind her back.

"Behave yourselves," their father said absently from the front seat, and they fell silent.

Back in the Philippines, Robert had registered for the draft but had not yet been called to serve. When fighting broke out, he had been interviewing for an English teaching job in the capitol. Manila fell swiftly and decisively. Japanese sentries closed the roads. Escaping ships were sunk in the harbor. Robert and other "civilian enemies" stranded in the city were rounded up and sent to Santo Tomas University, which had been hastily turned into an internment camp. Robert lived there, starved and ill, for the duration of the war.

Afraid she wouldn't be able to protect them alone, Naty sent their three small children to live with an elderly American couple at their summer home in the mountains. The Williamses, retired artists, had been friends of Robert's and assured her they were too remote and too old to be of any interest to the Japanese. Praying they were right, Naty remained with her parents and brothers in her hometown. Separated from her babies and her husband, Naty lived in an extended state of fear and hope. Months of agony turned into years.

By the grace of God, she, Robert and the children had survived, unlike so many others.

Stop. Don't think about that right now.

Now Naty felt guilty about her frustration. Her kids—who had been so affectionate and close to her before the war—didn't listen to her now, and they were shy with their father, who himself had become quiet and withdrawn. The children's English was strong, which would help them here in their new home in California. But their Tagalog was shaky from disuse, and the Williamses, though kind and generous, had let her children run loose. The kids were unrecognizable. Rude and loud and demanding. Robert's mother would think poorly of her as a parent.

Naty suppressed the urge to sigh. At the moment, nothing could be done.

Silently, she took a carefully pressed panyo out of her purse and dabbed the sweat at her temples.

"There it is," Robert said.

The car crested a hill, and they saw, at the end of the road, a tall Spanish colonial-style house, regal in the middle of the vineyard. Behind it stood some outbuildings, a few cottages, a barn, a carriage house, and the large winery itself, built of yellowish stone. Hot air shimmered over the red roof tiles.

"That is the hacienda." Robert turned to the kids. There were dark circles under his eyes. "My grandfather—your great-grandfather—planted these grapes and built these buildings. He sailed on a ship from Ireland, took a wagon across the country, and made his home here in California."

As they approached, Naty squinted. From afar, the house had looked as gracious as a picture postcard. Up close, however, there was no hiding its disrepair: flaked paint, crumbling plaster and sagging, sun-bleached wood. A carved stone fountain stood in front of the house, but instead of clear water, it was filled with sand and choked with devilish-looking weeds.

The driver took them up the curved and pitted driveway. When he opened the car door, the kids tumbled out. When Naty exited, a sudden blast of hot wind licked the sweat from her skin.

By the front door stood a tall, red-cheeked woman. She wore a seersucker pinafore and navy-blue sandals with high heels. Her hair—red as Robert's—was styled in neat waves and shone like a new American penny. Naty guessed she and this woman were around the same age, about twenty-five.

"Robbie," she said in a soft voice. Tears welled in her eyes.

"Sylvia." Robert gave a tentative smile and allowed the woman to embrace him. But Naty noticed he did not embrace her back, keeping his arms at his sides.

"Sylvia," he said stiffly, "meet my wife, Natividad. Naty, this is my younger sister."

Naty adjusted her gloves and shook Sylvia's hand. Robert's sister's warm expression was bright and sincere. "I'm so pleased to finally meet you all. What a beautiful family. Please, come inside where it's cooler."

On their best behavior, the kids walked into the old house, following their father and aunt. The curtains were drawn, and the interior of the house was dark and still. Polished wood furniture, old and expensive looking, populated the entry hall and the morning room where Sylvia led them now. The house, though showing its wear, was clean and smelled faintly of incense, like a church.

They sat on upholstered couches, and a white-haired Irish housemaid in a pressed uniform served them tea and sandwiches. The housemaid, whose name was Fiona, greeted Robert but eyed Naty and the kids with cold indifference. Naty adjusted her gloves again. Her cracked and peeling hands were still recovering from her work as a washerwoman during the last months of the war. Every day, she had washed kilos of dirty laundry and passed messages to Filipino guerrillas and American soldiers. What would this white woman think about that?

"Mommy, may I have another cookie?" Armando asked quietly.

"Of course." Naty patted her youngest son's head and placed a cookie on his china plate.

Robert and his sister chatted, shy from their many years apart. Naty focused her attention back on their conversation. Sylvia talked about her life in San Francisco with her husband, an attorney who practiced international law. Exempt from the draft, he had contracted polio as a child and used a cane to walk. Sylvia talked about their older brother, a member of the Seventh Infantry who had died in Leyte a year ago, and their father, who had died shortly thereafter.

They fell silent for a moment. Even the children seemed to hold their breath. The only sound was the ticking of the grandfather clock, loud and resonant.

Robert lowered his voice. "How is she?"

"As expected," Sylvia said. "I keep telling her she needs to come live with us. This big house, the vineyard, it's no place for her. And her heart—she needs more care than she's receiving here. There are specialists in San Francisco. We can get her all the appointments she needs. But she's made up her mind. It's no use."

"Will we see her today?"

Sylvia looked at him sideways. "What do you think?"

Robert said nothing. Naty sensed his pain. She longed to take his hand and reassure him, to feel the sweet connection they had once shared. But he wouldn't like that. He wouldn't like that at all.

When their food was finished, Sylvia stood. "Fiona will show you to your rooms. Have a rest. We'll have supper together tonight."

***

Naty finished her toilette, put on her cotton nightdress and climbed into bed next to Robert. Their room was too big, too luxurious. The too-soft pillows smelled of sagebrush and unfamiliar flowers.

Before she turned off the lamp, she studied her husband. The war had been hard on him. He'd lost fifteen kilograms, maybe more. The broad, healthy man she'd married was now rangy and scarred. A brutal bout of enteritis in the internment camp had whittled him down to sinews. His pajamas hung loose on him, making him look old and bent.

"My love," she whispered.

They were here in California, safe at last. This had once been a faraway dream.

Should she try again?

Under the bedsheet, Naty slowly reached for Robert's hand. For the first time in a long time, he let her. He closed his leaf-green eyes and drew a deep breath, as if pained. His chest rose and fell, ragged at first, then slow and steady as the seconds ticked by.

Naty's fingers tingled in his. Her body began to warm, melting at last like candle wax. She missed him. She missed what they used to do together at night. Before the war they couldn't get enough of each other, as if they were a fire that fed itself, endlessly hungry, endlessly lit. Intimacy had been a comfort to them both. In this strange place, far from a home that no longer existed, could it be again?

A gust of wind, hot and dry as tinder, blew in through the open window, stirring the valances. And just like that, the spell was broken.

Robert dropped her hand and stood up. "We need to close this window," he muttered.

"What?" Naty blinked. "Why?"

Almost angrily, he yanked the window closed and secured the old brass latches. "I need to check the rest of the house," he said.

"But why?"

He ignored her.

Perplexed, Naty sat alone in the giant bed as Robert left the room. In the dark she listened as he walked from room to room, closing and locking each window, checking and rechecking each door. *Latch. Click.*

As if Imperial soldiers had followed them here, over the ocean. Robert would not let them in—he wouldn't let anyone in.

Latch. Click.

Latch. Click.

Chapter Two

Of course, things weren't always this way.

Naty was the fourth of six children and the only daughter. Her family were innkeepers in a busy town north of Manila known for its growing business district. She'd grown up working in the inn, eventually handling her father's books and accounts. She loved people, music, dancing—anything fun, modern and lively.

She had a special facility for languages and could converse with visitors from all over the world. But she had no patience for school, and likewise, her teachers had no patience for her, much to her parents' disappointment. Her father in particular held college education in high esteem. He dreamed of enrolling her in one of the women's colleges in Manila and was sorry she did not share his enthusiasm.

In her town, the small number of wealthy landowners and gentry had been growing. Increased business with Americans had raised the demand for English teachers and private tutors.

Robert, disinterested in his own family's wine business, had recently graduated from Stanford in faraway California. A mentor of his, a professor and Thomasite who had come to the Philippines to set up American-style schools, recommended him to the wealthiest families in town, who promptly hired Robert to tutor their sons and daughters.

Upon his arrival in the Philippines, Robert stayed at Naty's family's guesthouse and proceeded to charm her father with his gentle, scholarly disposition. He charmed her mother with his politeness, and he charmed—annoyingly—all five of her brothers by simply attending a party as their guest, a giant red-headed American who spoke rudimentary Tagalog. Robert didn't seem to mind playing the clown. What a gas. Naty rolled her eyes. He was an instant hit.

He was definitely not a hit with her.

Why not? Where to begin?

First of all, he couldn't dance. She hadn't expected him to know the lindy hop or the jitterbug, but even the waltz and the rumba were far beyond his ability. There was only so much she could do to make him look good on the dance floor. Frustrated, she let him lead her to the punch bowl where she could more easily disentangle herself from him and hopefully save her poor smashed toes.

"Can you even do the hokey pokey?" she teased.

"What's that?" he asked, handing her a glass so gracelessly that a drop of it splashed on the lapel of her red party dress.

Even worse, her family insisted on playing matchmaker. They were enamored with him. Naty had always been an odd duck, not particularly beautiful, much too talkative and outspoken. The boys in town were as intimidated by her as she was unimpressed by them, but of course, rejection never felt good. She was eighteen and often doubted whether reality would ever meet her expectations for a romantic life. Naty preferred fantasizing about Filipino film stars, debonair and dapper, sharp dressers with dark, intelligent eyes and smooth moves. That her family thought the best she could do was this galumphing foreigner made Naty favor Robert even less.

One afternoon, she happened upon him sitting cross-legged on the patio on the ground floor of the guesthouse. He was dressed in linen trousers and a light green short-sleeved cotton shirt. His bare feet looked enormous on the blue azulejos. He was reading, bent over his own lap, poring over some old book from the guesthouse library.

Always outspoken, she said in English, "You look like a turtle."

Always gracious, he replied, "Thank you." He furrowed his brow and was quiet for a moment before his eyes lit up. He pointed at her and smiled. "Pagong."

Naty knew how to say turtle in seven languages. Playfully, she strode over to him and patted his red head like he was a toddler. "Good boy."

Before she could withdraw her hand, he reached up and grabbed her wrist. She jumped back in surprise but he held her, gently and firmly, and his sudden touch electrified her like a live wire.

Not letting go, he looked straight into her eyes, piercing her armor. His verdant irises matched the leaves of the bright green mango tree behind him, illuminated by the afternoon sunlight and trembling in the breeze.

"I like it when you call me a 'good boy,' Natividad," he whispered in perfect Tagalog.

Every nerve in her body sparked. Speechless, she watched as he lifted her hand and kissed the inside of her wrist. Then he smirked and let her go. She almost fell backward.

Stunned, she backed away from him and retreated into the house, unsettled by the way he'd taken control of her attention so quickly and thoroughly.

The notes began soon after that.

She found them everywhere: under her door, under her dinner plate, in her hat, in her shoes. Her brothers would pass them to her with a wink and a grin.

In the beginning, the messages were formal and flowery, leaving a too-sweet taste in her mouth. Over time, Robert began to understand who she was and what she loved. He mentioned he liked how she interacted with people at the hotel, treating everyone with the same kind courtesy whether they were a wealthy bigwig or the ragged son of the vegetable seller. He told her he admired how she treated her parents and brothers. He admitted he adored her laugh. And he said he loved to watch her dance even though he couldn't participate—observing her from afar, he felt the same thrill as being in her arms.

"Will you please teach me to dance?" he wrote.

"I'm not a miracle worker," she wrote back.

"You are miraculous to me, darling."

Every letter he signed not with his name but with a tiny drawing of a turtle.

And Naty began to feel—if not love—at least, a growing curiosity about what made this other odd duck tick.

On Sunday evenings after dinner, her parents allowed her to take a walk with Robert in the plaza. All of her brothers, five disinterested chaperones, lingered nearby, sneaking cigarettes or fighting over pulp magazines.

As she and Robert chatted and strolled, Naty often caught the disapproving glares of Filipinos and Americans alike. Not everyone was as accepting as her family, who were used to the company of people from around the world. She never thought too hard about the bad blood between the two nations. What did any of that have to do with her?

"Does it bother you when they look at us like that?" Robert asked.

She shook her head. "No. I don't care what they think. Do you?"

He held her hand in the crook of his arm. He wore short sleeves in the heat. The thrill of her hand on his bare skin made her lightheaded. He was warm, strong and solid, and he smelled so good—some kind of American shaving soap, clean and powdery. Up close, he overloaded her senses.

"I don't care what they think either," he said, "but I fear some of them don't know how to keep their biases to themselves."

At the time, Naty was too young and too intoxicated by Robert to fully understand what he was saying.

Under the mango tree, she taught him to dance. One afternoon, they dragged her mother's Victrola to the railing of the open ventanilla and paid her youngest brother in sticks of Wrigley gum to flip the records for them.

"Okay, my little turtle," Naty said, putting Robert's hands on the right places on her body as they grinned at each other like fools, "pay attention and you might learn something."

"Is it the hokey pokey?" he asked.

"Be serious."

Dappled sunlight migrated across the yard as Naty slowly taught him to waltz.

"Stop looking at your feet," she snapped, laughing. "Stop counting out loud! Count inside your head. You can do this, college boy."

When he could do a passable waltz, she taught him a slow foxtrot. By the time he'd mastered those steps, they'd been holding each other for three hours straight, and her brother had long forgone his gum, leaving them to dance without any music at all. The sunset had left traces of pink on the horizon. The moon made its early evening appearance, faint and low in the sky.

"I think you're ready," she said.

"Ready for what?" His voice was a soft rumble against her ear, like distant thunder.

Smiling, she stepped out of his arms. "Wait here."

Inside the house, she ran up the stairs two at a time. She put her favorite record on the Victrola, wound it up and dashed downstairs as the music began to play.

Outside, she ran into Robert's arms. He caught her and held her tightly. For one breathless second, she felt his heart beat hard against her chest.

"Let's dance," he whispered in Tagalog.

Glenn Miller's "Moonlight Serenade" filled the warm air along with the chirp and croak of the garden's usual nighttime suspects. With a steady confidence, Robert led her through the steps he had learned only a few minutes before. To her surprise, they fell into the steady rhythm of longtime dance partners while the sweet melody fell on them from above, just like moonlight.

And just like that, he was kissing her, and she was kissing him back, wide-eyed with wonder, her entire body on fire.

He pulled away gently and whispered against her lips, "Close your eyes, Naty."

"What?"

"Traditionally"—he smirked—"we close our eyes."

This was her first kiss. She didn't want to miss it. "No. Not me."

He shrugged. "Suit yourself."

They kissed until long after the music ended. They kissed until the moon had risen high over their tree. They kissed until, from far away, they heard Naty's brothers calling them inside the house for dinner, yoo-hooing and cackling from the open window like noisy pipit.

***

Robert and Naty were married three months later. Thrilled that their odd duck had found her turtle, her parents spared no expense. Even though a powerful rainstorm buffeted the cathedral, everyone in town seemed to be in attendance. The bells in the tower rang for her and her husband, handsome in his new barong Tagalog embroidered with green leaves to match his ridiculous eyes.

At their banquet, they danced to "Moonlight Serenade" and Robert got to show off his freshly acquired dance moves. Naty was a good teacher, after all. And later that night, while rain fell in heavy sheets outside their bedroom window, Robert showed her what a good teacher he could be too.

Crushed under his big body, panting and drenched and thoroughly loved, Naty caught a lightning bolt and rode it back to earth.

When she could breathe again, she whispered, "What was that?"

He propped himself up on one arm. She ran her fingers through his coarse red hair and traced his eyebrows and jaw line. With the tip of one finger, she gently stroked the ends of his long eyelashes.

"I'm not sure," he replied, "but I don't think it was the hokey pokey."

Chapter Three

Three days passed. Robert and Naty heard nothing from his mother.

Agnes Moore lived—presumably—somewhere in this gigantic house, but she hadn't made a sound or given any indication that she wanted to see them.

Sylvia, who was staying in a small cottage behind the main house, told them her mother had become extremely reclusive since her father had passed. Sylvia got almost all of her information from the household staff, who, on the sly, also kept her apprised of her mother's fragile health.

Naty had grown up in a tumble of noisy brothers, extended family and an endless parade of hotel guests. To her, the Moores didn't live in the hacienda—they haunted it.

"I don't understand," she said at breakfast after the children had run off to play. "She hasn't seen you in—what, ten years? You were separated by an ocean and a war. And now you're here. Why won't she see you?"

"Twelve," Robert said from behind his newspaper.

"What?" Naty asked.

Sylvia put down her coffee cup. "It's been twelve years since Mother has seen Robert. All the correspondence we sent to the Philippines was from Father or me."

"Or Ned," Robert said softly.

The siblings let the name hang in the air. They said nothing more.

Naty looked between them, Robert behind his wall of headlines and Sylvia, staring silently up at the rafters. Did emotions have such a costive effect on all Americans, or just this family?

Holding her tongue, Naty left the room and joined her children. Steering clear of their grandmother's wing of the house, Francisco and Armando set up a clever scavenger hunt for her and Luz. Checking off a list of knickknacks, spooky images in old paintings and various oddities like a tarnished gold pan in the livery stable and an unfortunate taxidermy quail in the library, Naty wondered at the enormity of the hacienda. Dozens of rooms seemed completely unused, holding only beautiful old furniture swathed in dust cloths. A mirrored ballroom, complete with crystal chandeliers, inspired a longing in Naty for fancy gowns and champagne. Playfully, she danced a swing with Luz across the ocean of parquetry, their laughter echoing against gilded ceilings.

What was Robert's grandfather thinking when he built this palace out in the middle of nowhere? What was he trying to prove?

Before bedtime and Robert's nightly window-locking foray through the halls, Fiona the housemaid delivered a note on a salver. Robert looked at it briefly and threw it in the wastebasket.

"Mother will see us tomorrow," he said flatly. Then he turned off the lamp and without another word, left Naty alone in the bedroom again.

***

Right after their wedding, Robert and Naty moved into a small house in the flower garden behind her family's main guesthouse. Each evening, Robert raced home from work. Then he and Naty proceeded to shake the foundations of that poor casita. In the early mornings, Naty ended the night shift and handed her duties over to the neighborhood rooster, who also had a knack for endless joyful screaming.

With parents who were frank about the birds and the bees, and with brothers who never censored themselves in front of her, sex wasn't a completely unknown concept. But with Robert's tutelage, sex quickly went from a curiosity to Naty's favorite pastime. Her husband's hunger for it was both bottomless and contagious. Now whenever he came home, she pounced on him as soon as he closed the front door.

In the candlelight, she studied his pale, smooth skin, dappled with freckles and covered with fine reddish-blond hair. He shaved each morning, and by evening his face was rough with stubble. For all his soft-spoken scholarliness, he was big and hairy and robust as a carabao.

"Barbarian," she whispered in his ear, delighting in the goosebumps that rose all over his body as he shuddered into her.

For all the words she knew—millions, it seemed—she didn't have any language for the things they did together at night. She loved Robert's kind heart and quick mind, of course, but God forgive her, she loved his body too. She loved his taste and scent. She loved the lusty sounds he made as he took his pleasure. Unexpectedly, she began to love her own body too—what shamelessness! She was both sensitive and sturdy, and dancing had made her flexible enough to indulge all of Robert's fascinating whims.

Early one morning, before Naty's coworker the rooster arrived, she and Robert lay tangled under the mosquito netting, holding each other close as the last rays of blue moonlight poured in through the open window. The scent of blooming dama de noche filled the room, heady and sweet. Lazily, Robert nuzzled her neck and kissed her softly while his hands roamed her naked body.

As he stroked the smooth skin of her belly, he stilled.

Languidly, she opened her eyes. "What's wrong?"

He smiled in the fading darkness. He ran his palm ever so gently over the new curve he'd found.

"Nothing's wrong, darling." His voice cracked a little. "Nothing at all."

***

Naty had kept all of Robert's letters and telegrams from California in a trunk under their bed. Upon their engagement, Robert's father had sent his son a kind letter and a very generous wire transfer. Sylvia and Edward—Ned—often sent letters with updates from home. The telegrams of congratulations arrived almost immediately when each of Naty and Robert's children were born. But none of those missives had ever been signed by Agnes Moore.

Heart beating fast, Naty fussed over her children in the hallway outside what Robert called the North Library. She clicked her tongue. Of course, she loved her children, but they were basically wild beasts. Their clothes would never be pressed enough. Their hair would never be neat enough. As they stood there, absorbing her nervous energy, they began to fidget.

"Call her ma'am," she reminded them. "Whenever she asks you a question, you reply with 'yes, ma'am' or 'no ma'am,' do you understand?"

They looked at her and nodded, wide-eyed.

"Practice," she said.

"Yes, ma'am," they said in unison.

Robert entered the hallway from the study. Dressed in a linen suit, he gave each of his children a cursory inspection and slight nod. For herself, Naty had chosen her best day dress, dandelion yellow gabardine, which she wore with a smart belt, high-heeled loafers and shortie gloves. Robert's gaze lingered on her throat, and for a moment, his expression softened. He couldn't quite meet her eyes, but the worry lines around his mouth disappeared, and Naty thought—hoped—he might even smile. But when Fiona suddenly drew open the doors of the library, his attention snapped away from Naty so sharply that she took a step back.

"Mrs. Moore will see you now," said the housemaid.

The children followed Robert inside. Naty entered last. Her heels were silent against a thick Oriental carpet, its colors muted with age. To still her jangling nerves, she scanned the room. Heavy draperies, half open. Dusty rays of sunlight. More old furniture. Drab portraits on the walls.

And in the rear of the room, a woman dressed in black, statue still. Upright in an armchair, a table at her elbow with a vase of lilies, a silver bell, some papers and two notebooks. A shiny fountain pen, silver like a dagger—a pen never used to write a letter to the Philippines.

Robert kissed his mother's cheek. She looked at him but did not smile. Her eyes were flinty as she studied his face.

"Mother," said Robert.

There was a chair set for Robert, but Naty and the children had nowhere to sit. Naty glanced down. There were crisp imprints on the carpet where other chairs, possibly even a couch had recently stood. Naty nodded to herself— Mrs. Moore was making a statement. Naty gathered the children close to her like a protective hen and looked up defiantly at the woman intent on ignoring her out of existence.

Robert noticed this slight. He stood next to the empty chair.

"This is my wife, Natividad," Robert said quietly. "And these are our children, Luzviminda, Francisco and Armando."

In turn, the children bowed and curtsied, as instructed.

Mrs. Moore looked them over, her mouth pressed tight. Her green eyes glittered in a sunbeam. Instead of acknowledging them, she turned to Robert. "Have you gone to see your father yet?" Her voice was rich and deep, surprising Naty.

"No, not yet," Robert replied.

"Go, at once. Take them." She waved her hand absently at Naty. "Let them see what their war did to our family."

"Mother, that is not—"

"He died of a broken heart, Robert. When we got word about Edward. Your father was dead within the week." Mrs. Moore's voice was emotionless. She took the large notebooks from her table and handed them to Robert. "There now. You'll need those. The old one was your father's ledger for the winery. The newer one was Edward's. Only the first few pages are filled."

Robert took them silently.

"And here, some paperwork from the War Department. It arrived today." She gave Robert the stack of papers. "On top is a pamphlet about burial options. 'Tell Me About My Boy,' it's called. Isn't that charming?" she said bitterly. "If you don't mind, I'll leave the repatriation process to you and Sylvia." She paused, and this time, her gaze lingered on Naty. "Bring his body home, Robert. I shouldn't have to mention that, but who knows what your thinking is now? Perhaps you think Edward should lie in some ghastly place across the sea, far from those who loved him." Mrs. Moore stared hard at Naty, who refused to buckle against her mother-in-law's hostile antagonism. "You people are a disease," Agnes Moore continued. "It isn't enough for Filipinos to take our boys' jobs in this country. You must also take their lives in your own."

Robert opened his mouth to say something, but, boiling with rage, Naty couldn't hold her tongue any longer. "Ma'am, you look unwell," she said, sweetly and overloud. "Shall I fetch the maid? The last thing we want to do is upset you."

Mrs. Moore produced a walking stick from the other side of her chair, and for a moment, Naty thought she intended to hit her in the face. Instinctively, she stood in front of her children. But Mrs. Moore only rose slowly to her feet.

"Oh," said the old woman, sneering. "So, you speak English. How handy." She rang the bell on her table, making the children jump. Fiona emerged from a side door and went immediately to her side.

Glaring at Naty, Fiona said in a sing-song voice, "Come with me now, madam. Yes, that's it."

They all stared as Fiona guided Mrs. Moore out of the room without another word.

~*~*~*~

Chapter Four

Naty changed the children into their play clothes and dismissed them into the gardens. Let them be feral—they needed to escape this suffocating house. They needed to breathe.

Back in the bedroom, Naty shook with anger.

"How could you let her talk to you that way? How could you let her talk to us—about us—that way?" She paced the floor, her heels clicking on the wood.

Her husband said nothing, sitting still on the bed with his hands on his knees. The notebooks and pamphlets sat on the bedspread next to him.

"I know you're angry," Robert said. "I'm sorry. I wasn't…ready…for her. I didn't anticipate how she would react."

"What were you expecting? A warm homecoming? After she's ignored you for so long?"

"I don't know what I was expecting. Nothing— I don't know."

"She didn't even acknowledge her grandchildren. Her own flesh and blood. Was she this cold to you growing up?"

"No. She wasn't." He was quiet for a moment. "We had nannies, certainly, but she spent more time with us than any woman of her station would be expected to spend with her own children. She was kind. Warm." Robert looked out the open window. "The house was filled with music. She sang, did you know that? She's a trained opera singer. She retired when she married."

"Well, I didn't like the song she sang today." Naty sat down on the bed next to him. "She called the Philippines ghastly. You know what's ghastly? Her behavior."

"She's grieving, Naty."

Naty frowned. Why did this old American woman get a pass for her grief? Naty didn't get to enjoy the luxury of sadness. She was expected to work, adapt, fight, survive and, most difficult of all, pretend to be optimistic—even though she, too, had lost so much.

Stop—don't. Don't think about that.

"We are all grieving, Robert," Naty said softly.

Hesitating, almost shyly, he put a hand on the back of her neck. The feel of his bare skin on hers stilled her. She reached up and placed her hand on his, pinning it in place so he wouldn't take it away. Close to him, she could smell his shaving soap again. When they were apart, she had kept some of his things in a suitcase. Sometimes at night when no one could see her, she would open the suitcase and take a deep breath, remembering the smell of his body. She'd allow herself one bright, vivid memory of holding him close. Then she'd shut the suitcase tight again, trapping the beloved scent so it wouldn't dissipate.

She closed her eyes so she wouldn't see him retreat from her again. "I miss you," she murmured.

His breathing, soft and jagged, stirred the air next to her cheek. Naty wished for a kiss, but that was a wild wish—even her tingling lips were too shy to ask for that. Instead, she leaned her head toward him and touched her temple gently to his jaw. Her eyelashes brushed his chin, still smooth from his morning shave, and the contact made her breath tremble on the exhalation. When he reached up to stroke her cheek, she jumped, surprised at his initiative.

Then, barely a whisper: "I miss you too, Naty."

Her eyes were still closed. She felt him shift slightly on the bed. Holding her breath, she waited. When his lips touched her temple at last, warmth suffused her body, and she trembled as if this were their first touch—as if they hadn't been married for seven years, as if they hadn't had three children together, as if their bodies didn't know each other as intimately as two people could ever know each other. This moment was a new moment. Finally, they were beginning again.

The knock on the door was soft, but it felt loud. It felt like a giant had snapped the wooden timbers of the house.

Naty opened her eyes.

When he let go of her, she felt suspended in midair. He stood up and opened the bedroom door a crack. Naty heard Sylvia's voice.

"I'm sorry to interrupt. Mother sent me to speak with you about the…paperwork from the war department."

And just like that, the real world flooded back into their room.

Robert cleared his throat. "Okay. I'll…I'll meet you in the library."

He shut the door again. Standing up straight, he smoothed down his shirt front and adjusted his cuffs. He gathered the papers from the bed and tucked them under his arm.

"Robert?" Naty said. But what would she ask? A million questions he wouldn't—couldn't—answer.

He couldn't meet her eyes. "I'll see you and the children at dinner."

Before he left the room, he went to the window, pulled it shut and locked it.

Latch. Click.

***

Sylvia asked if Naty wanted to hire a governess for the children since school wouldn't begin until September, but Naty turned her down.

Robert had begun to oversee winery operations, and the hours were long. Francisco, Armando and Luz provided a welcome distraction from Naty's loneliness. She rambled with them over the sunbaked hills, climbing oak trees and taunting the rattlesnakes hiding in the tall yellow grass. They found a box of ancient toys in the attic, including a top that reminded Naty of her childhood turumpo.

In the evenings, before supper, she did some halfhearted schoolwork with them. Thankfully, their reading was excellent. Their penmanship was atrocious. Naty figured as long as they learned their arithmetic they'd be all right. After supper, she and the children listened to radio programs in Sylvia's cottage. Before bed, she played records for them and taught them to dance.

As the summer days passed, Naty realized she had missed being a mother almost as much as she still missed being a wife.

What had happened to Robert at Santo Tomas? Why couldn't he touch her? She longed for understanding. She longed for him.

One Sunday after church, high clouds rolled into the valley, cooling the scorching air. After a big meal, the family rested under a fig tree in the back garden. The children played slapjack with their Aunt Sylvia on a picnic blanket. Robert and Naty sat on lawn chairs.

Naty put down the newspaper she was pretending to read. The family's driver had left the livery stable open after taking the afternoon off. The black Mercury Eight stood gleaming in the shadows, washed and polished. A longing for freedom struck Naty, so sharp she could taste it in her mouth.

"Robert," she asked, "could we please go for a drive? The kids are happy. They could stay here."

He closed his book and looked at the car. The idea was too enticing, even for him.

"Yes, all right."

Robert found the keys, and together, he and Naty pulled back the roof of the car and clipped it in place. She tied a scarf around her hair and snuck a bottle of wine and some glasses into a picnic basket. Sylvia and the kids waved as Robert steered them down the long driveway onto the dirt road. He stopped by the mailbox.

Naty put on her sunglasses against the rising dust. "Well? Isn't this a V8? Show me what this car can do, little turtle," she said, smiling.

Her heart leaped at the half smile he flashed her.

Robert pulled onto the paved main road. No one was around. He put the car in gear and hit the gas, throwing Naty back into her seat with a surprised whoop. They laughed all the way into the hills, where the car's big engine bested every dusty incline until they reached the place where the oldest and the thickest of the oak trees grew. The air cooled even further, and Naty took a deep, clear breath. Robert stopped the car at a wide overlook by the side of the road.

"Is this still part of the estate?" Naty asked when he turned off the engine.

"Yes," Robert said. He pointed out a distant ridge. "Our land goes from just south of the winery to the tops of those hills. There's an old spa resort up the road. Hot springs."

They climbed out of the car and found some granite boulders in the shade of some tall oaks. Naty poured the wine.

Looking more relaxed than she'd seen him in months, Robert talked with some pride about his work at the winery but shared he was worried about its ability to sustain itself. She knew he'd never wanted to inherit the business, but she also knew he felt responsible for his family's legacy. He wouldn't allow himself to fail.

Two hawks flew lazy circles over the valley. Soft sunlight illuminated the red feathers of their tails like stained glass.

"We'll make a good life here," Naty said. "We're very lucky."

Robert finished his wine. "We are," he said, but his voice sounded far away.

Naty took his empty glass and set it carefully in the basket with hers. She stood in front of him and took his hands. She remembered the last time they'd touched, in their bedroom after seeing his mother. She remembered his anxiety and wondered if there was some way she could help him feel calm.

"Close your eyes," she said.

To her surprise, he did it. In the soft shade of the oaks, she let go of his hands and slowly stroked the sides of his face. His skin grew feverish, and he blushed furiously at her touch. She stepped between his legs, and, putting her hands on his broad shoulders, she bent to kiss his lips. He jumped, but she held him still. He didn't move. His mouth, warm and familiar and fragrant with wine, tasted to her like heaven, and her body buzzed with desire.

"Don't move," she whispered. "Please."

She dropped a soft kiss on the corner of his mouth, then in the center, then in the other corner. She kissed his cheeks and each of his closed eyes. She kissed his forehead and the line where his straw hat had imprinted on his skin.

When Naty leaned against him, she felt the rise of his body against hers. This was not the distant memory of desire, but desire fresh pressed, like new wine.

Finally, he wrapped his arms around her waist. And the kiss he returned to her was ferocious. Green eyes wild, he stood and flipped their positions, pinning her against a rock and finding, at once, the aching spot between her legs. While he kissed her again, he ground against her with his hardness, igniting her through the thin fabric of her dress. Lightheaded, high on his kiss, she reached down at once and unbuttoned his trousers.

At last, Naty thought. *At last.*

~*~*~*~

Chapter Five

But moments turned like pages.

An old flatbed truck, heading down the hill from the spa resort, backfired as its driver accelerated around the corner.

The sound was loud, startling some sparrows resting nearby. They exploded out of the brush, screaming.

Robert let go of Naty and jumped back, stumbling on the corner of the boulder. He fell in the dust, his pants half off. His green eyes were bright and wild with terror.

For a split second, Naty didn't recognize him. He was like a stranger caught in time, trapped in some basement in Manila as the bombs rained down.

She got down on her knees and grabbed his powerful, trembling hands in hers. Since the war ended, he'd had attacks of the nerves before, but nothing like this.

"Robert," she said, loudly. "That was a truck. You are safe. You are okay."

His face frozen, he didn't speak. Ten frightening seconds passed. When he found himself again, he let go of her hands, turned away and fixed his clothing.

"Robert?" she asked.

Without a word, he gave her the keys to the car and got into the passenger seat.

Not knowing what else to do, she took the keys and started the car.

Silently, she drove them home as the sun went down. She swallowed everything she wanted to say to him, an ocean of words, until her stomach roiled with all the things she'd left unsaid. When they arrived at the house, Sylvia was standing at the back door, waving.

"Hey, you crazy kids," she called. "How was your joyride?"

Completely withdrawn, Robert had already started down the path to his office in the winery.

Naty closed the door to the garage, grateful for the darkness that hid the tears sliding down her cheeks. "It was wonderful!" she called, her voice crackling with fake cheer. "Just perfect."

***

A week later, Sylvia had a fitting at the dressmaker's shop in town and invited Naty along for an outing.

As her sister-in-law attended to her business, Naty walked around the deserted town square. There was an empty Chinese restaurant and a greengrocer with wilted vegetables in crates. Architecturally, all of the buildings were impressive but had seen better days. A grand hall had boarded-up windows and doors. Its faded sign made Naty sad—Napa Valley Opera House.

She dabbed at the sweat on her neck. The noonday heat was oppressive. Unseen insects vibrated in the trees, too smart to break siesta.

Heart aching with loneliness, Naty strolled down one of the streets leading away from the square. Here, small clapboard houses stood in a neat row, their paint peeling blithely in the sun. On one of the shady porches sat a young woman in pin curls and a housedress, shelling a big bowl of beans.

She squinted at Naty. Then she stood up.

By way of greeting, she shouted, "Hey! Hey, you! Are you Filipino?"

Naty took off her sunglasses and paused by the garden gate. "Of course, I am," she said in Tagalog.

"I knew it!" The woman spoke Tagalog with a friendly Ilonggo accent. "Wait there." She put down her beans and marched to the gate. Naty's heart leaped at hearing her native language again after so long.

Before Naty knew it, she too was sitting on the porch, shelling beans.

"Is this your special trick? Luring in strangers to clean your vegetables?" Naty asked.

"Yes! How did you know?" Lilibeth's laughter was easy. "You're not as good as the others I've tricked, though. Kind of slow."

As they shelled, Naty learned all about Lilibeth. She was twenty years old, a war bride, one of a small group of Filipino women granted permission to marry the Filipino American GIs who had enlisted to fight in the Philippines.

"The old-timers had a hard time here," Lilibeth said. "The manongs who came here first, who planted the entire valley? They were bullied, cheated out of wages, chased out of town. Sometimes they were beaten and shot, like in Watsonville."

"But why?"

"Take a guess." Lilibeth's fingers were long and quick. "White men thought Filipinos took too many jobs away from white workers. And they didn't like how Filipino men courted and married white women. It's against the law, did you know that? White people and Filipino people can't get married in California." She glanced up at Naty. "But love is more powerful than the law, isn't it?"

Naty didn't comment, wondering if her own marriage was still valid. She decided to change the subject. "Where's your husband now?"

"Rico and his uncle are working the fields. This is Tito Boy's house. He never married. He was the one who told my Rico to sign up. Fight for Uncle Sam, bring back a Filipina wife."

Lilibeth was one of nine children. Her parents met with Rico only once before agreeing to let her marry him and move to America. "They couldn't send me away fast enough! Only my mom cried—tears of joy!" She laughed. "I would have married him even if he looked like a lizard. But he's so handsome, Ate. Alam mo ba, he found a silk parachute while he was on patrol. He stuffed it into his pack. I sewed my own wedding dress from it. Do you remember how hard it was to get silk? The Japanese had a monopoly on it. It was impossible to get any. After we got married I dyed the dress green so I could wear it again and again. Rico loves it." Lilibeth smiled slyly. "He wants me to wear it in the bedroom. We put on music and dance all night, if you get my drift. He won't let me sleep! You know how these men get."

Naty felt herself blushing. She had been a newlywed once—an enthusiastic one.

"I'm not pregnant yet," Lilibeth declared, "but not for lack of trying!"

Lilibeth wrote down her phone number for Naty and promised to introduce her to the other war brides in town.

Imagining the sour face of Robert's mother, Naty invited Lilibeth and her family to the big house for dinner. Naty longed for company, and this joyful new friend lifted her spirits.

"My sister-in-law will be looking for me," Naty said.

"Wait!" Lilibeth said. "Before you go, come with me. I have something to show you."

Lilibeth grabbed her hand and led her to the backyard. Behind a tall, unruly hedge lay something that took Naty's breath away.

It was an enormous vegetable garden. Filled with every fruit and vegetable from the Philippines that Naty had been longing for since before the war, the small plot of land was a tropical paradise.

Lilibeth handed her an old rice sack. "Take whatever you want. The talong is almost ripe. We have sigarillas and sibuyas. Here's some garlic that's ready to use. What do you like?" With a small knife, Lilibeth harvested ripe vegetables and dropped them without hesitation into Naty's bag.

"Did you plant these?" Naty asked with wonder.

"Me? No." Lilibeth snorted. "I'm not that patient. This is Tito Boy's garden. He's worked on it for many years. Do you know what he told me? 'Almost anything can take root here in California, anak. As long as you know what it needs.' I think about this a lot, Ate Naty. It's like us. We're here now. It's time for us to take root."

***

After talking with Lilibeth, Naty started to hatch a plan.

At the bottom of her steamer trunk, she'd managed to save her favorite red dress, the one she'd worn to her first dance with Robert. In the evening, after everyone had gone to bed, she sewed under a reading lamp, altering the bodice where pregnancy and wartime famine had changed the shape of her body. She ordered some records in town and when they arrived, she stashed them in her closet. And on July 4, she conspired with Sylvia to have the children accompany their aunt to the Independence Day picnic in town.

After supper, the household staff left for the fireworks display. Robert and Naty sat together in the drawing room. She put one of her records on the gramophone and told him she would be back with a surprise.

Robert gave her a small smile. "What surprise?"

"You'll see."

She rushed upstairs and changed into her red dress. It fit perfectly, just as it had all those years ago. Heart thumping in her chest, Naty put on lipstick and smoothed her hair before tiptoeing down the stairs to the room where Robert waited for her. He stood next to the record player while "Moonlight Serenade" played softly in the dim light. She slid open the pocket door and stepped inside.

"Surprise," she said, beaming.

Robert turned around.

Chapter Six

Robert looked at her, and his smile collapsed.

"Oh," he said, less a word than the air escaping from his body in fear. "Oh, no."

Cold shame wrapped itself around Naty's heart. She had upset him yet again. How? Why? This was the opposite of what she wanted for their evening.

"I'm so sorry." Robert sat down in the armchair and covered his face with his hands. "This is not your fault, Naty. You don't deserve this."

Crying?

He wasn't supposed to cry. He was supposed to take her in his arms, waltz to Glenn Miller and be transported to that golden time of their early marriage, when the war was just a whisper across the ocean. When all that mattered was the desire they had for each other.

Love was stronger than sadness, wasn't it?

Wasn't it?

They had been wild about each other. What was wrong with her? Why couldn't she entice him? What kind of wife couldn't seduce her own husband, couldn't lead him to bed and help him forget all that was troubling him?

Naty switched off the player and sat down next to Robert on a footrest. She lay her head on his knee, listening to his quiet sobbing and waiting for him to speak.

At last, he took a deep breath. She took his hand.

"Naty," he said softly, "I think I have a problem."

The large house creaked around them. A door closed. A floorboard squeaked.

Robert waited for silence before he spoke again.

"The things I saw in Manila at the end—I keep seeing them again and again. Awake, asleep. Intrusive thoughts of the worst kind." He took both her hands in his and looked at her carefully. "This red dress makes you look so beautiful. I remember the first time I saw you in it." He paused, gathering strength to say the next part. "There was a woman—the wife of one of the suppliers for the camp. Filipino. They sold dry goods to the Japanese. One day, close to the end, her husband was taken in for questioning. They said he'd been sneaking intel about the camp to the guerillas. No one saw him for weeks. The woman grew desperate. She demanded to talk to the camp administrators. She offered money. She begged to argue on his behalf. They wouldn't listen to her. She put on her best clothes—a red dress, like this one. She stood at the gate. When it opened, she rushed inside."

Naty's blood ran cold.

"The new Japanese sentries—different from the ones we'd had early in the war—didn't hesitate to run a bayonet through her. She bled out next to the gate while they pretended to get medical staff to help. By the time the medics arrived, her eyes were closed. She was gone." Robert's voice was the barest whisper. "She had two small children. I don't know what happened to them."

Naty squeezed his hands.

"For days, I couldn't sleep. When I closed my eyes I saw her, lying on the ground. Her face became your face. And I couldn't do anything. I couldn't help her." He sobbed, once, then gulped down air until he could breathe again.

"I know we are safe here—I know that. But those thoughts, those memories, they aren't going away," Robert said. "The doctor who examined me before we left the Philippines told me some soldiers call this 'shell shock' or 'old sergeant's disease.' But I am not a soldier. I didn't put myself in the line of fire. I have no reason to feel these things."

Naty raised her head. "What? How can you say that? After what you have been through?"

She and the kids had been far from Manila at the time of the liberation of Santo Tomas, but she learned much later that the First Cavalry Division had rushed straight to the internment camp while Japanese forces held the rest of the city. Santo Tomas was surrounded, the sole American stronghold in a war zone. Artillery shells rained down on the university while the fighting raged around it. Retreating Japanese soldiers left a nightmare landscape of violence and gore, and American howitzers didn't differentiate between Japanese soldiers and Filipino civilians. The Battle of Manila crushed the city, and Robert had been in the middle of it.

"No, I have no reason," Robert said again. "I have no right."

With tears in her eyes, Naty thought of Tito Boy's garden, a patch of pure, beautiful life hidden behind that wild hedge. What had this old man said to Lilibeth? Anything can grow in California, if you understand what it needs.

Looking at Robert, Naty began to understand.

She wanted to comfort him with the kind of wild, escapist love they used to share. But that wasn't what he needed now. He needed time, and she needed to stop pressuring him.

"My love," Naty said, holding him, "you have been through hell. Your body—your mind—is healing."

He buried his face against her shoulder.

"I'm broken," he murmured against her. "What kind of man am I?" His tears wet her dress. His deep sob tore at her heart.

"You are my man, Robert," she said. "The very best man I have ever met. If you're broken, we'll help you heal together. If you need a year, ten years, a hundred years—I will stay with you. I'll wait. I'm in no hurry." She ran her hands through his coarse hair and kissed the top of his beloved head. "You are my turtle, after all. I go wherever you go—very slowly."

His sob became a soft, astonished laugh. He tightened his embrace, and Naty embraced him back.

For the first time, instead of seeing him from the outside, she tried to feel the weight of what he carried. For all the terrible things she had seen and learned during the war, she hadn't been as close to death as Robert had.

When he was calm again, Robert lifted his hand and cradled her cheek. "You have been so strong for so long, Naty. You saved our children. You kept a cool head. You didn't just find a way to survive. You found a way to fight back. In the face of unspeakable sadness. You fought back."

The guerillas had recruited her because of her language skills. She'd translated messages in code. If she'd been found out, she would have been killed.

"I know you miss your family," Robert said. "I miss them. They were my family too. If you ever want to talk about them again, I'm here to listen, darling."

Not for the first time, Naty's millions of words failed her. She sat completely still, unable to respond. Waves of grief—hot and acidic—threatened to spill over the rim of her heart. But she did not move. Soon the surface of her immense pain settled again, placid and glassy.

Robert kissed her forehead. "Thank you," he said. "Thank you for being so strong for me. For all of us."

~*~*~*~

Chapter Seven

Naty left Robert in the drawing room. She had held him until he'd fallen asleep in the armchair, calm at last. For the first time in a long time, she didn't feel the distance that had unspooled between them since they arrived in California. Their emotional intimacy had returned. She felt stronger and less alone.

With a soft click, she closed the door—Robert needed rest.

When she approached the stairs to return to their bedroom, she almost screamed.

There, standing like an apparition on the steps, was Agnes Moore, her walking stick in her hand.

Naty put a hand on her heart to keep it from punching its way out of her chest.

"Mrs. Moore," she said. "I'm sorry. You startled me."

Robert's mother's eyes were bright green in the electric lights of the hall. She had never looked more like her son.

"You snake," she said quietly. "You manipulative snake."

Naty was no saint but she certainly was not a reptile, either. Still feeling optimistic from her interaction with Robert, she stood her ground and didn't let the woman's words shake her. "Ma'am?"

Mrs. Moore tapped the wooden step with the metal tip of her cane. "I heard you both in the drawing room. 'I'm broken,' he said. You! You broke him. You broke my boy. You're smiling and satisfied with yourself, aren't you? What kind of harpy delights in breaking her husband?"

"Robert is fine," Naty replied. "He's sleeping. You can see for yourself."

"I spoke with my husband's solicitor, you know." Mrs. Moore pointed at Naty. "He told me it would be easy to draw up divorce papers. You need only sign them. You and your children would be entitled to an allowance. You needn't worry about that. That was your goal all along, wasn't it? Money? Or was the one-way ticket to the United States enough? Land of milk and honey. Is it what you expected?"

The woman's voice grew more forceful. Though she was angry, she seemed to relish telling this story she'd made up about Naty. As Naty listened, she could see the singer and actress Mrs. Moore had once been, commanding the attention of a rapt audience. Melodramatic. Mesmerizing.

"You made him cry," Mrs. Moore declared. She tapped her cane again. The wood rang out and echoed against the ceiling, accusatory. "You should be ashamed of yourself."

Naty shook her head. "I'm not ashamed of myself. He should cry. You should cry. He was a prisoner of war. You lost your son and your husband. What good is it to hold in your tears? Why do you let them poison you?"

"What good could crying possibly do? We aren't children, you little interloper." Mrs. Moore moved toward Naty but misjudged the edge of the step. Her walking stick clattered down the stairs and she grabbed at the banister with a shaking hand.

Naty dashed up the stairs and caught Mrs. Moore's arm.

"Ma'am," she said, "let me help you." She steadied the woman on her feet and glanced up the stairs. "Is Fiona upstairs? Shall I call for her?"

"No. She left to see the fireworks. They all did." Up close, Naty noticed Mrs. Moore was struggling to catch her breath. She remembered Sylvia mentioning her mother's heart problems. She could call Robert for help, but he wouldn't hear her from here. She could go and get him, but she didn't want to leave Agnes alone on the stairs.

"All right," Naty said. "Let's get you to your room. We'll go together. One step at a time."

"I don't trust you."

"That's fine. It's not required."

Slowly, Naty guided her mother-in-law up the stairs and down the long, dark hallway to her bedroom. They had nothing to say to each other. Naty waited for another diatribe or fictional tale about herself, but Mrs. Moore held both her tongue and, begrudgingly, Naty's offered hand.

Robert's mother's room was large, drafty and lonely. Naty turned on one of the lamps and helped the woman sit on her mattress. She unbuttoned the old-fashioned shoes, fluffed the pillows, and helped Agnes to lie down.

"Do you have something you can take?" Naty asked quietly.

Agnes nodded and pointed to a tray on her bedside table. "That tincture there. Two drops in half a glass of water."

Naty prepared the drink and Mrs. Moore dutifully swallowed it. She drew a deep breath and a little color returned to her cheeks. Naty put the empty glass back down on the silver tray. There was a framed photograph next to the tray, a handsome man in a suit. Naty picked it up.

"Is this Edward?" she asked.

Mrs. Moore leaned back and took the photograph. She touched a fingertip to the man's face. "No. That is my late husband. But Edward looked just like him. Sylvia and Robert take after me." She handed it back to Naty and motioned absently at the dark, empty room. "We shared this bedroom for forty years. Can you imagine? It just doesn't feel right without him in it. Sometimes I think I'll never feel warm again."

Naty looked around. She spotted a wool blanket folded on a nearby chest. She took it and spread it over Mrs. Moore, who stared at her with narrow, suspicious eyes. She hadn't said thank you once, but Naty didn't need anything from this woman. Not approval. Not gratitude. Not even good manners.

Naty sat down on the chair next to the bed, and now it was her turn to study Mrs. Moore's face. Showing vulnerability had opened a tiny crack in the older woman's tragedy mask. Behind the mask, Naty saw glimpses of a bright and horrible truth—Agnes Moore was heartsick, just as she was.

"I visited town a few days ago," Naty said quietly. "I saw the opera house."

A ghost of a smile touched Mrs. Moore's lips. "Ah. The opera house." She swallowed. "I was there, you know. Opening night. I was a new bride, and Robert's father had once been the richest man in the valley. I felt like a princess, such as my kingdom was." Her voice softened. "Gilbert and Sullivan. *HMS Pinafore.* What a ridiculous show—but what fun."

"Robert said you trained as an opera singer," Naty ventured.

"Of sorts. I was in the ensemble at the Tivoli Opera House in San Francisco. I danced a lot and sang a little." She closed her eyes and smiled. "There was a grand gaslit chandelier that hung above the audience. Everything gold and gilded and festooned with flowers. Every seat filled. The roar of applause. How grand. Just grand." She opened her eyes. "This was before the Great Earthquake, of course. All of that is lost now. All of it, gone." Her eyes bore down on Naty. "But you're young yet. What do you know of loss? It's just an abstraction to you now."

Naty looked down at her hands folded in her lap. The red fabric of her dress made her brown skin glow. Her mother was tisay, her father had dark skin. In complexion, she was a perfect mixture of both of them.

"Loss is not an abstraction, ma'am. Not to me."

Mrs. Moore grunted. "Is that so? Are your parents alive?"

"No, ma'am. Neither of them survived the war."

Naty paused. Should she?

Yes, let Agnes Moore hear the truth.

"After the bombings destroyed my family's guesthouse, we went to live with relatives in another village. My parents contracted malaria. There was a shortage of quinine and anti-malarial drugs during the fighting. They didn't recover."

Mrs. Moore said nothing.

"My two oldest brothers joined the guerillas when the Japanese occupation began. They were captured and executed in front of the cathedral. To frighten any Filipinos from joining the resistance." Naty fidgeted with the belt of her dress. Cold and matter of fact, her own voice sounded distant in her ears. She'd already cried an ocean of tears for her family—she certainly wasn't going to cry in front of this woman.

"The Japanese destroyed the infrastructure of our region," she continued. "My two younger brothers drank contaminated water. They contracted dysentery and died. Technically it was the lack of medical care that killed them. They were young and healthy. They would have survived with proper treatment." Naty looked at the photograph of the handsome man in the gilded frame. "Only one of my brothers survived the war. He is staying on the outskirts of Manila now. I'm trying to find a way for him to immigrate here. I want to keep him close to me." She paused. "We're all we have left of our past life. I don't want to lose him too."

Mrs. Moore had closed her eyes and lay so still, Naty thought she'd fallen asleep.

But she wasn't asleep.

"My world," she murmured, "used to be so big. Slowly, it shrank. To this town. Then to this house. Then to the walls of this bedroom. I suppose it's become too easy for me to forget all that lies beyond." Mrs. Moore opened her eyes and turned to Naty. The anger was gone. "Everyone here is either afraid of me or talks to me like a child."

"I'm sorry," Naty said, and she meant it.

"My husband was a businessman. We loved each other but we lived in two different worlds. Whenever we talked about our own interests, we bored each other to tears." A tiny smile glimmered on Mrs. Moore's face, then disappeared. "Edward was like his father. Sylvia—she's kind, but all she does is fuss and worry about me. The only person I could ever talk to about anything was Robert. And then he left me."

Naty thought about her own children. She and Agnes both had three—two boys and a girl. The pain of losing not just a child but her husband too? Unfathomable. For all the people Naty had loved who'd died during the war, her immediate family was still intact. This was not true for Agnes Moore.

"I'm sure Robert would like to talk to you again," Naty said, "when he's well. Until then, I can come up here and you can call me as many names as you like. If it makes you feel better."

Mrs. Moore chuckled, low in her chest—but just once.

They sat in silence. After a long time, Mrs. Moore said, "Natividad?"

"Ma'am?"

"Talk to Sylvia about your brother. Her husband's partner at the law firm specializes in immigration law."

Naty did not expect advice, offered like a thin and brittle olive branch.

"Now let me sleep," Mrs. Moore said. "Go."

Chapter Eight

Robert obsessed over weather reports.

He decoded the clouds, pored over his almanacs and scrutinized the refractometer again and again, checking the sweetness of the grapes. After consulting the stars and saying more than a few prayers, he and his staff determined the day of the harvest—the second Monday of October.

That morning, everyone on the estate and the neighboring properties showed up for the crush.

Naty had never seen anything like it.

Robert oversaw operations with his vigneron, a mustachioed Franco-American who'd fought in Europe. Their army of workers stripped the vines of big clusters of cabernet sauvignon grapes and piled them into big wooden flats.

The grapes were brought by truckload to the winery's giant press. But a special truckload of grapes was brought to the lawn outside the winery, where townspeople had set up a barbecue pit piled with oak logs. Huge sides of beef sizzled and smoked on the fire. A barrel of the Moore family's finest had been brought up from the cellar to share with neighbors and workers alike. A group of Mexican musicians strolled and serenaded the crowd with strings and brass.

The joyous abundance of food and people electrified Naty, who had always loved parties. She and the children watched as a crew of workers emptied the reserved grapes into a large wooden container.

"Are you ready?" Robert took her hand and led her to the vat, where townspeople were taking off their shoes and climbing in.

"Ready for what?" she asked.

"This is how wine used to be made," he said. "Take off your sandals."

Her children screamed with glee as their mother did as she was told.

"Mrs. Moore!" one of the workers called. Naty didn't answer for a moment, thinking they were looking for Agnes, but that couldn't be so—Agnes had left that morning with Sylvia on the train to San Francisco, one of their many trips back and forth from the city. Persuaded by Naty and Sylvia, Agnes had recently become a patron at the War Memorial Opera House near city hall. She had sat in the balcony for the most recent opening night, and Sylvia reported it was the happiest she'd seen her mother in a long time.

"Mrs. Moore!" called the worker again.

"Yes?" Naty said.

"Open your mouth!"

Confused and delighted, Naty opened her mouth as one of the women who worked at the winery squeezed a long stream of cabernet into her mouth from a fat wineskin.

"Now you're ready!" the worker shouted.

Two burly farmworkers lifted her into the vat. The grapes were cool and slick under her feet. The musicians started a fast, upbeat song, and the grape crushers began to holler and cheer. When Naty turned around, Lilibeth was in the vat next to her, cheeks glowing. They danced arm-in-arm, hearts racing, skirts tucked around their waists, their legs streaked with juice.

And Robert watched Naty as she danced, his green eyes glittering.

***

Still light-headed from the wine, Naty emerged from her bath. She'd scrubbed herself with almond soap, but the scent of crushed fruit seemed to cling to her skin. She sat next to the small fireplace in their room where Robert had lit a fire against the chill autumn air.

As Naty brushed her long, wet hair, she reflected on the three months that had passed since their family arrived in Napa.

The children were adjusting to their new school. Robert had invested in modernizing a few aspects of winery operations and signed on with the brand-new vintners' association.

Other problems lingered—particularly shortages of bottles and reliable rail lines to the East Coast.

But Robert and Naty were working together to address their most pressing shortage, labor on the vineyard—her brother was recruiting workers from the Philippines. With the help of Sylvia's husband's law firm, the first group, along with Naty's brother, would arrive early next year.

Naty put down her hairbrush and smiled to herself.

"What a perfect day," she said.

"Yes. A perfect day for our first harvest." Robert sat on the oriental carpet next to the fire and stretched out his long legs. He'd begun to put on weight again, and daily labor in the vineyard had made him tan and hardy. He'd grown close to his staff, who'd come to respect his willingness to learn and adapt. He still had nightmares. He still had moments of anxiety. But life here had brought a measure of peace to Robert Moore.

He didn't look like the young man she'd married. He looked like a man who'd walked through fire and emerged on the other side, stronger and more beautiful.

"I want to talk to you about something," she said in Tagalog.

"This must be serious," he replied in Tagalog. "Tell me."

Naty had anticipated this conversation for the past week. She had been walking the halls of the empty house when she realized Agnes was spending more and more time in San Francisco with Sylvia. Naty had studied the fading wallpaper and peeling paint and realized she and Robert needed to do something to preserve the house. It was in desperate need of care.

"I know that we have to be careful with our money," she began, "but I have an idea for restoring the house. It won't be quick, but I have been working on the numbers, and I think it is possible."

Robert listened carefully as she explained to him the potential she saw in the hacienda. There were no hotels in town, and the small motor court inns were utilitarian at best. The spa resort was too remote for most travelers, but the Moore estate was not far from the main road.

Naty gave him an overview of her ideas. They could rent out some rooms to guests and use the income to restore the house in phases—exterior, interior, plumbing, wiring. Slow but steady. She'd done the books for her father's guesthouse for years. She knew the difference between a pipe dream and a plan.

When she was finished, she held her breath as Robert considered what she'd proposed. She had prepared counterarguments for every objection he might have.

But he didn't argue.

"Let's do it," he said.

She beamed. "Really?"

"Really. You were always a better businessperson than I." He smiled. "I trust you."

She threw her arms around him and tackled him to the floor. The soft carpet padded their fall, and, as natural as gravity, their lips came together in a joyous, hungry kiss.

Since their conversation in the drawing room, Naty had contented herself with embracing and kissing, waiting patiently for her husband to find his way back to her. Now, as his warm hand lingered on her bare neck and he stroked her throat with the tip of his thumb, she wondered if the long road ended tonight.

A cool wine-scented wind blew in through the open window. Naty straddled Robert, and her silk robe fell open. His smile wavered for a moment as he stared at her cleavage. She waited, holding her breath.

Instead of touching her, he untied the belt at her waist and, with his fingertips, slipped the robe from her body. He caressed her bare arms and rested his hands on her waist. She leaned back, balancing herself on his hard thighs. At last, he reached up to caress her. Her nipples hardened against his fingers, and the sharp hunger in her chest settled low and deep in her belly.

He sat up and gave her one long, sweet kiss. His hand lingered, lovingly, on her breast. His other hand trailed down her body until his fingertips found her aching center. Staring into her eyes, he drew small, lazy circles on her, tracing her as she opened for him like a night-blooming flower.

Another kiss. And another. He whispered against her lips, "Thank you for waiting for me."

"For you? I would have waited a hundred years."

He laid her back on the soft carpet. Firelight licked his face, turning him golden. He spread her legs.

"I think you liked this," he murmured.

He slipped one long finger inside her and bent over her. Overwhelmed with arousal, she listened to the crackle of the fire and the click of his wet tongue on her tender flesh. His rhythm was steady and relentless. She took a deep breath and held it. At last, an orgasm, wild and enormous, rose out of the depths of her body and shook her. Locked between her thighs, Robert licked harder, and she came again, crying out with ecstasy.

She lay on the floor, shaking and wet, and watched as he took off his clothes. He dropped each piece in a pile— shirt, pants, boxer shorts, socks. And now he was above her, broad and lean and stronger than he'd ever been. He was everything now. An old friend. A new lover. Her partner in all things. Her fellow survivor. Her past, her present and her future—forevermore.

Eyes locked on hers, he parted her legs as wide as they would go, cracking her spine like a book he intended to read again and again. With yet another deep kiss, he slotted himself against her and moved his hips the way she liked, coating himself in her.

She closed her eyes, and lightning flashed in her mind.

When he pinned her hips to the carpet with his, a third tremor threatened inside her. She was ravenous for him, and when he snapped forward and entered her at last, deep and hard, she came yet again, tears of happiness sliding down her temples. His eyes were tender as he stroked her face and whispered beautiful words in her ears, but he took his pleasure roughly. Her body, fully aroused, savored the sweet, familiar pain. He was a big man. This had always turned her on. In appreciation, she grabbed his hair in her fists and pulled gently, making him growl.

"I missed you," she said.

"I missed you too," he gasped.

This time, when lightning flashed in the room, Naty's eyes were open. Thunder shook the side of the house, and the smell of wet earth filled the air. Naty heard the first drops of rain hit the ground, first in soft taps, then in driving sheets. An autumn storm poured in through the open window, soaking Robert's naked back as he made wild, frantic love to her on the floor.

Gently, Naty pushed him away as he blinked, disoriented with lust.

"My turn," she said.

She rolled him onto his back and straddled him again. With her hands, she fed him into her aching body, then she lay down on top of him, sheltering him from the cold rain. The raindrops sizzled on her skin. She closed her eyes and moved as if she were dancing to something slow and seductive. She drew long, lazy figure eights with her body. She flicked her hips upward, milking him so hard he gasped.

Soon, she imagined another song, wild and staccato.

A dance to get your heart beating again.

A dance to bring you back to life.

Naty arched her back, gripping him as tightly as she could. And Robert came at last, his hands digging into the muscles of her thighs. Another round of thunder shook the timbers of the house, drowning out his cries of pure pleasure.

That night, rain finally blessed the dry earth. It watered the hidden seeds and soaked the wandering dust, grounding it at last. Rain blessed the farmers and the vintners of the valley. Rain made this dry land a home. Most of all, it laid the vine to rest until springtime, when fresh green leaves would grow again, a promise fulfilled, year after year.

Drowsy, they lay tangled in each other's arms. The fire burned down to glowing coals.

"Robert," Naty whispered. "Let's go dancing again. We were so good at it."

"That's true," he murmured. "We are."

A minute passed. Was he asleep? "Robert?"

"Hmm?"

She stroked his bare chest. Rain continued to fall outside, soft and steady. They hadn't bothered to close the window. "Do you think…that everything will be okay?"

They looked at each other, reflecting each other's fascination. Then Robert kissed her once more, so thoroughly she didn't know if she was awake or dreaming.

"Yes, darling." He smiled. "I have a feeling that everything will be okay."

THE END

About Mia Hopkins

Mia Hopkins writes lush romances starring fun, sexy characters who love to get down and dirty. Her award-winning books have been featured by many publications including *The New York Times, The Washington Post, USA Today* and *Entertainment Weekly*. She lives in Los Angeles with her family. For more information, please visit www.miahopkinsauthor.com or connect with her on social media @miahopkinsxoxo.

Book List:

- The Eastside Brewery series
  - *Thirsty*
  - *Trashed*
  - *Tanked*
- The Cowboy Cocktail series
  - *Cowboy Valentine*
  - *Cowboy Resurrection*
  - *Cowboy Player*
  - *Cowboy Karma*
  - *Cowboy Rising*
- The Kings of California series
  - *Deep Down*
  - *Hollywood Honkytonk*

The Memory of You

ELLE CRUZ

The Memory of You

ELLE CRUZ

Blurb:

Once upon a time, a terrible mistake sparked the vengeful heart of a witch. Over sixty years later, the curse strikes its mark. Not only is Eli Amaro doomed to repeat the same day over and over again, but he is also forced to re-live the same excruciating sacrifice forever. To break the evil spell, he must give up what he loves the most, and he's not sure he has the heart to do it.

Emotional, angst-filled, and deeply romantic, *The Memory of You* is a speculative short story showing how love is powerful enough to cross time and space to triumph over even the darkest of forces.

Content Notes: Topic of non-consent (off-page); death of a loved one

Tropes and Sub genres: Amnesia, star-crossed lovers, cursed; Magical Realism

Heat Level: ⬤ (low heat)

Prologue

Eli

"The healers make their home deep in the jungle; in remote areas where the energy of nature is strong. Both healers and witches draw from the same energy. But take care. Never cross a witch, for it will take much more than the abilities of a healer to cure you."

—A Provincial Wanderer's Guide to the Philippine Islands (circa 1904)

Something strange happened the day before Vida and Rafa's wedding. It all started when Eli Amaro visited La Luna.

La Luna was strange enough itself. It was nestled into a crowded bank of shops in downtown Napa, and no one knew how to classify it. La Luna was a bookstore. A giftshop. An antiques dealer. The home of a spiritual medium. Whatever it was called, one thing was for sure.

La Luna dealt in the occult. Despite the rustic touches of eclectic antiques, art, and gifts, a creepiness hung in the air that set customers on edge. It was that same creepiness that drew them to the store. Shrunken heads and voodoo dolls dangled from the ceiling, archways, and shelves. The jars of preserved animals, shadow box displays of dead insects, and taxidermy animals were just there for show and didn't serve some sort of darker purpose just beyond the sphere of mortal comprehension. Right?

Just as it did to countless others, La Luna drew Eli in. He would never be able to explain why he drove directly to this strange shop right after his flight touched down from England.

The one thing he knew for certain? He was in love. That same love fueled him and gave his life the meaning he'd always been looking for.

He had no idea that love could also be a curse.

The woman behind the counter smiled when Eli approached. Her eyes glittered like those of a serpent about to strike, but the young man didn't see it. He was too busy scanning the glass display of antique jewelry, looking for the perfect ring.

And then he saw it.

He would never be able to explain why he chose that particular ring, or what drew him to it. All he would be able to remember was the woman's peculiar, unsettling smile as she took the chosen ring and closed her fingers around it. He didn't know who this woman was, or any of the motives afflicting her vengeful heart.

The trap had been sprung.

Love was a formidable power, but the woman had faith that her dark magic would triumph and carry out her revenge perfectly.

Chapter One

Eli

Montebello, California

Twenty years ago

Eli remembered the day his grandfather, his lolo, had changed.

It was a sweltering day in September. Seven-year-old Eli had been complaining of the heat. The small house he lived in with his parents, grandfather, and two older sisters did not have air conditioning. Lucky for his teen sisters, they were out with their friends at the community pool. Sadly, they refused to let Eli accompany them. His parents were both at work, so he was left with his grandfather.

"I have a great idea," Lolo said, his dark eyes twinkling. "Let's go to the drugstore to get ice cream."

To Eli, nothing beat drugstore ice cream on a hot day. Not even a trip to the toy store.

They hopped into the car and headed off. While Lolo was driving, he eyed his grandson carefully. Then he frowned. "Eli, where is your necklace?" he asked.

"Oh, I forgot it," Eli said.

Lolo was referring to the brown scapular necklace he'd made Eli wear for as long as he could remember. The scapular was a necklace worn by Catholics. It consisted of two small brown squares hung on a black string. Images of

Mother Mary and the sacred heart of Jesus were carved or stitched onto the squares. Eli wasn't sure why Lolo made him wear one. Lolo had also made his daughters and granddaughters wear them, but he wasn't nearly as strict on them as he was with Eli.

"It's okay." Lolo leaned over and fished another scapular necklace out of the glove compartment. "Just wear this one for now."

Lolo drove the short distance to the drugstore. They walked straight up to the ice cream counter. It was like heaven in here. Not only did the drugstore have the air conditioning blasting, but they had ten delicious ice cream flavors for only a dollar per scoop.

They bought their ice cream and sat at a small table. The scoops were so big Eli had trouble keeping up with them before they started melting. Lolo laughed at Eli's silly attempts to outlick the melting ice cream. He took a napkin and dabbed Eli's chin.

"What flavor is yours, Lolo? You're eating it really fast. It's not even melting."

"Pistachio," Lolo replied. "I'm not eating it fast. I just have a good technique."

"Pistachio? Yuck! That sounds disgusting."

"No, it's good," Lolo insisted. "You should try it."

Eli shook his head vigorously. Even though the thought of nut-flavored ice cream grossed him out, he loved hanging out with Lolo. He was so much more than a grandfather. He was a confidant and best friend. They'd always had a special bond, even though Lolo had six granddaughters. Maybe it was because he was the only boy? In any case, Lolo was Eli's favorite. He would never tire of hearing Lolo's folklore stories from the Philippines, or adventures he'd had when he was young.

"Lolo, can you tell me the story about the witches again?" Eli asked. "The one about the curse with the centipedes and cockroaches and spiders?"

Lolo didn't answer. Eli stopped licking his ice cream and looked at Lolo. He was frozen, staring at something in the distance.

"Hello? Did you hear me?"

Still no response.

Curious now, Eli craned his neck to see what had his grandfather's attention. It was a busy day in the drugstore, and it was hard to pinpoint what Lolo was looking at. And then Eli caught a glimpse of a woman in an odd dress, standing very still. He only glimpsed her for a split second before Lolo grabbed his arm and dragged him out of the store.

"Ouch! Lolo, you're pinching me."

Lolo didn't say a word. He opened the car door and shoved Eli inside. The heat seemed even more intense and oppressive as Lolo threw his cone aside, started the car, and zoomed out of the parking lot.

Lolo was breathing hard. He was covered in sweat. Fear shot through Eli as he stared at his grandfather. "Lolo, what happened?" he asked. "Is everything okay?"

Instead of answering, Lolo looked with wild eyes at Eli. "Are you wearing your necklace?" he demanded.

"Yes. I'm scared. What happened?"

Lolo's hand came up and fiddled with his own scapular necklace dangling around his neck.

"Hail Mary, full of grace, the Lord is with thee. Blessed art thou amongst women, and blessed is the fruit of thy womb, Jesus. Holy Mary, Mother of God, pray for us sinners, now and at the hour of our death. Amen."

Lolo continued his praying during the entire car ride. Eli was confused and scared. He lost his appetite. Lolo didn't even notice that Eli's ice cream had completely melted and made a mess all over the front seat.

***

Thirteen years later

Eli stood at the foot of Lolo's bed, gazing down upon him in his final hours. Eli was dressed in his student nursing uniform. He'd been about to leave for his clinical rotation at the hospital when his mother called him.

Needless to say, Eli wouldn't be going to clinicals today. As a matter of fact, Eli didn't feel like going anywhere. Since that mysterious day at the ice cream parlor, Lolo Gregorio had begun his slow, tragic decline.

Dementia had set in, starting with endearing forgetfulness. He'd forgotten names, and how to find his way to the bathroom, and how to wash his hands. But all the while, he'd been tormented by dreams and delusions. He'd raved about witches and dark magic and curses. He'd go into fugues where only frenzied prayers repeated over and over would eventually soothe his tortured mind. He would ask Eli and only Eli the same question on repeat: "Did you see that woman? The day at the drugstore? Did you see her face?"

Eli would think back to that day, which got more obscure with the haze of time. All he could remember was the profile of the woman and her rust-colored dress, which looked out of place.

"No, I didn't see her face."

Lolo had become obsessed with prayers. He would pray all day and force his family to pray with him. He would sprinkle holy water all over his room. He would make sure Eli was wearing his scapular.

Now, as Eli stood before his grandfather, a profound sadness seeped into him. This man, who had been his hero and friend, had become a delusional fanatic—a shell of who he once was.

Lolo's eyes were open, staring at the ceiling. He would blink occasionally, but Eli was convinced his mind was completely gone by now. Suddenly, Lolo raised his hand and beckoned Eli. Stunned, Eli looked around the room for reassurance, but he found none. He'd forgotten his family had given him a moment alone with Lolo.

"Come here," Lolo rasped.

Eli moved closer and looked down into Lolo's face. His eyes were still open, but not looking at Eli. Lolo said nothing for a few seconds. Then, without warning, tears welled up and trickled from Lolo's eyes.

"Always wear your scapular, anak ko," Lolo said. "Always pray to the Lord. Pray for protection against the evils of the world."

Eli's heart filled with pity. Even now, as his soul began its departure from the world, Lolo's demented mind gave him no reprieve. "Of course." Eli patted Lolo's withered hand. "I promise."

"I did a bad thing. A long time ago. She said you would pay for my sins. I'm so sorry, anak ko. I'm so sorry."

Lolo sobbed even harder, his thin frame shaking with effort. Eli went pale. Those were not the words of a demented man. He grasped Lolo's shoulders and tried to soothe him. "Lolo, shh, it's okay."

"No. No, anak, it is not. Because of my sins, you will suffer. She is not lying. She means it."

"What? What are you talking about?"

"The witch from Old Multo: Mangkukulam Lita Maria. I made a terrible mistake. I should never have crossed her. I was so stupid. For a long time, I never heard from her, then all of a sudden she started appearing in my dreams. She kept threatening me and telling me my loved ones would pay for my sins. Then one day, I saw her in real life—there at the drugstore on that hot day in summer. She wasn't in my nightmares anymore. She was real, and she found me. Worst of all, she found you. She knew what you meant to me. Oh, anak ko, please forgive me. Please, please, please forgive me."

Panic quaked through Eli. He covered Lolo's body with his own, clutching his thin body as if to draw the despair away from him.

His relatives burst into the room when they heard Lolo wailing. Eli straightened up while his mother and aunts and cousins surrounded him, crying out in distress.

"What happened?" Eli's mother asked, grasping Lolo's hand.

Eli's sisters crowded in beside him, but he wouldn't budge. He didn't even get a chance to answer before Lolo said his last words, uttered directly to him:

"Always wear your scapular and pray." The energy waned, and Lolo's voice thinned to a whisper. "The necklace will protect you and your loved ones. It can resist evil. Do not trust the moon, because it seeks to destroy you. Pray the rosary. Go to church and seek mercy. We are in God's hands now. I love you, anak ko."

Chapter Two

Holly

"'Tis better to have loved and lost than never to have loved at all."

—Alfred, Lord Tennyson, *In Memoriam A. H. H.*

Napa, California

October 7, 8:30 a.m.

Threads of a hazy dream clung to Holly's mind as she came out of a deep sleep. It was strange. Holly rarely dreamed, and when she did, they were more of nightmares. But this dream had been lovely. She couldn't remember the details, or anyone in particular. There had been no setting, just the ether of a dreamscape. She remembered someone, but she didn't know who they were. There had been no face…just the feeling of home. Completeness. A feeling of love so deep it banished the very concept of loneliness. The dream had been like drifting in a sea of warm clouds, and she'd never wanted to wake up.

But it was a good thing she had. "Oh no!"

It was eight thirty in the morning, and she was supposed to wake up at eight. She was due to meet her best friend, Sophie, at the Moonlight Diner at 9:00 a.m. sharp.

Holly sprang out of bed and threw on leggings and a pullover hoodie. She brushed her teeth and didn't bother to put any makeup on. Vida and Rafa's wedding wasn't until about 6:00 p.m. anyway. She had all day to spend with her friends and enjoy their company after being away from home for so long.

She took an Uber to the diner. It was clear on the other side of town, and it took almost ten minutes to reach her destination.

And there it was. Holly took a moment to gaze at the Moonlight Diner, a place that had been special to her growing up in Napa. It was across the street from the charming, rustic inn called the Oak and Vine.

She walked into the diner and smiled. It looked exactly the same after fifty years. The place filled her with nostalgia, especially when the familiar smells made their way into her senses. The aroma of hash browns, bacon, buttery toast, and coffee wafted through the air as Holly headed toward the booth where she'd spotted Sophie.

Sophie squealed in delight and enveloped Holly in a crushing hug. Holly returned the embrace with equal enthusiasm.

"It's so good to see you," Holly said.

"It's so good to have you back home!" Sophie replied. "Jeez, how long has it been? Over two years, right?"

"Yeah. I still feel bad that I couldn't make it for Grandlola's birthday last year."

"Don't worry about it. Grandlola will be attending the wedding, so you'll get a chance to see her. You know what? I think you're starting to develop a British accent."

Holly laughed. "No, I don't think so."

"Yes! See? Did you hear the way you said 'no' and 'so'? Totally British."

Holly chuckled and shook her head. After graduating from nursing school, she'd accepted a job abroad as a nurse in London. It was meant to be temporary, but it had become a permanent situation. It had been difficult leaving America behind, but she'd fallen in love with London. It had taken hold of her soul and hadn't let go.

"What about you?" Holly asked. "How is the podcast? Where's Travis?"

"*She Vibes* is doing great," Sophie replied. "Travis is working on a case right now in the city, but he'll be attending the wedding tonight."

The server came by and took their orders. Holly sipped her coffee, smiling at the thought of childhood friends Sophie and Travis finally admitting their true feelings.

"I still can't believe you two are together," Holly said. "I thought it was going to be a disaster when Ron found out, but I'm so glad everything worked out for the best."

"Speaking of love, what about you?" Sophie smoothly turned the tables on her. "What is taking you so long to find your hottie London boy?"

Holly opened her mouth to answer. For some reason, the words lodged in her throat. The thought of finding true love at home in London sparked something inside her—as if she was trying to recall an important word, its identity perched on the tip of her tongue.

"Holls?" Sophie's eyes filled with concern. "What's wrong?"

Holly blinked a few times. A wave of sadness passed over her like a dark cloud. It disappeared in a moment, its trail fading away like a plume of smoke. Shaking off the strange feeling, she adjusted herself in the seat and accidentally knocked a fork off the table. A man with a green scarf was passing by just then. He picked up the fork and put it back on the table.

"Thank you," Holly said, but the man was practically out the door before she'd finished talking.

"Seriously, is there something wrong?" Sophie placed her hand on top of Holly's, giving her a squeeze.

"No. No, not at all." Holly willed a bright smile back onto her face, ignoring the strange feeling. "I'm fine. I just can't believe Ate Vida is finally getting married. I'm thrilled for her and Rafa."

***

Later that evening

The moon and stars shone brightly through the windows of the chapel as Vida and Rafa sealed their marriage with a kiss. Everyone applauded while the happy couple beamed from ear to ear.

They retreated down the aisle, fingers entwined. The lilting strains of "Forevermore" accompanied them. Holly knew their story, and the odds against them. Seeing the happy ending of their tale made Holly's heart swell with joy, but something held her back. It was happening again— that strange tinge of sadness, like a dark shadow limning the edge of a cloud.

Holly dismissed it. Maybe the jet lag was rearing its ugly head. Or perhaps she was homesick? In any case, she forced herself to ignore it. She was only here for a few days, and she was determined to enjoy herself, weird depression be damned.

***

"Holly! Oh my God! Come here and give me a hug."

Holly's head swiveled toward the voice. She spotted Sophie's mom, Liz, standing near a decorative trellis in the outdoor area next to the reception site. She enclosed Holly in a fierce embrace. Sophie stood by, chuckling in delight.

"I'm sorry I missed you when you came to the bridal suite earlier. How is life in London?" Liz asked. "How is work?"

"Everything's going great."

"Which hospital do you work at again?"

"Greater Hamilton Children's Hospital."

"Oh, I remember now," Liz said. "I think Sophie told me you work in the cancer unit?"

"Yes, that's right."

Liz grimaced.

"God bless you for doing that," she said. "When I was in nursing school, I cried every day during my pediatric training. That's why I work with the elderly."

As Liz and Sophie chattered away, Holly noticed the beauty of this night in Napa. It was otherworldly, as if the veil of another dimension draped over the atmosphere, shifting worlds back and forth in invisible colors and waves. Suddenly, the sadness descended again. Instead of waving it away this time, she let it sit. Simmer. She came to the disturbing realization that it wasn't the sadness that bothered her—it was the familiarity. She'd felt this way before, and not just today. This sadness went more than deep—farther than the depths of her heart. It was a part of her. It was a stain on her soul she desperately wanted to scrub away.

"Holly, I wanted to introduce you to Jake."

Holly snapped to attention. A handsome man stood next to Sophie, his friendly eyes trained on Holly.

"It's a pleasure." He extended his hand.

Holly shook his hand on reflex. As handsome as he was, she felt nothing—no stirring of her heart, no awakening of the dormant parts of her soul.

"He's Rafa's nephew," Sophie said. "I thought you two would hit it off."

"Yes, I heard you're a nurse," Jake said. "I'm in my last year of nursing school. I want to work in the ER."

Holly's face lit up. She had a soft spot for her fellow nurses, especially new ones. "Really?" she said. "Good for -you. That's a great career choice."

Before she could say another word, the trellis they were standing next to went up in flames. Holly and Sophie screamed. Liz and Jake jumped back.

They were outdoors. It wasn't the trellis that had caught fire; it was the decorative chiffon curtain draped on it. The Hacienda employees swept in immediately and attacked the flames with a fire extinguisher.

"That was a close one," Liz said. "I knew all these candles were going to be a problem. I warned Vida, but she didn't listen to me."

Holly was about to respond, but a quickly retreating figure caught her eye. A green scarf streamed behind them as they disappeared into the bushes at the edge of the property.

"Holly! Where are you going?"

Holly would never have ignored Sophie, but she had a feeling in her gut that she needed to follow. That instinct made her rush past the bushes toward the vast vineyard beyond.

The rational part of Holly was well aware that following a stranger into a remote vineyard was a bad idea. Despite that, she couldn't help but believe, with every fiber of her being, that this person with the green scarf was the culprit behind everything she felt today. It made no sense, but she believed it down to her very soul.

She spotted the figure, whom she could see was a man, fleeing past the ripe vineyards. He ran past the thick outline of acacia trees, all the way to the pond at the periphery of the property.

"Wait!" Holly shouted.

The man stopped.

Holly approached. She forced the breaths in her chest to slow down. Her footsteps were slow and deliberate so as not to disturb this moment. "Who are you? I saw you at the diner today, didn't I?"

The man didn't answer. Didn't turn around.

"What's going on?" Holly asked. She didn't like the way her voice sounded. It was shrill, out of control. "Who are you?"

He turned around. A thousand emotions descended upon her, like falling sparks. His dark eyes spoke of anguish. Of loss. Despite the aura of sadness surrounding him, the sight of his familiar and unfamiliar face chased away all the shadows.

He was but a stranger, and it broke her heart that she didn't know him. Or…perhaps she couldn't remember him? "Am I supposed to know you?" Her whispered question mirrored the despair in his eyes.

Wordlessly, he shook his head.

"No. No, you're lying."

No response.

"You're the one, aren't you?" Holly demanded. "I saw you at the café earlier. You set the fire at the wedding. I know this makes no sense, but I can't help it. You know what's going on. You know everything."

The man gazed into her eyes, each second ticking by increasing the sorrow in their depths.

"Why won't you talk? Say something!"

They stood there for a brief eternity. Holly waited until the waiting became unbearable. She couldn't stand his silence. She wanted something from him, but she didn't know what it was.

All she knew was that he was a bright, incandescent presence. He lit up every part of her, and she wanted to do the same for him. She wanted to know him—she wanted him to spill all his secrets into her like an endless draft of sweet wine.

She ran up to him. Despite the fear in his eyes, she continued on. She wanted to dive into the alluring darkness pooling in his gaze and swim in its depths until she lost herself. Her arms wrapped around him, and her lips found his. When their lips met in a kiss, everything changed.

The universe shifted…

Love bloomed…

Life reset.

The world as she knew it began again.

Chapter Three

Eli

"No matter how much time passes, no matter what takes place in the interim, there are some things we can never assign to oblivion, memories we can never rub away."

—Haruki Murakami, *Kafka on the Shore*

October 7, 7:30 a.m.

Eli always dreamed. He was one of those rare people who could not only remember his dreams but control them. He had grand adventures and saved countless worlds as the sole hero of his imagination. There was never a shadowy beast or ruthless killer who could thwart his dreams and turn them into nightmares. Eli defeated them all.

That was why Eli woke up the morning of October 7 with a feeling of dread stirring in his chest. He had no recollection of his dream the previous night. It was as if someone had cleaned the slate with one powerful swipe.

But the lack of dreams was half the struggle.

He had no idea where he was.

Alarm shocked his body into wakefulness. He'd been here before. There were no memories telling him where and how and why he'd been here, but his heart knew. He'd been here more than once. Maybe even a hundred times.

The thought stirred terror in his chest. Was there truly a gap in his memory, or was his imagination going wild? Fighting the rising panic,, he forced himself to calm down and take stock of his surroundings.

The room was cozy. Themes of grapes and wine and vineyards intertwined with the rustic aesthetic. He was in some kind of hotel room, but he didn't know where. Despite the strange surroundings, he did not get the impression he was in any immediate danger. There were no signs of struggle. He was unharmed. Whatever happened to him the night before, he had a strong inkling there had been no foul play involved. It had to be something more insidious.

Eli grabbed his phone and opened the navigation app. The location made his eyes widen in shock. "Napa?" he whispered. "Why am I here?"

He got up and took stock of what he knew. He was a nurse at Greater Hamilton Children's Hospital in London. His mother's name was Mary. His father's name was Antonio, but he'd passed away when Eli was a child. As a result, his grandfather Gregorio had stepped in and assumed a greater role in his life. Gregorio had been an amazing father figure...in the beginning. Before the illness had set in, he would keep Eli entertained with stories of life back home in the Philippines. He had loved to talk about folklore and mythology. Even when he'd descended farther into darkness and lost himself, Eli never forgot the loving man Gregorio had once been.

Eli let out a shaky breath. So, he hadn't lost his long-term memory. He could easily book a flight back home to London, but he wouldn't. Not until he found out why he was here.

Determined to solve this mystery, he showered and got ready for the day. Before he left, he clenched the scapular necklace in his fist as reassurance that somehow his grandfather was watching over him. Protecting him.

Before he left, he threw on a green scarf to curb the morning chill. He made note of the hotel's name: the Oak and Vine.

He paused on the street corner and breathed in the stinging cold air. His breath turned to mist, and it reminded him of how time was fleeting. Every moment passed by, only to disappear and never repeat again.

There was life on the streets at this time of the morning. People were out, strolling down the avenues of this old town part of Napa, heading toward cafés and eateries. He saw couples strolling arm in arm, hand in hand. The sight of them sparked an empty feeling within, as if a fundamental part of him was missing.

He spotted a diner across the street. The aroma of bacon and coffee and buttered toast beckoned to him, helping ease the strange feelings of emptiness flowing through him.

Without another thought, he headed across the street and entered the diner. The scene was benign—people eating, families chatting, friends smiling at one another. But a strange sense of weariness descended upon him. There was something cruel about the scene unfolding. People were happy. Content. Going about their lives without a care in the world. He could have this kind of life. This was the life he wanted, but instead here he was, struggling to unfold this mystery.

The hostess led him to a booth, and a server immediately approached. "What can I get you?" Her welcoming grin had a relaxing effect on him. She had a youthful air that defied the gray hairs covering her head. A grain of recognition sprouted in Eli.

"Have we met before?" he asked.

The woman blinked at him.

"I don't think so, honey," she said. "But maybe? Lots of people come in and out of here. It's possible."

Eli breathed deep. Forced himself to calm down. *Just go through the motions*, he told himself. *Figure out why you're here, and then you can go home and get on with your life.*

"Just coffee. Black."

"You betcha."

Eli leaned against the booth's vinyl cushions. He focused on his hands as he fiddled with the silverware on the table, taking a moment to gather his thoughts. He'd woken up this morning with no recollection of his dreams. Did that have something to do with being here? What was the significance of Napa? If he just dropped everything right now and went home, it would all be over. He could forget about this disturbing gap in time and get on with his life.

It could be easy.

He glanced up and saw a woman sitting a few rows down.

And suddenly he knew it wasn't easy. Nothing would be easy from that moment on. In fact, just encountering this woman here and now could ruin everything.

Panic erupted in his heart. He didn't know why, but he needed to get away from her. For reasons unknown, he didn't want to talk to her or look at her or touch her.

Unfortunately, the only path out of the diner would take him past her. The narrow aisle seemed to thin to a thread as he got up and hurried out of the diner.

A fork clattered to the floor. He stopped for half a second, but it might as well have been half a century. He wanted to pass by and ignore it, but he couldn't. He wanted some acknowledgment that he was really here in the presence of this woman. He picked up the fork and placed it back on the table without turning to look. He heard her voice. She thanked him, but he couldn't bear it. The sound of her words was the worst part of this whole ordeal. He knew this woman. And somewhere in his heart, he felt she knew him too.

Eli left the diner. It took an enormous amount of strength not to fall to his knees as a torrent of memories collided into him.

A children's hospital ward.

Him as a new nurse walking onto the ward for the first time.

A beautiful nurse approaching him, introducing herself as his preceptor.

Eli staggered to a stop on the curb as the memories kept coming.

The nurse's beautiful smile as he brought her coffee and pastries.

A fleeting touch of his finger against her hand on the last day of his training.

The looks that grew bolder with longing as the weeks passed, until finally an innocent dinner turned into a kiss he'd dreamed of since the moment he first met her.

And then the name appeared to him from the echoes of love and longing and passion.

Holly.

And suddenly Eli knew. He should not have figured out Holly's identity so soon, but somehow, impossibly, it all came back to him.

A new emotion took over, replacing the emptiness.

Rage. Despair. The pure misdirected hatred that had sparked this whole series of events, and the trap he'd fallen into.

Eli knew where he needed to go.

La Luna.

***

The rideshare dropped him off on the outskirts of downtown Napa on a street lined with old shops. It was within a short walking distance from the old courthouse, and just across from the Veterans Memorial Park, where the deep-green Napa River meandered in a lazy path between the town and the valley. Tourists came here to take pictures and experience the old-world charm. But not Eli. He came here to settle a score.

It was oddly deserted here. A few shoppers walked by, drifting with blank stares as if in a dream. Eli ignored the chill running up his spine and searched for his destination. He spotted it immediately. The wooden sign hung above the door: *La Luna—curator of mysteries.* He noted the small paper sign taped up to the glass door: *Enter here with your soul open,* with a decal of the Philippine sun and three stars next to it. The sight of the icon unsettled him because it confirmed what he already knew:

Everything happening to him had something to do with his grandfather.

Eli strode through the tight aisles in the shop. The scent of cloying incense filled his nostrils as he navigated this tiny, maddening maze. Tall shelves crammed into the narrow space, making the store seem even smaller than it was. The shelves were filled with books and strange objects, like shrunken heads, unidentifiable body parts preserved in jars, real animals preserved in various positions, and jars and bottles of things Eli couldn't identify. It all added to the dizzying and overwhelming nature of this place.

"Excuse me." Eli squeezed his way past a customer, who jumped in surprise at his abruptness.

Finally, he entered a small open area toward the back of the store. His sudden appearance startled the two nearby customers. The woman standing at the counter did not flinch. She didn't even look up at him.

Recognition tickled his brain as he studied the woman. Since the moment he'd seen Holly at the Moonlight Diner, memories had started trickling back. He remembered everything about Holly, and the entire story of how they'd fallen in love. She'd been a head nurse at the children's hospital—a fellow expat with a background similar to his.

He'd thought she was a lovely person, inside and out, when they'd first met. But after the first week of training, Eli had known he was falling for her.

It had been a gradual kind of love. He'd kept his feelings at bay for almost the entire four weeks of training. He'd always heard it wasn't a good idea to date a coworker.

But true love had other plans. He hadn't known that Holly had felt the same way. He'd never known she harbored a secret crush on her American trainee. He'd been clueless about her own stolen glances and silent longings until that fateful day they'd shared a kiss.

However, there was more to this story. It was the final missing piece he couldn't capture no matter how much he racked his brain. And this mysterious woman behind the counter could help him uncover the truth of everything.

"I know you," Eli said.

Something in his voice jarred the other two customers. They froze in place, their concerned gazes bouncing back and forth between the woman and Eli.

"Is everything okay?" one of the customers, a young man, asked the woman behind the counter.

The woman smirked, her eyes not even sparing a single glance at Eli. "The store is closed," she said. "Leave."

Strangely, the other two customers turned and left without a word. Eli stood there. He wouldn't be moved, no matter what.

When the door shut after the last customer left, the woman finally looked up at Eli. Thick dark hair framed her heart-shaped face. Her flawless brown complexion and full black brows added to the sharpness of her impossibly dark eyes. Any other time, Eli would have found her pretty. Beguiling. However, the lethal power uncoiling in her gaze told him she was anything but.

"Who are you?" Eli asked. The question made him feel foolish, as if he was the only person left in the dark.

The woman's red lips quirked up in a dangerous grin. "My name is Lita," she replied. "I must admit. You have surprised me, Eli Amaro. You are much stronger and more courageous than I expected."

Eli's body stiffened in fear. This stranger knew his name.

Lita's heels clicked on the wooden floor as she walked a few steps toward the far left of the glass counter. The skirts of her rust-colored dress swished with every step. She opened the door and removed a small velvet tray of antique jewelry.

"What exactly do you remember?" Lita adjusted the beautiful pieces with care, her slender fingers playing upon the gold and jewels with a gentle nature that belied her malicious aura.

"I remember Holly," Eli said. "And my life before her. What I can't remember is…you. And why you are doing this to me. I've never done anything to you."

Lita sighed and looked up at Eli. "Strange how you only remember certain things," she said. "Let me jog your memory. Did your grandfather ever tell you stories about the Philippines? I'm sure he told you about the witches and healers. The ones from his province. They called my part of town Old Multo."

A cold sweat trickled down Eli's back. The names *Lita* and *Old Multo* brought back memories of both sadness and terror. "Yes, he did."

"What did he tell you about the witches and the spells they cast?"

Eli paused, searching his memory. "It's hard to remember exact details," he said. "I remember him saying something about dark magic, and how they used animals or bugs to attack their enemies."

Lita's expression hardened. "Old tricks and old magic from an ancient land," she muttered. "We can do much more than that. And did he ever tell you about the young witch he deceived? The one he tricked into falling in love with him?"

Lita's tone made Eli's blood run cold. He had no response. Her words sparked familiarity in Eli, reminding him of the mysterious things Lolo had said the night he'd died.

"Of course, he didn't tell you the truth," Lita spat, her voice dripping with derision. "Why would he tell his precious grandson about his horrible sins?"

Lita took the jewelry case and threw it back into the display. She slammed the glass door. A jagged crack spidered across the surface, but it didn't shatter. Eli stepped back.

Lita took a breath. Composed herself. She rested her hands lightly on the counter and looked up at Eli again. This time, he saw it: the look of a predator sizing up its prey. He remembered this look. He'd seen it when…he'd first come to the shop the day before.

"I remember now," Eli whispered. "I flew in from England separately, two days after Holly. I came here yesterday and bought an engagement ring for her because she always said she loved antique jewelry—because each piece has a story behind it." He lifted his hand. There it was: the round ruby atop a gold ring on his pinky finger. This small piece had much more than a story behind it—it held a force of dark magic within. He yanked the ring off so fast he almost dislocated his finger.

Lita laughed. The ring made a hollow sound as it rolled across the wooden floor.

"You could throw that ring into a fire and it still wouldn't help," she said. "It's already done its job. Do you really want to hear this story? Again?"

The way she said "again" made Eli shiver in dread. She couldn't possibly mean he'd been here more than once. Could she?

"One day, when I was hanging clothes out to dry, and my nanay was performing healing at our bungalow, I saw a handsome boy walking by." Lita slowly came around the counter and stood in front of it, her hands tucked demurely behind her. "It was strange seeing this boy out in the country, especially dressed as smartly and carrying himself the way he was. He was classy. From a richer family in town.

"He showed interest in me. Every day, he came, and slowly he won my heart. I fell in love. For nearly a year, he'd come to visit, bringing me gifts and promising me he would propose."

Lita's face grew dark. An ugly anger swirled in her eyes as she continued. "Then one day, I went to town to surprise him. I'd brought him and his family special kakanin my lola and I had made. I got to the gates of his house…and I saw him near the front door. With another girl. His friends were there too, and they saw me first. They knew who I was, even though I didn't know them. Do you know what his friends did next? They laughed. At *me*. They called me a bruha, and they laughed so hard at the thought of Gregorio with me. How could anyone be afraid of the witch who'd been fooled by the even more foolish Gregorio? They'd said it was a dare. He'd had a reputation as a coward. To prove them wrong, he'd told them he would pretend to love me, then break my heart. He was not afraid of witches. Everyone in town was afraid of them, but Gregorio wasn't. And he'd proved it."

Lita turned. The soft swish of her long skirt was almost hypnotizing as she walked to a shelf and started rearranging the jars and books on it. "I was humiliated. I was forced to go back home, so ashamed of what had happened—so ashamed of how I'd allowed myself to be fooled."

Lita's fingers trailed over the skeleton of a snake, so gracefully displayed on a small wooden pedestal. "For years after, I was so sad. There was a perpetual cloud over me. Everyone said I was different, and it was true. Gregorio had not only taken my innocence—he'd robbed me of my trust in anyone.

"Many years later, I was surprised to realize that the sadness had gone away. Just faded, like a distant memory. It had been replaced by anger. Rage. But in honor of my healer grandmother, I was forbidden from activating the dark magic from my father's mangkukulam side of the family.

"When she finally passed, I was free to take my revenge. But it would have been too easy to torment Gregorio himself. I had to get creative. What was the worst thing I could do to him?"

Lita's frightening gaze fell back on Eli. His heart stuttered as fear took deeper root. "I watched him. I watched as he grew older, had children, and then grandchildren. It wasn't long before I understood what would destroy him— what would really rip out his soul. The answer was…you. Eli Amaro, his treasured only grandson. You were precious to him above all. Cursing you was the answer. Tormenting his dear Eli…that would truly break Gregorio the Courageous."

Lita laughed again, the sound punching into Eli's gut like a fist.

"No," Eli said. "This can't be true."

"Of course, none of this makes sense to you," Lita replied. "You would never understand our world, and how our souls live on forever. You and your westernized eyes look down on us. You look at us as poor, uneducated, superstitious people from a third world country. Things are happening all around you that defy your explanation, so you ignore it. Miracles and wonders and curses happen every day, and you assign some scientific or logical rationale to it. But what if I told you…it's all magic? Do you ever wonder why there are some days where only bad things happen? Oh, there's a good explanation: it must be bad luck. It's funny that none of you ever stops to think…what if it's a curse? What if I angered the wrong person, and my loved ones and I are paying the price?"

Every fiber in Eli's rational mind told him this woman was wrong. Her imagination was wild, and she was delusional. But as much as he didn't want to believe any of it, his heart knew the truth. Lita was the mangkukulam his grandfather had been afraid of. She had never been a figment of his dementia-riddled brain. She was real.

"Wait." Eli struggled to control the shaking in his voice. "You've put a curse on me and my fiancée because of my grandfather? How is this right? How is this just?"

"It is just in every way." Lita's harsh voice made Eli step back. "At this very moment, Gregorio is watching from the great beyond. He's seen the dozens, maybe even hundreds, of times you've repeated this day, forever stuck in this agonizing cycle…and there is not one thing he can do to help you. He must deal with the consequences of his sins. He shoulders the burden of your ruined life. This torment he feels…it is just a fraction of what he did to me."

Eli settled into anguished silence. The darkly gleeful tone with which Lita described the curse threatened to douse the fire of hope in his heart. This curse had destroyed the fabric of everything he understood to be reality. Even now, though his rational mind told him to fight, or flee, or rage at the injustice, he knew in his heart it wouldn't help. He wondered about the existence of multiple timelines, especially the ones where he'd experienced this situation countless times before. Had he tried to fight Lita? Tried to destroy this evil place and crush every artifact that powered this dark curse? Had he fled in tears, powerless to do anything against forces he couldn't even begin to understand?

"Lita." Eli raised his hand as if to ask for mercy. She shot him a disdainful glare, and he lowered his hand. "I can't begin to understand the hurt you feel. I'm so sorry for the pain my grandfather inflicted upon you. But I'm begging you—from the bottom of my heart—to let me go. Let *us* go. Hurting me and Holly isn't the answer. Please."

For a moment, Lita looked almost remorseful. But then her eyes flashed with hatred again. "I beg to differ." Her voice was a venomous whisper. "This is the only answer. In war, there are casualties. The only thing I am sorry for is the day I met Gregorio Solano. He leaves a trail of destruction in his wake. He was not the man you thought he was. And how poetic is it that I've carried out my revenge on the day of a wedding? A day of new beginnings and the start of love everlasting?"

Lita laughed her cruel laugh again. "I've told you this countless times, but I never tire of saying it. You will live the same day again and again. The day resets at midnight. It also resets if you and Holly touch each other. But take care. If you speak to her—so much as utter one word—not only does the day reset, but she will lose all memories of you. For good."

Eli's body tensed. Every muscle, every part of his soul screamed, *No, this can't be true!* The unfairness churned in his gut like the most excruciating visceral pain. And yet he simply stood there. To have his entire life at a standstill, cursed to repeat this torturous day without end—how could this be happening? How was this possible? He wanted to tear the shelves down and raze the entire store to the ground, but he didn't try. Lita wanted to see him writhe in agony, but he would not give her the satisfaction.

"The only things that last forever are legacies," she said. "We choose what we leave behind. Your grandfather chose to leave a legacy of ruined lives and poor choices behind him. How sad."

Lita's dark mockery made Eli's hands clench into fists. This was the culmination of Lolo's fears. He'd been caught in Lita's trap. Eli couldn't even begin to fathom the repercussions of this curse—how many people it affected, and how long he'd been caught in it.

And even more tragic—how Lita had been affected. Eli's anger made him want to hate Lita and perceive her as nothing but an evil, hateful witch—but his heart wouldn't let him. Lolo had been so ashamed of what he'd done that he couldn't admit the truth to Eli. But now that Eli knew the truth, it tore him apart. At the heart of this curse was an innocent girl who'd been deceived and violated in the worst of ways…by his very own grandfather. Through the fog of pain and helplessness, he forced himself to see the world through Lita's eyes—to imagine how she'd felt all those years ago when Lolo and his friends had laughed at her and called her a fool.

Eli's stomach turned. He gulped back the bile in his throat as he forced himself to look into Lita's fiery gaze. "Lita. What my grandfather did to you…it's unforgivable. The thought makes me sick. You did not deserve to be treated that way, and I can't blame you for how you feel.

But for what it's worth…I am so sorry. From the bottom of my heart."

Lita's eyes shimmered. Her bottom lip trembled. Eli's hopeful heart waited for her to respond—to find whatever shred of humanity was left in her heart. But her gaze turned stony once again, her eyes practically freezing the air with their hatred.

"Well said, Eli Amaro," she said. "Remember what I said about legacies and choices. Only when you choose to learn the true meaning of loss will you finally be set free."

~*~*~*~

Chapter Four

Holly

Napa, California

October 7, 8:00 a.m.

Holly woke up later than she'd planned on the morning of Vida and Rafa's wedding. She got up, brushed her teeth, and got ready for her breakfast with Sophie.

She locked eyes with herself in the mirror. Her dream had been so vivid. She remembered details about the man in the green scarf that should have been impossible: his dark-brown eyes that had held her in their thrall. The sumptuous curve of his lips. The way his muscular form had filled out the gray coat and jeans. And the most peculiar thing that stood out—the scapular necklace dangling around his neck. It had been years since she'd seen any Filipino American person wearing one. Some Fil-Am teens wore one as a sign of cultural pride, but she noticed the style tended to fade away with time. Yet he wore it with a sense beyond pride—like it was a vestige of something from the past he desperately held on to.

Holly took an Uber from the Hacienda to the Moonlight Diner. She spotted Sophie sitting at a booth.

"It's so good to have you back home!" Sophie said as they embraced. "Jeez, how long has it been? Over two years, right?"

Holly and Sophie ordered breakfast and chatted, catching up on the last few years since they'd been separated. All the while, Holly remained on the lookout for the man in the green scarf.

Soon, Holly got swept away in her conversation with Sophie. It was like old times—they laughed and acted silly, picking up right where they'd left off. Holly and Sophie were so close they were almost like sisters. Nothing as trivial as time or distance could tear them apart in any significant way.

An hour passed. The bill came, and after a brief fight, Sophie won and insisted on paying. When the giggles and laughter died down, the strange notion hovering in the back of Holly's mind suddenly came to the forefront. The man in the green scarf. She'd seen him in her dreams, and something inside her told her his presence was strong here.

She would see him here, and she hoped he'd be able to answer all her questions.

She searched the whole restaurant—but he was nowhere to be found. Had he left while she was distracted? But no. That was not how it was supposed to work. He was supposed to walk down this aisle, stop briefly at their table, and keep walking.

But he never appeared. Holly left the diner with Sophie, wondering what had happened to the man…and why each passing moment without seeing him worsened this feeling of emptiness inside her.

***

4:00 p.m.

Holly followed Sophie through the Hacienda as she walked toward the bridal suite. Even though Holly wasn't even related to Sophie, Vida had treated her like family since the beginning. She remembered visiting the Hacienda on weekends or after school with Sophie when they were in elementary school. They would run around the vineyards and play by the lake near the property. Vida would feed them and bake cookies for them. Holly hadn't played at the Hacienda since she was eleven, but it had still been a formative part of her childhood, filled with nothing but joyful memories.

Sophie knocked on the door of the bridal suite. "Ate Vida? Can we come in? Holly is here. She wanted to say hi."

Footsteps approached. Vida Moore opened the door dressed in a beautiful lilac silk robe. Some members of the bridal party were gathered in the room as well. The photographer snapped photos of her dress, which was hung on a hook by the French doors. Vida was already in full makeup, with her dark hair swept up in an elegant coif. Holly beamed. She was breathtaking.

"Holly!" Vida exclaimed. "I'm so glad to see you again. Look at you! You're so beautiful."

"No, you're the beautiful one," Holly said as they embraced. "Thank you so much for inviting me. It's so good to be home again—to be here again. Gosh, being at the Hacienda makes me feel so nostalgic. I love it here."

Vida pulled away. A puzzled look settled on her face as she stepped back, glancing back and forth between Sophie and Holly. "This is so peculiar," she said. "I'm getting this strong sense of déjà vu."

"Yeah, I kind of feel that way too," Sophie said. "How weird is that?"

Holly felt it too, but she didn't say anything. She knew it was so much more than déjà vu, but she couldn't explain it. Instead, she tried to focus on Vida's big day.

"Is that Eden and Auntie Nancy?" Holly asked, her face lighting up as she saw familiar faces emerging from an adjoining room.

The two ladies rushed over to hug and greet Holly. She got lost in the moment of coming back home, but even still, the memory of the man in the green scarf always lingered in the periphery.

***

Holly couldn't believe the brightness of the moon. Its huge round face soaked up the distant sun's rays and translated its daytime glory into a hushed glow that suffused through the tall chapel windows.

She'd never seen a more stunning couple than Vida and Rafa. It went beyond their amazing looks. The connection, passion, and love between them were palpable. They washed the atmosphere in an invisible current of sparks that stole everyone's hearts.

Later, out on the huge patio overlooking the vineyard, they all watched as Vida and Rafa took the stage for their first dance. The gentle, passionate strains of "Forevermore" slipped through the air as Vida and Rafa moved together as one on the dance floor. Sadness pricked Holly's eyes. Looking upon a love so beautiful should have made her happy, but there was something missing.

The man in the green scarf and the scapular. She was so certain he would have shown up sometime during the wedding.

But he never did.

Earlier, during the reception, Sophie had introduced her to a nice man named Jake. He was handsome and charming and kind. Yet Holly felt no spark in her heart for him. Instead, she found herself looking for someone who didn't exist. She felt if she tried hard enough, she could somehow will him into existence.

"I'm going to the ladies' room," Holly whispered in Sophie's ear. "I'll be right back."

Holly left the ballroom. She peeked over her shoulder to make sure no one was watching, then she went on an exploration of the property. She walked purposefully down the hallway toward the restrooms, checking to see if the man would pass by. She went upstairs to the second floor, pretending to head toward her room, when in reality, she hoped against all hope she would run into the man.

She never did.

***

Time was running out. Sophie would start to wonder where Holly was. Desperate now, she hurried down the stairs and went through the side door that led out to the vineyards. There was a slight chill in the air, but Holly didn't need her jacket as she strode over the grass, down the low dirt slope, toward the lake beyond the trees. Her heart raced, and anticipation sparked across her skin as she closed in on her destination.

She wasn't expecting to see him—she wanted to believe her imagination had run wild and everything would go back to normal—but there he sat by the lake's edge, framed in moonlight.

He looked almost unreal, like dreams made corporeal. The darkness somehow made his green scarf glow with a deep emerald hue. She was afraid a breath could scatter his image into a million particles, so Holly held hers until he made the first move.

The man stood up the moment he saw her. His eyes lit up, but she didn't miss the sadness behind the light. "Who are you?" Holly asked.

The man didn't answer.

Somehow his silence didn't surprise her. Slowly, carefully, she moved toward him. He kept his eyes on her, never moving. Finally, when she was close, he reached into his pocket and held out a folded piece of paper. She gave him a puzzled look for a moment, then reached for it. She was afraid to take her eyes away lest he disappear into the ether, but the words drew her gaze.

Holly,

> *You might not believe me, but we've waited a long time for this moment.*
>
> *You don't remember me. My name is Eli, and in a past life, we were in love. We ended up this way because my grandfather made a grave mistake in his past.*
>
> *We've fallen into an endless loop. The day will repeat over and over again. We will remain in this cycle until I can find a way to break this curse. The witch told me that the only way I can break free is if I choose to learn the true meaning of loss.*

Holly paused. She looked up at Eli, speared by the sadness on his face. She continued on.

> *You don't remember me, but I remember you. I look back at the moments we shared. If I knew this would happen, I would have held you closer...held you longer. Held your hand more. Spent more moments listening to your voice, with you in my arms. Spent more moments making you laugh, knowing I could bring you joy.*
>
> *Because I know how to break this curse...how to release us.*

They were just words on paper, but they had the power to alter the course of Holly's life. With trembling hands, she looked up at Eli. He closed the space between them. He was right. She did not know him, and it wasn't fair. She had no memories of who he was, or the moments they'd spent together, but she was certain of one thing.

She was in love with this man, and she would do anything in her power to not let him go.

Eli pulled his scarf away. With the most exquisite care, he lifted his necklace and looped it over Holly's neck, avoiding her touch. She looked down at it, resting so peacefully against the warmth of her chest. It was the scapular she'd seen in her dreams. She looked at him with hope in her eyes.

In that split second, she learned, with heartbreaking clarity, what he was doing. He was letting her go. It was the only way to break the curse.

A scream gathered in her throat.

No, no, no. Don't do this, Eli. Don't let me go. Don't give up.

But it was too late. She didn't know how any of this worked—how magic and things beyond explanation could manipulate reality—but she knew he was going to sacrifice their love to set her free.

"I love you, Holly."

She tried pulling away, but his words stilled her. They were the last words Eli uttered before he kissed her, and the world fell apart for the last time.

~*~*~*~

Chapter Five

Eli

London, England

October 8, 6:00 a.m.

When Eli woke up the next morning, he remembered his dream.

He and Lolo were strolling by the lake. It was a beautiful place, filled with tall acacia trees through which you could glimpse fertile vineyards beyond. A full moon hung in the sky, solitary, with nothing but a black void pinning it in place. Its peculiar red sheen frightened Eli. He looked at the water and was surprised to see thousands of stars floating peacefully on the surface, like tiny diamonds. Eli gave Lolo a questioning look, to which Lolo answered,

"Some things change."

Then, one by one, he reached for each star floating on the water and placed them in the sky. At first, Eli was puzzled. Then he saw how his grandfather moved: with such exquisite care, as if he was an expert crafter adorning his artwork with the purest heart. Even still, there was a slowness to his movement, as if the sky itself was hurt and he was trying to soothe it. And before long, the moon was no longer solitary. It was made all the more brilliant by the beautiful stars in the sky. Suddenly the red sheen of the moon faded, and it turned bright once more.

Eli shook off the powerful imagery of the dream and got up to start his day. He went through the motions. Every morning, he would grab his pre-brewed cup of coffee, then walk to the window of his flat in London and look down at the charming line of shops below. He loved watching the owners open their shops. It was as if watching them transferred some of that morning energy to Eli and hyped him up for his shift at the hospital.

He ate a quick breakfast, brushed his teeth, and got dressed. He took the bus to the children's hospital and clocked in for his shift.

He walked onto the ER ward, greeted the familiar faces, and received his patient assignment. He went over to the nurse roster to see who was on duty today. Twelve nurses, one charge. There was no Holly Evangelista on staff today. As a matter of fact, according to the manager, there never had been a Holly who worked at this hospital.

Eli excused himself and hurried into an empty patient room. He locked the door and paced the room as panic tore him to shreds. He'd been so certain that everything would go back to the way it was, with one exception: Holly wouldn't remember him. He hadn't even fathomed that the curse would deposit him in a world where Holly didn't exist.

Lita was crueler than he could ever have imagined.

Eli pulled his phone out and used the search engine to look for Holly. He found dozens of Holly Evangelistas scattered across the world, but none of them were his.

He crouched in the corner of the room, overcome with grief. This couldn't be happening. After everything he'd gone through, and how much they'd endured, this was how their story ended?

"Eli? Oh, my goodness, are you all right?" One of his coworkers found him cowering in the corner, pale, his brow beaded in sweat.

"I'm sending you home, Eli," the nurse manager said. "You're not well. Get some rest."

Eli didn't have the strength to refuse. The world was a blur when he took the bus back to his flat. The grief was all-consuming. He didn't even remember walking up the steps and entering the door. He stood in the kitchen for so long his knees started trembling. He propped his hands up on his kitchen sink and finally gave in to sobs.

A pool of tears formed on the floor. Unable to bear the grief, he picked up his phone once more and did another search. This time, he typed in, *Holly Evangelista RN Napa, California.*

He hit search.

Eight tenths of a second later, Holly's name appeared at the top of the search listings. He clicked on it. Her smiling face appeared, along with a blurb about her.

Holly Evangelista, RN—Northcoast Memorial, RN Manager, Pediatric CTICU.

Eli couldn't move. He stood there frozen, his hand gripping the phone so tight it turned numb. He took a slow breath. Counted to ten.

There was no telling what kind of universe Lita's curse had placed him in. Holly could be anyone and not the person he knew and loved. Even so, he would never be able to rest until he found out. At the very least, he wanted to hear from her and rest assured that she was happy. That was the most important thing.

Two hours later, he was on a flight bound for California.

***

Napa, California

Five days later

"Eli Amaro?"

Eli stood up. Smoothed his hand over the front of his white button-up shirt and nodded in acknowledgment to the man calling for him. "Yes, sir."

"We're ready for you."

Eli's heart tripped in his chest. Heat flushed up and down his neck. He prayed against all hope that he wouldn't perspire through his shirt.

He walked into the conference room. It was quite large, but only three people sat at the table, serving as his interview panel at the children's hospital. They introduced themselves: Dr. Kia, the medical director. Bill, the VP of human resources. Holly, RN manager of the pediatric CTICU.

Bill gently closed the door behind Eli as Eli tried not to fall to his knees. He made brief eye contact with Holly, desperately searching for some flicker of recognition. There was a warm gaze and a nod.

But nothing else.

Eli sat, fighting against his instinct to stare with hopeless longing into Holly's eyes.

"It's a pleasure to meet you, Eli," Dr. Kia said. "How are you today?"

"I'm wonderful, thank you."

"We were so impressed with your experience and certifications," Dr. Kia said. "According to your cover letter and résumé, you moved from the US to England to work as a nurse. What made you want to return?"

Eli's gaze flicked over to Holly. "I just…wanted to come home," he said.

***

As Eli drove down the road, he thought about the interview. It had gone as well as could be for anyone trying their best to get hired. As for someone on his particular quest, however…

It had been a failure. He had left as a broken man. The entire time, Holly had rarely spoken. She let Dr. Kia do most of the talking, and when she had spoken, there'd been no inkling of familiarity or intense emotions buried deep within. There was only one conclusion:

She didn't recognize him.

Eli parked his car in the lot of Hacienda Luz and entered the lobby.

He didn't know why he wanted to torture himself. He could have stayed in any other hotel in Napa, but he chose this place. It was painfully familiar, even though he'd technically never been here. He remembered all the details from being trapped in the cursed universe: The giant, elegant chandelier dominating the lobby, and the terraces traversing the top floor in grand, sweeping lines. The French doors showcasing a stunning view of the grassy lawn with the rolling vineyards beyond.

Eli ventured through the doors and onto the grass. Peace pervaded this place. He could feel the generations of love and hard work that permeated the very atmosphere. He knew about the Moore family, and the epic love story that served as the foundation of the Hacienda's success. This place, after everything that had transpired with Lita's curse, should have planted some sort of traumatic response within him. Yet it didn't. It served as the last reminder that the love between him and Holly had been very real. He would carry those memories with him forever.

He looked down to the woods by the lake. Eli had a choice to make. He could stay and find out more about Holly. She might even be married with kids in this particular world. During the interview, he'd never got a chance to see whether she wore a ring. But the truth was…if Holly was spoken for, he wouldn't try to win her back. He would go away and let her live her life. What was the old saying? If you loved something, you had to let it go.

Eli heard a commotion when someone opened the doors of the Hacienda to come outside. There were some chatter and giggles, then the voice of someone who sounded familiar.

Sophie.

Eli spun around. He could remember so many details from the cursed world with vivid clarity, including voices. Sophie stood there, a short distance away, with three other women. One of them was Holly.

Once again, he froze. What would she think if she saw him here? That he was a creep who was stalking her? It didn't matter. This time, he didn't bother averting his gaze. He watched as she tucked a lock of hair behind her ear, smiling at something Sophie said. Suddenly she looked up and caught Eli's eye. Her smile faded.

Eli stayed rooted as she told her friends she would join them later. Then she walked toward Eli, her hands in her pockets. She looked lovely in her green cashmere sweater and cream-colored slacks. He wanted to capture the way she looked and freeze it in his memory forever because this might be the last time they'd ever see each other. She stopped about three feet away from him. Once again, her expression was unreadable.

"Hello," Eli said. "So, we meet again."

Holly didn't respond. A peculiar expression crossed her face, as though she wanted to say something but held it in. Eli didn't want to waste another moment. He shifted on his feet, looked away to gather courage, then faced Holly once more.

"I have to be honest," he said. "It's not a coincidence I'm here. This is going to sound wild, but I came here for you. I was hoping that maybe…you're single, or not attached, or not married. Ugh, this is awkward. See, there's a reason I sought you out. If I'm making you uncomfortable, let me know and I—"

Holly suddenly reached up and pulled something from the neckline of her sweater.

A scapular.

The world as he knew it turned upside down. He was overwhelmed. Confused. Despite the chaos of emotions, hope shined the brightest of them all.

"Eli." Her voice was a whisper as her dark eyes shimmered with unshed tears. "I saw your name on the list of interviewees this morning. I didn't want to believe it. But then I *saw* you when you came into the room. I couldn't react. I couldn't do anything, because I thought my mind was playing tricks on me. I wanted to break down and cry, but I couldn't. I know who you are. You leaped across timelines and defeated the most powerful of curses. The witch altered time and space, and she destroyed our past…but she couldn't touch our love. I remember you, Eli. I remember the first day I met you, in a past life, all the way to the moment you kissed me to release us from the cycle. I love you."

They reached for each other at the same time. Eli enclosed Holly in his arms, their lips meeting in a kiss that redefined passion. All this time, he'd thought the scapular was some empty religious symbol, but it was so much more than that. It held the magic of Lolo Gregorio's love, and had somehow protected Holly and Eli's memories as they'd fallen victim to the worst part of the curse.

Lita was right. Eli would never understand the inner workings of the magic and the powers beyond mortal comprehension, but he did know one thing: somewhere beyond the grave, Gregorio had atoned for his sins. Even though Lita was to blame, Eli let go of his hard feelings and prayed she had finally found peace.

He held Holly for a long time, feeling their hearts beat as one, until the sun sank beyond the horizon, making way for the brilliant face of the moon.

THE END

About Elle Cruz

Elle Cruz is an author of contemporary romance. By day she works in the medical field, but at night she writes swoon-worthy stories perfect for all the hopeless romantics out there. In addition to being an author, Elle is active in the writing community and loves to mentor and give advice to new authors. She lives with her husband and two kids in Southern California.

Book List

How to Survive a Modern-Day Fairy Tale

Catching Feelings

Pasko Na, My Love

Forevermore

Social Media IDs:

Instagram: @ellecruzauthor

TikTok: @ellecruzauthor

Threads: @ellecruzauthor

To sign up for Elle's newsletter and get exclusive content, go to http://ellecruz.com

Maybe This Time

KAYE ROCKWELL

Maybe This Time

KAYE ROCKWELL

Blurb:

Gabriella Alonso and Cole Williams used to be best friends who were secretly in love with each other. Until one night changed the course of their lives forever. Now ten years later, Gabriella, who is hiding a dark secret, is surprised to find out she will be working with the guy who ghosted and abandoned her when she needed him the most. Cole is determined to make things right. He spent the last two years looking for her but he's shocked to find a complete stranger instead of the girl he used to know. Can Cole win Gabriella over? Or will the ghosts of their past destroy any chance he ever had?

Content Notes: Profanity; Abandonment; Mention of physical abuse

Tropes and Sub genres: Second-Chance Romance, Multicultural Romance, Workplace Romance

Heat Level: 🔥 🔥 (fade to black)

Prologue

Gabriella

High School Graduation

Ten Years Ago

"Cole! "

A lock of his jet-black hair falls across his forehead when he turns his head and his gaze finds me in the crowd.

A bright smile automatically spreads across my face and I have to bite my bottom lip at the sigh I want to let out at the sight of him.

We've known each other since we were ten and even though it's been eight years now, he still takes my breath away. He really is quite beautiful with his piercing green eyes and coal colored hair. I'm surprised no one has scouted him to be in one of those teen dramas my friend Sofia is so fond of. He looks like he jumped off the screen except Cole has always been on a whole different level.

He's not just good looking. He's breathtaking.

And he's left quite a few broken hearts in his wake. Including me. The girl-next-door strictly stuck in the friend zone. So okay maybe my heart is only hurt a little bit, wishing he would see me in a different way. In a not so friendly type of way. But it is what it is. At least we're friends.

At least I have that.

But again.. he did kiss me last night.

I tear off my cap as I make my way across the sea of families celebrating the end of high school.

"Hey!" I say, nearly out of breath at having to catch up to his long strides because even though he saw me, he kept walking. We're nearly at the parking lot by the time I do and he doesn't say anything and simply looks down at me.

He isn't frowning. He isn't smiling either.

He's just looking at me with a deadpan look on his face while I'm bent over, clutching my knees, struggling to catch my breath. His eyes that are usually a bright emerald green have dulled that they look almost black. Nothing like how he looked at me last night.

I straighten suddenly feeling awkward. I've never felt that way around Cole before.

He's been the one constant in my life. The person I went to at the end of the day when a guy blew me off or a friend talked about me behind my back. When I was in middle school and my parents were struggling, he would always bring me an extra lunch. He would even go as far as sneaking in snacks in my locker so I would never go hungry.

So why is he looking at me like that? Instead of how he usually greets me. With a smile and a quip about how I need to brush my hair?

My mind flashes back to last night.

Our families had thrown a joint graduation dinner and afterwards when all the adults were drinking and talking, Cole and I climbed into the treehouse in his backyard.

We stared up at the ceiling, reminiscing about our childhood. We joked about old relationships and scoffed at friends who became strangers. Talked about what our future would look like and what our dreams were.

And when our moms had called out to us telling us to come down and go to bed, he leaned over just as I sat up and kissed me.

It wasn't a peck either. It was a full-on kiss. Exactly what you dream first kisses to be.

Full of promise. It spoke of years spent longing and crushing on your best friend.

But now he looked at me like he didn't even know who I was.

"Are you okay?" I whisper. I would normally go straight for a hug but in this case with him looking at me like that… doubt is making me self-conscious.

And frankly, a little worried. Did the kiss not mean anything?

"I'm good." He turns to look over his shoulder before looking back at me, this time his face has transformed into annoyance, "Did you want something?"

I know that look. I've seen it many times, mostly when he talks about his dad or a girl who bothered him way too much when she couldn't take a hint. Sometimes even directed at me but only when I made him watch a cheesy Filipino Rom Com or I'm dating some random dude at school that he didn't like.

Never out of context like this. Never for no reason.

"I–ah," My eyes sweep the parking lot behind him, trying to make sense of what was happening and searching my brain for a memory of what I could have said or done for him to be so callous like this towards me.

"I just wanted to say congratulations… on.." I wave my hand holding my cap.

He raises an eyebrow in acknowledgement, his impatience breathing life into his every movement. He sighs like he can't be bothered and mutters a thank you. He abruptly turns as if to leave and my hand goes to his arm reflexively.

He flinches at my touch as if it caused him physical pain.

"Cole?" I drop my hand and go around him to see his face. He stares past me and when I look over my shoulder, I see a young woman I don't recognize idling in what I recognize as his dad's SUV by the curb obviously waiting for him. The car has a big 'Congratulations Cole!' written on the windows.

I feel bitterness claw at my chest at the sight of another girl who gets to be with him while I stand here yet again, a spectator in a dream I've had since I met the usually cheerful next-door neighbor of mine. But now I get it. He's got a new girl, a college girl by the looks of her and I'm cramping his style by keeping him here instead of wherever they're off to.

My head is muddled in confusion and questions demanding answers but my embarrassment over his cold shoulder wins over everything else.

I take a step back and throw my hand up in a wave, "Looks like you gotta go so… yeah high school was fun. See you around!"

"Bri."

I clench my fist tighter around my cap and plaster on what I hope is a bright smile before turning back to him.

Cole is looking directly at me now, his hand flexing steals my attention. He almost looks as if he wants to reach for me and his eyes roam my face like he's memorizing it. Almost like he's sad but then as quickly as it came, his face turns blank before he straightens.

"Take care of yourself," he says softly, his eyes trailing down the side of my face before he abruptly turns away.

I tilt my head in question, confused. I'm about to ask him what's going on when the girl yells out his name and now I'm definitely certain she's waiting on him, "Cole, hurry the hell up."

Cole cusses under his breath before he storms toward his dad's car. My mouth drops open at his brush off. He's usually the one dragging me places or making me hang out and now he's walking away without so much as a goodbye? It isn't like him.

Especially after last night.

But then again... Maybe this girl does mean that much to him. We had always joked about how one day he was going to meet a girl who was going to completely spin him out of his axis. Someone who would make him chase instead of run away from.

Maybe it finally happened.

Little did I know that the sight of him getting into that car with that girl would be the last time I ever saw him again or that in the span of just a few hours, my life would change forever.

And not for the better.

~*~*~*~

Chapter One

Cole

Present Day

"It's her." I breathe out as I stare at Rafa's phone in disbelief.

My friend says something but I ignore him as my finger traces the image of my childhood friend on my phone screen. The picture that Rafa had taken is slightly blurry since he took it in haste but there's no mistaking that lopsided smile and those eyes that have haunted my dreams for the last decade we've been estranged.

Bri.

"I knew she looked familiar and last night it clicked, man. The new Banquet Manager at Hacienda Luz is that Gabriella girl you wouldn't stop talking about back then. The one you've been trying to find for the last two years."

I finally look up at Rafa, my hand gripping his phone tight. The look on his face mirrors my astonishment.

"I-How–" I stop short when it dawns on me that Gabriella is in this very city. Hacienda Luz, the hotel and vineyard owned by the family of Rafa's fiancée is twenty minutes away from this restaurant we drove to after Rafa picked me up from the airport. If I leave now, I could see her. Talk to her. Hug her.

The thought of finally seeing the girl who used to be my everything, sends a sudden wave of heat through my whole body while simultaneously chilling me from the fear that she may not remember or forgive me.

When I sure as hell remembered her. Thought about her. Dreamed about her.

Memories of us as kids, of that one single kiss we shared has gotten me through some of the toughest times in my life since leaving home.

I owe Gabriella an explanation.

I make a move to stand when I spot Mason, and Ruby, entering the restaurant headed straight towards us. Mason is the owner of Atout, the restaurant we're currently dining in and Ruby owns a catering company. They are both in charge of cooking the food for Rafa's wedding reception. I recognize them from the video chats we've had through the last few months while we brainstormed dining options and menu plans for all the festivities surrounding Rafa and Vida's wedding. My stomach sinks knowing I can't just leave now that they're here.

I paste on a polite smile and do my best to not look like I have one foot out of the door.

Ruby smiles brightly at me as she takes a seat on my right. Mason raises his hand at me in greeting before taking a seat alongside Ruby. I give both of them a friendly nod.

"Nice to finally see you both in person."

"Same!" Ruby moves to pick up the menu on the table when her eyes fly to Rafa's phone laying on the table, Gabriella's picture still displayed on his screen. She exchanges a confused look with Mason who is now looking between me and the phone in curiosity.

"Why do you have Miss Alonso's picture on your phone?"

Alonso?

I pause at the unfamiliar name and look back down at Rafa's phone.

Yup, that's definitely her. She's going by her Mom's maiden name now?

When I stay silent, trying to wrack my brain, Rafa answers for me. His hand goes to snatch his phone from the table, the corner of his lip curling up in amusement.

"Cole grew up with her. He's been trying to find her for the last…?" He waits for me to finish the sentence.

"Two years. And we didn't just grow up together. We were …" I search for the proper word to describe just how close we were and just how much she meant to me but I come up short. The last two words come in a whisper, my head filled with memories and my heart, regret. "… best friends."

Before they can question me further, we're interrupted by the waiter coming to our table, notepad in hand.

We put in our orders all the while my mind is still stuck on the girl next door who apparently now went by the name Alonso.

Chapter Two

Gabriella

One week later

"Miss Alonso?"

A stack of papers is dumped in my line of sight and I have to shake myself from the memories I allowed myself to get lost in.

I thought for sure I had buried them deep enough but one trick of my eye brought them all to the surface.

I look up and find Dave, my Banquet Captain idling by my desk with a worried look on his face.

"Are you all right? I said your name three times."

I force a smile, trying my best to channel the boss woman persona I've adapted ever since I took over this job a few months ago and push back any wayward thoughts of the most painful time of my life away. I wave my hand in a dismissive manner and tap on the space bar on my keyboard to get it to power back on again. I must have been sitting here for at least thirty minutes buried under memories for it to have gone on sleep mode.

I had picked up some coffee at a café on my way to work today when I thought I saw Cole but the second I had turned around, that person was nowhere in sight.

I've been spending way too much time at work and not getting enough sleep. That is the only explanation for why

I conjured him up then allowed myself to even think of him afterwards.

Breathe, Gabriella.

"I'm okay, I was just thinking about Miss Vida's rehearsal dinner and wedding we have coming up in two months."

He nods in understanding and I gesture toward the seat in front of my desk.

Dave is a recent transfer from one of the owner's properties so we were still getting acclimated to each other's way of working. He is a few years younger than I am but with his extensive background in hospitality and event management, he was overqualified to replace my vacated spot as Banquet Captain. I feared he would challenge me at every turn but so far we've seen eye to eye on almost everything.

Crossing his left leg over his right, he sets his padfolio on one knee and grabs the first Banquet Event Order, BEO for short, from the top of the stack he had just placed on my desk.

I pull up my desktop folder for the Fall Event season and give Dave the nod to start.

We have a meeting at the end of the third week of every month to discuss where we're at with the current month's events and what's to come for the next. We just recently concluded our summer season and it's about to be even busier with Harvest Season coming up.

Dave and I spend an hour going through each BEO, making notes on which vendors to contact, dietary restrictions and client requests. We also make the necessary adjustments to the bottom line after tallying the cost of equipment rentals, food and beverage costs.

"There's a request here for Filipino food for Miss Vida's wedding." Dave frowns as he pores over the requests that include a separate golf cart for Lola Naty, the owner of Hacienda Luz. "Do we even know if the person they hired to help Ruby and Mason can do this type of cuisine before they approved it?"

One of our big events this upcoming season is the wedding of one of our owners, Vida. It's a pretty big deal for both of us. Especially since we were still both new to the property. We feel a certain level of responsibility and privilege at being given the opportunity to execute this.

It will also be my biggest event as the new Banquet Manager at Hacienda Luz so I'm feeling the pressure of proving myself capable and deserving of the title I now hold.

I smile at him in assurance but on the inside I'm worried. I have zero information on this new chef. All we know is that he is an external hire and was sought after by Vida, herself.

"I might have to work with him on this menu. I spent years in my mom's kitchen so I know my way around the lumpia table."

Dave smiles, his eyes casting back down to his BEO before coming back up to meet mine.

"I can help, you know? I grew up helping my Lola and I gotta say my adobo is better than hers," he whispers, pressing a finger against his lips as if playfully asking me to keep it between us.

My mouth hangs open in shock, "You cook?"

Dave chuckles, shutting his padfolio and setting it on top of his BEO stack.

"And here I thought the Filipino part would shock you. Yes, I cook and my mom's Filipina so I spent so much of my childhood either eating or cooking the food. I can help. This is a two hundred guest list."

I smile at that and offer him an apologetic smile. To be honest, I had known he was Filipino.

"I actually knew you were Filipino." I admit.

He raises an eyebrow in question.

"The phone calls with *Nanay* tipped me off."

I overheard him on the phone talking. I found it endearing.

He grins while leaning on my desk, "Well then all I need to do is convince you that I'm a good cook." He maintains eye contact for longer than he usually does before his eyes dip lower, pausing at my lips, "I can cook for you. We can call it a taste test."

My eyebrow quirks. He's flirted with me a handful of times but always in passing and never quite so forward like this.

I'm about to respond to him in warning when I hear someone knock. We both turn to look at the door and I have to blink a few times before what I'm seeing completely registers.

By the time the shock wears off, Dave is already on his feet shaking the hand of the black-clad newcomer.

What I saw before was not an illusion. He really *is* here.

Cole.

My eyes eat up the sight of him. He looks taller somehow, definitely broader. A hint of a tattoo peeks from underneath the white shirt he's wearing underneath his black coat. His hair no longer flops to the side, instead gelled and shorter. The style accentuates his chiseled features, highlighting his emerald eyes that pop out even more now that his hair isn't hiding them.

He's mumbling 'nice to meet you' but his once-familiar eyes are locked on mine, a library of emotions clouding them.

Everything comes rushing back, the longer I hold his gaze. My insides churn and my chest aches. The familiarity of the pain I've hidden since I last saw him rush to the surface. It isn't until Dave clears his throat, his head ping ponging between us that I once again wear the mask I've so carefully crafted over the last decade.

A hint of a smirk lifts one side of Cole's lips before he quits his inappropriate staring and actually spares Dave a cursory glance.

"Cole Williams."

I rise to my feet and extend my hand out, my eyes flashing with warning. Now is not the time to rehash the past and definitely not the time to reminisce with old neighbors.

"Gabriella Alonso. Banquet Manager."

Cole stares at my hand for a fraction of a second that certainly feels like it's longer. For a moment there I'm scared he'd pull me in for a hug. I bite back the sigh of relief when he shakes my hand but when I pull back, he holds on daring me to say something other than my name and title.

"Cole." I snap, without thinking.

"Yes, Bri?" He chuckles out, his face splitting into a handsome grin.

Damn it. I forgot how freaking gorgeous he was. My memories did not do this man justice.

Bri.

He's the only person who's ever called me by that nickname. It was something he came up with when we were eight and he complained about my name having too many syllables.

I force a laugh out, not wanting to prolong this awkward exchange. I shrug out of Cole's hold and take a much-needed step back.

"Dave?" I turn back to look at my Banquet Captain who's staring at me, his eyes burning with questions I don't have the answer to right now, "Could you take the corrected BEOs down to Sales and make the necessary adjustments with them?"

Dave hesitates but nods, his movements slow as he gathers his stuff from my desk along with the BEOs with annotations on them.

Cole stuffs his hands into his pockets, his shoulder leaning against the doorframe. He watches me watching Dave and I feel the tension practically come off him in waves.

"We'll talk about the taste test later then?" Dave asks, lingering next to Cole by the door.

I nod and give him my best smile even though all I want to do is grab my purse and take an early day. The thought of being alone with Cole after years of radio silence and built-up resentment makes my skin crawl and my heart sink to my stomach.

Finally, Dave takes the hint and goes, leaving me with the person I used to know.

Chapter Three

Cole

"Long time no see, Bri." I let my eyes wander the length of her and damn, she's even prettier than I remember. Even better than that blurry picture Rafa had taken.

Her black hair that used to come down to her backside in unruly curls is now dark brown, wavy, and shoulder length. Her cocoa eyes that remind me of nights spent in front of a fire roasting smores are shifting around the room, almost in a panic now that Dan-Dave-Dean or whatever his name is left. She's sexier now too and definitely dressing it. Her pink suit jacket does nothing to hide those curves she used to hide behind sweatshirts and baggy t-shirts in high school. Her white button-up top molds itself perfectly onto her bigger-than-a-handful chest that leaves little to my imagination. The matching pink suit pants hugs her backside so tight and so right, it looks painted on.

Gabriella sighs, muttering something to herself that sounds a lot like *let's get this over with*. Running a hand through her hair, she sits back down and gestures toward the office chair in front of her desk.

Holding my smirk, I ignore her. It takes me three steps to get to her and when I do, I grin when her eyes widen realizing just a few moments too late what I'm about to do. Turning her chair slightly, I push it until it's between her computer desk and the L shaped table beside it. One of my hands goes to the desk and the other on the table essentially trapping her between my arms. I bend until I'm leaning over her and our noses practically touch, our lips inches away from each other.

She emits a gasp as her eyes fly up to mine. She places a hand on my chest in an attempt to shove me away but I don't budge. She *will* hear me out.

Her brown eyes flare, "What do you think you're doing?"

"You're mad at me."

I know she's mad at me. I know *why* she's mad at me.

Hell, looking at her now, I've never been more angry with myself for wasting so much time. When I could have been spending it making it up to her in inventive ways.

"*No shit, Sherlock.*" She mumbles once again under breath, both her hands are splayed across my chest now, attempting to push but her attempts are feeble. She's not even giving me a healthy push, just like she did when we were kids. Because even though it's been a decade now, she likes my proximity. Maybe missed it even but she's adamant on pretending she doesn't like it.

Damn, I really missed this girl.

"Cole, seriously. I'm at work. I don't want to give anyone the wrong impression here."

I feel a slight twinge of jealousy remembering how I overheard that jerk flirting with her just moments before I let my presence be known.

"By anyone, you mean like David Lopez?"

That's right, I did in fact know his name. I knew her whole department employee roster by heart after obsessing over it for a week now.

Gabriella's eyebrows rise and just when I think she's finally given up on pushing me away, she ducks underneath my arm before I can stop her. She straightens her suit jacket and goes to the door to shut it before turning back to me.

Pointing at the office chair again, she glares at me.

"Sit down or see yourself out, Cole."

She said all that with a straight face. I let out a low whistle, my hand immediately going to the back of my neck. As much as her bossiness irks me, it fucking turns me on too.

After all these years, Gabriella still has a viselike grip on me. I observe her for a minute, letting my eyes drink in the sight of my old friend. I missed so much of her life when I left San Diego and since then I've always felt like my life was missing something essential. Then one day, there she was again.

And now she's actually standing in front of me. Within touching distance. That missing piece that left a gaping hole in me and the dreary feeling I've been living with for the last decade is gone. Even in this cloud of resentment and words that were left unsaid, somehow everything feels right. Less lonely, even.

I have to fix this.

I thought pushing her was the answer but clearly her affection for me is gone and somehow hate replaced it. I need to play by her rules if I want to get through to her.

So, I do what I'm told. I sit and wait. Watch as she takes a heaving deep breath before rounding her desk and sitting opposite me. She takes her time, her eyes drifting towards my knee when I cross it, clearly hyper aware of my movements.

"What are you doing here, Cole?"

I pat my breast pocket and point at the words *Chef Williams*. She must have missed it because she was too busy staring at my face.

"Wait. You're the new chef?" she asks incredulously.

"That I am," I answer.

"Chef Williams… This can't be hap…" She trails off, sliding down her chair a little all while shaking her head like she can shake this truth away.

"What's the matter, Bri? It's been ten years but didn't we say someday we'd own a restaurant together? This is almost like that."

"Don't call me that, my name is Gabriella and we're not kids anymore."

I lean over her desk taking in every inch of her, "I've noticed."

Sighing, she shuts her eyes for a moment, resting the back of her head on the chair. Her exhaustion is evident in her movements, like she hasn't taken a breather in years. If what I've heard about her struggles is true, I'm here to remedy that. I never thought of myself as the white knight type of guy but if that's what it takes to take care of this woman in front of me after everything she's done for me and what she's had to endure, get me a horse.

"What are you really doing here, Cole? Of all the places in the country, hell even in the state, you just happened upon the one I work at?"

Judging by the cold reception she's given me since she first saw me, I know she's not ready for the whole truth yet.

"Must be fate."

"Cut the crap, Cole."

I simply grin at her because even though I like seeing her riled up, pushing her buttons too much might not be the best way back into her good graces.

That gets to her, it seems. She sits up straight in her chair and shoots me a look that makes my heart pick up speed. I've never seen her like this before. Even during the times I sat beside her in our treehouse while she complained about a backstabbing friend or a douchey guy behind those eyes still held a sadness only someone as kind as her could have even after betrayal. But right now? That look she's giving me holds a multitude of emotions but I don't have in me to decipher everything quite yet. The pain swimming behind them gets to me first then the anger pierces me but it's everything else that makes me second guess this plan.

"What happened to you, Bri?" I swallow hard, unable to look away.

For the first time since I found her, I'm uncertain. This reunion didn't happen the way I thought it would.

I thought she'd run into my arms the second she recognized me. That she'd break into one of those infectious smiles when she realized we'd be working closely together.

Instead, she tried to rush me off, displaying anger and hurt.

"I grew up, *Chef*," she bites out. "Now if that's all, I'll walk you out and introduce you to the rest of the team."

She starts to stand but stops when she sees me rounding the desk. I'm moving before my brain catches up to my movements but I don't care. I've wasted so much damn time that I'm not willing to waste any more.

"I'm here for you, Bri." I go to kneel next to her chair and take her hand in mine.

She's too shocked to resist, her eyes stuck on how I'm holding her hand.

"Do you know how long it took me to find you? What I've had to do to be here right now?"

"C-Cole. What? I don't understand what's going on right now."

"I messed up–" The sudden sound of an alarm coming from Gabriella's phone that's sitting on her desk interrupts me just as a knock on the door comes through. We hear a throat clear from outside and the distinct voice of Dave comes through the door.

"Miss Alonso, we're needed for the weekly standup."

I really don't like that guy.

~*~*~*~

Chapter Four

Gabriella

"Cole?" I huff out as I enter the banquet kitchen. I've been looking for him for the last half hour having exhausted my search through the grounds and the main kitchen. He looks up at the sound of my voice from where he's plating desserts for our event tonight with Ryan, the sous chef. I feel my eyebrows pinch together when he barely spares me a glance before going back to drizzling caramel on top of the salted caramel cheesecakes our client special ordered for the dinner we're hosting.

I don't know why I'm surprised, in the last few weeks that Cole's been here, he's been hands on with every event, even the small ones like the one tonight. Even going as far as staying during events to make sure the clients are happy with the food and being available for all nutritional questions or concerns. I was so used to having to tag team smaller events with Ryan, that I did not realize just how valuable having both the Banquet Manager and an Executive Chef present can be. For the first time in our Hacienda's history our GSS score, which is our Guest Satisfaction Survey, is almost at a 100 percent and it's all because of how seamlessly Cole and I work together.

Without even meaning to do so, he's managed to make me look good in front of the owners and I no longer felt compelled to compare myself to Dave who had more experience than I did.

"Give me a second, Miss Alonso, we're almost done here." Cole murmurs inspecting each plate as Ryan starts placing the plated desserts on the sheet pans.

Wordlessly I grab the pan rack and position it next to Ryan and help him stack them on it. I reference my BEO and do a silent plate count, noting the three extra desserts they plated. I bite back a smile at that.

The old Banquet Manager, Leo never let us do extras claiming he was controlling food cost but Cole always made sure we had them. It's been such a relief to have the backup. Sometimes shit happens at events and we're left scrambling to come up with an extra dessert for a headcount mistake or accidental drop.

Ryan does a final plate count before placing the rack in the insulated box, "Twenty-eight plates, Chef."

Cole pats Ryan's arm, "Are you good with transport while I chat with Miss Alonso?"

"Yeah and you're good to go. I got this." Ryan salutes both of us before rolling the box outside. I wait until I hear the distinct sound of the box attaching to the golf cart and it leaving before turning back to Cole.

He has his back to me as he goes about cleaning the area they just used. I grab the used utensils and dishes, place them in a dishwashing rack and send them through the conveyor dishwasher.

"So, what can I help you with, *Miss Alonso*?" He asks with a grin as he tosses all the dishrags in the dirty linen basket.

"It's just us now, Cole." I clear my throat and hand him an updated BEO for the Moore wedding, "Sales missed the rehearsal dinner request when they sent us the BEO for the 200 plus wedding. Vida wanted me to make sure you were up to date with those changes."

He reads the updates I highlighted and gives me a thumbs up, "Got it. I'm friends with Rafa -. I'll let them know I got it."

I let out a huge sigh of relief. It's been an adjustment being the one in charge but also working with someone as easygoing, assertive, and meticulous as Cole.

Leo hated changes after the initial BEOs had been made and oftentimes as Banquet Captain I had to play mediator between him and the sales department just to get anything done.

"Well, that's all I wanted then, thank you." I go to grab the BEO from him because it has all my notes when his hand goes to grab mine instead.

My eyes jump to his in surprise and his answering smirk tells me everything I need to know. He's done being patient with me. Over the last three weeks, Cole has attempted more than a handful of times to get me to sit down and talk to him. Each time I've managed to give an excuse due to the steady stream of events we've had but tonight we only have this small dinner that Dave and Ryan could handle on their own.

"Not so fast, Bri." His thumb rubs my knuckles in a gentle manner, the gesture causing goosebumps to prickle my skin.

Damn this guy. Ten years later and I revert back to an adolescent with her first crush.

"Cole." I start while I try and think of an excuse to get me out of this. I really do not want to rehash our past. I've worked way too hard and I'm not going to let what was or what could have been damage all the work I've done to come out of the last ten years unscathed.

"Gabriella Anne Alonso *Cruz.*" Cole says with the same affection in his tone he used on me as kids whenever he needed to placate me after an argument, "I think it's about damn time you and I talked, don't you?"

My hand is still wrapped up in his, somehow his hold becomes firmer yet gentler like I'm some prized porcelain doll he wants to take care of. His eyes are softer now that it's just the two of us and he looks at me with a hint of fear and sadness.

The sadness gets to me then I realize what he just called me and I relent.

Chapter Five

Cole

I peer over my menu at her. We're sitting in a little cafe called Moonlight Diner, about ten minutes from the Hacienda. No matter how hard I try, I can't seem to keep my eyes off her. This is the most time we've spent together in over ten years.

Her eyes meet mine and I struggle against the need to cross the few feet separating us, to hold her in my arms. She looks exhausted and overworked. Now I'm wondering if she's taking time to care for herself or if all she does is work.

I dip my head, purposely avoiding her vacant stare. I try to concentrate on the menu in front of me but I can't for the life of me focus on anything other than her proximity.

The fact that I'm close enough to see her yet unable to touch her is killing me. The memory of the only time I was ever brave enough to act on my feelings is burned into my brain. I've chastised myself enough over the last few years for not doing more. How different our damn lives would have turned out if I didn't push away the one person who had been my constant.

"Stop staring at me, Cole."

I smirk and drop the menu on the table. I give her my full undivided attention now that she's finally spoken a word.

"Stop being so beautiful, Bri."

Her eyes flash with warning before she places her menu on top of mine. She glances behind me and waves at the waitress to come take our orders. The second we got there she headed straight to a two-person table at the corner of the restaurant by the bay windows overlooking the sprawling garden. And if that didn't clue me in to this being her regular spot, the waitress who approached greeting her by her first name did. As I look around the bistro style cafe, I can tell why she favors this place. It's definitely her style. It was quiet and quaint but clearly popular with the locals given the steady stream of customers coming in and out even on a Tuesday night when most people favored tacos or pizza.

The waitress, Mia, an older woman of short stature with red hair and a cherubic face who instantly made me feel comfortable, strides over to our table, taking the menus off the table.

"Are you having your usual, honey?" she asks Gabriella who smiles warmly at the older woman.

"Yes, but swap the Sprite for a glass of your best white, please."

Mia raises an eyebrow but says nothing before looking at me, "And what can I get this handsome fella?"

It's then I realize I didn't even look at the menu to know what they have to offer. My eyes scan the small restaurant and land on what the man at the next table is eating. I'll have what he's having, I guess. Better than admitting to being too enamored by Gabriella to read the menu.

"I'll have the salmon and a red, please." As soon as I say it, I inwardly cringe.

"Actually Mia, he'll have the Lechon Barbeque burger with an IPA." Gabriella interjects.

Mia and I both look at her in surprise but the older woman recovers faster, leaving before I can even respond.

Gabriella raises an eyebrow at me as if daring me to argue because even though it's been years, I can't argue that what she ordered for me sounds a lot better than fish and wine.

But I want to hear it from her.

"Care to explain why you changed my order up on me, Bri?"

"You threw up when we had our first communion. Since then, you've had an aversion to wine which doesn't really make sense now that I think about it since you work in a vineyard. And you absolutely hate eating salmon because your mom cooked it at least twice a week so every time your mom made it, you would make up some excuse to have dinner at my house. You love it when my family hosted parties because the lechon and barbeque skewers were your favorite. Also, junior year, bonfire at Mission Beach. You had beer for the first time and you drank like three of the Stone IPAs before I had to drag you home. That's exactly what they have on tap here."

She's absolutely right, of course. Salmon, I can have sparingly but I would never touch wine unless I'm cooking with it.

"You know me too well, Bri."

At the reminder, Gabriella sits up straight, her smile slipping. She doesn't say anything in response, her eyes dipping down to her lap.

But I don't let that deter me. Even though she's worked hard to give me the impression that anything she might have felt for me back then is gone, flickers of the old Bri have made appearances every now and then. It's kept me going. Strengthened my resolve.

I have nothing to lose when I've already lost her. All I can do is try and get her to understand. My best bet to get her to talk to me and not shut down is to tread slightly. Test the waters with something simple so as not rock the boat.

"I take it you come here often?" I gesture around the restaurant. "Got your own table and everything."

"I come here a few times a week, especially when work runs late." She answers vaguely.

"Alone?" I can't help but ask, thinking about the Banquet Captain who acts like her annoying shadow at work. Always around. It's one of the reasons I haven't been able to get her alone to talk.

Gabriella rolls her eyes at that. But I'm seriously asking her. I have no idea if she is single. I certainly have only seen her at work these past few weeks and she has zero social media presence. All I know about her is hearsay at this point so I continue to look at her, waiting for a response.

"Yes, Cole. I come here alone."

"And?" I press.

"I don't date."

"Good."

She stares at me, bewildered, questions swimming in her eyes. Ones she refuses to ask me, possibly in fear I'll hit back with my own.

Her cellphone pings and she turns away to grab it from her purse to check it.

I take that moment to study her more freely while she's occupied. Her hair is up in a ponytail, tiny tendrils framing her face. My hands itch to touch her. Then she chews on her bottom lip as she answers a text message and it takes everything in me not to groan at the sight. I'd give anything for another taste of her.

"I miss you."

"I'm right here, Cole." she replies, sighing as she drops her phone back in her purse.

"You know what I mean."

Mia chooses that moment to come back with our drinks and for a moment I watch Gabriella drink the wine. I feel a heavy weight settle in the pit of my stomach as I recall my journey to finding her again and how when I finally did, she turned out to be a complete stranger.

It made me both mad at myself and sad at the same time. Mad that my actions led to our estrangement.

"What happened to you, Bri?" I echo my question quietly, hoping my tone conveys the heartbreak and sheer longing I feel. That I am in no way judging her. Hoping she understands that I in no way blame her for how she's acting towards me.

The fact that our friendship has turned into distance, awkwardness, and resentment is all on me.

"Life, Cole. Life happened." Her harsh sigh, the second one she's released in a span of minutes, has me leaning over the table and taking her hands in mine.

She doesn't try to take them away and I take that as a sign. I curl her hands around mine until I can intertwine our fingers together.

"What did you mean by what you said?" She whispers, her eyes drifting back up to mine. She searches my face for a moment before she continues, "When you said that you looked for me and that I didn't know what it took for you to be here?"

I decide to let blind faith lead me because even though I don't think she's ready to hear the answers, I let my heart decide and go for it.

"I've looked for you for over two years, Gabriella. I almost gave up too. You're a hard woman to find. You weren't on any social media sites. Out of sheer desperation and fear that you may be gone, I hired an investigator but he came up blank until–" I pause, worried this next part might make her angry, "–I had him run Sofia's information."

Her eyes widen and I watch as her throat bobs.

"It took me a few tries to even get her to agree to meet me but when I pleaded my case, she relented. She told me you were still in California."

"What–what else did she tell you? And why were you looking for me?"

This is where it gets tricky. Sofia, her best friend from high school, had been adamant about not sharing too many details so most of what I found out was from Ruby and Vida.

I didn't want to break their trust in me but I also didn't want to lie to Gabriella.

"Not much. Just that you had been on your own since high school and it's been rough." My grip on her tightens, "I've been actively looking for you for over two years, Gabriella but I've been waiting for you to come back into my life for a lot longer than that."

She's quiet for a moment so when she pulls her hands back, I let her. Her gaze falls on her lap. I take a sip of my beer then another to calm my nerves while I wait for her response, not wanting to rush her even though everything in me is fucking screaming to push.

"I'm not the one who left, Cole," she says quietly.

"I didn't have a choice, Gabriella."

"Right," she bites out, her arms crossing across her middle as she regards me with a look of disbelief.

"Bri. There's a lot you don't know about what happened back then."

"Go on then. You've gone through all this trouble to find me just to explain it to me, so do it. Tell me why you kissed me only to act like you couldn't get away from me fast enough the next day. You left with some girl then disappeared and ghosted me. Let's see you talk your way out of *that*."

My eyes narrow at her but my heartbeat kicks up a notch. I got a lot of room to make up for.

The memories of that time in my life pierces through the armor I built around my heart and no matter what I fucking did to try and forget, the memory of what went down still hurts like hell.

"That girl? She was my dad's girlfriend."

Gabriella drops her arms, her perfect lips parting in shock. I'm distracted by the sight for a moment before I realize she's waiting for me to continue.

"The night before graduation, after our dinner party and the treehouse." I give her a sad smile, "My parents sat me down. They were getting divorced. Apparently, my dad had been having an affair with his teacher aide. He was getting transferred to a college in New York and since he made more money than Mom, they decided I was going with him."

"But–but you were eighteen and going to college, you could have stayed with your mom or gotten a dorm in school," she stammers.

I shook my head, rubbing at the slight heartburn this trip down memory lane was giving me.

"She was selling the house and I couldn't exactly go to school as the son of the professor who was sleeping with his TA." I open my palm out on the table hoping she'd take it. Hoping she'd know I needed a little bit of her support to get through the next part of my story.

Her eyes soften when they land on my palm and she reaches out, giving it a squeeze.

"I'm sorry I acted like a jerk on graduation. I woke up that day to my mom gone. I was pissed that my dad sent his girlfriend to pick me up while he packed up his things back at the house and angry with my parents for missing graduation. It was a shitty day that led to even worse weeks. I'm even more sorry for not responding to your calls or texts. After moving to New York, I didn't even last a month with them before I enlisted in the Air Force. By the time I got out of training and tried to contact you, it was too late. You had changed your number and all your social media had been deleted. What happened, Bri?"

"I guess my story is not far off from yours. My parents also sat me down but they at least waited until after graduation to let me know they were selling the house and moving back to the Philippines."

I nod for her to continue. My PI discovered that much.

"They paid for school but everything else, I had to figure out on my own. I had to juggle school and work. Anything beyond that was too much for me so I canceled my phone line and deleted all social media."

"Why did you change your name?"

She starts to run her fingers through her hair then realizes it up. In frustration she yanks her ponytail off, her hair cascading to one side of her shoulders. The sight of it nearly knocks me off my feet but then she starts to speak and the crack in her voice when she does is my undoing.

"About a year after college… I met this guy. I had mutual acquaintances with him, he knew people I had gone to school with and worked with. On paper, he was perfect. Charming, sweet, attentive, and understanding with my busy schedule. I was working multiple jobs by then to afford my own place. At first everything was good. So good that he ended up moving in with me but not long after that he changed. It was a gradual change and he started slowly showing his true colors…" she trails off, her gaze taking on a distant look.

"Did he hurt you?" I ask, a man on the edge.

She shuts her eyes and nods once. Her small hand trembles in mine and I don't think about it. I'm at her side in an instant. Crowded restaurant be damned.

Mia comes back to the table with our food and I silently mouth the words, *to go* and *check*. Thankfully she sees Gabriella slumped over my arm, her hand clutching me and Mia takes the hint, scurrying away to box up our food.

I stick my hand in my pocket and pull a few bills out. I throw a hundred and twenty-dollar bill on the table just as Mia comes back with our plastic bag of food.

I give the older woman a grateful smile mouthing, *Thank you.*

She dips her head in response, casting a cautious glance at Gabriella before waving a silent goodbye.

Gabriella straightens in my arms, patting my shoulder to release her. Even though that's the last thing I want to do, I let her go. She offers me a small, teary smile.

I grab her purse, slinging it on my shoulder before I gently grab her hand, guiding her outside. Thankfully I insisted on taking my car here. I don't like the idea of her driving home when she's upset. I don't like the thought of her being alone, period.

Besides, there's still a lot of things that are left unsaid between us. Now that she's finally opened the gate of communication between us, I don't want to risk leaving her for fear she might shut it on me again.

As soon as she's safely inside my car and buckled up, I set my phone on the holder and click on the maps app.

"What's your home address, Bri?"

She was resting against her car door but snaps out of her reverie and looks around. Something seems to click and her frown comes back.

"Just take me back to the hotel. I can drive myself home Cole."

"We can go back and forth on this until you finally give it to me or come with me to my place? Ultimately it's up to you, Bri but please let me be here for you."

Please.

Her address was something I didn't ask Vida for. I was too afraid I'd give in to temptation and turn up at her door.

She eyes the door handle and I chuckle, knowing immediately she's thinking of bolting.

"I'm not leaving you alone without making sure you're alright and I'm not going anywhere until we finish this conversation."

Gabriella glowers at me, muttering her address so low I strain to hear it but I do.

"I know you've managed on your own for a long time, Bri… but please let me take care of you. Let me do this much for you." I say quietly.

I'm not the type to hold anyone against their will but Gabriella is and will always be my exception. I need her to understand that I'm trying to fix my mistakes.

"Take me home, Cole."

She goes back to resting her head on the car door, her eyes slowly shutting as she relaxes into her position. She tucks her legs under her and releases a slow, deep breath.

I don't know if she meant for me to hear it because she practically breathed out the words. "Thank you."

I relax in my seat, hope ballooning in my chest.

Chapter Six

Gabriella

"Bri?" A whisper cuts through the fog of sleep. I feel a hand on my shoulder and I jerk, my hands instinctively going to the top of my head.

I hear a voice so familiar that it makes my chest ache, "Gabriella, it's just me. It's Cole. You're safe."

"Cole?" I whisper as goosebumps prickle my skin. The lump that had lodged itself in my throat loosens and I'm able to breathe freely again.

"Yeah, it's me. We're here at the address you gave me. I parked on the street because I didn't know the gate code."

Oh.

Reality sinks in and I remind myself that my memories are merely that.

I'm safe.

My earlier conversation with Cole brought about memories I had fought so hard to forget and I fell asleep from the burn out of my brain going into overdrive. When I woke up, for a moment there I was transported to a time when I would wake up the next day still exhausted from not just the physical trauma of my previous relationship but the emotional as well.

Trauma is a tricky thing to navigate. For the most part, I feel like I've managed it just fine but there are times when the memories of what happened assault my brain and I surrender unwillingly to it.

"Thanks for dropping–"

Before I can finish my sentence, Cole is already out of the car and opening my door in mere seconds. He carefully unbuckles me from my seat, taking my purse and the takeout bag from the floor then he offers me his hand.

Confusion muddles my brain so I take his hand and let him lead me to the side gate without question. He releases my hand so I can enter the code and he follows me inside, his eyes scanning the surroundings like my own personal bodyguard.

When we reach the stairs, I look over my shoulder at him. He meets my eyes, his hand going to my lower back as he urges me to keep going.

Uncertainty makes my steps falter but I know deep down, he's right. We were a book left unfinished and if we didn't do it now, we'd have to finish it another day. I'm not sure I can live in a constant state of anticipation when we could sit down and finally find some resolution. Move on from these feelings we let fester. I've never properly moved on from him and the resentment that followed his departure was not something I want to live with any longer.

It was too heavy. Too much of a burden for me to carry.

I suppose he's feeling the same way if he went through all this trouble to find me.

It doesn't take us long to walk to my apartment. The complex I live in is small and only has two floors with a handful of one-bedroom apartments on each floor. I chose it because it isn't far from the hacienda and it is in one of the safest neighborhoods in the area.

After what had happened with Peter, my sense of security is shaky at best.

I unlock my door and Cole follows me in but lingers behind me waiting, watching as I secure the locks on my front door. The apartment came with two locks but I had installed two additional bolts just so I could sleep at night without having anxiety attacks.

I kick off my heels, placing them on the rack by the door. I pressed my lips together, fighting a smile when I see that Cole has already taken his shoes off and placed them there as well. Years spent in my house have trained him well in the ways of living in a Filipino home.

The apartment opens up straight into the living room. I take off my gray tweed topper jacket and set it on the back of my couch, leaving me in just my sleeveless crewneck black dress and tights.

Cole heads straight for the barstools I have at my breakfast bar, taking the dinner he had boxed up at the restaurant out of the bag. I still can't believe I froze up back there. Fifteen minutes with him and I let my guard down.

Holding back a sigh, I go around him to the kitchenette.

"Can I get you anything to drink?"

Taking off his jacket, he tosses it on top of mine.

"Anything cold and not wine will do. If you have beer or Coke, that's preferable." He moves to stand next to me, raising an eyebrow with his hand on one of my drawers as if asking for silent permission to snoop around my kitchen.

Nodding, I point at the drawer next to his hand. "Utensils are on the right."

I grab two cans of Coke from the fridge and sit on one of the stools. He hands me a set of utensils and I hand him his drink. We dig into our still warm food in silence for a few beats before he clears his throat halfway through his burger.

"Tell me what happened, Bri."

My gut twisted.

I set my fork down, pushing the plate of alfredo away from me. My eyes stung from having to fight back the tears but even though fear is practically coursing through every pore in my body, I felt safe. Cole always had the ability to make me feel that way. Even at sixteen when a boy broke my heart for the first time and I sat in the treehouse with him, I knew he wouldn't tease me even if that was his go to. I knew he would set everything aside to be there for me, no I-told-you so's, just the comfort and safety of his arms.

"A job saved me. I was working in San Jose for a golf resort as a hostess. Chef Karl, the Food and Beverage Director there, set me aside one morning and flat out told me that he knew I was in a bad situation. Said he saw through the makeup and the excuses then he gave me an ultimatum. He told me he saw potential in me and would do everything he could to make sure I had all the tools I needed to have a career but that I needed to save myself first. Then he took me to the police, helped me fill out a police report." I swallowed, my eyes drifting towards the hand now squeezing my knee. "Anyways, after all was said and done. He started training me to do paperwork and inventory. Then I trained with the other managers in the department and learned the ropes, started doing events."

"What happened to…?" he asks carefully.

I shook my head and shrugged, "It was my word against his. The police believed him but the police report spooked him enough that he packed up and left. He left a letter apologizing for everything, promising to leave me alone and that was that. But I wanted to be certain he never found me so when my old boss let me know about a property that was looking for a banquet captain, I took the opportunity. I filed to have my name legally changed and thankfully my old boss is good friends with Vida. I was able to make the transfer effortlessly within weeks and well, here I am."

I attempted a shrug but the urge to cry started to overwhelm me. Tears blurred my vision and blinking didn't help. It only made them leak out of my eyes faster.

"Bri…" Cole's arms scoop me up and before I can protest he's lifting me. He carries me to the couch, setting me gently on his lap. I bury my face in his neck and his arms tighten even more around me. It's like balm to my battered soul. He had always been my undoing, my calm, the one person capable of both tearing me apart and putting me back together.

I feel his lips everywhere. On top of my head, my forehead, my cheek. One of his hands is on my waist but the other is running a path down my hair and back.

For a moment he just holds me, whispering words I can't make sense of in the fog in my brain. I could tell they were beautiful words, ones I wished for and had always hoped I would receive from him.

Then in the aftermath of the most painful of breakdowns, I feel a sense of peace wash over me. The wracks that had torn my body cleansed my soul.

As the tears slowed down to just a roll down my cheeks, I felt the pressure in my chest ease. For the first time in years, I felt like I could breathe. Like someone had lifted the heavy burden off my chest and allowed me the space needed to lose a little bit of the weight of my trauma. It was enough.

My eyes fluttered open and there he was. Looking at me with tears swimming in his own eyes. He brushed the flyaways that stuck to the wetness coating my cheeks. The gentleness of his touch has my chin quivering but he grips my jaw in the palm of his hand, his thumb brushing over my chin up to my lower lip. His hooded eyes drop to my lips and he swallows.

I don't think, I lift my head and press my lips against his. He doesn't even hesitate, his grip tightens on me and he kisses me. It isn't a gentle kiss or one of timid exploration like the one he planted on me when we were eighteen. It's urgent, possessive like he's marking me as his.

I break away, gasping for air but the second we part, we move back in again.

Like we can't get enough. Like we had been deprived of oxygen and the only way to survive is to steal it from each other. It is a battle for dominance, one I knew he would win. One I would surrender completely to if it meant he'd be the prize. He turns me in his arms and instinctively I move to straddle him.

Burying his hand in my hair, he uses it to tilt my head as his mouth descends. He trails kisses across my cheek down to my neck.

I tip my head back even more to give him access, trembling from the force of my own need.

"Cole…" I whisper, intoxicated from his touch, from the feel of his lips on my heated skin.

"Fuck, you don't know how long I've waited to hear you say my name like that."

His lips move to the spot behind my ear and I don't know how he knows but he does and he sucks on the spot that makes me shiver and moan. His answering grunt as he once again ravages my mouth makes my hips move on their own, seeking some reprieve. Suddenly Cole flips us both and I'm lying with my back on the couch and he's hovering over me. He rolls his hips forward and I feel just how much this man wants me.

"Is this okay?" His voice comes out breathy, laced with lust as his lips skim my ear and collarbone.

Before I can answer, he bucks his hips again, making me moan his name louder. The sound of it spurs him on and he curses against my skin. His kisses grow frantic against my neck as his hips speed up.

I pull his head up and crash my lips against his, my hands sliding under the hem of his t-shirt feeling the abs I fantasized about as a teenager.

I've prided myself on always doing what was right. This felt more than that.

Felt more than need. Than want.

It felt inevitable.

Chapter Seven

Cole

In between kisses and fervent touches, in the back of my mind there's a small voice cautioning me to slow down but having a writhing Gabriella under me is not something I can easily ignore.

She's my every dream come true and now finally being able to kiss her after years of not even knowing if she was even alive has to be some cosmic sign from the universe.

This was more than fate.

It was inevitable.

And that thought is what pierces through the cloud of lust.

As I lie here on her couch, with her tucked into me asleep with nothing but a fleece blanket covering us, I think about everything we had both been through. I wish I had done more to find her but I can't undo what was and the only thing I can do is to do better.

I knew it at sixteen, when she cried in my arms about a boy that wasn't me.

I knew it at eighteen when I finally worked up the courage to claim her with a kiss.

Ten years later it hasn't changed, she's it for me.

We were destined since the moment we ended up in houses next to each other and she climbed into my tree house to introduce herself with fried bananas and mango juice.

The girl with the missing front tooth and crooked pigtails wormed her way into my heart that day and never left.

I already lived a life without her in it.

That's not an option for me anymore.

Chapter Eight

Gabriella

I woke up the next day from the best sleep I've had in years to the smell of spam and garlic permeating the air.

I sit up, stretching when I hear a groan and a chuckle.

"I have to say that's the best sight to wake up to."

I drop my arms in surprise, my eyes flying open and I realize way too late that I had fallen asleep on the couch completely naked. My bare chest and torso are on display and I clutch the blankets on my lap to hide but I'm too late.

"Don't cover up on my account, Bri. I will definitely not be opposed to naked breakfasts."

I feel my skin heat and I know I'm turning red. My eyes are fastened on my lap and I have yet to meet his eyes but I feel him move from the kitchen before he's kneeling in front of me.

His eyes and smile are brighter today, his happiness evident.

"Good morning, my Bri. I made you your favorite spamsilog." He presses his lips against my forehead, breathing me in before he pulls me completely onto his chest, his fingers tickling a path down my bare back.

"You're still here," I whisper as memories of what we spoke about and did come flooding back.

After what had happened the first time we kissed, there was a small part of me that worried he'd be gone come morning. Waking up to him making me breakfast felt like a dream.

"There's nowhere else I'd rather be than with you, Bri."

Surprisingly the feeling of calmness I had last night is still present and the once familiar pressure against my chest is nowhere to be found.

His hand plays with the ends of my hair as he maneuvers us both so I'm once again sitting on his lap. He pulls off the sweatshirt he's wearing and puts it on me.

I look at him in question as I push my arms through it and pull it down my thighs to cover up.

"I keep a bag of spare clothes in my car, I hope you don't mind that I borrowed your keys so I could go get it."

I shake my head and play with the hem of his sweatshirt.

It smells like him. Like how it smells after it rains. Like hope after a storm.

"Cole?"

"Yeah?" He tucks me into his chest as if knowing we're veering into a serious turn in our conversation.

"Why did you look for me?"

"Because I'm in love with you, Gabriella Cruz."

My head knocks into his chin when I whip it towards him so fast. My eyes widen at the way he just says that like it's a fact rather than a confession.

He laughs, his hand grabbing mine that's rubbing his jaw almost absentmindedly.

"Yes, Bri. I've loved you for two decades now. When I got out of training and realized you had disappeared, I did everything I could to nurse my broken heart. I buried myself in work and did everything I could do to advance my career. Even when I got out four years later that was my fallback. I pushed myself to the brink of exhaustion. I went to culinary school, did internships around the world. But at the end of the day there was nothing I could do to ignore the piercing ache your absence in my life had caused. That became more evident when my dad moved overseas and shipped me the only thing I had asked him to keep safe for me. One box, Bri. The only thing I had left that was of any value in my life was a single box with memories of you. Concert tickets, movie tickets, everything you had ever given me, I had kept in there and when I opened it again, I knew. There was no escaping the truth anymore. I had to find you. I had to find my missing piece."

I move on instinct, I straddle his hips. My hand goes to his chest, just above his heart and the feel of it racing against my palm makes me smile through the tears now flowing down my cheeks. He thumbs my tears away, cupping my face in his palms and I lean into them silently urging him to continue.

"I had almost given up on finding you, having exhausted all my options."

"How did you find me?"

He smiles sheepishly, "Remember when I said I knew Rafa, Vida's husband to be?"

I nod and wait for him to continue.

"I had known Rafa back when I was still in the Air Force. He became kind of my mentor at a time when I was struggling to figure out whether I should continue my service or find something else to do with my life. He was actually the one who noticed that I liked to cook and encouraged me to take a few culinary classes to see if I could find my passion in that." He tucks a strand of hair behind my ear, "I had mentioned you a few times to him and he saw a picture of us that I had hung up at my house but because he had known you as Gabriella Cruz he didn't put it together until a few weeks ago when you had sat down with him and Vida about the wedding. I flew in the day after that and the second he showed me a picture of you, I knew it was fate. Regardless of what I did to try and find you, we were always destined to meet again."

He tucks me into his chest with a grateful sigh.

"I had every intention of ambushing you, getting on my knees if I had to just for a moment of your time. But then I met Mason and Ruby. I told them everything, Bri. But they were hesitant. Ruby told me I needed to tread carefully if I had any chance of getting you to forgive me and give me a chance. That me showing up out of the blue after years of silence wasn't enough. I needed to prove myself to you. So, she suggested I ask Vida for a job." He smiles, giving me a quick kiss. "It didn't take much convincing for Vida to agree to let me work with you."

There were so many emotions running through me. Astonishment and gratitude being at the forefront.

"I can't believe they all did this for me. For us."

His hands tighten around me, "Do you want to know what Vida said when I asked her?"

I nod as I sit back, staring up at him in awe.

"Sometimes all you need is one chance. Maybe this time, your love won't end."

A tear rolls down my cheek and Cole quickly wipes it away.

I love Vida. I'm still young and inexperienced yet she has entrusted me with so much.

"I knew there was a chance you wouldn't forgive me. I figured this way, I get to still be a part of your life even if it was just in the professional sense."

I clutched Cole's shirt in my first, feeling his heartbeat speed up when my other hand goes to trace a path down the side of his face.

"Are you mad?" He whispers, uncertainty lacing his tone at my continued silence.

I shake my head as I trace his eyebrows, his nose, cheeks before my finger goes to his lips.

His eyes blaze, his hands moving to my hips as he watches me take a moment to work up the courage to tell him my most guarded of secrets. My arms snake around his neck.

"I've been in love with you since the moment I realized boys weren't as yucky as I thought, Williams."

His eyes light up, the love in them making them look like green embers.

"Get used to saying that name, Bri. It's going to be yours soon." He grins before crashing his lips against mine and claiming me again.

Epilogue

Gabriella

Cole nudges my shoulder with his as we watch Rafa and Vida dance their first dance from the cake table.

"You did it." He proudly tells me.

"*We* did it." I look over at Cole and find him already staring back at me.

My heart bursts with so much love for the boy I used to know. Now the man I can never live without again.

The second he walked back into my life, it was like finally seeing colors after only seeing black and white for so long.

I could not have done any of this without him.

I'm about to steal him away to show him just how grateful I am, when a gentle hand touches my shoulder.

"Vida! You look so beautiful!"

My boss pulls me into a warm hug. "Excellent work Gabriella. Thank you for making our special day all the more so."

Rafa pats Cole on his shoulder, "I second that. Thank you to you both."

I feel a tear roll down my cheek, a sudden rush of emotions have me tightening my arms around Vida. I have so much love and gratitude for this woman.

"I want to thank you, Vida and Rafa. For trusting me, and for bringing Cole and I back together." I reply softly.

"And congratulations on the marriage." Cole adds with a grin as he wraps an arm around my waist.

The newly married couple exchange smiles as he presses a kiss on my temple.

Vida winks and playfully points to her wedding ring, "Maybe this time next year this will be you."

I feel my cheeks flush at Vida's playful suggestion.

My moment of fluster ends as someone yells out, "Kiss!"

The sound of spoons clanging against champagne flutes fills the room.

As we watch Rafa and Vida share a sweet kiss under the stars, I feel Cole's fingers wrap around mine.

I lean against him and feel certain that this is what I want our future to look like.

Forevermore.

THE END

About Kaye Rockwell

Kaye is a Romance Author who spent the majority of her childhood falling in love with fictional characters and daydreaming about her own Happily-Ever-After which eventually led to her writing her own love stories.

She has made it her mission to diversify bookshelves with Romance reads that are packed with just enough tension, swoony lines, lingering looks and riddled with life lessons that have you reaching for the tissue box.

Book List:

Glad You Exist

In Case You Didn't Know

Honest With You

When I Met You

More Than Anyone

Social Media Links:

https://linktr.ee/authorrockwell

Someone's Always Saying Goodbye

MAAN GABRIEL

Someone's Always Saying Goodbye

MAAN GABRIEL

Blurb:

As a bestselling romance author, Carisa "Carrie" Bloom knows the formula for happily ever after. It's the reason she is living one of her own. But when her beautifully crafted fairy tale ends tragically, she is left both fragile and broken.

For years, Carrie stays away from the limelight, abandoning her career to live a quiet life, until she receives a proposal from a British film producer, Joshua Grant, to turn one of her books into a movie. It only takes one day and a night in London for this opportunity of a lifetime to change their lives forever.

But is Joshua ready for this? And is Carrie brave enough to take a chance again? She must choose to stop believing that in her life, *Someone's Always Saying Goodbye.*

Content Notes: vehicular accident, on-page death of spouse

Tropes and Sub genres: One-night stand, surprise pregnancy; Multicultural Romance

Heat Level: 🔥 🔥 🔥 (open door intimacies, euphemistic description)

Prologue

Carrie

The car tumbled twice, veering to the side of the highway upside down, the screeching metal a deafening sound. It happened terrifyingly fast, and yet, for Carrie, everything moved in slow motion, the texture of the moment vivid and crystal clear. Death was looking her in the eyes.

The airbag had cushioned the blow somehow, and the seatbelt kept her locked in place, but everything around her was mayhem. Screams were coming from the back seat, their friends being thrown around like ragdolls.

Then, in the middle of pandemonium, his hand found hers. Their hands clasped tightly, holding on to each other because without saying a word they knew it was the end. She couldn't even see his face to say goodbye. She wanted to scream, but she couldn't.

Suddenly, the car stopped, and the screaming ceased. The silence that followed was eerie. There was blood all over, a sharp pain was digging into Carrie's thigh, and she couldn't move. Her neck was trapped, pinched between the debris, and she started to shake uncontrollably.

"Paul..." she whispered, her voice hoarse and trembling. There was no response, and she waited a few more seconds before saying his name again. "Paul..." A sudden flash of coldness encased her, fear taking over, and all she wanted was to hear her husband's voice. She needed to know that he was okay, that he was going to be okay.

She never heard his voice again.

By the time she gained consciousness after a month-long coma, their families had already laid him to rest. She didn't even have the chance to say goodbye.

~*~*~*~

Chapter One

Carrie

Five Years Later

Carrie Bloom arrived in London with nothing but her passport and a change of clothes.

"This is going to be a quick meeting," Lara, her Los Angeles agent and best friend, wrote in an email with a plane ticket attached two nights ago. Without question, Carrie hopped on the plane, because she knew it was time to step out of her shell.

Dressed to the nines in black wide leg trousers, a black turtleneck top, Manolo Blahnik boots, and a heavy black coat, Carrie stepped out of her hotel in the center of town, a slight limp not noticeable to most after years of therapy, and braved the balmy London air to meet a man named Joshua Grant. Joshua, as Lara explained it, was a British film producer interested in optioning the romance novel Carrie penned more than five years ago.

Carrie, with her deep brown eyes and loose curls cut in a short bob, was a vision of sophistication, of glamour, but inside, she was a complete mess. She ran her fingers across the fading scar above her right eyebrow, something she often did without thinking. She wore it like a badge of honor, a reminder. Carrie's smiles were timed, her movements choreographed, her clothes always intentional. And she was *exhausted*. She had been exhausted since the day she lost Paul. Without her heart, without love to give, she stopped writing romance and decided to pursue a quiet career as an editor.

She jumped into a blue Mercedes Benz–quite a fancy Uber, Carrie thought. They drove along the bright lights of Piccadilly Circus, traffic barely moving. At the center of the rotunda, a band of musicians serenaded the crowd, a group of tourists on top of a stalled red double-decker bus applauding in admiration. If Carrie was being true to herself, she'd jump out and party with the mob. She needed to feel this energy, to feel this buzz, to be reborn wild. The idea made her chuckle–she would never do such a thing. It would be laughable, really, she thought. Still, inside, somewhere deep, she really wanted to let loose.

A few minutes later, the Uber dropped Carrie in front of a restaurant named Romulo's. Carrie was pleasantly surprised to discover that it served Filipino fares, a big sign said so on its doorsteps. "Mr. Grant did his homework," she muttered under her breath, a small smile forming on her face.

She walked into the quaint joint, admiring the art on the wall that showcased scenes depicting Filipino culture. But it was the aroma of the sumptuous dishes she grew up with that plunged her into deep nostalgia. She inhaled with a smile, even lightly closing her eyes, transported back in time.

She was ripped from her daydreams by a slight buzz in her tiny black purse; a call. Pulling out her phone, she saw Vida's face plastered across the screen. Her good friend rarely called without prior notice, so she knew this was not for chitchat.

"I'm getting married!" her fifty-year-old friend uncharacteristically whisper-screamed from the other end. Surprised, Carrie jolted backward. Her phone slipped her hand, and she caught it with another, only for it to bounce off her arm until she was able to finally grab it like a master juggler.

"What?" she gasped, putting the phone back to her ear, one hand over her mouth.

"I know," Vida replied, clearly suppressing a giggle.

"How did it happen?" Carrie asked, trying to sound cheerful, but obvious worry laced her tone. Selfishly, her immediate thought was that she was about to lose her to her soon-to-be husband, Rafa, who was the perfect man for Vida.

The friends met one night when, after hours of driving, Carrie stumbled into the peaceful quiet of Hacienda Luz. It was the most harrowing phase of Carrie's life, and Vida helped her through it. Though ten years apart in age, they struck up a quick sisterhood–both of them being Filipino added an easy familiarity to their friendship.

"I fell in love," Vida declared.

"Vida, no one should *fall* in love. One should rise with it…" Carrie complained, but she knew it was a moot point– Vida truly loved Rafa.

"Oh, stop with your romance novel lines. This is real life. I fell in love, and I think it's time."

The bells chimed as the door opened behind her; turning around, Carrie was almost knocked out by the vision of a tall man, a very tall man, dressed in a dark suit, with a face that could brighten anyone's dark day.

"Vida, I'll call you back."

For a split second, her heart skipped a beat.

It skipped.

A beat.

Her heart, which she thought had stopped beating a long time ago.

Chapter Two

Josh

It was an impulse call, but his mother made him do it. Now, Josh found himself getting out of his town car to meet this woman who wrote, according to his mother, some of the greatest romance novels of all time. How would Josh know that? He has never, not once, read a romance novel. He looked at his watch, planning to cut the conversation short soon after his last bite.

"Bollocks," he muttered under his breath, patting down his trouser pockets after realizing he must have left his phone at work. His driver, Steve, had just zoomed out of view.

"Here goes my wasted hour," he sighed, annoyed, as he walked toward the restaurant his mother chose.

In frustration, Josh pushed the door more forcefully than he intended, almost hitting someone standing on the other side. Immediately, Joshua pulled the swinging door back with one hand and grabbed the woman toward him with the other, his arms protectively wrapping her to his chest.

No one moved for a hot minute, processing what just happened. Then, Joshua bent his head down to make sure the woman wasn't hurt, only to be faced with the most beautiful amber eyes he'd ever seen, along with parted luscious pink lips just waiting to be kissed.

"I'm sorry," Joshua said as he immediately released her. Something in his core tumbled, and his heart pounded in both fear and confusion.

"Oh," was all the woman said. She looked startled, for good reason, still clutching a phone tightly close to her chest.

"Are you Carrie Bloom, by any chance?" Josh asked, his hand rubbing the back of his neck in embarrassment.

"Yes, I am," she responded hesitantly, slowly putting her phone away.

"I'm Josh Grant. I think our people arranged this rendezvous."

"Carrie Bloom," she said, taking a few steps back and extending her hand for a more formal introduction, which Josh gladly returned.

She looked cute, Josh thought. Pretty, with freckles scattered like stars across her face. When their hands touched, he felt a little something – a spark, likely the effect of dry heat inside the restaurant fighting the cold weather outside. Still, whatever it was, it unnerved Josh a little. No, actually, it unnerved him a lot.

They stood there awkwardly, motionless, gazes locked. Josh narrowed his eyes, trying to grasp the intensity of this interaction, his heart still beating ferociously.

"Hello, welcome to Romulo's. Do you have a reservation?" The hostess finally came to greet them, breaking their awkward silence, and they both followed down a narrow hallway toward the back of the restaurant.

Josh, still feeling uneasy, pulled the seat out for Carrie, who smiled as she sat. For reasons unknown, that small smile made him happy, and he didn't take happiness lightly. At forty-two, he knew what happy was not.

"How long are you in London?" he asked, settling himself in the chair across from her–surprising himself with the question. Like an idiot, he immediately turned on his stoic façade to hide his own shock.

"I fly back tomorrow night," she responded, methodically unfolding the crisp white napkin before settling it over her lap. Josh couldn't help himself–he stared at her, watching her movements, noticing the sadness in her eyes. This woman was pulling him in–a pull so strong, it confused him.

Could this be love at first sight? Josh frustratingly pondered. Even the thought of it riled him more than he cared to admit.

"That's a shame." He didn't know why he said that out loud, only furthering his exasperation. Still, it was out there, and he saw–what he thought, what he hoped–was a flicker of both hesitation and thrill in Carrie Bloom's eyes.

He averted his eyes to avoid any more sudden outbursts, moving them to the table in front of him. Reading through the menu, Josh felt his stomach grumble; thankful for the distraction, he realized his mother, Rose, was spot on when she suggested this restaurant.

Josh rubbed his palms together like an eager teenager. It was the first time in a long time that he felt this excited– Filipino food was a comfort cuisine for him.

"Did you stalk me? Or your people, maybe?" Carrie asked slowly, skepticism obvious in her creased forehead. Josh lifted his head instantly, brows furrowed, even more confused now.

"What do you mean?" he asked, staring at his dinner companion, squinting his eyes in curiosity.

"Did you know I was Filipino before we met?" she added, supplying more context.

"Actually, no. That's why I was a little surprised to meet you. Perhaps my mum knew and didn't bother to share. This restaurant was her idea."

"Your mother?" Folding her arms across her chest, Carrie leaned back in her chair, sizing Josh up further.

He nodded. "She's Filipina. Born and raised in Manila."

Carrie quirked a brow. "But…"

"Stepmum. My biological mother is Irish Norwegian."

"I see. So, did you grow up eating Filipino food?" Carrie bent forward, resting her elbows on the table, accepting Josh's explanation, her expression changing to amused interest.

"Sinigang and adobo are my absolute favorites," Josh offered, his chest puffing a little with pride, and Carrie smirked. "How about you? Parents?"

"My mom is from Manila, and my dad is from Ilocos. They met in California, at the beach, actually. In Malibu." Carrie's smile faded, sadness clearly overriding her mood at the mention of her parents.

"Bloom?"

"My husband's."

That hit was hard and unexpected. She was married, and intuitively, Josh wanted to take a few steps away. *Far* away. What was he thinking? That she might be single and this was some sort of fate? He faked a smile as the thoughts bubbled up inside him.

"I kept it even after he passed," she explained further. Josh sighed, then stopped himself mid-breath, hoping it didn't look like he was glad her husband had died.

"Then you disappeared…" His mother had told him the story. Five years ago, the four-time #1 New York Times bestselling author disappeared without a trace. Her last book was a smashing success, and fans were clamoring for more, but a year later, nobody had heard anything from her.

"Then I disappeared, yes."

"Well, I found you." Josh wanted to touch her cheek and take away the sadness in her eyes, but he controlled the urge to give her a hug.

"You did," she responded softly, and for some reason, her words tattooed themselves on his mind.

He did.

~*~*~*~

Chapter Three

Carrie

Josh chucked loudly. His laugh was so loud, Carrie had to turn around and smile at the patrons next to them to apologize. In truth, though, if she was being honest with herself, she didn't care. For the first time in a long time, she didn't care about anything except for this moment, where everything seemed light and free.

They'd just opened their second bottle of wine, a spread of half-consumed tiny plates of pork sisig, kare-kare, and chicken adobo gracing their table. It was a small table, a tiny space in the corner, lit by sunlight that got fainter and fainter as the night progressed, conducive for intimate conversations.

Their faces were mere inches apart, both of them leaning on the table, the wine bringing down their walls bit by bit. When they both reached for the bottle of wine, their hands brushed–and it was dynamite for Carrie, an explosion of feelings she thought she'd lost years ago. Normally, Carrie would have jerked away, but tonight was different. Carrie let her hand linger in Joshua's, letting his hand stay on top of hers. Slowly, in stunted motions, they moved together in harmony, like a dance, until their palms touched.

They were both quiet.

It was too fast, too soon, Carrie thought, but all her cares had vanished the moment she'd laughed harder than she had in years with this intriguing man. Thrill was coursing through her veins. Perhaps it was the way he bit his lower lip, or the way his eyes landed on hers with intense awareness, or maybe the slow grin forming on his face. She sighed because she wasn't prepared for whatever he was about to say. She had a sudden urge, a want – no, a need, buried within – to be intimate, to be touched, to be owned again.

"Why was there sadness in your eyes when you talked about your parents?" he asked softly, his eyes glued on her.

She shrugged, trying to deduce whether to tell him the painful story.

"When I was five years old," she started before she paused, looking away from Josh. "When I was five, my dad walked out on us, and we've never heard from him again." She pulled her hand away gently and rested it on her lap.

"Do you know where he is?" Josh asked, the compassion in his voice clear as he leaned in even further.

She shook her head, eyes turning glassy, face taut.

"I'm sorry," Josh whispered.

"Don't be. It's been a long time. I don't talk about it much. When I lost Paul, I realized everyone who matters in my life is just going to say goodbye anyway."

Josh quirked a brow. "So, you stopped believing in love, and in turn, stopped writing about it?"

"Yes. It's hard to put your heart into something when it's empty. It's a glass case with nothing in it." Carrie slunk further into her chair. Josh's hand jerked closer, trying to grab her back, but she stayed slumped.

"I'm sorry I asked. I shouldn't have…"

Carrie interrupted his apology. "The thing is, we feel sad about losing anything, especially a person we hold dear. I remember how my sister lost her favorite doll the week my father left, and she cried more over that than losing a parent. I didn't know what losing my dad at that age was going to be like. It wasn't sudden–it was slow, lingering, and then the hole got bigger and bigger. You'd think someone could fill the gap until you lost that someone too."

In the long silence that followed, Carrie pulled herself tall and propped her elbows right back on the table, resetting her mood, hoping to recapture the freedom from minutes ago. Although sadness still floated in her eyes, she smiled generously. She knew she needed to; she knew it was time. "Forget about me. How about you? What's your story, Joshua Grant?"

"No story here, really," he muttered, reaching back to hold Carrie's hand.

Surprising herself, she let him. His warmth brought absolution to her weariness. She looked up at him, straight into his eyes, coaxing him to speak, to open up like she did.

"I'm tired," he finally revealed. Carrie knew he wasn't talking about tonight. She could tell from his eyes that he meant his soul, and to her surprise, she stroked his cheek with the back of her hand. He leaned into her touch, and Carrie felt she had passed the threshold that finally sprung her from her void.

Chapter Four

Josh

They were the last people at the restaurant, the bar scene by the foyer already winding down. Joshua and Carrie had finished their second bottle of wine, with only a few sips left in their respective glasses, but there was no indication they were ready to leave. In fact, from the way they were looking into each other's eyes, they didn't want to let each other go. It was most apparent in Joshua's sighs – heavy and deep, which made Carrie smile each time. Joshua felt different, nervous, but also blithe in a way he had never felt before.

With their hands still clasped together, Joshua made the surprising move to brush his lips across the back of Carrie's hand. She didn't hesitate–it even looked like she welcomed the intimate gesture, giving Joshua the much-needed confidence to pursue her further. The problem, though, was Joshua didn't know how to do it, not with her. He had done this hundreds of times with many women, but Carrie was different. He didn't want to screw this up–he was *scared* to screw it up. He took a mental note to thank his mother tomorrow, first thing.

"Are you tired tonight, too?" Carrie asked gingerly; it was obvious she was as nervous as he was.

"No, not tonight. I want to stay here for a while. I want to stay the entire night." Joshua's voice was gruff but sensual, a soft whisper, an invitation.

"They're closing down soon." Carrie matched the tone of his voice, and again, Joshua signed. He didn't know what to say next, what to do, without pushing her away.

"Is there someone waiting for you at home?" she asked, wide-eyed, staring at their tightly clasped hands, looking ready to pull away at a moment's notice.

"No. No one."

"I'm glad," Carrie beamed, and Joshua sighed again as if he'd been waiting to exhale.

"Where to next, Carrie Bloom?"

"How about you show me your place, London boy?"

This London boy was hooked. So hooked, he didn't want the night to end. So hooked, he called on the waiter immediately, paid as fast as he could, and flagged down the first cab that crossed their path.

As soon as they got into the car, their lips found each other's, and no one said anything more.

Chapter Five

Carrie

The moon was bright enough to cast playful shadows across the beautiful night sky. Carrie, head laying heavily on Joshua's arm as she watched the moonlit sky from Joshua's bedroom floor, had never felt this peaceful–as if the world was perfect. It was like she wasn't hurting anymore, like she was… happy.

In this moment, as Joshua gently touched the scar on her brow with affection, she was.

The scar was deep, and so was the pain with it.

"It's a reminder," she murmured at the touch, moving her head away, hiding the sudden burst of sadness that embraced her. Still, Joshua pulled her in tighter, his strong arm pinning her closer to his chest.

"Of the nightmare?" Joshua whispered, his lips finding her temple, referring to the story of her accident.

"Of the pain," she retorted with equal gentleness.

"Is there anything I can do…" His tone was playful, as if another round of wild sex was what she needed to forget. Perhaps it was.

"Tonight has been perfect," she smiled, gratitude in her tone. She knew this was as far as they could go. She knew that before anyone could say goodbye, she had to put a lid on it.

"It's not over yet, you know."

Carrie smiled and faced him, but in the back of her mind, she knew it was the closest she'd ever be to this man, a man who chose to listen to her story, a part of her she never willingly talked about. With him, she felt safe enough to speak her heart, safe enough to talk about the night she lost herself.

"Carrie, you're alive, and it's a beautiful thing. I've never read your books, but it will be the first thing I'll do tomorrow." He chuckled.

"Today is tomorrow," she teased, poking him playfully in his side.

"I'll read them every day until I get to know you better." His tone had changed. There was seriousness and genuine compassion in Joshua's voice, and Carrie felt it, like she was all that mattered. Instead of answering, she pulled herself up and kissed this man—a complete stranger—with intense yearning. She had never felt more alive until tonight, in his bed—er, floor—in his arms, in his kisses. For one more night, she wanted to feel this much-needed freedom. To forget. To forget and not feel any guilt.

"You're a smooth talker, you know that?" Her lips playfully caressed the side of his lips. "How about you do what you just did to me again?" she asked. She never asked for anything, but tonight, with this man, she wanted more.

"Now we're talking." Instantly, he was on top of her again, but he stopped suddenly and stared into her eyes, cajoling her to want more, to ask for more. Though she felt there was more she could ask, all she could give him was tonight. "Will I see you again after this?"

She didn't respond. She couldn't. She didn't have it in her to ask for more, to be this happy, because the pain of goodbyes had been a constant shadow, and she knew it would never go away.

***

When she woke up the next morning after only a few hours of sleep, the usual morning surge of anxiety welcomed her. She rubbed at her chest, looking around, trying to remember where she was. Turning around, she found Josh next to her, and the calm that washed over her was unexpected.

"No regrets," she whispered under her breath with a smile. In fact, she thought she owed him gratitude.

Then, panic came knocking in a sudden rush.

She still didn't know how to face him after the uninhibited acts of indulgence from last night. It was one thing to do it with a little liquid courage; it was another when everything was so vivid in the light of day. Carefully, she pulled the covers off her naked body, slid out of bed, and quietly put her clothes on. *It's better this way*. It had always been the plan, to walk away quietly, as if it never happened.

"Hey, you heading out?" It was the sweetest forty-year-old man's voice Carrie had ever heard. She turned around and looked at Josh in broad daylight, and it didn't disappoint. Without his fancy clothes and his well-styled hair, he looked doubly charming. This, right here, was a man of true beauty, the kind you only see in a movie. The kind you want to run toward and make mad love to all over again. The memory of her many orgasms from last night betrayed her–she could feel the heat rising on her face.

"Yeah. I need to work a little before my flight tonight," she offered. Her voice was cold as ice, but a slight quiver trembled underneath.

Josh snickered playfully, one eye shut and a hand blocking the sun beaming across his face through his floor-to-ceiling window.

"What time is your flight?" he asked nonchalantly, getting out of bed with, thankfully, the white sheets draped around his waist.

"Ten," responded Carrie, turning around for fear of getting caught staring at Josh's abs.

"Let's meet for dinner?" Josh asked, his words sounding more like a plea than a question. "I'll have my driver take us to the airport at seven?" he added.

Carrie sighed –though she acknowledged the many things that could go wrong if she said yes, the idea still stirred something in her chest. *Just dinner, and then they go their separate ways and never see each other again.* She knew her book adaptation was never going to be made–at least, not by this man.

"Sure."

~*~*~*~

Chapter Six

Josh

Josh should thank his mother for this one. Rose didn't always get it right, but she was on the mark with Carrie.

"You want to take a shower and I'll make breakfast?" he offered. He *never* did breakfast after one night with a woman, but here he was, almost stumbling like an idiot, putting on his jeans and a white shirt, heading down to the kitchen exploding with excitement. He cleared his throat, using his fist to cover his mouth. "The studio sent me a rack of women's clothing for a fitting a few weeks ago. It's in the guest bedroom," he added, stopping at the door. "They're all brand new. Some might be in your size." Josh didn't offer that it was for his ex-girlfriend's television show–she didn't need to know that.

"I guess a shower would be nice," Carrie conceded.

While Carrie was in the bathroom, Josh pulled out a carton of eggs, a fresh pack of Canadian bacon, jam, and butter from the fridge, and put bread on the toaster. He opened the fridge once more to check if he still had those expensive truffles he liked. Josh loved breakfast and always had it alone. It was his favorite time of his schedule–not because it was the most important meal, but because it was the one moment he could think and plan his day. If he didn't get to do breakfast, he'd be all over the place.

While the eggs cooked in the skillet, Josh poured orange juice into two glasses and placed them on his long, mahogany table, grinning with delight. He was nervous and couldn't explain why; he laughed at himself and shook his head to reset.

Carrie walked down the stairs in jeans, a white button-down shirt, her black boots, and slightly blow-dried hair. She literally took his breath away, and he had to hold onto a chair to steady himself. She looked younger make-up free, even more beautiful than last night, he conceded. Josh suddenly felt a stirring in his gut; he exhaled and turned around to the counter to gather himself.

"Do you need a bag for your clothes? You know what? I'll get them dry-cleaned and you'll have them this afternoon," he offered, closing the drawer harder than necessary. He was being awkward, not himself, terrifyingly clumsy, and Joshua Grant was *never* clumsy. He was a film producer for a major house, for crying out loud. On instinct, he grabbed his cup of coffee to keep his hands busy.

"It's fine. I can just pack it." Carrie smiled, pulling her hair up in a short ponytail.

"Joshua!" a voice reverberated from somewhere inside the townhouse. "Are you home?" Josh spat out the coffee he was slowly savoring.

"Mum?" Josh smacked his forehead and hurriedly walked to the front door. "Why are you using your keys?"

"You weren't answering last night. I was so worried. I called you more than twenty times and texted you maybe about fifty. Where were you?" Rose, in all of her four-eleven glory, was a force of nature. She was in plain black pants and a black sweater over a white shirt, looking put together, as if on her way to a fancy brunch. She stopped mid-scolding when she laid eyes on Carrie, who stared at both mother and son from the kitchen in shock.

"I invited her to breakfast," Josh hastily reasoned, thankful they were both decent and fully clothed.

"Why? You stood her up?" she asked pointedly, glaring at her son, disappointed.

"Hi. I'm Carrie, and he did show up last night." Carrie extended her hand to Rose for an introduction.

"Thank goodness. I didn't raise a man who disrespected women." Rose added.

If only she knew what filthy things Josh did to her last night, respect would be the last word on her mind.

"I asked you a number of times not to do that," Josh complained, though his voice was full of affection.

"Carisa Gonzales, in person." Rose stretched her arms wide and wrapped them around Carrie for a tight embrace. Josh immediately looked at his guest, recognizing the discomfort written all over her face. Rose was too much, and it was one of the reasons Josh adored her, but this might be pushing it.

Before he could stop his mother, Carrie was already bending down to receive her. Rose, all pure excitement, could barely contain herself.

"You have written some of the most riveting love stories of all time!" Rose screamed in Carrie's ear.

To his shock, Carrie smiled, and things felt right all over again, and Josh sighed with relief.

***

Five hours later, they were at it again in the family bathroom at the airport. He was no exhibitionist–in fact, he loathed promiscuous behavior–and yet, here he was, moaning to his lust's content inside this woman he had only met last night. His need for her was utterly unexpected, and she was all he thought about the entire day.

"God, what are you doing to me?" he whispered, his lips on her cheek, her eyes wide in ecstasy.

"I'm coming, Josh, right now. Take me there. Take me there now…" Together, they screamed, groaned, and grunted, sighed and heaved.

"I can't get enough of you. I want to do it all over again," he groaned as he rocked her back and forth on the sink, her legs around him.

"God, this is hot…" she whispered as she bit her lower lip.

Still inside her, Josh was gone again.

~*~*~*~

Chapter Seven

Carrie

Three months later

"Breakfast at Bruno's?" Carrie heard her best friend, Lara, ask as she walked into the office. Well, more like a small room inside Carrie's sixty-year-old, three-bedroom, home she once shared with Paul. She'd been meaning to move, but no time was ever the right time. Now, she had to drive up to Vida's to help her with the wedding, so it would have to wait again.

"Sure," she said. "Why not? I'm stuck anyway." She gestured to the book she was working on for one of her long-time clients.

"Is it Sylvie's?" Lara asked, and she nodded.

Sylvie's new book was romance, and though Carrie was good at pulling herself away from her projects, the storyline reminded her so much of her own tryst with a tall stranger a few months before. The memory and the feelings were still so fresh that there were times she had to pleasure herself to calm herself down enough to pretend it didn't happen. She even had to buy one of those fancy pink vibrators from Gwyneth's Goop store. That man changed her. For the first time in a long time, her sexual appetite was heightened, aroused, and she didn't know how to deal. It wasn't like she just wanted sex–no, she wanted sex with one particular man, and *that* was a problem.

"Earth to Carrie Bloom," Lara called, bending her head in front of Carrie's face, brows furrowed, pretending to be annoyed with a smirk on her lips, teasing her best friend. "What did that guy do to you? You've become a ticking time bomb."

"Stop it." Carrie brushed her best friend's face away gently and stood to get ready. She felt the room spin, and her hand shot out to grasp the desk for support.

"Hey, are you okay?" Lara caught Carrie's arm. "Hey, hey…"

Carrie shook her head. "I probably just need to take my iron supplements again. I've been feeling out of sorts a lot lately."

"I think you're overworked. Maybe you need a break. Go back to London for a couple of weeks. Heck, take a whole month off. You can work from anywhere."

"I don't plan to go anywhere."

"Well, at least answer his email." Lara was referring to the two emails Josh Grant had sent before flying to Africa, apart from the email his people sent Lara regarding the book they didn't even get to talk about.

"What's he doing in Africa, anyway?" Carrie nonchalantly asked, pretending to be uninterested but failing miserably.

Lara quirked a brow. "Do you really want to know? I mean, you kept telling me not to tell you anything about him unless it's about your book."

"Fine." Carrie rolled her eyes, giving in. In truth, she'd been dying to know–she just didn't want to admit it to herself.

"Joshua Grant is a patron of a children's organization in Ghana. He travels there twice a year to visit the facilities and the children. His mother told me," Lara explained, which surprised Carrie greatly.

"Rose called you?"

"Rose and I are best buds, girl." She laughed softly. "Let's go get you some food." Lara pulled Carrie's purse off the back of the chair and pushed her out the door.

***

The nights were the worst. Carrie had showered more than a hundred times since she got back to the States, washed her clothes, and stowed away her luggage, but she could still smell him on her. She knew it wasn't possible, but it was as strong as if he was in bed next to her.

With her laptop propped up on a pillow, she worked on Sylvie's highly sensual romance novel. Her client *had* said she wanted to try something different, but this new project was definitely turning out to be more erotic than Carrie was ready for. She could feel the heat rising on her cheeks, and as she read about the main character taking a woman on the dining room table, Carrie was tempted to pull Gwyneth's little pink contraption out from its hiding spot in the bedside drawer. Her nipples perked up, and a throbbing sensation at the tips hurt a little. She'd been having fuller, heavier breasts lately.

"It's what thinking about sex all the time does to you," she jokingly muttered to herself. She knew that once her period came, it would be a restart, and she would feel decidedly non-sexual again.

She stopped short at the thought.

Her period.

Her period?

Her period!

She grabbed her organizer and flipped it open to the present week before flipping it backwards to the previous month, then the month before that. As clear as day, she'd missed it twice now.

Twice!

She jumped out of bed, both her hands over her mouth, willing herself not to scream. Then, she stumbled down and sat on the floor. She didn't know what to feel, and so the universe threw it at her–she felt her stomach rumble, and she ran to the toilet before she was sick all over the floor.

***

"Why are you doing this here, of all places? Are you sure you're Carrie?" The second person Carrie confided in about her condition was her younger sister, Robyn.

"I don't know what has gotten into this woman!" Lara doubled down on Carrie.

"I don't want to do this at home. I don't want to be alone."

"We can all go home together. You're not going to be alone," Robyn offered sympathetically, giving Lara a sideways, knowing glance.

"I'm not going to wait. I'm doing this right now after we finish our meal." They were at Community for dinner–their favorite eclectic, fine-dining Asian restaurant in downtown Los Angeles.

"Who are you and what did you do to my sister?" Robyn gave Carrie a wide-eyed glare. "You've been acting super strange lately. First this…" Robyn pointed her finger at Carrie's belly and started drawing circles in the air. "And then this casual sex thing. You're many things, but casual isn't one of them."

"If this stick proves that I am what I think I am, then I'm nothing but casual. I had casual sex with a stranger," she whisper-screamed as she moved her eyes from left to right, hoping no one could hear them.

"Well… Josh Grant is not really a stranger," Lara pointed out.

"Whatever. I still had sex with a person I met not even two hours before. I think that counts as very casual."

"Are you drunk right now?" Robyn chimed in.

"I might be pregnant, so of course I'm not drunk!" she quiet screamed again. There it went–Carrie finally said the word. *Pregnant.* Since the realization hit her a few nights ago, she had not once said it out loud.

Pregnant. Fuck.

Chapter Eight

Josh

"Is this all?" He was not in the greatest of moods today, jet-lagged after just returning from Morocco last night and utterly frustrated after receiving his messages from his assistant, Frannie, revealed that the one message he was looking forward to wasn't there.

He had emailed that woman twice. *Twice.* He didn't usually contact women after one night. His friend, Digsy, told him not to do it, but he did anyway because he felt what he and Carrie shared was special.

The past few weeks had been hectic–from location shoots in Casablanca to his visit to the Kids We Educate and Feed office in Ghana. He thought a distraction would be the best antidote for his Carrie disease. That woman was everywhere he went or looked, and she was even invading his dreams.

Raking his fingers through his hair, he turned around, heading to his desk with the breathtaking view of the London Eye. Even though it was a gloomy London day, Josh sat in his office in his pinstripe navy suit, crisp white dress shirt, and blue Ferragamo tie, ready to seize the day.

"Get yourself together, Joshua. You're not a teenager," he told himself before dumping his mail on top of his perfectly organized desk.

Frannie walked in then, a mug of steaming hot coffee in one hand and a clipboard in the other. "Here's your coffee. Dark, like every Monday morning."

"Thanks," Josh grumbled again under his breath.

"Let's go through your day, shall we?" Frannie continued. "It's not light."

"I need my week to be busy," he instructed, taking the big leather chair behind his massive glass desk as Frannie stood across from him, ready to fire away.

"You have a nine thirty with marketing, ten fifteen with Larry, and lunch with Ms. Viviane."

"Huh?" Josh lifted his head in surprise at the mention of his ex-girlfriend's name.

"Your…your girlfriend, V," Frannie reminded him with a hint of sarcasm.

He looked at her in shock. "We broke up."

"You did, but we all suspected it wasn't final. Like always."

"Who's we?" Josh sighed at the realization that he and V never really spoke about breaking up. They just seemed to have drifted apart and away. Again. So technically, he didn't cheat on her with Carrie. "When was this lunch arranged?"

"She called two weeks ago, and she insisted that I put it in your calendar as soon as you got back to work."

Josh quirked a brow. "At whose discretion, Frannie?"

"I'm sorry, Josh. Would you like me to cancel?"

"Where is the lunch?"

"Simone's," Frannie said loudly, a reminder that it was his favorite restaurant to frequent near the office.

"Fine."

"I didn't put anything in your calendar until three thirty," Frannie uncomfortably stated. She knew about Josh's noontime nookies with V and even arranged a time in his schedule for sex. The very thought of it veered his mind to the woman he had been trying to forget.

"I don't need extra time in the schedule," he curtly responded. "Have Carrie Bloom's people called yet?"

"They called back, yes. They said Ms. Bloom is very busy for the next few months and that she will not take any meetings until next year."

He furrowed his brows. "Are you serious? Who does she think she is, Steven Spielberg?"

"More like Nora Ephron, I heard." Frannie chuckled at her own joke. "Can I ask why you are mad at Ms. Bloom? She came to London for a night to meet with you about the book. If there's someone who should be annoyed, it should be her, no? Since nothing came out of the meeting she traveled thousands of miles for?" Frannie ended this line of questioning with a smile, which earned her snarky, squinted eyes from Josh in warning. "Also, your mum is on her way."

"Now?"

"Joshua!" Rose's voice rang through the hallway, almost as if summoned. "We should stop meeting like this, Joshua. You have to make time for me. Take my calls. Your dad is also worried about you, and so are your brothers."

Josh rolled his eyes as she rushed into his office. "I just got back late last night."

"And you're at work first thing the next day? You should make time to relax, not all this work, work, work!" Rose was love at its most volatile. It was rough and tough, but it was true and real and all-encompassing. "We're going to breakfast." She insisted with a stern look on her face–but her adoring and sympathetic eyes betrayed her.

"I can't. I have a nine thirty, mum."

Rose looked at her watch. "You have an hour, so let's go." She clapped her hands twice like a soldier commanding her troops.

"I can cancel the nine thirty. It's an internal meeting. I bet the marketing team will be relieved," Frannie jumped in.

They didn't go very far. Josh was able to convince his mother to grab a coffee and a sandwich at Zosimo's across the street.

"Josh, I'm sixty years old. Last week, I went to see Dr. Chung…"

"And?" There was both panic and anticipation in Josh's tone.

"I'm healthy, but he wants to watch my blood pressure. I guess it's expected of women my age. I'm not getting any younger, you know." Rose looked into the distance, being melodramatic, and Josh was gobbling it up like the adoring son that he was. "I want to see my sisters in California. It's been years."

"Mum, go to California. You deserve a vacation." Josh took a slow sip of his steaming coffee before looking at his mother with an encouraging smile.

"That's why I'm here to see you."

"Okay?" Josh was well aware this was not about money. His parents were independently wealthy; it was the reason he was able to go to Oxford and Yale, and why he lived a privileged life growing up.

"Would you come with me and visit my family?"

Josh's eyes went wide. "Mum, I just got back."

"Exactly. If your office has survived without you for two months, what's one more?" Josh didn't like where his mother was going with this. "Plus, you haven't seen your cousins in more than four years."

"How about Dan and James? Why don't you ask them?" His brothers would surely be better choices for this.

"Leila is about to give birth any second now, so Dan is out. James already has a trip planned with Steph and the kids. You are my only hope."

"Is Dad okay to be left alone?"

Rose rolled her eyes. "Your father would be happy to be at home with his books and his garden."

Josh sighed heavily. "Mum, you know I can't just up and leave. I have a company to run."

"I don't ask for much, Joshua. Just tell me where you are so I know you're okay and spend a little time with your mother before it's too late."

"Stop saying that." Josh reached for his mother's hand on the table with a sigh, knowing he would have to rearrange his entire month to accommodate Rose's request. "Let me see what I can do."

~*~*~*~

Chapter Nine

Carrie

"Are you going to tell him? *How* are you going to tell him?" Lara asked, panic-stricken after Carrie came back from the bathroom, sat down quietly, and discreetly showed them the white stick with two very pink lines.

"Holy moly." That was all Robyn could utter, staring at the stick wide-eyed.

Carrie found out two nights ago that she could be pregnant. She already knew she would carry the baby, and she already knew she would make space–a very big space, the biggest–for this new person in her life.

"What does this mean?" Carrie asked her sister quietly, pointing at the stick.

"It means you're almost done with your first trimester. You came back from London three months ago."

"Okay," she replied mechanically. Carrie and Paul had tried to have a baby for years after they got married. They married young, and they couldn't wait to spend the rest of their lives together. The universe had other plans, obviously, because Carrie couldn't even begin to comprehend how this happened.

"Were you not being safe?" Lara asked carefully, noticing Carrie's fragile state of mind.

"We were – all three times," Carrie responded.

Then there was quiet.

Carrie mindlessly placed her hand over her stomach, and no one spoke as the women watched her with both worry and joy.

"I'm keeping this baby," she whispered before bursting into tears, a smile forming on her lips. "God, this is the best news I've had in a very long time." Again, quiet. Shock. "I'm going to be a mommy," she quietly sobbed.

"You're going to be a mommy," Robyn affirmed, enveloping her sister's hand with her own.

"You're going to be a mommy," Lara echoed, standing up and bending down behind Carrie, putting her arms around her best friend.

***

"Mom! Your eldest daughter's got news," Robyn screamed as both sisters walked into their mother's house in Bel Air.

"Stop it! Carrie pulled Robyn back, giving her a silent warning with her eyes.

"We're in the garden," Pilar replied, her voice faint as the girls nervously made their way to the backyard. It looked like she had visitors, to Carrie's intense relief. She could at least prolong the inevitable. It wasn't like she was twenty-five–she was already pushing forty, so really, it shouldn't be that much of a shock.

Carrie nearly dropped her purse when she saw who was standing next to her mother by the swimming pool.

Joshua Grant.

She started coughing, practically choking on nothing, and she couldn't stop. Rose, whose presence shocked Carrie even more, stood up and handed her a glass of water, which she hurriedly consumed. Wide-eyed, she looked from Josh's dumbfounded face to Rose's and back, and then at her mom and Robyn.

"Are you alright?" Robyn asked, grabbing the glass of water from Carrie's trembling hands and mouthing, "what the fuck" while widening her eyes.

"Yeah, yeah, yeah, I'm fine." She waved her hand to appease her audience. "I'm good. Thank you. Allergies, maybe."

"Carrie Bloom?" Josh spoke her name so softly, as if only to himself, and Robyn and her mom all turned to look at him.

"Carrie Bloom?" Rose clasped her hands together in pure delight. "What a coincidence!"

"I guess so," Carrie replied with a forced smile, shock still written all over her face. Carrie prayed under her breath that she and Josh were not related, even by affinity, because *that* would be horrific.

"These are my daughters, Carrie and Robyn," Pilar said, introducing the girls with pride. Carrie's mom was the rock of their family, raising them as a single parent after their father fled when they were mere toddlers. She was the thread that pulled them all together, the constant nagging voice in her head, a woman whose sad eyes hid under a veil of ferocity.

"Carrie Bloom is your daughter?" Rose asked in wonder, a big smile on her face.

"Yes. How do you know her?"

"Her books!"

"Oh, yeah, she stopped doing that," Carrie's mom offered. "Girls, Rose Grant was my classmate in high school. No, actually, my best friend, but she moved to England, and we lost touch. This is her son, Joshua," she added to which Carrie obviously sighed in great relief.

"We know Carrie. We met briefly in London a few months ago. This is an absolutely wonderful surprise," Rose beamed.

"Oh?" Robyn said as she turned to Carrie with a questioning glare. "Oh!" Robyn was able to put two and two together as Carrie gave her another wide-eyed warning.

"Mom, remember my trip to London a few months ago? It was to meet Mr. Grant and his team about my last book."

"Oh, that's wonderful!" Pilar said as everyone turned to Josh, who still seemed stunned, glued to the spot.

Finally, he spoke. "Hello again, Miss Bloom."

Carrie's eyes could no longer avoid Josh's pulling gaze, and so she stared right back–and then she almost stumbled backward.

Chapter Ten

Josh

No words could explain the violent pounding of his heart–even more so because he was not a heart-pounding kind of man. But as soon as he saw Carrie, in jeans and a white t-shirt, her hair tied back, simple and striking at the same time, he was a goner. Gone.

Was it possible to fall in love so quickly? he wondered. The dryness of his mouth, the never-ending sighs, as if running after his breath, and the sweat forming on his palms–somehow, he knew they were tells. He had fallen in love with this woman, and seeing her right now, he knew he could never lose her again. He closed his eyes, trying to gather himself, strategizing his next move. He would try his very best to keep seeing her–no, for her to want to keep seeing him.

"What's the big news?" Pilar asked her eldest daughter, and everyone turned around to look at Carrie.

"Oh," Carrie responded with hesitation.

"Oh," Robyn echoed. Josh noticed as they looked at each other nervously, alarm obvious in their eyes.

"You said Carrie has some big news." Pilar tried to refresh her daughters' memories. Everyone was left staring, waiting for either of the girls to speak.

"Vida is getting married!" Carrie declared.

"Yes! Finally!" Robyn echoed her sister's excitement, but something wasn't feeling quite right to Josh. Carrie was oddly flushed, and her sister was clearly trying to cover something up.

"Oh goodness, this is great news! Great news indeed," Pilar exclaimed, her hands clasped together in extreme delight. "Rose, Vida is a wonderful woman who took care of Carisa when her husband passed away."

After so many years, Carrie and her family were comfortable talking about what happened to her husband, but for Josh and Rose, who were hearing it with fresh hearts, it was still a tragedy that deserved a moment of silence.

To everyone's surprise, Rose slowly walked the five steps to Carrie and hugged her tightly. It was exactly what Josh wanted to do–take care of her, if she'd let him. Yet, Josh knew that, though there was vulnerability about Carrie, she was also strong and sturdy and stable.

"What are you cooking, Mom?" Robyn inquired with furrowed brows. A strong, pungent smell suddenly emanated from the kitchen.

"Rose here wants to try my paksiw na isda," Pilar proudly declared.

"The slimy fish in vinegar juice?" Robyn asked, wrinkling her nose. "We need candles inside the house fast. That smell is going to stick to the curtains."

"Remember when we used to say the exact same thing, Pilar? Look at us now, missing it." Rose chuckled, eyeing the girls with a glimmer of understanding.

Joshua didn't appreciate the smell either, but his eyes stayed glued on Carrie, having noticed the sudden change in her expression. She was turning pale, uncomfortable, clutching on her stomach as if she was about to be sick. She stood in silence as Robyn ran around the house lighting candles, and Rose and Pilar carried on with their discussion about food and memories. Joshua started to walk toward Carrie, wanting to simply talk, but as soon as he stopped a foot away, she almost threw up on him and ran inside the house in a hurry.

Pilar, in a panic, followed her fleeing daughter with her eyes and then turned to Joshua, who looked just as worried. Not getting any answers, she ran inside the house to follow Carrie, with Robyn not far behind.

Suddenly, a glass shattered on the floor.

"You're pregnant?" Pilar's voice reverberated through the house and out to the patio, where the Grants waited for their return.

"Mom!" both daughters shouted in unison.

Silence.

Josh cracked his knuckles anxiously as he absorbed the information in shock. There was no question in his mind that Pilar was referring to her older daughter.

Carrie Bloom was pregnant.

Chapter Eleven

Carrie

There was something about the Napa Valley air that nourished Carrie's soul. She always found peace in the company of the Moores, and having Vida here lightened her heart some.

"You're going to be a great mother, Carrie," Vida said, her eyes sparkling with what looked like hope. Dressed in a flowy white dress, a shawl around her shoulders, Vida had never looked more radiant.

They were hidden in the back of the main building of Hacienda Luz, sitting in a row of colorful hammocks, feet dangling in the air like young girls, the moonlight providing reprieve in the darkness.

Carrie's head was bent down, deep in thought. Decisions had to be made. She couldn't erase the vision of the restrained fury she saw on Joshua's face as she left her mom's house. Without a doubt, she concluded, he had heard everything–heard that she was, in fact, carrying his child.

"Does the father know?" Vida inquired softly.

"I think so. By some freak chance, his mother is a friend of Mom's, and he was at the house yesterday. What are the chances, right?"

"Fate can be tricky, you know? Sneaky." Vida laughed a little, putting her arms up in the air as if welcoming whatever the universe had to offer them tonight.

Carrie lifted her head to look at her friend and graced her with a smile, Vida's playfulness a much-needed comfort. She sighed before speaking. "I want this baby, Vida. I want this baby so bad that I feel selfish. I don't care what Mom thinks." She paused, letting the silence embrace her. "I don't even care how the father feels. I will do everything, anything I can, for this child's happiness. I think that's probably the reason I survived."

"Are we still looking for that?" Vida asked, a hint of obvious disapproval in her slightly forceful voice. "Carrie, you're alive, here, with me and your mom and your sister and friends. That is your purpose. You don't need to question why you exist. You should never, ever question that."

Carrie's heart fluttered. For so long, she'd been convinced she didn't deserve to survive, questioning why Paul and Laine and Eugene died while she walked the Earth with no reason. Carrie bent her head and cried–the ugly cry she'd been holding in since she got here.

"You can cry here, you know. You can be as weak as you need to be in front of me, and I will still tell you that you're worth it. You can lock yourself in the room for days, and I'll let you do it, but I will also continue to remind you that you are a gift. All I ask is that you give yourself a chance to see that." Vida jumped off the hammock, walked to her friend, and hugged her as tight as she could muster. "You're a miracle, Carrie, and you shouldn't question that." The wind swirled around them as if it too wanted to embrace Carrie and whisk away her grief. The crickets had stopped singing, and the silence of the night was their only companion as they poured their hearts out to each other.

For five years, Carrie had tried to stay in her lane, to do the right thing–always walking on eggshells, terrified to get too close, too attached to people, because she couldn't afford to get hurt again. In her life, someone's always saying goodbye. She had accepted that. Now, she had to deal with this. Joshua. This baby. So much was at stake.

"Do you love him, the father?"

This was the question Carrie wasn't ready to face. She didn't know, didn't *want* to know. "I can't do love anymore. I'm too wounded for that."

"You should give love the chance to work its magic. Love isn't pain, Carrie. It heals, but you need to give it the chance." Vida touched Carrie's forehead with her own, and, under the moonlight, they both prayed with all their hearts.

***

Vida's wedding was an amalgamation of heart and soul, of east and west, of light and love, and happiness abundant in every corner. The vineyard was full of both laughter and tears, and as Carrie stared at her friend, carefree and radiant, she couldn't help but think of her own wedding.

That day defined her as a woman, and when her other half was snatched away, she faltered. Disappearing was the only way she knew how to exist, but that life seemed so far away now. Carrie rested her hand on top of her stomach and sighed, as if finally able to breathe again. She bent her head down, emotions overflowing like a river in the wild. She wanted to burst into a million little pieces–this time, because of the generous amount of happiness she couldn't seem to contain. She laughed to herself.

Sitting on a dilapidated bench between two vineyard rows, away from the crowd, Carrie enjoyed the solitude. She needed time to herself after the whirlwind of the past few weeks–from finding out about her baby, to seeing

Joshua again unexpectedly, to all the events leading up to this beautiful wedding.

"I feel like I've been waiting for you all my life," she whispered into the wind and lifted her head up to the sky.

The vineyard was both quiet and loud–the laughter and the music, although lively, were muffled inside Carrie's head as she tried to imagine her future. She smiled, knowing this was the perfect moment for her and her baby. It was the moment they finally found each other, the connection more real–as mother and child.

A light breeze kissed her cheeks. She closed her eyes and savored the moment, letting the wind encase her, as if it was whispering back. Was this Paul telling her to finally move on, letting her heart go, washing away all her guilt and pain? Perhaps he too was happy to learn of this baby. Perhaps this was him encouraging her to live, to wholeheartedly love. When she opened her eyes, she gasped in surprise.

Josh.

~*~*~*~

Chapter Twelve

Josh

Josh stayed where he was for as long as he could, staring at the only woman who had ever captured his heart. A lump formed in his throat as soon as he recognized the emotions on her beautiful face–he wanted to run to her, tell her that everything would be alright, that he was in love with her and had been going crazy for weeks trying to figure out how to get her to love him back.

Still, he stayed there, behind one of the vines, just looking at her. The chill of the night wasn't gentle, and with the dress she had on–a sheer, off-the-shoulder number–Josh worried she might catch a cold. The sun had fully set, the night sky already glowing with the sparkle of stars.

A few minutes had passed with his heart violently beating under his chest when he finally conjured the courage to walk up to the woman he knew was meant for him.

"Hey," he finally said as Carrie lifted her head. He smiled, but he could feel his lips quivering behind his façade.

"Hey," Carrie responded, her eyes wide, fear apparent. Immediately, Josh wanted to touch her, to appease her, but he didn't. He knew they had so much to talk about, but all he wanted was to be with her–to be hers.

"Can I join you?" he asked as Carrie gathered her long skirt and moved to one side so Josh could sit next to her. He was in jeans, not thinking he would catch her at the wedding reception. He thought he would have time; Robyn wasn't very clear about what time the wedding was when they spoke this morning.

They were quiet for a few minutes, the faint song in the background the only sound–they were playing *Forevermore*, a Filipino ballad, a staple at weddings, one his mum used to sing. It was fitting for what he was about to say to Carrie.

"Why are you here?" Carrie finally asked, leaning backward while giving him a sideward glance. She looked skeptical, or maybe hopeful. Josh couldn't quite place which one.

"I just want to see you again." Josh exhaled, turning his head and meeting her eyes for the first time. He needed her to see that he was here, present, for her, forever.

"Why?"

"Because I love you." He held onto her eyes, no matter how much he wanted to blush and hide.

She gasped, putting both her hands over her mouth, but Josh saw her eyes turn glassy, tears threatening to spill. "Why?"

He took a deep breath before answering. "Because something in me wants to make you happy…if you'd let me." He slipped sideways to face the woman of his dreams, and, with shaking hands, reached out for hers. "Your hands are cold. It's chilly." He got up, removed his black sports jacket, and wrapped it around Carrie, her doe eyes looking up at him.

"Josh, I'm pregnant."

He just nodded. "I'll take care of you and the baby if you'd let me. We'll face the father together. Robyn told me he doesn't even know about it yet. I won't be in the way if you're in love with him." Josh paused. "If not, and I have a chance with you, then I'm taking it."

He'd rehearsed these lines over and over on the drive to the Hacienda. He knew it wasn't enough, but he also didn't want it to sound like those lines in the movies he'd made. Carrie should hear *his* truth, who he really was, not some fabricated spiel from his award-winning screenwriters.

"Hold on. What did Robyn tell you?" Carrie stood up in a hurry, her creased forehead looking terribly confused as she faced Josh with hands on her hips.

Suddenly, whispered giggles sounded from a few feet away, and out came a couple with hands all over each other, stopping short upon seeing Carrie and Josh. They looked more than a little surprised and supremely embarrassed. It was obvious they were making out.

"Hi, Car," the man said.

"Hello, Senator Hizon," Carrie responded. "Hi, Gel." She waved at the woman next to him.

"If you'll excuse us…" The young senator bid them farewell and reached for the woman's hand to make their escape.

The incident gave Joshua pause, providing him some time to think his spiel through. After watching her friends walk away, Carrie finally turned around to resume their conversation.

"So, what did Robyn say?" Carrie repeated her question.

Josh sighed. "When I asked her about what I heard, she wouldn't give me the time of day. I had to chase her around town, and Mum had to explain to her husband that I was not after her at all."

"Rose talking to Chase? Geez!" Carrie rolled her eyes. "And?"

"But when I told her I'm in love with you, she finally agreed to meet me for coffee."

Carrie looked at him, almost shocked at what she was hearing. "What if we don't work out?"

"What if we do?" he countered pointedly. *Was she saying she loved him back?*

"Didn't you hear the part where I said I am pregnant?" she whispered softly.

He nodded. "Loud and clear. I want to be in your life, Carrie. These past months away from you were the most emotionally destructive of my life. I didn't know love until I met you. I want to be in your baby's life too… if you'd let me."

Carrie shook her head. "It was one night. How can you be so sure?"

Josh stepped in closer, towering over her, but at the same time, just wanting to gather her in his arms.

"I'm not. What I'm sure about is that seeing you makes me feel good, and at peace, and I have this profound need to make you happy. It doesn't make sense, but nothing about any of this makes sense. I'm in love with you. You're like a lifeline, an extension of my breath, a part of my heartbeat. It may be selfish to dump this on you like this, but I have to say it. I have to try, or I will forever be walking this Earth wondering…"

"It's ours," Carrie quietly interrupted.

"Huh?" Josh was taken aback, confused. "What is?"

"The baby. It's ours."

"What do you mean?" It was his turn to stare at her with wide-eyed hope. "The baby is mine?"

Carrie nodded slowly, making sure Josh got the message loud and clear. "Yes. The baby is yours."

"I'm going to be a dad?"

"If you want to be, yes."

Within half a second, Carrie was off the ground and wrapped in Josh's tight embrace. "We're having a baby?" he asked again, this time with unwavering disbelief.

"We're having a baby."

"Together?"

Carrie giggled and nodded this time. "Yes."

"I love you, Carrie." He set her down, both hands on her arms.

"I love you too, Josh. I can't wrap my brain around how fast my feelings have evolved, but this beautiful life changes everything. I'm no longer afraid to love. I love you, and more than anything else, though I'm still terrified of goodbyes, I want to take the chance if it means we'll both fill the empty space in my heart."

Josh beamed, his smile so wide, he felt it was about to rip his face in half. "Well, can we tell your mom that we're having a baby and that it's not a mistake? It's a miracle, and our mums will finally be related when we get… I mean, you know, sharing a grandchild and all. But, if marriage is in the cards, I'm throwing my bet at it too."

Carrie laughed at his eagerness. "Let's take it slow, tiger."

"Well, as history may have it, we don't do slow."

Finally, without another word, Carrie jumped into his arms and kissed him. Josh was in heaven, the happiest he had ever been in his life.

He didn't do happy, but with Carrie, he would try every single damn day for the rest of his life.

THE END

About Maan Gabriel

Maan Gabriel is a mom, wife, dreamer, writer, and advocate for women's stories in literature. She earned her BA in communications from St. Scholastica's College in Manila and MPS in public relations and corporate communications from Georgetown University. She has lived in Manila, Brussels, Dakar, and Mexico City. During the day, she works in strategic communications. Gabriel, along with her husband and son, currently calls suburban Washington, D.C. home.

Book List:

After Perfect

Twelve Hours in Manhattan

Pasko Na, My Love

Social Media IDs:

Facebook - @MaanGabrielAuthor

Instagram - @maan_gabriel

Threads - @maan_gabriel

Moments In The Vineyard

AURORA PAIGE

Moments In The Vineyard

AURORA PAIGE

Blurb:

Ava

The Russos are ruthless and want my vineyard. No amount of money can buy what's mine. I'm making sure of it. Until I run into Sebastian Russo. My enemy. I'm supposed to stay away from him. What happens when the moment we have in my vineyard changes all that?

Sebastian

I have one task—take Maldonado Vineyard. It'll be easy. I'm irresistible. Ava Maldonado will hand it right over.

I'm wrong– Ava makes me forget why I initially approached her. I'm forced to choose between my love and my family. Whatever I choose, I'm losing someone I love.

Content Notes: Profanity, open door love scenes

Tropes and Sub genres: Billionaire, Alpha hero; Enemies to Lovers

Heat Level: 🔥 🔥 🔥 🔥 (explicit sex)

Chapter One

Ava

"Tell me you're kidding, Ned," I panicked. My accountant pulled out multiple spreadsheets with numbers for all aspects of my father's–err–now *my* business. Most numbers were in red, and according to the older man in front of me, red wasn't good. Ned analyzes my finances and books every quarter. It's August, and he finally had time to meet with me to discuss quarter two revenue and margins.

"Ava, this isn't a joke. You're losing money. With the way Maldonado Vineyard's running, even cutting staff, you'll only be able to survive for a month," he said, factually.

I covered my face with my hands, sighing. *Is this really happening?*

"Maybe it's time to consider taking the offer that the Russo family has been trying to get you to sign for years—"

"No! Absolutely not," I snapped. I glared at him, and he quickly looked down at his paperwork. "I'm not selling to that family. They think they can take over the entire Napa Valley. That's not going to happen."

My father and I built our vineyard and winery from the ground up ten years ago, after my mom passed away, learning the entire process of wine making with the help of my mentor, Vida, who owned Hacienda Luz Vineyard, which had been in Napa Valley for over eighty years. At one hundred-fifty acres, it was way bigger than my tiny ten-acre lot. Her Filipino family was so kind to Papa and me, inviting us to family gatherings. We even attended Lola Naty's one-hundredth birthday last Christmas Eve.

The first time the Russo family approached Papa with an offer to buy our land was two years into our business. Papa respectfully declined, but they continued to harass us through the years, offering more money than I knew what to do with. We continued to decline their offers.

I'd only seen Aldo Russo and his son, Lorenzo, come by to talk business with Papa. Aldo was the patriarch of the family and started their business. Lorenzo and his wife, Lilibeth, had five children. I barely interacted with their children despite how close we all were in age. They went to private schools and ivy league colleges. I, on the other hand, worked hard—getting good grades in school and a full scholarship to UC Davis. I was happy.

"Just think about it, Ava." Ned avoided eye contact with me as he packed up.

Meeting him on a Monday left me in a sour mood, my week already ruined. "Sure," I scoffed.

He glanced up, then walked out of my office.

The Russo family took over most of the smaller wineries in the area. Mine was small potatoes compared to their empire, but Maldonado Vineyard was built during a rough time in our lives—we did this for my mom.

I was proud of what my father and I built. I wondered if the Russo family could say the same about their business. After all, no family dynasty was built without stepping on, and in some cases, stomping on, others. When Papa passed away three months ago, it nearly destroyed me. I almost gave up the vineyard and signed it away to the Russos. I was out of fight, but Papa's dying wish was to keep our vineyard in the family. I'd never let him down. I just needed to figure out how I could get it making money again. I couldn't let my family's vineyard go bankrupt—it was all I had left of my family's legacy.

Chapter Two

Sebastian

"We've doubled our profits since last year," my father, Lorenzo, said during our family meeting.

I had no part in building the family dynasty of Russo Estates Vineyard, but I had a huge part in expanding it.

"Sebastian, what're your plans to expand our company this year?" Dad asked.

My role was in acquisitions, finding ways to grow our holdings. Over the past year, I managed to prove my worth by coming up with a plan to better utilize our land. My grandfather, Aldo, tasked me with finding more.

"I'm looking at some open lots toward the hills. It's promising and a great opportunity to do something different. Picture gondola rides up to our winery at the top of the hill, like Montserrat in Barcelona," I said confidently.

"That's something we can do in the future. We want something immediate, like taking over these smaller businesses—the first one being Maldonado Vineyard," Dad said, sternly.

"That family has refused every offer. We need to move on," I said, watching my dad pace.

"No, we're getting that prime land. They're growing a variety of muscat grapes other than Muscat Blanc for their secret Moscato blend." Dad glared at me.

"How'd you suppose we do that? Money doesn't seem to be important to them." Irritation laced in my tone. I gave him an idea I thought he'd approve of, but instead, he mentioned taking over Maldonado Vineyard… again.

"Well, that's where you come in," Grandpa said, pointing at me.

I swallowed a lump in my throat.

"Jomar Maldonado died three months ago and his daughter, Ava, has been running the winery on her own since. Apparently, she bottles her own wine, runs events on her own, and continues to resist every reasonable offer we've given." My grandfather's expression was grim.

I chuckled. "Good luck resisting me."

"That's what I wanted to hear," my father said sharply. "Don't fail this time like you did with Weston Wineries."

My father doubted my ability to seal the deal. Doing that successfully, my family would be wildly impressed. All I wanted were the accolades. I wanted to be taken seriously by my father and grandfather. I might be my father's eldest son, but I was also the eldest grandson, and I wanted a real seat at the table, which was still headed by my grandfather.

"Don't worry, it won't happen again."

***

My siblings and I left my parents' private estate and headed back into town for lunch. We decided to go to Atout, a reservation-only, fine dining restaurant near one of our family's wineries.

Lucas made a phone call, and we were seated at the chef's table. Matteo, Layla, Lucas, Gianna, and I surrounded the table in the kitchen, watching the chef and his staff prepare our dishes.

"Kuya Sebastian, now that Dad and Grandpa aren't around, what's your plan to get Maldonado Vineyard?" Layla asked.

With me being half-Filipino, our mother ensured that we knew our Philippine roots. We were never taught Tagalog; but she taught us how to properly address older siblings and our Filipino relatives as a sign of respect.

"You know, Kuya, I'm sure Ava's going to smell you right away and know what you're up to," Matteo said. "And I'm not saying it's because you stink—"

"Because we all know you smell," Lucas added.

My siblings laughed out loud, echoing in the bright kitchen.

I pursed my lips and rolled my eyes. Being thirty-six years old and the eldest, I was always teased by them.

Matteo was the second oldest, then Layla, Lucas, and Gianna. We were all three years apart, but were close.

"Seriously, Kuya, what's your plan?" Gianna asked.

"I'm going to ask Grant to do some background and recon on Ava. I want to know everything about her, win her heart, and take her business," I said snarkily.

"Sounds like the same plan you had for Everly Weston, except it backfired. You fell for her, and she broke your heart," Matteo reminded me.

"That's different. Everly lied to me, using me to get our trade secrets for Weston Wineries," I defended.

"This isn't any different. Anyway, it's done with. We need to move on," Layla snapped.

"This situation doesn't involve any family—just Ava. It's going to be a piece of cake. I'll take her vineyard and make everyone proud," I said confidently.

"Don't get in too deep, Kuya," Matteo said. "Have you seen her? She's hot."

"Kuya Matteo's right," Lucas said. "Ava's hot. I'll take my shot and she'll hand everything to me when I'm done with her." He smirked.

"Oh my god, Lucas." Layla smacked his arm.

I shook my head, laughing.

This time around, I wasn't going to let my emotions and feelings interfere with my plan. I'd win her over and get what I wanted.

As my siblings laughed and talked about everything but business, I pulled out my phone and got my plan in motion.

Sebastian

Hey, Grant. I need you and your team to run background and do recon for Ava Maldonado of Maldonado Vineyard.

Grant

Got it, boss. When do you need my report?

Sebastian

Friday end of day.

Grant

Copy that.

Sebastian

Thanks.

I trusted Grant, the head of security for Russo Estates, to get me all the intel on Ava. Getting Maldonado Vineyard was a challenge, and I wasn't going to let that woman stop me from getting what should've been part of Russo Estates years ago.

~*~*~*~

Chapter Three

Ava

Since meeting with Ned a week ago, I worked endlessly to figure out a plan to save my family business. My best friend, Chiara, had time to step away from her public relations business to meet with me today.

"Hi, Chiara." In front of Sweet Pea Bistro, I greeted and hugged her petite frame tightly.

"Hi, Ava. I've missed you," Chiara said.

We entered the quaint family-owned establishment, ordered, and seated ourselves in the corner.

"What's going on? You sounded so anxious on the phone." Chiara's expression filled with worry.

"I met with Ned on Monday, and he said if things continue to stay stagnant with my business, I'm going to lose it in a month. What should I do?" I propped my elbows on the table and buried my face in my hands. "I can't lose everything."

"I'll go back with you to the winery and help you come up with strategies to get business booming again," she reassured me.

I lifted my head and smiled.

"Thanks, Chiara."

***

Chiara and I laughed the entire lunch, catching up. Having our own businesses to run, it'd been hard to manage time for us to hang out.

"Did you hear that Vida and Rafa are having their wedding at Hacienda Luz?" I asked. Chiara met Vida when Papa and I were learning about the wine business.

"I'm sure their wedding will be amazing." Chiara's face lit up. She was a sucker for romance. When it came to her own love life, like mine, we weren't so lucky.

Chiara's last boyfriend cheated on her, like mine did. I'd given up on looking for Mister Right. *I was one year away from being thirty and maybe I was destined to be alone forever.*

"I'm sure it'll be beautiful," I said with a wide grin. "Let's get back to the winery. I can't keep Ninong Fernando and Ninang Reyna in charge for too long. They'll sample everything for themselves."

My godfather, Fernando, and godmother, Reyna, were my dad's younger brother and sister-in-law. They'd been retired for a couple years, and when Papa died, they began helping me out while I ran operations.

"You signed up as a vendor for the Food and Wine Festival this weekend, right?" Chiara asked.

"Yeah, I did. I hope that drives up more business for me."

"It will. You're beautiful, charming, and your wine is damn good." A sparkle flared in Chiara's eyes.

"Thanks." I smiled wide. "Shall we go?"

Chiara nodded.

Something caught my eye as we walked out. Not paying attention, I ran into someone … literally. He was a tall, broad man with a warm and spicy scent, one I could get addicted to. He wore a well-fitting suit, and by the feel of the material, it was expensive. His arm was around my waist, steadying me. An electric jolt ran through my body.

"My apologies," I said, tilting my head up, looking at him closely. His sharp jaw was covered in dark brown scruff. My eyes widened and heat rushed to my face. With pursed lips, I stepped back.

I recognized him. Who wouldn't? His family loved the camera; they had commercials and billboards all over California. While he might not be in any of them, his face was part of the website. His dark brown eyes glimmered.

"Sebastian Russo," I said, low, eyes narrowed on him.

"How are you, Miss Maldonado?" he asked, smiling.

"I was good before I ran into you," I snarled, side eyeing Chiara, hoping she'd save me. Chiara stood nearby, watching us with a wicked smile. *Traitor.*

"Well, if it helps bring you to better spirits, I'm very happy running into you. You've made my day." His gaze held mine.

I rolled my eyes and scoffed. If he wasn't part of the family that wanted to take my vineyard, I'd flirt back. He was sexy. Women did whatever it took to get his attention, but I wasn't one of those women. I got another whiff of his intoxicating scent, and I hated to admit it, but I got aroused. There was a crackle in the air between us as he stared at me. If I didn't hate him so much, I'd say was eye-fucking me. As much as I tried to resist the urge, I did the same thing to him.

"Tell that to someone who cares. Don't you have girlfriends on rotation or something?" I mocked.

His brow lifted, then he chuckled.

"I need to go. Goodbye, Mr. Russo. Hope we don't run into each other again." Before he could get a word in, I turned on my heel, grabbed Chiara's arm, and practically ran out of there.

I wasn't going to let that man try to charm me—no matter how gorgeous he was.

~*~*~*~

Chapter Four

Sebastian

Grant sent his report on Ava by the deadline, and to my surprise, she lived a simple life. She didn't go out to fancy restaurants, spend money on frivolous things, and if she wasn't at work, she was at home. Ava frequented Sweet Pea Bistro every other day. During Grant's reconnaissance, she wasn't dining at the bistro, so she'd most likely be there for lunch the day I ran into her—and I was correct.

Since bumping into her a couple of days ago, I couldn't get her out of my mind—her scent, curves, and beauty. She was alluring and so attractive. Her eyes were sultry and hypnotic. I'd follow her anywhere. She was probably in a relationship. How could she be single? I needed to get her out of my mind for the sake of my business. I wanted to run into Ava again and have a decent conversation, but didn't want her to think I was stalking her.

This morning, I decided to grab coffee and get some work done at one of the local coffee shops in Napa Valley. Arriving at Moonlight Diner, I entered the small family-owned café, ordering my usual black coffee and croissant. I scanned around for an available seat on this busy Friday. All seats were filled, except for one in the back corner. It would share a table with a woman sitting alone—Ava. *My lucky day.*

I smiled widely, walking toward her. She lifted her head, glaring. She shut her laptop and started to pack up when I reached her.

"Ava, may I join you?" I asked.

Her hand extended out, gesturing to the empty seat. "I was just leaving," she snapped.

"Please don't leave." I sat down.

She stopped and stared at me in confusion. "Why are you doing this to me, Mr. Russo?"

"Please call me Sebastian. Enlighten me. What am I doing to you?" I picked up my coffee cup and took a sip.

"Following me. Everywhere I've gone in the last couple of days, you've been there. What do you want from me?" Annoyance in her tone.

Except for today, all encounters were because Grant tailed her. "Do you believe in fate?" I lied. I couldn't tell her the real reason I wanted to talk to her—not yet, anyway.

"Fate? You've got to be kidding." She laughed mockingly. "You must use that pickup line on all women, am I right?"

"Never." I held my gaze on hers. "You're the first."

She pressed her lips together, hiding her amusement.

"What's the real reason, Sebastian? Why are you so desperate to be in the same room with me?" she asked.

"Since we're talking about being in the same room, there's one room I haven't had you alone in." I smiled slyly.

"That's bold of you to say."

"I was talking about my winery." I winked, chuckling.

She rolled her eyes; her cheeks turned a dark pink. She was adorable.

"I wanted to talk to you and apologize for my father and grandfather's persistent offers to buy Maldonado Vineyard. I hope your father wasn't upset about it. I'm also truly sorry for your loss. I wish I had a chance to get to know Jomar," I said genuinely.

Her chocolate brown eyes watered, gaze softening.

"Thank you," she said softly, looking away shyly.

"Please don't leave, Ava. Stay and keep me company. I won't disturb you." A small smile tugged at my lips.

Her head tilted to the side. After a few seconds, a lopsided grin appeared across her face.

"Okay." She nodded. She placed her laptop back on the table.

Ava and I sat at the table doing our work and minding our own business. I took quick glances at the beautiful Filipina woman in front of me, admiring her concentration and focus on her work. As soon as she looked up, I glanced down at my laptop screen. I caught Ava sneaking glances at me, too. I smirked, making her blush. *Are we in middle school?*

As she bent down to get something from her bag, I got a whiff of her scent, my cock twitching immediately. I'd rather take this woman to bed than take her business away from her. Heat rushed through my body, getting a hard-on as I thought about fucking her. I cursed under my breath, shifting in my chair to ease the strain against my pants.

A ruffling sound distracted my thoughts and throbbing dick. I saw Ava packing up her belongings.

"You're leaving?" I asked disappointedly.

"Yeah, I need to go to the winery. See you around." Ava smiled.

"I'm hoping sooner than later and in a more intimate setting." I winked.

She blushed again.

This woman has an effect on me—I'm hoping that the feeling's mutual.

Chapter Five

Ava

I couldn't stop thinking about Sebastian. He knew how to charm and flirt with women. I didn't reciprocate when he tried, but his deep, amorous voice turned me on every time he spoke. I could get an orgasm just listening to him talk dirty to me.

"Ava, anak, we're done setting up. Are you okay?" Ninang Reyna asked, brows furrowed. "You seem distracted."

"Ninang, I'm fine." I gave her a small smile. "I just have a lot on my mind." It was a lie. I wasn't going to tell her who I was daydreaming about. My godparents knew the Russo family and their proposal.

"Don't think too hard, anak." Ninong Fernando chuckled. "Your ninang says that causes wrinkles."

I laughed. "I think we're ready. Do you mind if I walk around to check out the other booths?" I asked.

"Of course, take your time." Ninang nodded, grinning.

A few streets of Downtown Napa were shut down for the festival. Over one thousand visitors were expected to be in attendance for the two-day event. I hoped this would drive up business for me.

I strolled down the street, glancing at the different booths. The mixture of savory and sweet aromas filled the air from food vendors, making my mouth salivate.

Stopping at a jewelry booth, I browsed bracelets and picked up a silver one with tiny crystals around it. Sunlight beamed on it, making it radiate and sparkle. I put it back down.

"That'll look pretty on you," a familiar, deep, raspy voice whispered in my ear. *Sebastian.*

A shiver went down my spine, a response from his breath and scruff tickling my ear. My breathing and heart rate increased. My body responded to his presence instantaneously. I turned, our faces and bodies were close. He dressed casually in dark, fitted jeans and a gray sweater. His hair was slightly messy, as if he just got fucked. *Maybe he did.* I eyed down his body.

Our gaze met, a sizzle in the air between us. Butterflies fluttered in my stomach.

"Do you really think so?" I asked.

"I think you'll look incredible in whatever you choose to wear." He smiled, eyes darkening. He leaned into my ear. "And not wear."

My face heated as this man continued to use his charisma to shake things up.

"You're really direct, aren't you? Is this how you talk to all women?"

"Only to the ones I'm attracted to—which is only you, Ava." Sebastian winked. "Can I talk to you alone?"

Say no. Don't do it. "Sure," I said softly, nodding.

His large, muscular hand enveloped mine, guiding me to a spot away from the festival. Electricity ran through my veins from his touch. I pulled my hand away and crossed my arms in front of my chest. My gaze narrowed on him. I stepped back, and he paced forward simultaneously. My heel collided with something, unsteadying me. Sebastian caught me before I could land on the ground, pulling me into his arms. I gasped as my body pressed against his.

My hands gripped the swells of his biceps. His eyes were intense, remaining on mine. Then he shifted my body to stand, keeping his hands around me.

"What did you want to talk to me about?" I asked breathily.

"Obviously, there's a connection between us. I know you feel it, too." His eyes searched into mine. "Go on a date with me, Ava." *I'll go anywhere with you.*

"Umm…" My mind told me to let him go fuck himself, but my libido said otherwise.

"I don't bite." He chuckled, then leaned to my ear. "Unless you want me to," he growled.

That did it. Arousal pooled between my legs.

"I'm not going to take 'no' as your answer," he said persuasively. "Please let me take you out."

I sighed. "Okay."

"Perfect." He pressed up against me. "Ava, look what you do to me. I'm rock hard and all you did was stand there looking beautiful."

His bulge felt huge. I couldn't believe I had that effect on him. Thinking about his cock had my pussy throbbing, craving for it to be touched by him. My eyes lowered to his erection; heat spread across my cheeks.

I cleared my throat. "I need to go back to my booth."

He reached into his pocket and handed me his card, grinning.

"Let me know when you're free next week for dinner." He flashed his sexy smile, then walked away.

This may be a bad idea. I don't know if I can control myself around him.

~*~*~*~

Chapter Six

Sebastian

It'd been a week since I saw Ava at the Food and Wine Festival. I gave her my number and told her to call me when she was available for a date, but I hadn't heard from her. When I held her, desire hazed her eyes. Her body's reaction showed interest in me, but here I was waiting like a fool for her call. *I wasn't a fool—and didn't like being ignored.*

I wasn't going to wait any longer and drove to Maldonado Vineyard.

I arrived at the small vineyard, stepping inside the winery, and scanned the room. The voluptuous goddess was on the other side of the tasting room. Our eyes met, then I strode toward her.

Her body stilled as I stood in front of her.

"Hi, Sebastian," she said with a lopsided smile.

"Ms. Maldonado, have you forgotten about me? I thought we would've gone on our date by now," I said brusquely, eyes fixed on her.

"Can we discuss this later?"

"No," I snarled.

"Sebastian, I'm sorry I haven't called you. I've been busy," she said, turning away.

Oh, no you don't. I took her hand and spun her back around to face me. "That's a weak excuse. I'm busy, too, but want to make time for us to have a date," I said irately.

"Wow," she gritted. She pulled her hand away from my grasp. "I *have* been busy. Since the festival, business has picked up. Unlike *your* family, who can afford to hire hundreds of employees to work for you, I do *everything* on my own. Sometimes I don't sleep, so I can keep up with everything. So don't tell me that I'm giving a lame excuse," she snapped, nostrils flared.

I felt like an asshole.

Tension crackled between us.

"I apologize, Ava. I didn't know—"

"That's right. You don't know all that I've gone through and what I do to make my business thrive. I considered calling you later today, but you've changed my mind. I'll never go out on a date with you." Her cheeks flushed.

I grinned, amused. Taking a step toward her, she moved back. She tried to act cold, but her eyes were filled with heat.

"Why are you smiling like that?" she scoffed.

"You're so cute when you're mad." I reached out to her face, taking a loose strand of hair, and placed it behind her ear.

"Quit trying to charm me. It's not going to work—"

My arms snaked around her waist, and I pulled her into me. My lips crashed onto hers. Electricity sparked my nerve endings. She draped her arms around my neck, kissing me back. My tongue brushed against the seam of her lips. They parted, inviting my tongue into her mouth. Our tongues curled around one another, fighting for dominance. Our kisses became hasty; my breathing and heartbeat quickened.

I embraced her tightly, my hard-on strained against my pants. My cock wanted to be set free—to be touched, sucked, and fucked by her. She moaned into the kiss.

Releasing our lips, I stepped away from her.

Ava stared at me, speechless.

"Text me your address. I'll pick you up at six o'clock tonight. Wear something dressy." It came out more like an order.

Not giving her a chance to respond, I turned around and strolled out the door with a sly grin.

Chapter Seven

Ava

Watching Sebastian walk away, all I thought of was that kiss. It caught me by surprise, but I wasn't mad it happened. I liked it and kissed him back. A spark blazed through my body. I shouldn't be giving Sebastian the time of day, let alone have him take me on a date. He didn't give me any opportunity to refuse, but deep down, I didn't want to.

I asked Ninang and Ninong to handle closing the winery this evening. I told them I wasn't feeling well and not to worry about me. I was glad they didn't see Sebastian and me kissing—they would've made a scene.

I arrived at my small Tuscan-style home that I inherited when Papa passed away. I didn't have plans to sell it unless I had to. If my business tanked, then I'd be forced to sell and move elsewhere. *That wasn't going to happen.* Diverting my thoughts back to my date later, I texted Sebastian my address. He responded quickly.

Sebastian

Hi, Ava. Thank you for texting your address. I'll see you in a bit, beautiful.

Ava

See you soon.

Sebastian told me to wear something *dressy* for tonight. What did that even mean? Rummaging through my closet, I found the perfect outfit—a sleeveless black dress. It had a plunging neckline and the bottom hem hit slightly above my knees. It was sexy and classic. I paired the dress with black leather ankle booties and a navy blue peacoat.

I curled my long black hair in loose curls and kept my make-up simple. My palms sweated as it got closer to six o'clock. I couldn't believe I was actually going out on a date with Sebastian Russo.

Sebastian. Fucking. Russo. *This is a bad idea.* He was a womanizer and playboy. Out of all the women he wanted to take out, why me? I wasn't wealthy or famous. My family didn't come from money. I wasn't anyone special.

The doorbell rang, startling me. My hand trembled opening the door.

"Hi." My breath hitched as I ogled the tall, dark, and gorgeous man.

He wore a tailored dark gray suit that fit him perfectly, making him look powerful. I forced my best smile, trying to hide my anxiety about going out with him.

"Ava," Sebastian said, deep and raspy. His gaze slowly went down and up my body. "You look amazing. Ready?"

"Thank you. I'm ready."

He extended his hand as I stared into his eyes.

I smiled, placing my hand in his, energy sparking inside me.

I shouldn't have let him kiss me or take me on this date, but my body craved his touch and addictive scent.

I'll give him a chance.

***

I slid into the passenger side of Sebastian's luxury sports car. He was a gentleman, opening and closing the door before he entered the driver's side.

The car smelled like him; an aroma I was already addicted to. Sebastian started the car and drove off.

"Where are we going?" I asked, staring at his side profile.

"It's a surprise." He turned his head to me, smiling sexily.

Did he think flirting and charming me would work? My cheeks heated. *It's working.*

We pulled up to the valet at Atout. My jaw slackened, knowing the reputation of this Michelin-star restaurant.

The valet opened the door, and Sebastian quickly went around the car, assisting me out. The touch of his hand sent shivers of delight down my spine. His scent lingered in my nose, getting me wet.

We entered the restaurant holding hands with fingers interlaced. We were led to a private table—the chef's table—in the kitchen, where two dozen red roses laid.

"Surprise; hope you don't mind," Sebastian said.

"Not at all. It's a very nice surprise." I gave him a genuine smile.

***

I hadn't laughed so hard in months, ever since Papa passed away. We talked about growing up here, our Filipino families, college, and goals in life.

Throughout dinner, our eyes locked several times, an intense energy between us. Once our meal was done, we seemed to be more comfortable around each other.

Sebastian was really funny. He told me stories of how he and his brothers would prank their sisters, and how his sisters retaliated against them when they were children. I thought he'd be really arrogant, making this date awkward and uncomfortable, but it was far from it.

We drank wine with our courses, but surprisingly, it wasn't from our vineyards. There was a different wine pairing for each of the eight meals prepared. I wasn't drunk, but I had a nice buzz.

I looked at the time, and it was nearly closing time.

"We should go," I said.

Sebastian took me back home, and like the gentleman he'd been all night, he walked me to my door.

"I had a great time." I smiled.

"Same here. I'll call you and hopefully we can go out again?" he asked, tilting his head, peering down at me.

"I'd like that. Good night, Sebastian."

"Good night, beautiful." He leaned down, placed a chaste kiss on my cheek, one hand around my waist. His other hand caressed my cheek. He gave a smoldering look, increasing the arousal already pooling between my thighs. *I'm definitely in trouble.*

Chapter Eight

Sebastian

Ava and I had been seeing each other almost every night for the last few weeks. I enjoyed our conversations and her company; she relaxed me. When I didn't see her, I missed her; when I heard her voice, my heart melted.

Surprisingly, we hadn't had sex yet. In my past, I'd fuck on the second date… that's if the woman made it to a second date. Something about Ava had me taking things slower with her. I wasn't going to ruin what we had between us.

We flirted and made out a lot, leaving us breathless every single time. Ava made me hard whenever our lips touched, and I'd catch her lowering her gaze to the bulge in my pants. When the time came, I'm sure sex with her would feel incredible. I planned a weekend getaway to San Francisco for Ava and me.

Sebastian

Hi, angel. I'm on my way.

Ava

Hi, Casanova. See you soon.

I smiled. The first time Ava called me "Casanova," I chuckled. I asked her why she chose that nickname for me, and she said it's because I was known as a womanizer. I didn't blame her for thinking that because it was the truth, but my playboy ways were in the past—now I wanted Ava for my future. I'd give up my past lifestyle for her. She had me wanting to be a better man.

My phone rang. *Dad.* I groaned, then answered.

"Hi, Dad. How are you?" I asked, watching the road.

"Sebastian, I'll be better if you tell me something good. How's it going with the Maldonado girl?" His words were sharp.

"Her name's Ava," I defended.

"Hope you're not falling for her. Just get me that land."

"Don't worry. Let me take care of it." I couldn't keep the annoyance from my tone.

He reminded me why I pursued Ava in the first place. Things were different now. I really cared about her, and she felt the same way about me. There was no way I'd ever hurt her. I approached her house, refocusing on us being together this weekend.

She opened the front door, flashing a wide smile, instantly brightening my day.

"Hi beautiful. You ready?" I pulled her into me, embracing her tightly. My nose nuzzled into her hair, inhaling her intoxicating scent.

She laid her head on my chest.

"Mhmm. I'm ready," she hummed.

I leaned down, placing a gentle kiss on her lips.

"Let's go." I held her hand and picked up her luggage.

Ava smiled sweetly. "I'm excited."

***

I took the scenic route so Ava would enjoy the two-hour drive. Taking her hand, I interlaced my fingers with hers. Then I lifted our adjoined hands to my lips, kissing the back of hers. She turned her head, smiling.

"Sebastian, please tell me our plans this weekend," she whined adorably.

"You're so impatient. You'll see." I laughed.

She sighed.

"You're not getting anything out of me, angel." I winked.

Ava lifted a brow, grinning mischievously. She pulled her hand away. I frowned, knowing I upset her.

"You know, Casanova," she started, "I was thinking…"

"About?"

She placed her hand on my thigh, surprising me. I swerved in my lane briefly as her hand stroked my thigh. *Fuck.* An erection grew.

"This weekend… I thought of being intimate with my Casanova," she said seductively.

I twisted my head toward her, eyes wide. She smirked, then poked my chest hard.

"I changed my mind," she snapped.

She pulled her hand away, but tensed when I gripped her wrist.

"You're not getting away that easily, angel. You think you can tease me, then leave me hanging?" I growled.

She relaxed, sighing loudly.

"We're almost at the hotel." I released my hold on her wrist. Then held her hand, lacing our fingers together. "I'm sorry, baby. It's our first getaway and I want to make it special." I kissed the back of her hand.

"Okay, I won't ask again," she said sweetly.

"So, you had something planned?" I smiled coyly.

"We'll see, Casanova."

"It's on," I said in a playful tone.

I pulled up in front of the Palace San Francisco Hotel, and the staff greeted us as we entered the luxurious hotel. Ava's eyes beamed.

"Mr. Russo, your room's ready," the hotel manager said as we approached the check-in desk, handing me the keys. Then we headed to our room.

***

Ava looked in awe at the penthouse suite. We stood by the window overlooking the blue skies of the San Francisco Bay.

"Do you like the room?" I asked, my hand on the small of her back.

"I do, but it's a little much for just the weekend." She gave a lopsided smile.

"I wanted to do it." I placed a gentle kiss on her lips. "Today, a private chef will cook us lunch, and tomorrow, we'll have a couple's massage… and the hours in between, we'll think of something." I grinned, then winked. "How does that sound?"

"Amazing," excitement filled her voice.

After lunch, we spent the rest of the afternoon sitting on the couch, snuggling and talking.

"I've been meaning to ask you something," she said, my attention on her. "I'm not sure if you know Vida, the owner of Hacienda Luz, and my mentor."

"I know Vida and the Moores."

"Well, Vida and Rafa's wedding is next month and I'm planning to go. Would you be my plus one?" she asked.

"Of course, angel. I'd love to go with you." I smiled wide. *I wanted her as my forever plus one.*

Her face brightened.

"Did you want to stay in for dinner?" I asked.

"Sure. I'll be right back, then we can order," she said, getting up and heading to the bedroom.

I scrolled through my phone, waiting. A few minutes went by, then a clicking sound on the marble floor caught my attention. I looked up, breathless. Ava stood in a black two-piece lace lingerie set and high heels. I slowly raked my gaze over her smoking hot body. My cock responded, hardening.

"Wow." That was all I could muster.

"Like what you see, Casanova?" A sinful smile curved on her lips.

"Mmhmm." I licked my lips. My gaze lowered to her lips, to her breasts, then up at her face. "Damn, you're gorgeous."

I got up and closed the distance between us. Grasping her waist, I pulled her against me, kissing her passionately. She kissed me back, deepening the kiss. She ran her hands through my hair, tugging some strands.

A low growl rumbled through my chest. Electricity spurred and awakened my body.

My cock twitched from her tantalizing scent. I trailed kisses down her neck, then sucked by her collarbone, marking her mine.

A breathy moan escaped her lips.

I swiftly removed her bra, my gaze lowered to her perky breasts. I licked my lips and cupped her mounds. My mouth devoured her breasts, lapping and sucking her nipple while my hand squeezed and played with the other one. I alternated between each breast, giving each the same attention.

Ava tugged on my shirt, pulling it over my head. Her hands grazed down my chest, lowering past the waistband of my jeans and cupping my erection.

I groaned, then swept her off her feet, carrying her to our room, kissing her fervently.

I gently laid her on the bed, admiring her. "I'm a lucky man."

~*~*~*~

Chapter Nine

Ava

Sebastian's eyes were evident to how he felt about me. When I first met him, I didn't even want to be in the same room as him because of his surname. His family wanted what my family worked hard to build. I assumed Sebastian was just using me, but he was different. The playboy façade wasn't there.

He kissed my stomach while hooking his fingers under the thin waistband of my thong, tugging it off my body as he hungrily eyes my body.

"You're beautiful and perfect," he said adoringly.

"Thanks, baby. You're so sexy but overdressed."

He quickly stripped the remainder of his clothes. My eyes widened, taking in the view. *He was incredibly gorgeous.* No wonder why women threw themselves at him. His cock was bigger than any of my ex-boyfriends. My pussy soaked, thinking about his cock inside me.

We took our time with foreplay, exploring each other's bodies for the first time, and making each other orgasm several times.

Sebastian claimed my lips in a firm kiss as if our life depended on it. I straddled his lap, and his cock hardened once again before he flipped me on my back and released our kiss.

"Wait here, beautiful. I'm getting a condom," he said.

"Wait. I'm free and clear and on the pill. You?" I asked.

"I'm clear. Just had my check up."

"If you're okay with it, can you go bare?"

He smiled devilishly. "I'd prefer that, too."

His tip grazed my opening, teasing my entrance.

"Please, Sebastian," I pleaded.

I gasped as his cock inched inside, filling me up and stretching my walls.

"You're so tight," he groaned.

He thrusted slowly, moving in a steady rhythm. His hot mouth took each breast, sucking and flicking my nipples. I arched my back, moaning.

He gripped my hips, thrusting faster and slamming into me balls deep.

"Fuck!" I whimpered, playing with my tits.

Our bodies beaded with sweat, glistening under the lights. The scent of sex and our moans filled the room. An orgasm brewed in my core, getting closer to my climax.

My lower belly tingled as my pussy clamped around his cock. My body quivered with my release. I rode out my orgasm as he chased his.

He grunted, thrusting one last time before emptying out in my pussy and shuddering with his release. The mixture of our juices dripped from my entrance as he pulled out. He rolled onto his back next to me, holding me close and fitting perfectly against his body.

He left for the restroom and shortly returned with a small damp towel. He gently cleaned me up between my thighs.

His cheeks were flushed, and mine felt the same.

"Are you tired, angel?" he asked.

"No, why?"

"Because we're just getting started." He kissed the top of my head.

*****

Since our getaway in San Francisco, we hadn't been able to stay away from one another. Over the following few weeks, our sexual appetite grew. We fucked almost every night until the early morning hours, craving more of each other.

Sebastian and I had dinner with Ninang and Ninong last week. Since they were my "parents," I thought it was time for them to meet someone special to me. They seemed to really like Sebastian.

Today was Vida and Rafa's wedding day, and I was so excited.

Chiara

Have fun at the wedding!

Ava

Wish you were going.

Chiara

Me too.

Getting nervous having Sebastian with you?

Ava

> Kind of. Women will stare at
> him and curse at me.

Chiara

Be flattered. You're with him and
they're not.

Ava

> I need to finish getting ready.
> TTYL.

Chiara

Bye!

I started getting ready for the evening wedding. Autumn was the most beautiful season to get married in Napa Valley with the warm colors of oranges, yellows, reds, and browns embellishing the landscapes of the many vineyards in the valley. With the couple's champagne gold wedding theme, I chose to wear something matching the season—a burgundy cocktail dress. I curled my long black hair, applying a natural look with a burgundy lipstick to match my dress, and wore black strappy heels, finishing the look with gold accessories.

Sebastian arrived a bit early, making me breathless. My gorgeous man was fitted in a charcoal gray suit and burgundy tie, purposely matching me.

"Wow, Ava." Sebastian's mouth gaped as he ogled my body.

He stepped forward, kicking the door closed behind him. His arms hooked around my waist, pulling me into him. A bulge pressed against my belly.

"You look stunning. All the men will be jealous that you're mine." His lips lifted wickedly. "All mine."

"Women are already jealous, giving me the evil eye when we're out together."

"Don't worry about them, angel. I'm yours and no one else's." Sebastian tightened his embrace, reassuring me.

"And I'm yours."

He leaned down.

"Nuh-uh, I just did my make-up. I don't want it messed up."

"So, a quickie is out of the question?" He chuckled.

I looked up.

He wiggled his eyebrows, playfulness in his eyes.

"What do you think?" I laughed. "We should go."

He pouted, then kissed the top of my head. "We'll pick up where we left off later."

"You can count on it, sexy." I winked.

***

We arrived at Hacienda Luz; the chapel was decorated beautifully with flowers matching the warm colors of the season.

"It's so beautiful."

"It sure is," he said gently.

Looking at Sebastian, he stared at me tenderly. "So beautiful."

My cheeks heated.

I grasped his hand, fingers intertwined, then took our seats for the ceremony. His thumb stroked the back of my hand. That simple gesture was so endearing.

Guests took their seats, then the room became silent as the wedding ceremony began. Soft music serenaded the wedding party as they walked down the aisle, smiling. We stood after the music changed, watching Vida in awe as she strolled down the aisle, gorgeous in her Filipiniana gown, and gaze fixated on Rafa. The off-white dress was adorned with delicate details and embellishments.

Tears welled in my eyes during their vows. I'd always dreamt of having a traditional Catholic wedding like my mother and father wanted for me, wearing a white ballgown with a long train, veil, and tiara, and meeting my Prince Charming at the altar. That was a little girl's dream. I glanced at Sebastian, who seemed enamored by the wedding. Who was I kidding? I couldn't imagine Sebastian the type to get married, let alone be with one woman in a committed relationship. He was a playboy, and eventually, he'd get bored and leave me. I fell for him hard and fast. I didn't even know what *we* were. I was just one of his many women.

A tear escaped from the corner of my eye, then another. My tears weren't only of happiness; I felt for the couple but also of sadness that I wasn't worthy of being with Sebastian. Before I could grab a tissue from my purse, Sebastian handed me one, then held me close. I didn't want him to see me crying, since part of it was because of him.

He comforted me with his embrace, molding perfectly into him like we were meant to be, but I was still insecure.

After the ceremony, Sebastian and I strolled around the outdoor reception area overlooking the vineyard during cocktail hour. Fairy lights hung above, twinkling in the night sky. We sipped our glasses of wine as I admired the décor, while noticing women gawking and eye-fucking him. He probably knew and liked it. *Were any of his ex-lovers here?* I became disgusted thinking about it. I was here to celebrate Vida and Rafa tying the knot, not pity myself.

"Angel? Are you okay? You look pale." Sebastian's deep voice cut through my negative thoughts.

"I'm fine." A lopsided smile formed, then I finished my wine.

He studied me carefully. "Did you want another drink?"

I nodded. "Yes, please."

He smiled. "You got it, baby." He kissed my forehead, then walked to the bar.

I stood there, people watching until I saw a woman stand next to Sebastian at the bar. She was laughing, leaning into him, but he didn't budge. My hand balled into a fist. Why was I getting jealous? We weren't exclusive.

I breathed deeply, calming myself.

A handsome man approached me, diverting my attention away from Sebastian.

"Hi," he greeted, smiling. "Did you try the wine they're serving?"

"I did," I commented. "It's very good—"

Sebastian strode toward us, fire in his eyes, and stopped in front of the man I chatted with.

"She's with me. Find another woman to flirt with," Sebastian sneered.

"Look, man, it's just small talk." The guy stepped back. "I'll just go. Enjoy the wedding."

Sebastian turned to face me, grinning. It fell the moment he saw my expression.

I glared at him, jaw clenched.

"What?" he asked.

"Let's talk."

We moved to a spot away from everyone.

"Why are you upset?" he asked.

"I don't understand why you embarrassed me in front of the man I was talking to." My brows furrowed.

"I saw the way he looked at you. He wanted more. He's not going to have what's mine," he growled.

"What's yours?" I snapped.

"You're mine, Ava. I thought I'd made it clear. I'm not sharing you with anyone. We spend every day together. When I'm not with you, I miss you. When I'm with you, I don't want to let you go. You're always on my mind and it kills me to see you with another guy—even if it's only talking," he confessed with a pained expression.

I stared at him silently.

"Don't you have anything to say?"

I sighed. "Let me ask you something,"

"Anything." He tilted his head to the side.

"Are we exclusive?" I asked.

"Isn't it obvious?"

"I don't want to speculate." I gazed at him.

"We are exclusive. You're the only one I want to be with." He touched the tip of my nose with his finger.

"I was jealous when I saw a woman at the bar getting close to you. I wanted to rip her eyes out. You're mine, and I'm definitely not sharing you with anyone. I want women to know that I've claimed Sebastian Russo and that I'm yours." My voice was thick and raspy.

A devilish grin tugged at his lips. He stepped forward, wrapping his arms around my waist.

"I'm so turned on right now. Your feistiness is getting me horny," he said, grinding his hard-on against me. "When we get home, I'm going to show you that I own that pretty pussy of yours," he growled in my ear.

A soft moan escaped my lips, arousal soaking my panties from his dirty talk.

"I own your cock. It's all mine," I said greedily, knowing he liked dirty talk too. "I'll use it to fill my tight pussy, milking and draining all the cum from your big cock."

He groaned.

"We need to wait until the wedding's over before we can go back to my place."

"Let's continue to enjoy the wedding." He placed a gentle kiss on my lips. "Then I'll have some fun with my woman at home." He smirked.

I can't wait.

We returned to the reception, enjoying our dinner and the program for the evening. When it came time for the bouquet toss, I stood in the middle of a large group of single women. Vida smiled and winked, then tossed the bouquet. To my surprise, I caught it; no hair pulling involved. I looked at Sebastian, who wore a wide grin.

I stood by Vida, getting our picture taken together.

"Congratulations, Tita. I'm so happy for you." I hugged her. "You look absolutely stunning."

"Thank you, Ava."

She pointed at the bouquet in my hands.

"So, Sebastian Russo, huh? Looks like you need to start planning your wedding soon." She chuckled.

"No wedding bells yet." I laughed. "Sebastian's amazing and has made me so happy. I hope we can be as happy as you and Rafa."

"Seems like you both already are." Vida glanced at Sebastian, who was still smiling.

"Thanks, Tita. Congrats again." I hugged her once more, then returned to my seat.

Next up was the garter toss—I wondered if he'd catch it.

Chapter Ten

Sebastian

I'd attended many weddings, but Vida and Rafa's was the most romantic. You felt the love in the room for them and the love they had for each other. It wasn't a wedding to show off your wealth and social status. I imagined it was Ava and me up at the altar. Although we'd known each other for a few months, I was falling in love with her.

This was the first time I could see myself with one woman for the rest of my life. When Ava cried during the wedding ceremony, I couldn't tell if it was because of the wedding or something else. I'd never want to make Ava cry. I wanted to be the one that she chose to love forever, to make her smile, laugh, and feel loved. Ava caught the bouquet from the bride, and I caught the garter from the groom. If that wasn't a sign Ava and I were meant to be, then everything was pure luck.

We rushed to her house after the reception. We would've stayed longer, but I couldn't wait any longer. I was going to explode in my pants if Ava continued to brush against me while we danced. I followed her inside, closing and locking the door behind me. Ava was leaning against the wall, smirking. Her lust-filled gaze fixed on mine. I stood in front of her, caging her with my hands.

She gripped the lapels of my suit jacket, pulling me down. Our lips crashed; passion ignited. Her lips parted, allowing my tongue access to her hot mouth and deepen the kiss. She moaned, my cock responding with a hard-on.

I panted softly after releasing our kiss, then grinned.

"What's that look for?" she asked.

I hoisted her over my shoulder, her ass next to my face, as I climbed up the stairs. Ava squealed, laughing so hard.

"Sebastian! Put me down!"

"Baby, I'm taking you to your bedroom." I chuckled.

"You know I could walk," she protested.

"This is way better. I have a great view," I teased, slapping her ass.

I threw her onto the bed. She giggled as she propped herself up.

I watched her infatuatedly. "I love your laugh. You're adorable and beautiful."

Her cheeks turned pink. "You're so sweet. But right now, I need you to strip for me, baby. Let me see your sexy body." She turned the music on.

I laughed nervously, blushing. With all the women I'd been with, I'd never had that request. I was excited that this was a first I had with Ava. I wasn't going to let her down.

I stripped down to nothing, swaying my hips and giving Ava a private show.

She squealed and clapped, eyeing my body.

Her eyes lowered to my lips, then to my erection. She bit her bottom lip, her gaze traveling up meeting mine.

"Like what you see, angel?" I smirked.

Her eyes darkened.

I joined her in bed, wrapping my arms around her and gently kissed her lips. I laid down and lifted her to straddle me.

"It's your turn to strip," I growled.

Ava unzipped her dress, then pulled it over her head, leaving her in matching lace undergarments. She removed her bra, exposing her perky breasts. The cool air stiffened her nipples. Her thong was nothing more than a tiny piece of fabric.

"Do you have any attachment to your panties?" I asked.

"No—"

With the flick of the wrist, it snapped, and I threw it off the bed.

I admired the goddess in front of me, ready to worship her.

"Let's try something different tonight," I suggested.

"Like what?"

"I want to make love to my girlfriend." I caressed her cheek. "Because I love you, Ava." My heartbeat raced and my stomach fluttered with my admission. "I know we haven't known each other—"

She looked at me affectionately and smiled. "I love you too, Sebastian."

I was in bliss when she professed her love back. I pulled her down, kissing her fervently. I flipped us over, then I trailed gentle kisses down her neck, sucking on her skin and marking her to show everyone she was mine. She squirmed underneath me, moaning as I played with her tits. Taking each one in my mouth, I sucked and lapped her nipples with my tongue.

My knees pushed her inner thighs, spreading her legs wide. I settled between them, positioning my throbbing cock at her entrance.

"I need you inside me. Please, baby" She whimpered.

I eased inside her slick sex.

"You're so tight," I groaned.

A sharp breath escaped both our lips when I stretched and filled her pussy completely. I let her body adjust to my size before I retreated, then slid back in with ease.

I caged her head with my hands, kissing her slowly and sensually, matching the speed of my thrusts. I took my time, wanting to make this moment last—the night we confessed our love. Her hands stroked my back.

She bucked her hips, meeting my every thrust, and a heated gaze locked with mine. Our moans resonated in the room.

I thrusted, slowly increasing speed. Her breasts bounced, sweat glistening on her chest. Sweat dripped down my forehead. Our bodies melded into one, moving together seamlessly.

Her walls throbbed around my pulsating cock. Pleasure grew inside me, getting me closer to my orgasm. I tried to hold out as long as I could, wanting to make this loving moment last.

Ava gripped the bed sheets and cried out, her body shuddering. A warm fluid covered my cock. She rode out her orgasm while I chased mine.

I had pent-up sexual desire from earlier today, needing her both physically and emotionally. My balls clenched and my body quivered with my orgasm. Our juices commingled as I emptied out.

I collapsed on her, panting. Then I pulled out and rolled onto the bed next to her.

She turned her body, facing me. Her cheeks were flushed in the afterglow of sex. I stroked her long strands of hair.

"I love you, baby," she said, whisper-like.

"I love you more, angel." I placed a tender kiss on her lips. She was everything to me. I was going to prove it to her every single day.

I cleaned us up before I held her in my arms, then drifted off to sleep.

***

We were spent after a few rounds of sex last night, but I wasn't sated. I couldn't get enough of her. I wanted more. I managed to get out of bed without waking her and took a quick shower. With a towel around my waist, I went to the kitchen, wanting to surprise her with breakfast. There was barely anything in her fridge. I called my assistant, asking him to get groceries and a breakfast spread delivered to Ava's house. I wasn't going to let my girlfriend starve.

Groceries, breakfast, and a flower arrangement were delivered to the house soon after. Setting up the breakfast bar, my phone rang. *Dad.* I cursed under my breath, not wanting to deal with him, especially with Ava here.

"Hi, Dad," I said lowly.

"Sebastian, how's the plan?" he asked, gruff, getting straight to the point. "Are we taking over Maldonado Vineyard?"

"Dad, about that… umm—"

"Don't tell me that you've fallen for the Maldonado girl—"

"Her name is Ava," I gritted, blood boiling inside.

"Watch your tone, Sebastian," he snapped.

"The plan's no longer in motion." Irritability laced in my tone. "And yes, I'm in love with her."

"I see. I know where your loyalty lies."

My hand ruffled my hair. "I was hoping you'd understand, but you're all business."

"I've built Russo Estates for *our* family, so I can give you the best in life."

"Thank you for everything you've done for our family, but I won't follow through with this plan."

"Alright, then, don't bother coming back to work until your priorities change," he said. "I won't accept your relationship with Ava."

What the fuck! My jaw clenched and my hand curled into a fist.

"As you wish," I barked, then hung up.

I needed to find a way to not lose my family and Ava in the end.

Chapter Eleven

Ava

I couldn't stop smiling since Sebastian and I expressed our love to each other last week, but I felt Sebastian was hiding something. The morning after the wedding, Sebastian surprised me with breakfast, flowers, and even groceries, but he was distracted, saying he was fine.

We'd spent every minute we could with each other. I haven't felt this giddy in so long. My phone pinged while I restocked the shelves at the winery.

Sebastian

Hi, angel. I miss you.

I grinned; butterflies fluttered in my stomach. He affected me even with texts.

Ava

Hi, Casanova. I miss you more.

Your place or mine tonight?

Sebastian

I'm sorry, baby, I'm working late tonight. I won't be able to see you later.

My smile fell. I didn't want to be the needy girlfriend who wanted to be with him twenty-four-seven. We both had obligations running our businesses.

Ava

No worries, baby.

Sebastian

I love you.

Ava

I love you more.

I frowned.

We'd been dating for a couple months and even though we were exclusive, I was still insecure no matter how many times he reassured me. Was he really working late? Maybe I wasn't satisfying him enough, and he was slowly cutting me off.

Stop the negative thoughts, Ava. I needed to trust Sebastian.

"Excuse me?" a woman asked.

I looked up to find a tall, leggy blonde standing before me. I recognized her—Everly Weston of Weston Wineries.

I gave a tight-lipped smile. "How can I help you?"

"You're Ava Maldonado, right?"

"Yes."

"I'm Everly Weston. My family owns—"

"I know who you are," I interrupted. "What can I do for you?"

Her expression remained as a resting bitch face. *Get straight to the point, lady.* Her vibe instantly killed my mood.

"I heard you're losing money and selling this place. Is it true?" she asked.

What the fuck! "No, where'd you hear that from?" I snapped.

"From Aldo and Lorenzo Russo. They met with my father, telling him they're buying out your business." Her tone was haughty.

"Really?" I grumbled.

"Sebastian's in charge of making that buyout happen," she said.

"Excuse me?"

"Sebastian's in charge of acquisitions," Everly mocked.

"There's no proof my business is bankrupt. This place isn't for sale," I gritted out.

"I heard that you're dating Sebastian. So you know, he dated me with intentions to take my family's business. You don't have to believe me," she said, then left my winery.

Sebastian used me. *I knew it.* He didn't love me. He played me like a fool.

I felt like vomiting. *How could I be so stupid?*

I walked over to Ninang and Ninong, their expressions worrisome.

"Ava, bakit parang galit ka?" Ninang asked.

"I'm not upset, Ninang. I'm not feeling well and need to go home. Are you going to be okay here?"

"Of course, anak. Go home," Ninong said.

"Thank you both. You're the best." I forced a smile, hoping they couldn't tell it was fake.

I headed home, figuring out how to keep Sebastian out of my life.

***

I arrived home, opened one of my bottles of Cabernet and started drinking. I didn't have much of an appetite. For the last hour, Sebastian was non-stop texting and calling me, but I ignored him. He stopped, finally getting the hint.

There was pounding on the front door. Looking through the peephole, my body stiffened—it was Sebastian. I pursed my lips, opening the door. He rushed inside, practically knocking me down.

He hugged me tightly. "I was worried when you didn't pick up any of my calls. Are you okay?" he asked.

I pushed away, glaring at him. "Get out!"

"You've been drinking. What the hell's going on?" A deep crease settled between his brows.

"Didn't you hear me, Sebastian? Get out of my house!" I yelled.

"Why?" He stepped forward.

I stumbled backward. "You used me," I snapped. "Everly Weston came by my winery, saying I'm losing money and your family's buying it out. The kicker—*you're* the mastermind of the plan."

He ran his hands through his dark hair.

"Let me explain—"

"No, you need to leave," I barked.

"I'm not leaving until we talk about this. I'll tell you everything. I promise," he pleaded.

"You've been lying to me since day one, including being in love with me." My heartbeat increased. "It's over Sebastian. Now leave." Tears blurred my vision, rage burning inside me. I was embarrassed to let my guard down for a Russo to deceive me. I should've known better.

"I do love you," he said with desperation. "I'm not leaving, angel."

Tears escaped my eyes. "Please leave or I'll call the police," I sobbed.

Sadness clouded his eyes, a pained expression across his face. Then he left.

I shut the door, locking it. Then slid down to the floor, leaning against it.

I picked up my phone, still sobbing.

Sebastian

I'm sorry, Ava. I'll tell you everything. Please talk to me, baby.

I need you, angel. More than anything in this world. I love you so much. I don't want to lose you.

I let my guard down, allowing him into my heart. *What do I do?* I dialed my best friend.

"Hey," Chiara answered cheerfully.

"Chiara," I sniffled.

"Ava, what's wrong? What happened?" she asked, worried.

"It's Sebastian," I said, softly.

"Did something happen to him? Is he okay?" she asked.

"He's fine."

"Then what's wrong?"

"I broke up with him." I sighed.

"Why?"

"At the winery, Everly Weston came by to tell me that the Russo Family was buying out my vineyard, and it was planned by Sebastian." Tears streamed down my face. "He fucking used me. He even told me he loved me."

"I'm so sorry. Did you talk to him about it?"

"Why should I?" I snapped.

"Hear his side. You don't know Everly's intentions. Maybe she wants you guys to split up." *What if Chiara's right?* "You know I'm here for you always, but stop shutting people out the moment you hear something you don't like. Just talk to him, okay?"

"Fine." I pouted.

"I'll call you later, okay?"

"Okay." Our call ended.

I needed to calm myself down before I talked to Sebastian. I didn't want to say anything I'd regret.

Chapter Twelve

Sebastian

My whole world fell apart because of what my dad wanted. Ava and I declared our love, but it came crashing down. Dad lost his shit when I backed out of the plan. Everly couldn't mind her own fucking business.

It'd been a week since Ava broke up with me. I haven't gone to work—hell, I didn't know if Dad called his bluff, whether I had a job or not.

I asked my siblings to come by this afternoon. When I opened the door, they were speechless. My scruff had grown out, looking disheveled.

"Kuya Sebastian, what the hell's wrong with you? When's the last time you slept and showered?" Layla asked.

"A week," I said hoarsely.

Her brows raised high. "A week?!"

The rest of my siblings had the same surprised expression on their faces.

"Before we make you take a shower, Kuya, what happened?" Gianna asked.

My hand ran through my hair. "I messed up," I said.

"What're you talking about?" Lucas asked, brows knitted.

"You guys warned me about the takeover plan—"

"You fell in love with Ava?" Layla asked.

"Yeah. Dad knows. I won't follow through with the plan. I can't do that to her. I love her and she loves me, but not anymore. Everly told Ava about the plan. Now Ava's ignoring me. I miss her."

"What the fuck?" Matteo blurted out. "Everly's a bitch. Why would she just go up to Ava and tell her?"

"Do you think Dad or Grandpa have anything to do with this?" Gianna asked.

"Someone told Everly," Lucas insisted.

"Pull yourself together, Kuya," Matteo urged.

"Go shower and get dressed. You look disgusting." Gianna scrunched her face.

I rolled my eyes.

"We'll help you get Ava back," Layla said. "Now go. You stink."

I returned to my siblings after showering and getting ready.

"There's our Kuya," Gianna squealed.

I grinned. "So, how do I get Ava back?"

"Confront Everly, then Dad," Matteo said. "Call Ned and get more info on the buyout."

I nodded. "Thanks."

I met Everly at the bistro. She was already seated when I arrived.

"Everly," I barked.

"What's this about, Sebastian?"

"About you confronting Ava. Where'd you get the information about the buyout?" I sneered.

"My dad and I met with Ned and ran into your father. Ned told him the status of Maldonado Vineyard," Everly divulged.

My father was the worst. I was ready to face him, and if I was removed from the family business, then so be it.

***

I called Ned, discussing Ava's situation and ways to save her business before going to my parents' house.

I desperately needed to see Ava later.

Sebastian

Hi, Ava. I miss you so much. Can I come over?

Ava

Hi. Okay, I'm ready to talk.

I grinned, happy she finally responded to me.

Sebastian

I'll be there in an hour. I'm going to see my parents first. See you soon.

I rushed inside the family home, startling my parents and grandfather.

"Sebastian, anak, are you okay?" Mom asked, concerned.

"I'm sorry, Mom, for interrupting. I'm here to speak with Dad." I narrowed my gaze at him.

"What the hell's gotten into you?" Dad snapped.

"Dad, you're not going to take over Ava's business. I'm not letting you do that," I protested.

He glared at me. "Look at what she's done to you. You're disrespectful."

"She makes me a better man. I'll leave everything to have a future with her. I love her and would give her the world if I could," I proclaimed.

My dad's mouth opened, but I interrupted.

"Ava broke up with me because she found out about the plan, but I'm getting her back. I'm not letting anyone take her vineyard away. Even you. If that means I need to leave our family's business, I will."

The room went quiet.

He opened his mouth again, but Mom placed her hand on his arm. He closed his mouth, pressing his lips together.

"Anak, do what you need to do. We're not going to stop you from being happy. We'll continue to support you. Isn't that right, Lorenzo?" Mom said, giving him a knowing look.

"Yes, of course," Dad agreed. I questioned the validity of his agreement by his expression.

Look who's the alpha in their relationship. I pursed my lips, hiding a smirk.

"I'm going to step down from my position at Russo Estates, effective immediately. Don't worry about me," I said, reassuringly.

"If that's what you want," Dad said.

"It is," I said, then left, heading to Ava's house.

I picked up some flowers for her along the way. My palms were damp as I got closer to the door. I was nervous. *You got this.* Ava opened the door. I gasped at her beauty. Although it had been a week since I last saw her, she still took my breath away.

"These are for you." I handed her a bouquet of long-stemmed red roses.

She stepped aside, inviting me in. We sat in the living room on opposite sides.

"Ava, I'm so sorry for hiding the truth from you." A pained expression on her face. "It was true, at first. I was supposed to find a way to take over your business, but I couldn't follow through with it." I gazed at her, feeling guilty.

She sat silently, staring at me.

"You probably don't believe me, but the plans changed when I started falling in love with you."

"I'm so in love with you, Sebastian. I should've talked to you first. But I was so angry. I couldn't control my emotions—the vineyard and winery mean so much to me." Ava frowned.

"I know," I said softly.

"After finding out about the plan, I called Ned, and he confirmed my financial situation. I need to sell it to keep my assets. I guess your father's wish came true." Tears brimmed in her eyes.

"I need to tell you something." I peered at her.

Her eyebrows raised in curiosity.

"I left my family's business—"

"What? Why?"

"I called Ned, too. He told me the options to save your business. So, I bought Maldonado Vineyard and am going to help you run it. We're going to make it successful *together*." I stood up, extending my arm. "Whatever your vision for your business, we'll make it reality."

She got up and took my hand; electric energy sparked between us.

"Are you being serious right now?"

"Yes. I'll do anything for you. I love you, Ava." Tears pricked the back of my eyes.

"You're incredible. I don't know what I did to deserve you, but I'm the luckiest woman in the world. I love you, Sebastian."

THE END

About Aurora Paige

Aurora Paige is a healthcare professional by day and a Filipina American writer of steamy contemporary romance with sassy heroines and sexy heroes at night. Each Aurora Paige story delivers a variety of Curvy Heroines, Multicultural relationships, Alpha Heroes, Steamy Heat, and a Guaranteed Happily Ever After. You can find updates on her website (www.aurorapaige.com) or subscribe to her newsletter (www.aurorapaige.com/newsletter-sign-up) where she shares her upcoming releases, writing updates, exclusive content, and giveaways.

Book List:

Playing for You (Hot on Ice, Book 1)
https://mybook.to/PlayingforYouHotOnIce

Playing for Keeps (Hot on Ice, Book 2)
https://mybook.to/PFKHotOnIce

Playing for Always (Hot on Ice, Book 3)
https://mybook.to/PlayingForUs

The Christmas Rental (Holidates Series, Book 1)
https://mybook.to/TheChristmasRental

The Love Prescription (Holidates Series, Book 2)
https://mybook.to/TheLovePrescription

Moonstruck at Mardi Gras (Holidates Series, Book 16) https://mybook.to/MoonstruckAtMardiGras

The Game Changer (Hot Streak Series, Book 1)
https://mybook.to/TheGameChangerRockets

Unmasked: A Fairytale Retelling
https://mybook.to/UnmaskedFairytale

Jingle on the Bay https://mybook.to/JingleOnTheBay

All Wrapped Up https://mybook.to/x3Vp

Secret Kisses https://mybook.to/YG0y

Merry in Mykonos
https://mybook.to/MerryinMykonos

Social Media IDs:

Instagram - @xoaurorapaige

TikTok - @xoaurorapaige

Facebook - @xoaurorapaige

Facebook Group - @thesmittensquad

Bookbub - aurora-paige

Goodreads - Aurora_Paige

Double Exposure

JUNE GRAY

Double Exposure

JUNE GRAY

Blurb:

When twenty-seven-year-old Roxie flew to California to photograph the Moore-Balmaseda wedding, the last person she expected to see among the guests was AJ, the man who broke her heart almost a decade ago.

The moment AJ saw Roxie again, he knew she hadn't forgiven him. But he was determined not to waste this second chance. This time, he would prove that he was no longer that same kid who made foolish but well-meaning mistakes.

But can AJ earn her trust again? And can Roxie find it in her heart to forgive?

Content Notes: Profanity, sexual situations, mention of death

Tropes and Sub genres: The One That Got Away, Second Chance Romance

Heat Level: 🔥 🔥 (fade to black)

Chapter One

Roxie

Present

"We know many of you have traveled a long way to be here with us. Your presence means the world to us and we are so grateful for your love and support," Rafa, the groom-to-be, said during the rehearsal dinner inside the tasting room at Hacienda Luz. He turned and gave his fiancée a warm look. "Tomorrow, Vida and I will embark on a new journey as husband and wife."

Roxanne Morales zoomed in on the scene and snapped shot after shot, framing the couple to emphasize the loving glances between them. She'd photographed many weddings before but, as a Filipino American herself, events that celebrated Philippine traditions were her favorite. She loved watching big families come together, laughing with each other, singing karaoke, or doing the latest viral dance together. These events always filled her with a bittersweet feeling and made her wish for something she herself didn't have.

For Roxie, photographing weddings was as close to a big family as she was going to get.

Ignoring the ache in her chest, she moved around, making sure to capture the reactions of the guests. Through her lens, she found Lola Naty, the matriarch of Vida's family, and snapped several photos of her warm, teary-eyed smile.

Roxie zoomed out as everyone raised their glass for a toast, until the table full of guests became a soft blur at the edges of her lens while the happy couple remained in sharp focus.

She covered the room, taking photos of different groups of people, stopping at a group of kids and instructing them to yell out "Sausages!" before clicking away. She moved again and pointed her camera to a group standing by the bar who looked to be in their late twenties. She tried to snap pictures of everyone but her gaze kept lingering on one face that gave her an uncomfortable feeling of familiarity.

When he looked over and she saw those dark, piercing eyes that seemed as if they could see right into her thoughts, she knew.

"AJ?" With a pounding heart, she lowered her camera and stared across the room at AJ Kim, the half-Filipino, half-Korean ghost from her relationships past. The last time she'd seen him was almost a decade ago, when he'd deliberately broken her heart.

Her eyes stung at the memory, but even she could see that the man across the room was different from the person she remembered. This person bore only a passing resemblance to the boy who used to make goofy faces to make her laugh. Gone were the soft boyish edges; his face was more angular now, his jaw more defined. His body, too, had changed drastically, no longer lean and lanky, but taller, more solid. His black hair was longer, falling over his eyes and curling behind his ears.

The guy who'd once described himself as "too nice to be hot" had grown into a striking, uncomfortably attractive man.

She didn't know how long she stared at him but her heart stopped when she realized he was starting to walk towards her. In her panic, she hid behind the camera, changing locations as casually as she could manage so as not to be found out. Maybe then she could get out of this situation with her pride and heart intact.

"Roxie?" She almost dropped her camera when she heard the voice beside her. It was deeper than she remembered, but she'd recognize it anywhere. With the camera still concealing her face, she asked, "Who?"

He bent down to try to peer at her face but she turned away, snapping pictures at random. "Roxanne Morales?" he asked.

She shook her head. There was no way she could face him. Not right then, when she wasn't ready. "I don't know who that is. Sorry."

"My mistake. I thought you were someone else."

***

The event ended an hour later. Roxie stayed until after all the guests had left to make sure she wouldn't run into AJ. After packing her things in her camera bag, she headed out of the tasting room to the balmy night, relieved to find the parking lot mostly empty.

She was almost at her rental car when she noticed a man leaning against a white sedan. "AJ," she blurted out then realized too late she'd given herself away.

"It *is* you." He pushed away from the car and took a step closer, eyebrows drawn together. "Why did you pretend not to know me?"

"I didn't see you."

"I don't believe you," he said, eyes dark and sharp.

Her ears burned. How was it that, after all this time, he still had the uncanny ability to tell when she was lying? "I didn't recognize you," she replied, craning her neck to meet his gaze. Had he always been this tall?

Something like regret flickered over his features but was gone the next moment. "Well, it's good to see you."

"Yeah, you too." She lifted her keys and pressed the unlock button on her car. "So, good night." She hurried over to her rental, anxious to make her escape. She needed to get away before the years of lingering resentment cracked her cool facade.

"Grab a drink with me," AJ said suddenly. "I hear the wine here is really good."

She bristled. How many nights had she cried herself to sleep over this guy and, now, he had the audacity to ask her to grab a drink? But as she turned to tell him to fuck right off, she found herself asking, "Why?"

He shrugged. "Just to take a stroll down memory lane?"

She'd rather walk barefoot down a path of Lego pieces than revisit the past with him but, even as she opened her mouth to say no, a different answer came out and surprised them both. "Okay."

Chapter Two

Roxie

Past

Roxie sat on the plastic seat of the swing and wrapped her hands around its metal chains, finding them cold to the touch. In hindsight, coming to the playground at ten p.m. probably wasn't the best idea, but she had no choice.

It wasn't long before she saw a figure emerging from the shadows, walking towards her in that half-swagger, half-goofball way of his. He wore a black hooded sweatshirt and basketball shorts, his feet in flip-flops, the official outfit of someone who'd just gotten a text from his girlfriend and had hurried out of the house.

He stopped in front of her and bent down, dropping a kiss on her lips that made her stomach flutter and her eyes sting. "Hey," he said with bright eyes and a wide smile, like this was his first life and everything was new and full of possibility. Like everything was perfect.

And it had been… until a few hours ago anyway.

"Hey." She wondered if he could see the swollen skin under her eyes, but it was dark and the streetlights could only illuminate so much.

He took the seat beside her and kicked off the ground, setting his swing in motion. "Bet you I can go higher," he said, kicking his legs out to gain momentum.

Willing to put off the inevitable for one more minute, Roxie joined in. Pretty soon they were both swinging, laughing as they egged each other on to go higher. The wind rushed through her hair and, for a few heartbeats, they moved in tandem. But, all too soon, they were out of sync again.

Eventually, they had to slow down or risk yanking the metal frame right out of the ground. The laughter died in Roxie's throat as her swing slowed, swaying lower and lower until her feet were back on the ground. "AJ, I'm moving," she blurted out before she could lose courage.

"I know. I am too," he said, laughing when one flip-flop went flying off into the rubber mulch.

She reached out and grabbed his chain, making his seat sway haphazardly. "I'm serious."

He dragged his feet on the ground, finally noticing her change in mood. "Hey, what's wrong?"

She didn't realize until then that tears were already sliding down her cheeks. She swiped at her face with her sleeve and took a deep breath. "My mom got a job in Virginia."

"What…" he asked, his eyebrows drawing together.

"I'm moving, AJ."

His eyes grew wide as her news sunk in. "What… why? When?"

"It's apparently a really good job in Washington DC. A once-in-a-lifetime opportunity or something." She couldn't meet his eyes, so she stared at his bare foot.

"You're really moving? You're not joking?"

"In three weeks."

"Three weeks?"

She couldn't bear it anymore; she crumpled over, burying her face in her hands. "I don't want to go. I want to stay here and finish high school. And go to prom." A fresh onslaught of tears came as she thought of all the things she'd been looking forward to doing with her boyfriend but now couldn't.

It wasn't fair. She had spent most of her high school life alone and now that she'd finally found her person, the one who made her feel like she was worth loving, she had to leave.

AJ began to pace. For one second, she panicked as he walked away, but he only retrieved his flip-flop and came back.

"AJ?" she asked in a small voice, tilting her head up to look at him. "Say something."

He faced her with a determined glint in his eyes. "We can figure this out, Rox. Maybe we can convince your mom to take another job." He took out his phone, no doubt to search for jobs in Dallas.

"She already accepted it," Roxie said in a whisper.

"Then…" He blew out a frustrated breath, jabbing his fingers through his hair. "Then we'll do long distance for a while. We can take turns visiting. We can do this."

She hung her head, unable to keep the cloud of despair from descending over her. A lot of people had made long-distance relationships work, but they were barely eighteen. Were they even emotionally capable?

He crouched down before her and put his hands on her knees. "Hey, we'll be fine."

"Will we?" she asked, tears streaking down her cheeks.

He tugged on the sleeve of his sweatshirt and swiped it over her face. "Of course. This is us we're talking about." He stood up and pulled her to her feet. He cradled her face in his hands and tilted her head back so he could look into her eyes. "We'll figure this out, Roxie. I'm not going to let a little distance keep me away from you, okay?"

"Okay," she said with a sniff.

AJ had confidence in them and, for now, that was enough.

~*~*~*~

Chapter Three

AJ

Present

AJ couldn't believe where the night had taken him. One minute he was at the rehearsal dinner for Tita Vida's wedding, spending time with a family he hadn't seen in a while and the next minute, he was heading back to the tasting room with a girl from his past.

Not just any girl. *The* girl.

Roxie had started out as a childhood family friend who'd become something more when he'd asked her for help. It was like straight out of a rom com where the guy asks his friend for help with wooing the popular girl in school, only to end up falling for that friend. And that friend had become his girlfriend, who then moved away and, inevitably, became an ex. And who, now, felt like a stranger.

Still, it was promising that this almost-stranger followed as AJ led the way to the tasting room. Unfortunately, the doors were already locked.

"Well, crap," he said, looking around to figure out an alternate plan.

Just then his Tita Vida and soon-to-be husband Rafa walked by, he whispering in her ear and she laughing softly. "Hi. Did you leave something in there?" Vida asked when she caught sight of AJ and Roxie.

"We were hoping to get a drink," AJ said.

"That's okay. I should probably get going anyway," Roxie said, taking a step back. "Still have a big day tomorrow."

"No, wait," Vida said, her phone already out. She dialed a number and spoke for a few moments before turning back. "You can go to the verandah. I've instructed the staff to turn on the fire pit and leave a bottle of wine."

"I don't want to keep the staff here later than necessary…" Roxie hedged.

"Nonsense," Vida said, her eyes practically glittering as she smiled at the pair. "You're welcome to stay as long as you'd like."

"Thank you, Tita," AJ said, reaching up and kissing her on the cheek.

Rafa winked as AJ shook his hand. "Have fun."

***

"Wow," Roxie said as she entered the glass-enclosed verandah that had a one-hundred-and-eighty-degree view of the vineyard. The moon was high in the black sky, gently illuminating the rolling landscape below.

Roxie walked around the sofa and took a seat, eyeing the bottle of wine and two glasses sitting on the edge of the stone fireplace. He sat beside her, putting plenty of space between them. He could feel her eyes on him as he uncorked the bottle and poured the 2013 Cabernet Sauvignon into two glasses. "To old times," he said, handing her a glass.

She took a sip, not returning the sentiment.

He studied her by the flickering light of the fire, taking note of what had changed and what stayed the same. Her face had matured a little, her wide-eyed innocence now replaced with wariness, but she was more beautiful now. Her hair was still long and black, though instead of ponytails and braids, she now styled it wavy and swooping over one side. He hated that it concealed half her face and badly wanted to reach out and tuck it behind her ear. She wore a little more makeup now too, a far cry from the girl who couldn't even get the hang of eyeliner.

"Remember when you were practicing your makeup for your debut but you couldn't get the mascara right so you practiced on me?" he asked with a grin.

She blinked at him, not a hint of a smile on her lips. "I remember."

He sighed and took a large swig of wine. "So where do you live now?"

"Arizona," she replied without looking at him. She was quiet a moment, then, "You still in Dallas?"

"I moved to San Jose after college. Doing the whole Silicon Valley thing."

She nodded, fingering the stem of her wine glass. He could tell she had more questions but her stubbornness, as always, held her back. At least that part of her hadn't changed.

"So you're a photographer?"

"Yep."

He sat back. "Huh."

"What does that mean?" she asked, her eyes flicking up to his.

"I was just thinking how you said it was a hobby and nothing more."

"People change, AJ."

"That they do." Another glance and a swig. "That they do." He didn't really know what he'd expected to happen when he'd invited her for a drink, but it definitely wasn't this. He supposed he'd always held onto hope that, when he and Roxie reunited, there would be fireworks and tears and maybe PDA. What he got instead was anger. Lots of it.

Which, in the grand scheme of things, was better than apathy.

"You're right, you were more likable back then," he said with a smirk.

Her eyes sparked. "I'm not the only one who's changed. The guy I knew would never be intentionally mean just to get a rise out of me." She drained the rest of her wine and stood to leave.

He almost let her go. But, at the last minute, he grabbed hold of her wrist. "You're right. I'm sorry."

She looked like she might leave anyway; he wouldn't have blamed her if she had. But, after what felt like forever, she finally met his gaze, a wary expression on her face. "What do you want, AJ?"

He tried to breathe around the sudden lump in his throat. "I want to catch up. It's been a hell of a long time."

An emotion rippled over her face but was gone before he could decipher it. "I'm here to work. The day after tomorrow, I fly back home. We have no time to catch up."

"We have right now." He held her gaze, willing her to accept his offer. "So?" He raised his eyebrows and stuck out his lower lip, the goofy little expression that she'd never been able to say no to.

She rolled her eyes but, to his relief, sat down. "I can't believe that still works on me."

***

It took exactly half a glass of wine for the thaw to begin. Little by little, the Roxie he knew started to peek through the wall of ice she'd built around herself. She talked a little bit more, offering tidbits about her life. She may have even cracked a joke.

He caught the way her eyes sparkled in the firelight as she talked about how she got into photography and all of the places it had taken her. He couldn't help but feel a sense of pride at her success, even if he'd had no hand in it.

His Roxie had grown up. The Sour Patch girl he knew from high school had grown into a beautiful, but no less sweet and tart, woman.

When he noticed goosebumps on her arms, he shrugged off his navy sports jacket and held it out to her. Before she could refuse, he said, "Just take it. You get chilly anytime the temperature dips below seventy."

She eyed him quietly as she slipped her arms inside the sleeves. "You remember that?"

"How could I forget? You used to steal my hoodies every chance you got."

"I still have the one you gave me. That blue one with the soft lining."

"That was my favorite." His throat tightened as the memories returned, the pain he'd repressed rising back to the surface. He locked eyes with her and realized she, too, was thinking of the past.

"I still have it if you want it back," she said, her voice barely above a whisper.

He couldn't look away from her if he tried. "Keep it. It's yours."

She broke the connection, her eyes flicking down to the dark liquid in her glass, her hair falling over the side of her face. Without thinking, he reached over and tucked it behind her ear. The move caught her by surprise and she stilled, eyes wide as she stared at him. The air between them crackled with unsaid words.

He leaned in just a fraction, every muscle in his body straining to get closer. "Roxie, I…"

Before he could continue, his older sister, Mina, appeared out of nowhere.

"Oh my God, AJ, there you are." She barely glanced at Roxie before continuing. "Can you do me a huge favor?"

He straightened, swallowing down his frustration. "What's up?"

"Mama and Appa's rental got canceled and now they're saying there are no cars available." Mina's eyes flicked over to the wine bottle on the edge of the stone fire pit. "Wait, can you even drive?"

"I'm fine, but…" He stopped and jerked his head toward the woman beside him.

"Oh. Hi." Mina did a double take when she recognized the face. "Wait… Roxie?"

Roxie broke out into a smile as she stood up and gave Mina a hug. She and Mina had always gotten along. She'd even told AJ once that she wished Mina was her older sister too. "Nice to see you again."

Mina held her at arm's length and gave her a once-over. "Look at you!"

Roxie laughed. "I heard you just had a baby. Congratulations, little mama!"

Mina held up the baby monitor in her hand. "I did. And she doesn't sleep well in unfamiliar places." Her eyes landed on the jacket Roxie was wearing. She spun around and smacked her brother on the arm. "You didn't tell me you two are back together!"

Roxie coughed out an awkward laugh. "No, no. I'm actually the event photographer. We're not together."

"That's right, Mom mentioned that she referred you to Tita Vida."

Roxie nodded. "Please thank her for me."

"Will do." Mina's eyes flicked between the two. "Anyway, I'll let you two get back to your conversation. I'll find someone else to go to the airport."

AJ knew the moment Roxie glanced at her watch that it was all over. "Actually, I should be going. I still have to prepare for tomorrow."

"Good to see you again," Mina said as she and Roxie embraced.

"Are you staying at the Hacienda?" AJ asked, a frisson of panic shooting through him.

"No. At the Spring Vines Hotel."

"That's on the way to the airport. I can take you."

She held up a black key fob. "I'm all set."

He tried again. "Are you sober enough to drive?"

"Yes, Officer." She lifted one foot off the ground and touched her nose with a finger. "See?"

He couldn't help but smile even as he sighed. "I'll walk you out then."

They left Mina sitting with the wine and the baby monitor, strolling through the courtyard where string lights glowed overhead. They wandered through an arbor walkway covered in pink bougainvillea flowers, the silence between them restless and uncertain. He walked slowly, trying to extend the moment but, all too soon, they were stopping at her car.

"So, I'll see you tomorrow?" AJ asked, trying to tamp down the foreboding feeling that this might be the last time he'd see her again.

The corners of her eyes crinkled. "I'll be the one with the camera, running around like a panicked chicken."

Belatedly he noticed that she was still wearing his jacket but he said nothing, only opened the door for her and said goodnight. At least now she had a reason to find him again.

Chapter Four

Roxie

Past

"How was school?"

"Fine." Roxie didn't bother to look at her mother. She just continued to push food around her plate.

"Anything good happen?"

"No."

"Anything bad?"

"No."

"Did you make any friends yet?"

"No."

"Why not?"

"Because *no*."

"Roxie…" her mom warned.

Roxie dropped her fork with a clank. "What do you want from me?"

Her mother's eyebrows shot up. "First of all, I want you to fix your tone," she said, a warning in her voice. "Second, I want you to give Virginia a chance."

"I'm here, aren't I?" The truth was, people here were more or less the same as back home; she just didn't want to make friends. Because having friends meant accepting she was never going back to her old life in Texas.

"Yes, but you're not trying."

"I *am* trying," she said, afraid her voice would crack and tears would spill out. Before they'd moved here, Roxie had promised herself that she would be supportive of her mother. After all, this was a big change for her too, and she was only doing her best to provide for their little family. But with each passing day in this unfamiliar place, this place that definitely *wasn't* home, Roxie couldn't help but feel the resentment start to seep in.

"It'll get better. Promise." Her mom reached over and tried to take her hand, but Roxie jerked back.

"I'm going to start homework," she said and pushed away from the table.

***

Roxie couldn't sleep that night. She lay in bed, staring up at the ceiling through tear-blurred eyes, the homesickness so strong, her bones literally ached from it.

You awake? came a text from AJ.

Roxie

No.

AJ

Me either. :) What are you doing?

Roxie

Just lying here.

AJ

I miss you.

Roxie

Me too.

AJ

Wanna video chat?

Roxie

Not right now. My face is a mess.

AJ

Okay. So, hey, did you ever find that surprise I left in your luggage?

She glanced across the room to her hardshell luggage in the corner of her room, still unpacked.

Roxie

What surprise?

AJ

Check the lining.

Roxie rolled off her bed and turned on her desk lamp, wincing when the floor creaked as she made her way across the room. She sank to her knees and opened the luggage, wondering how AJ had managed to access the lining. It took a moment but she found the zipper and slipped her hand inside, her fingers making contact with something soft.

She pulled it out, choking back a sob the moment she saw the sky-blue fabric. She held it up to her nose and inhaled AJ's familiar scent.

AJ

Did you find it?

She pulled the hoodie on, its fleece lining immediately enveloping her in warmth.

But this is your favorite, she texted back.

AJ

Your favorite too, judging from how many times you've stolen it. Keep it. It'll be like I'm there, keeping you warm.

Tears stung her eyes for what seemed like the hundredth time that day.

Roxie

Thank you.

She stared off into space, wishing like hell she still lived in Dallas. As she zipped up the lining of her luggage, an idea struck her, one so obvious she wondered why she'd never thought of it before. With renewed hope, she went to her closet and began to yank clothes off hangers, folding them haphazardly before throwing them into her luggage.

Guess what, she texted AJ.

AJ

What?

Roxie

I'm coming home.

She reread the text with a wide grin. It was so unlike her to be this spontaneous and reckless, but it felt right. She jumped when her phone started chiming with an incoming video call. "Hello?" she whispered.

AJ's face came on screen, a huge smile on his face. "You're coming here? Really?" he asked, eyes wide with excitement.

Roxie bit her lip, her head bobbing up and down. "I have enough money in my bank account. And I'm eighteen now, so I can buy my own ticket. My mom won't even know I'm gone until..." The thought of her mother coming home to an empty house gave her pause, but she shoved it away along with the rest of her guilt. "Anyway, I'm coming home!"

His smile faltered. "You're running away?"

"Can you really run away if you're already eighteen? I'm legally an adult now; I can live wherever I want."

"I know but…" He stared at her through the screen as if trying to read her thoughts. "What will you do once you get here? What about school?"

"I'll re-enroll."

"Where will you stay?"

"I don't know. I don't care." She waved the thought away and resumed packing with one hand. "I'll figure that out later."

"Roxie…" The way he said her name indicated he wasn't on board with the plan.

"I thought you said you missed me?" she asked.

"I do. But—"

"But what? I'm coming home. We can be together."

He blinked for a few moments and she knew he was about to do that annoying thing where he said something rational. AJ Kim: Mr. Nice and Sensible.

"You can't talk me out of this," she said, determined to protect the first happy thought she'd had since she came to this miserable state.

"Rox…" he said again. "Think about this for a second."

She sank to her knees, her resolve deflating. She turned away, hiding her crumpling face from view.

"Roxie?" When she didn't reply, he said, "You know that I miss you so much it hurts. Like, missing you gives me explosive diarrhea."

Despite the tears, a chuckle slipped out. She had always loved that about him, how he could make her laugh even during her darkest moments.

"But you won't be able to return to school without an established address."

"I can live with you," she said weakly.

"I don't know that your mom would allow that. And if your mom is not on board, my parents won't be either."

"I'll get a job and an apartment." Even as she said it, she knew it wasn't a realistic solution. She'd have to work to afford an apartment anywhere in Dallas, which would leave her almost no time for schoolwork or AJ.

"It's only a few more months till graduation," he said with a smile that was meant to encourage her but made her miss him even more. "Who knows, maybe we can attend the same college."

Her eyes lifted to his on the screen. "Did you get your acceptance letters already?"

"I got into Rice University. What about you?"

"I haven't received any yet. I don't know if I'll get accepted."

"Are you kidding? If I can get in, then you're definitely in. Your acceptance letter is probably engraved on glass and it'll arrive to you via special delivery and the box will burst with glitter when you open it."

She smiled, her heart clawing in her chest. "You're so annoying. I wish I was there to bite you."

"In the fall, you can bite me any time you want. Promise."

She nodded and, for the first time since moving to Virginia, she felt a little sliver of hope. She only had to survive for a few more months. "I'm going to hold you to that."

Chapter Five

Roxie

Present

Roxie had never been good at being part of a group. In high school, she was just *there*, the kind of person who lingered in the periphery, who did everything possible to avoid being the focus of attention. She supposed it was why she was so good at event photography because she could melt into the shadows and be invisible if she wanted.

The only person who had noticed her back then, who'd made her feel *seen*, was AJ Kim. And it pissed her the hell off to realize that he still had that ability to this day.

Roxie sat on the hotel bed with her laptop in front of her, flipping through the photos she'd taken the night before. AJ was in many of them and, in each one, he was always looking away as if searching the room. But there was one shot where he was looking directly at the camera with eyebrows drawn, almost as if he could see past the lens straight through to her.

She'd tried to keep her defenses up last night, had flung out sharp words to keep him back. But she should have known that AJ wouldn't be deterred. He had always been that way, stubbornly running headlong into a goal no matter the harm to himself.

It was probably for the best that they'd been interrupted at the verandah. Because Roxie knew that whatever he'd been about to say would devastate the defenses she'd spent years constructing, walls that she'd built *because* of him. AJ was the reason why she had trouble trusting men, why the last decade of her life was littered with failed relationships.

She needed to keep her distance. She couldn't have him breaking her down again. Losing AJ had been agonizing enough the first time; she wasn't sure she had it in her to lose him again.

***

After Roxie picked up her assistant, Kayla, at the airport, they returned to the hotel room and prepared for the wedding. Roxie changed in the bathroom and came out to find Kayla giving her strange looks.

"What? Is this outfit not appropriate?" Roxie asked. She'd put on a pair of taupe wide-leg pants, a white halter-neck top, and comfortable strappy heels. She normally threw her hair up in a bun when she worked but, today, she'd added loose curls that framed her face.

"No, you look gorgeous," Kayla said with a knowing smile. "Almost as if you're trying to impress a guy."

Roxie's heart leapt in her throat, her eyes flicking around the room. "What guy?"

Kayla walked over to the desk and motioned with both hands to the navy sports jacket that hung off the back of the chair. "The guy who owns this, perhaps?"

"That's mine," she said and tried to play it off by putting the jacket on. It was way too big but when she folded up the sleeves, it looked almost intentionally so. "See?"

Kayla was not convinced. She had worked with Roxie for several years and could tell when the truth was not being told. "Uh-huh."

The moment Roxie caught a faint whiff of AJ's cologne from the jacket, the words spilled out of her. "Fine, it's a guy's. Remember me telling you about my high school boyfriend?"

"The one whose heart you broke?"

"*He* broke *my* heart," she said, annoyed. "Anyway, it turns out, the bride is his aunt."

Kayla's eyes grew wide. "He's here?"

"He's here." Roxie slipped her hands into the pockets and sighed. "And I stole his jacket."

***

315

It wasn't hard for Roxie to keep her distance from AJ for most of the day. She stayed busy throughout, beginning with the photoshoot with Vida getting ready in her hotel room, and not letting up until halfway through the reception.

While the guests ate at the outdoor location overlooking the vineyards, Roxie wandered around and took photographs of each table, making people call out random words to get a smile. Before too long, she arrived at the table full of Kims.

Tita Liza stood up right away and drew Roxie in for a deep, familiar hug. "How are you, Roxanne?"

"I'm good, thanks." Roxie looked around the table, ignoring AJ's empty seat. "Wow. Looks like the family has grown."

"Oh, yes," Tita Liza said and introduced her son-in-law before scooping the toddler out of Mina's lap. "And this is my grandbaby, Charlie."

Roxie touched the baby's little hand, nostalgia and envy washing over her. She'd felt like a part of this family once, too. She'd spent many nights eating dinner with the Kims while her mother was at work. They had taken care of her and treated her like one of their own. Then she would return to her own home, to a mother who was only doing her best, with a stomach full of rice and guilt.

"How have you been, Roxanne?" Yae-Joon, AJ's father, asked in that gentle way of his.

"I'm doing okay," she said with a wry smile. "Keeping busy."

"We miss seeing you," he added.

"I'm sorry we couldn't make it to Carol's funeral," Tita Liza said.

Roxie's eyes pricked at the mention of her mother, but she pushed it away like always. It had been years since her mother had died; she didn't know if the regret and grief would ever completely go away. "It's okay." Roxie shook off the encroaching emotions and managed to smile. "Well, it was great to see you all again."

She turned away from the table and froze when she spotted AJ across the way, chatting animatedly with Kayla. A streak of jealousy shot through her, but she just as quickly shut the feeling down because she and AJ were nothing to each other. At least, not anymore.

***

A while later, while Roxie photographed kids playing with the colorful streamers on the ground, AJ sidled up to her and whispered, "Nice jacket."

Her finger faltered on the shutter release button. She took a deep breath before lowering the camera and facing him. "Here," she said, moving the camera strap aside to take the jacket off.

He stayed her hands. "Keep it as long as you need. Don't want you getting cold."

"Thanks." She took him in, admiring the fit of his black suit, the way it accentuated his wide shoulders and narrow waist. His hair swooped casually over one side, falling over his eyebrow. For a split second, she felt a pang of regret that she hadn't been there to witness his transition from teen to full-blown man but, then again, she remembered why and the regret reverted to anger once more. "I have to get back to work."

"Wait. Let me make you a deal," he said, producing a plate from behind his back. "Cake for a dance."

"No, thanks." She'd only had one protein bar the entire day, but he didn't need to know that. "I'm sure Kayla's up for dancing," she added, the jealousy adding to her *hangriness*.

AJ's eyes flickered with amusement. "I'm sure she is."

"So…" She threw a hand to the side, motioning in the general direction of her assistant. "Ask *her*."

His eyebrows quirked and the corners of his mouth tugged up. "I was talking to her about your schedule. To see if she could cover for you while you eat and dance."

The anger seeped out in a sigh and she found herself glancing down at the plate in his hand. Her stomach grumbled. "Fine. One dance."

***

Roxie inhaled the cake. One minute AJ was handing her a fork and, the next minute, the plate held nothing but crumbs.

"You want another slice?" AJ asked, taking the empty plate, and handing it to a passing waiter.

"I'm good. Thanks."

He quirked an eyebrow. "So, you ready for that dance?"

"Fine," she said with an exaggerated sigh. "A deal's a deal."

AJ took her hand and led her to the dance floor just as the opening notes of "Fade into You" by Mazzy Star began to play.

"Did you plan this?" she asked through narrowed eyes.

One side of his mouth quirked up. "I may know someone in the band."

She shook her head, biting back a smile. "Of course, you do."

He brought her closer, resting one hand on the small of her back, the other holding onto her hand. They swayed together, the song's melody floating around them, wrapping them in amber-hued memories.

"We were good together once, right?" she asked in a moment of weakness. "I didn't imagine that?"

His eyes flicked over her face as he shook his head. "You didn't imagine it."

The heat of their gazes proved too much and Roxie turned away. He bent down and touched his cheek to her head and, for a time, they moved in perfect harmony while the rest of the world faded into a blur.

"Roxie," he whispered, his warm breath on her cheek. "We're still good together."

She swallowed, too afraid to speak. The song, the dance, the boy—they were all dangerously close to breaking through.

"I have never once stopped thinking about you." He brought her hand up to his chest and, with a voice thick with emotion, asked, "Did you think about me?"

I will never not think about you.

"I didn't want to," she said, her chin trembling. "Thinking about you hurts."

His hand slid higher up her back, drawing her even closer. "How about, for now, we forget the past? Tonight, let's focus on the here and now. Then, tomorrow, you can go back to hating me."

"I don't hate you," she said, her vision starting to blur with tears.

Relief rippled over his face as he let out a breath. "Good."

When his lips drifted closer, she was faced with a decision: allow this kiss to happen, knowing what pain would inevitably follow, or step away and protect her heart at all costs.

She chose the latter. Because, despite her tough words and bravado, she was still that same girl who had her heart broken years ago.

"I can't do this," she said, untangling her fingers from his and taking a step back. "I might not hate you, but I haven't forgiven you."

~*~*~*~

Chapter Six

AJ

Past

AJ wondered if it was possible to pass out from excitement. Because the closer the taxi got to the house, the faster his heart pounded and the more lightheaded he felt. He'd spent a month saving up for this trip, had picked up every extra shift at work, and now he was finally in Virginia.

Then the car turned the corner into an older neighborhood lined with two-story Colonial houses. He stared out of the window, having trouble imagining Roxie existing anywhere else but in their neighborhood back home.

Would she be different? Was a month long enough to change?

But there she was, standing on the sidewalk with her long hair and sardonic smile, looking every bit like the girl he'd fallen in love with. The car barely came to a stop before AJ opened the door and jumped out with his bag, belatedly throwing a quick *thank you* to the driver before running towards Roxie and scooping her up into his arms.

He laughed, discovering she smelled the same, felt the same. Even her laugh was the same.

"Put me down, you nerd."

He set her feet back on the ground but kept his arms wrapped around her. "Hey," he said, sure that his smile started from his eyes and went all the way down to his toes.

Her cheeks were pink as she reached up and gave his lips a soft peck. "You made it."

"I missed you."

She tilted her head back, her eyes full of emotion. "I missed you more."

"It's not a competition," he said with a chuckle and dropped a kiss on her nose. "But if it were, I'd win because I missed you the most."

She started to laugh but AJ swallowed it with a kiss, and everything was right with the world once again.

***

After lunch, Roxie drove him around the area and took him to her new school.

"I kind of thought it would look historic," he said, squinting up at the nondescript brick building that could be any high school in the country. "I thought everything in this state was old?"

"What, you were expecting the school that George Washington attended?" she teased.

He grinned over at her. "Kind of."

She rolled her eyes, still grinning. "Speaking of schools, I got my acceptance letters."

"You did?"

She nodded, bouncing on the balls of her feet. "I got into Rice University!"

"You did?" He couldn't help himself; he picked her up and spun her again. Finally, after everything they'd endured the past few months, the future looked bright again.

***

That night, while trying to sleep in the basement guest room, he received a text from Roxie.

Roxie

Still awake?

AJ

I was almost asleep.

Roxie

You know, if you wanted to, you could come upstairs. Just walk on the right side of the hallway so the floor doesn't creak.

AJ

On my way.

He crept upstairs but as soon as he reached the first floor, the lights turned on. Roxie's mom rounded the corner, seemingly unsurprised to find AJ there. "Couldn't sleep?" she asked, shuffling past him into the kitchen.

He glanced at the stairs to the second floor before following Tita Carol. "I, uh, I was thirsty."

"You want hot cocoa?"

"Water, please."

She went to the fridge and returned with two bottles of water. She set them on the breakfast table and motioned AJ to sit. "I know it's been hard, you two being separated," she said after they both sat down.

"I wanted to ask…" He stopped and cleared his throat. "Did you move because of me?"

Her eyes flickered in surprise. "No, of course not."

"I thought maybe you didn't approve of me and Roxie…"

"No, no. You're a good kid, AJ. I've always thought that." She sighed. "But being a single parent is hard. It's a constant struggle to make ends meet. Sometimes I didn't have money for new school supplies or clothes. Some days, all we ate for dinner was ramen. So, when this job came along, I knew I had to take it. It wasn't an easy choice, but sometimes you have to make the difficult decisions for the good of those you love."

He nodded, a lump stuck in his throat. He blinked fast, hoping his tears wouldn't fall. "I get it. I don't resent you or anything. Just so you know."

"Thank you. I hope, one day, Roxie feels the same." She got up and took her empty bottle to the recycling bin. "Did she tell you about her acceptance letters?"

He brightened. "Yeah."

She stood at the sink, staring out of the window. "I hope she picks Duke."

His head jerked up in surprise. Duke University was the school Roxie had always dreamed of attending. He remembered a ten-year-old Roxie bragging that she'd one day be a Duke Bear. "I didn't even know that was an option."

"I thought it was always the first option. But who knows what's going on in that head of hers? She hardly talks to me these days." She pushed away from the sink and, for the first time, AJ noticed how bone-tired she looked.

"Roxie acts all tough but I think, deep down, she understands," he said.

She sighed, a sound straight from her weary soul. "I hope so." She started to leave then turned back. "Oh, and AJ?"

"Yes?"

"You might want to rethink your trip upstairs."

His eyes grew wide and his cheeks went up in flames. "Oh, um, I was just—"

She flashed a knowing smile. "Thirsty, I know."

He ducked his head, more uncomfortable than he'd ever been in his entire life. The very last person he wanted to talk to about sex was his girlfriend's mom. "I was… uh…"

"Believe it or not, I was once a teenager in love too," she said, then added in a tone that felt both like a blessing and a warning, "I can tell you and Roxie have a long future together. I just hope that you don't rush into any decisions that might jeopardize that future."

***

AJ didn't go upstairs that night. He took his water bottle and went back to the basement. Even though every part of his body wanted to sneak up the stairs, tiptoe on the right side of the hall, and enter the doorway at the end, he stayed put, Tita Carol's words swirling around in his head, about love and responsibility and making the difficult decisions.

Chapter Seven

AJ

Present

AJ kept his distance, pretending Roxie's words hadn't just hit the mark. For years he'd stewed in regret and had almost reached out many times to apologize, but something had always held him back, some fear that he hadn't been able to name until tonight, when Roxie said she hadn't forgiven him.

Still, he held onto the hope that one day she would.

***

AJ waited until the end of the reception, after Tita Vida and Rafa had made their getaway and the guests dispersed, to try again. With the hacienda staff fluttering around, AJ approached Roxie while she and Kayla packed their gear.

"Hey," he said with a smile, hands firmly in his pockets to keep from touching her. "Can we go somewhere to talk?"

Roxie started to refuse but Kayla dragged both bags out of reach. "I've got this. Go."

Roxie still looked as if she wanted to argue but then she sighed and faced AJ with pursed lips. "I don't really feel like talking."

"What do you want to do then?"

She looked around for a second before she turned back to him with a glint in her eyes. "Swim."

"I didn't bring a swimsuit."

"Neither did I."

The corner of his mouth tugged up as he grabbed her hand and started towards the edge of the reception area. They ran, laughing like children, as they made their way past the rows of bushes and the flower-adorned gazebo. They started down a grassy hill but Roxie stopped a few steps in. "My heels are sinking."

He crouched down and offered his back. "Get on."

"What the hell," she said before grabbing his shoulders and hopping on his back. He straightened up and hooked his hands under her legs, securing them around his waist before starting back down the hill.

He carried her, relishing the feel of her body pressing against his back, of her warm breath brushing against his ear. For those few moments, he could almost believe they were the same kids again. But, all too soon, they arrived at the pool, and he once again had to let her go.

She looked around at the dim area, lit only by the soft, blue glow from the underwater lights, before turning back to AJ. "Not chickening out, are you?" she asked with a grin.

He snorted and began to tug on his tie. "Not a chance." It became a race, both trying to kick off shoes and slip off pants as quickly as they could, stopping only when she was down to her top and underwear and he in his boxer shorts.

"Ready?" he asked and, before she could answer, cannonballed into the pool. Roxie was laughing when he surfaced, getting ready to jump in herself. "Wait, it's really dee—"

She jumped in without hesitation.

He waded over, ready to grab her when she flailed. He began to panic when a few heartbeats passed and she didn't surface until, finally, she emerged with a smile.

"I thought you were scared of the deep end?" he asked, watching her arms and legs moving gracefully underwater. The Roxie he knew had been terrified of water deeper than four feet and had always held onto his shoulders for dear life.

She shook her head as she drifted around him. "I've been swimming for some time now."

"Competitively?"

"No." She raised an eyebrow, her eyes sparkling with a challenge. "But I bet I can beat you across the pool."

He eyed the length of the pool, then the tiny bit of a woman beside him. "You're on."

They swam to the side and held on, fake glaring at each other.

"You ready to lose, Kim?" she taunted.

"As much as you are, Morales," he said, biting back a laugh. They were still terrible at trash talk.

"*Setgo*," she said and took off in a freestyle.

"Hey!" He took off after her, sweeping his arms above and through the water, his legs kicking as fast as they would go. He caught up halfway across the pool, catching sight of her as he turned his head for a breath. They were in tandem for a few strokes before he slowed and she passed him.

He touched the wall a few seconds after Roxie. "You cheated," he gasped as he swept his palm down his face.

"You let me win," she retorted, slicing her hand across the water and splashing him. He lunged at her and they wrestled for a few, breathless moments. He tickled her sides while she tried to dunk him underwater and, for that moment, it was like they were those innocent kids again, before distance and time came between them.

They stopped and faced each other as the laughter died in their throats, the playfulness giving way to something more heated. With a burning in his chest, he took in the sight before him: Roxie's skin glistening with water, tendrils of hair curling around her face, lips slightly parted.

"I bet I look like a complete mess right now," she said, swiping her finger under her eyes.

He cradled her face in his hands and dragged his thumb across the length of her bottom lip, unable to spend even one second taking his eyes off her. "You've never looked more beautiful."

She blinked at him, her face colored by uncertainty. But he also saw desire there, in the way she nibbled on her bottom lip, the way she nuzzled into his hands. He could see the conflict in her eyes, the two versions of her battling it out: the young and the old, the girl who still loved and the woman who still hurt.

AJ drifted closer, surrendering to the powerful tug he felt toward her. He only meant to graze his lips against hers but, then, she met him with parted lips and liquid wildfire rushed through his veins. He surged forward and deepened the kiss, his tongue easing past her lips and plunging into her mouth.

He kissed her fiercely, holding nothing back. It was an apology, a prayer, a promise. He kissed her as if it were the first time, and he kissed her like it was the last time.

They were both gasping when they finally broke apart.

"Do you want to take this inside?" he rasped, leaning his forehead against hers.

Her nod was all the answer he needed. Without wasting another second, he all but carried her out of the water. He grabbed their clothes and held his hand out to her, letting out a breath of relief when she took it.

They ran again, but the mood was different now, their footsteps more frantic and urgent. He led her around the back of the property, running alongside the vineyard, away from prying eyes, until they reached the little bungalow where he was staying. They stopped at the door, while his jittery hands fumbled around in his clothes for the key.

When he found it, he let out a triumphant sound before unlocking the door and stepping inside. Then he held the door open and waited.

Chapter Eight

Roxie

Past

It was near the end of May before Roxie was finally able to fly to Texas on her own, to attend what was supposed to be her senior prom.

AJ was all smiles when he picked her up at the airport, with a cardboard sign that said *Miss Morales* in his hands. On the drive home, he took every opportunity to look at her. "I can't believe you're here." He reached over and grabbed her hand, bringing her knuckles up to his lips.

"Me either." She looked out the window as they passed places she used to know by heart. "It's weird. Everything looks familiar but different. Like double exposure in photography, when you overlay two images. It's like that, like I'm seeing the new images over my memory of it."

He smiled at her. "So, it sounds like you're enjoying your photography elective."

"Yeah, it's fun. Not something I want to do long term, but fun."

"You still want to be a marine biologist?"

"Yes."

"You know, I hear Duke has one of the best marine biology programs in the country."

Roxie flashed him an exasperated look. She didn't know where he'd gotten the idea from but, a few weeks ago, he'd started suggesting she forgo Rice for Duke. "I still have no idea how you managed to convince my mom to let me fly here for prom," she said to change the subject.

"I don't know if you know this about me but I'm a pretty convincing guy," he said with a knowing look.

She sat back in her seat and fixed her eyes back out the window. "I'm going to Rice, AJ. And you're not convincing me otherwise."

"What?" he asked with an innocent expression. "I was talking about prom."

***

Mina helped Roxie get ready later that day, styling her hair and doing her makeup. When, at last, she was ready, Roxie walked out to the living room, to their smiling parents and a dumbstruck AJ.

"Wow," was all he could manage.

"You don't think it's too much?" she asked, smoothing out the front of her gown. She'd worn one other gown in her life, but this one was form-fitting and showed more cleavage than she was entirely comfortable with. Still, it was their senior prom and she wanted it to be a night AJ would never forget.

"Not too much." He sucked in a deep breath and then let it out slowly. "It's… uh…"

"He means you look beautiful," Tita Liza said then pinched his arm that held the corsage.

He blinked back to the present, stepping forward and slipping the corsage on her wrist. After she pinned the boutonniere on his lapel, they took the obligatory pictures in front of the fireplace, and then they were off.

***

Roxie didn't think she had very many friends at her old school but, that night, people came up to her, greeting her and asking where she'd been. She hadn't thought anyone would even notice that she was gone, but it seemed she was wrong.

They spent the rest of the night dancing, sometimes slow, sometimes fast. At the end of the evening, she and AJ drove to the Marriott hotel, where they'd planned to spend the night.

They were silent on the elevator ride up, both lost in their thoughts. She sneaked a peek at AJ's face and realized he looked as anxious as she felt. When she reached out and took his hand, he flashed her a nervous smile.

Once in the room, they faced each other, both a little scared to make the first move. "We don't have to do anything you're not ready to do," AJ said.

Even though her stomach trembled, she nodded. "I want to."

And then she turned around and he began to unzip the back of her dress, his knuckles trailing along her spine. Goosebumps bloomed on her skin when he leaned down and pressed his lips to the back of her neck.

When her clothes were in a pool by her ankles, she turned around and pushed his jacket off his shoulders, then turned her focus on the buttons of his shirt, taking her time, noting the way his chest rose and fell, the way his Adam's apple bobbed as he swallowed.

She felt self-conscious for only moments before he was laying her gently on the bed, preparing her as best he could until she was squirming and then, suddenly, quivering all over.

He carefully put on a condom before settling over her, elbows on either side of her head. "Ready?" he asked, brushing hair away from her face.

And with her heart pounding in her chest, she nodded.

Later, they lay staring at each other, unable to believe what they'd just done. In a moment of embarrassment, Roxie pulled the covers over her head and hid. AJ followed her under, a concerned wrinkle to his forehead. "Are you okay?" he asked, touching her face.

"I'm just…" She let out a shaky breath, her entire body so full of emotion, it was leaking out of her eyes. "I'm just a little overwhelmed with everything."

"Do you regret it?"

She shook her head. "No. I'm happy we did it. I'm happy you're my first." She bit her lips together, realizing that being her first didn't necessarily mean he would be her last.

"Me too."

Her eyes flicked over his face. "Why don't you want me to go to Rice?" she whispered.

"I just… I want you to go to your dream school."

"Dreams change, AJ."

"I think you need to take me out of the equation and go to the school that's best for you."

"Even if it means we'll be apart?"

He took in a ragged breath, the skin around his eyes growing red. "Even then."

Chapter Nine

Roxie

Present

"Rox?"

Roxie stood just outside the door, torn between her heart and her mind. She had gotten carried away at the pool, pretending they were their old selves again. Her brain had shut off the moment their lips touched, and she'd chosen instead to focus on the tangible, on the taste of his tongue, the rumbling sounds emanating from the back of his throat, the warm solidity of his body.

All of it had carried her along, made her believe that reliving the past with AJ was a good idea. It wasn't until she was standing at his doorstep, watching the wide expanse of his back as he searched for the key, that she finally had a chance to breathe. And remember what brought them here in the first place.

She shook her head. "I… can't."

"So, what, you're just going to leave again?" he asked, his voice edged with frustration.

All the anger she'd suppressed over the years roared to life. "What did you say?"

He released a breath through his nose, his jaws clenched tight. "You heard me."

She stomped inside the room, her chin held high as she squared up to him. "You're the one who broke up with me, remember? I may have left physically but you fucking *abandoned* me."

"I did it because I knew you wanted Duke. You worked so hard to get into that school," he said, his entire face red as he jabbed the air with a finger. "And for what? For you to throw your future away because of me?"

"I wasn't throwing anything away," she cried, her voice rising in volume. Did he really not know that she had considered him her future?

He slammed the door and threw their things on the ground. Then he grabbed her head and kissed her, tangling his tongue with her to keep her from speaking more painful truths. Her hands slid up his bare chest and, for one second, she couldn't decide on her next move. Finally, she decided to push. "You are such an asshole," she said, even as her body throbbed with want. "I would've done anything to be with you."

He held his hands out. "Well, I'm here now," he said, the thick cords of his arms bulging, the ridges in his stomach taut. "But you keep pushing me away."

"I. Don't. Want. You. Anymore." To prove her point, she pushed at him again, but he was an immovable wall.

He bent down to get in her face, his eyes narrowed. "I. Don't. Believe. You."

"Believe what you want." She was a second away from losing her cool and she couldn't have him seeing that. She turned to go but, somehow, his hand was on her elbow, dragging her back, and she found herself wrapping her arms around his neck as their hungry lips met once more.

She tore herself away with a sob. "I can't do this again."

"One more chance, Rox. That's all I'm asking for."

She turned her face up to him, tears sliding down her cheeks as she showed him all her cards, revealing all the hurt and longing she'd endured over the years. "I don't know how to forgive you. After what you did to me."

"I thought I was making the right decision. I thought I was doing what was best for you," he said, his voice thick with emotion, his face etched in pain.

"You didn't even give me a choice."

"That's exactly what I was doing. I was trying to make it so that Rice wasn't your only option."

"But that wasn't your choice to make."

His face crumbled and he sank onto the edge of the bed, holding his head in his hands. "I'm sorry," he said, his voice hoarse. "I fucked up. I fucked everything up."

To see him like that, looking so broken and desolate, ripped her heart in two. Roxie found herself reaching out and sliding her fingers through his hair. Despite it all, she still loved him. Maybe she always would.

His arms went around her waist and he pressed his face into her stomach. She held him, both of them crying for so many things: for the kids they used to be, for all the time they'd lost, for what could have been.

When he looked up, his eyes were red. He opened his mouth to apologize again but she bent down and kissed him, hoping it would put an end to the painful squeezing in her chest. She didn't know she was capable of forgiveness until that moment, until she saw the agony in his eyes, until she felt the thread of heartbreak that kept them tethered to each other over the years.

She took a step back and, with tears sliding down her face, peeled away the remaining layers of her clothing until she was bare. He rose to his feet and did the same, until they were both exposed and vulnerable, staring at each other through tear-blurred eyes.

He waited for her, stood stock still until she was ready, until she flattened her hands to his stomach and rose on her toes to kiss him. Then the world blurred as he lifted her in his arms and carried her to the bed, as he settled between her legs and held her face in his hands, as he lowered his weight onto her, and, finally, as he slid home.

***

Later, she lay on his chest, tracing a finger along the bridge of his nose and down to his lips, his eyes following her every move. "Roxie…" he said, his voice pitted with gravel.

"Mm?"

"That day at graduation—"

She covered his mouth with her fingers. "No. I don't want to go back there."

He pressed an apologetic kiss on the center of her palm before tugging her hand aside. "I just want to say I'm sorry. If I could turn back time, I would do so many things differently."

"Me too."

His hand slid up the length of her spine and tangled through her hair, bringing her head down so he could kiss her. "Stay, Rox," he whispered against her lips.

"Tonight?"

"Tonight. And forevermore."

The way he said those words, the earnestness in his face, made her wish she could say yes. "I don't know about that…"

"I'll make you a deal: Stay with me a few more days."

"And? What do I get in return?"

The corner of his mouth lifted, his eyes soft at the edges. "Maybe a happy ever after."

Chapter Ten

Roxie

Past

The second and last time Roxie came to Dallas was during the weekend of AJ's graduation. She hadn't planned it until their fight the night before, when he'd once again insisted that she go to Duke and she had snapped at him before hanging up. Filled with guilt, she had booked a ticket, hoping to surprise him and apologize in person.

But he still hadn't answered any of her texts by the time she arrived, nor did she find him at home. Roxie had to enlist Mina's help to find his whereabouts, eventually locating him at a classmate's house. When they arrived, they found the entire place filled with teens, the music so loud, the thumping could be felt down the block.

"Roxie, is that you?" somebody called out as soon as they went inside. Lacey, a girl from her old class, ran over and wrapped her arms around a stunned Roxie. Lacey, the girl AJ had been crushing on when he'd asked Roxie for help.

"You came! Can you freaking believe we're done with high school?" she practically squealed.

Roxie made a half-hearted attempt at smiling. "Yeah. Finally."

While Mina went off to find her brother, Lacey led Roxie through the house, past different rooms brimming with kids drinking and dancing. The pain in Roxie's stomach intensified when she saw people making out, and she had to double-check to make sure none of them were AJ.

They stopped in the kitchen, where Lacey handed Roxie a red plastic cup. Roxie was sniffing the questionable liquid in the cup when AJ stumbled into the room and slung an arm over Lacey's shoulders.

"Hey, Lace, do you have anymo—" He froze when he saw Roxie, his eyes growing wide. "Rox?"

She gaped, hardly recognizing the person before her. If the AJ she'd known the past few months had been wound tight, this one was the complete opposite, so loose-limbed and mellow, he had to hold on to someone else to stay upright.

"What are you doing here?" he asked, arm still draped over Lacey.

Roxie couldn't keep it together any longer. She turned on her heel and ran, pushing past people to get to the front door.

"Hey, did you find him?" Mina asked as she passed.

"Kitchen," Roxie managed to say before her throat closed up.

"Where are you going?"

"I have to get out of here," Roxie said, rushing out the door.

***

Roxie walked back to her old neighborhood with tears running down her face. Her mom would have a conniption if she knew her daughter was wandering alone this late at night, but Roxie was beyond caring. She had spent the rest of her savings coming here only to find the love of her life with someone else. What else was there to lose?

On the way back to AJ's house, she stopped across the street, staring at the house she'd grown up in, taking note of what had changed and what remained the same. She stared up at the window that used to be hers, wishing she could climb back up there, curl into bed, and go to sleep. And maybe in the morning, she'd wake up to her old life, when things were perfect and the boy across the street loved her back.

Eventually, her feet carried her over to the playground and the swings. She sat down, her fingers wrapping around the cold metal chain, the breeze whipping around her and raising goosebumps on her skin. She shivered, chilled down to the bone, as she stared into the dark street, willing herself to feel nothing but the cold.

Chapter Eleven

AJ

Past

AJ woke up with a sick feeling that had nothing to do with his hangover. He crept out of the house early, texting his parents that he had to be at the school to get ready for the ceremony. In truth, he was running away, afraid of what would happen if he were to come face-to-face with Roxie again.

When he'd seen her at Lacey's party the night before, he had been so shocked, so overcome with emotion that he'd shut down. The alcohol had only made things worse, amplifying his confusion. He'd forced himself to stay detached because it was easier than dealing with his warring emotions.

If Roxie went to Duke, the distance between them would be too much. And if she went to Rice with him, she'd inevitably start to resent him when she realized what she'd given up.

Any way he saw it, he was going to lose the person he loved most in the world.

So, he decided to take the fastest way out, maybe the coward's path, and opted to push her away. Even though it hurt like hell, he ignored her presence and acted like he no longer cared. At least, this way, she'd still have Duke.

When he and his classmates walked into the gymnasium at the start of the ceremony, he looked to the stands, searching for Roxie. He wondered if it would always be like that, if he'd search every crowd for her face, if his heart would break each time she wasn't there.

But he pushed the thought away and graduated. It wasn't until he was saying goodbye to his friends that he realized what he was truly leaving behind. This school, these people, this life. Again, he searched the crowd for Roxie, needing her comfort and familiarity, but she was already gone.

***

When he came home, he ran into Roxie on the way to the front door, her luggage rolling behind her.

"Wait, already?" he blurted out then carefully tucked away his emotions again. "That was quick."

"It was last minute," she said through stiff lips. She refused to meet his eyes. "I wanted to surprise you."

His chest threatened to cave in, but he took a fortifying breath. "Well, have a safe trip back home," he said and headed to his room, his eyes already prickling with tears. He hated this, hated himself for hurting her, but he was doing the right thing. His only hope was that, one day, Roxie would see it too.

"That's it?" she called out.

He kept his back to her, afraid his face would give him away. "What more is there?"

"How about an explanation of why you haven't been answering my texts or calls? Or why you've been treating me like I don't matter? Or why you were at Lacey's house, fawning all over her?"

Shrugging was all he could do.

"After all we've been through, that's all you got? I think I deserve more than that."

She did. She deserved the world, way more than what he had to offer. Way more than he could give. "I don't have anything left to say," he bit out.

"This is it, AJ. When I go, I'm never coming back," she said with a quiver in her voice.

He bit his trembling lips together. His fingernails dug painfully into the palms of his hands. "Bye, Roxie. Have fun at Duke."

Then he did the hardest thing he'd ever done—he walked away.

Chapter Twelve

Roxie

Present

AJ took Roxie back to her hotel the next morning and kissed her goodbye, doing what he'd failed to do a decade ago: give her a choice. So, she chose to return to Arizona and leave the weekend at Hacienda Luz behind as a fond memory. At least this way she could go home knowing her rift with AJ had been repaired. And maybe, now, she could move on and live her life.

But as she sat at the boarding gate, with Kayla beside her, she could feel the tug on the thread, trying to pull her back to the vineyard.

"You all right?" Kayla asked.

"Fine. Why?"

"You're doing the thousand-yard stare."

She let out a hollow laugh. "Just thinking."

"About Mr. Jacket?"

Roxie let out a sigh.

"I still don't get why you two aren't going to try to make it work. The chemistry was there. Everybody could see it."

"It wouldn't work. We live clear across the country from each other," Roxie said, repeating what she'd told AJ earlier. "And we have a terrible track record for long-distance relationships."

Kayla shook her head and rummaged in her bag, pulling out her work laptop. She opened it up and flipped through wedding photos until she found what she was looking for. "There. Tell me those two dummies don't belong together."

On the screen was a photo from the reception, in the foreground a blur of candlelight and flowers, but in sharp focus in the middle ground stood AJ and Roxie with their arms around each other. Roxie's heart hammered in her chest as she gazed at the couple in the photograph, with their eyes closed, their heads bent toward each other, the yearning evident in their body and their faces.

There was something honest there, the kind of bond that survived time and distance. How could she walk away from a love like that?

Hope filled Roxie, lifting her to her feet. "I... I should..."

Kayla pushed Roxie's bag into her hand. "Yes, you should. Go."

***

The Uber ride back to the Hacienda felt like hours. Her stomach was in knots as she stared out the window, willing the scenery to pass by faster. Finally, Roxie reached her destination and she got out and hurried toward the verandah, which had been rearranged for breakfast. With her heart pounding in her ears, she entered, seeking out AJ's face among the guests, wishing she had her camera to hide behind. It struck her then that she'd been using her camera as a crutch, a way to hold the world at a distance instead of taking part.

She took a deep breath and made her way into the crowd, leaving behind her armor and her walls.

"You came back," said a familiar deep voice behind her.

She turned, a thousand emotions pulsing through her veins as she faced AJ, the boy and the man overlayed, forming the image of the person she loved. "I'm back," she said with a wavery smile.

His eyes glimmered with hope as he took a step closer. "How long?"

"Two days. Maybe forevermore," she said with an incredulous laugh and, then, the rest became a blur as he pulled her into his arms and kissed her.

THE END

About June Gray

June Gray is the author of the bestselling Disarm series. She loves to tell stories that excite and enrage, that break the reader's heart and put it back together again. June is a storyteller, a graphic designer, a fitness freak, a military wife, and a dedicated fangirl. She was born in the Philippines, raised in Australia, and now calls the United States home. She can currently be found dodging tornadoes in Oklahoma with her husband and two daughters.

Book List:

Disarm

Illicit: books2read.com/JuneGray-Illicit

Bad Blood:

Finding West: books2read.com/JuneGray-FindingWest

Heading East: books2read.com/JuneGray-HeadingEast

North Star: books2read.com/JuneGray-NorthStar

Taking Heart: books2read.com/JuneGray-TakingHeart

Untamed: books2read.com/JuneGray-Untamed

Under The Wishing Tree:

Under The Winter Sky:

Social Media IDs

Website: authorjunegray.com

Facebook: @JuneGrayAuthor

Instagram: @authorjunegray

TikTok:@authorjunegray

Stay With Me

LIZ DURANO

Stay With Me

LIZ DURANO

Blurb:

It's been three years since landscape painter Tallie Vicente walled off her heart after losing her husband and the scandal that followed. But when car trouble while driving from New Mexico to Napa Valley to attend her cousin's wedding ends up with her having to share a room—and a bed—with a young, gorgeous doctor, unexpected sparks fly between them, proving that it's never too late to fall in love again.

Content Notes: Mention of death, some profanity, open-door intimacies

Tropes and Sub-genres: Age gap, Later in life, One-night Stand; Multicultural Romance

Heat Level: 🔥 🔥 🔥 🔥 (Explicit sex)

Chapter One

Tallie

"I'm so happy you're on your way here, Tallie. I just can't believe you're driving here instead of flying," my cousin Vida Moore-Aquino says on my car's speakers. She's been my best friend since the day my mother married her uncle and we became family. "But I get it."

"I'm so sorry, Vida, but thanks for understanding." I glance at the vast expanse of desert around me as I speed along the interstate. Flying sure looks better right now.

"Oh, no! Don't apologize, Tallie. I'm so grateful you agreed to be my matron of honor," she says. "I just hope coming back doesn't... trigger things."

"Vida, it's been three years." I hope my confidence translates well over the phone as I continue, "I've healed, and I'm ready."

Forget that it took a phone call followed by a formal letter and another phone call from my cousin to nudge me out of hiding, but I'm here, and that's what matters. "It's a pleasant drive and the stops along the way were amazing. Sedona was breathtaking. I just might stop by again and stay for a few days on my way back."

"I know you're planning on driving back as soon as we fly to the Philippines for our honeymoon, but I hope you stay awhile," she says. "At least, until we get back."

A month in Napa? Most likely, I'll be gone by the time they leave for the airport, but I can't disappoint her. "I'll think about it."

"I hope you do." She pauses. "But you being part of my wedding is more than I can ask for, Tallie. Where are you now?"

"The last sign I passed said no rest stops or gas for the next fifty miles, but I'll arrive by tomorrow evening at the latest." I sigh. "Vida, I should be the one apologizing, considering everyone's already there. I should have started sooner, or at least, not stayed a day in Sedona."

"You're fine," she says. "Just get here."

What should have been a three-day trip has turned into a five-day drive, and I've got no one to blame but myself.

Still, Vida's right. I could have flown.

But when crumpled, burning metal is all you see at the thought of getting on a plane, you do the next best thing to declining an invitation to be the matron of honor at your cousin's wedding.

You drive.

But I'd be lying if it was the only reason I decided not to fly. I figured driving would give me a chance to turn around in case I decided at the last minute I couldn't go ahead with it, that even after three years, I can't go back.

But for Vida, I will.

I'll brave everyone's pity.

I'll deal with my shame like I did before I left.

"I just wish I could get there sooner to help you with everything."

Vida laughs. "Are you kidding? That's what my whole extended family is for. They got everything nailed down months ago."

"Oh… right." How could I forget the extended Moore clan—my clan now, too, even if my marriage—that would have been involved the moment Vida got engaged? Her wedding is the first grand wedding to be hosted at Hacienda Luz Hotel & Vineyard in decades, and with cousins like Ruby, a chef, and Eden, an event planner, they have most of the things nailed down.

"No, your job is to get here as soon as you can so we can spend time together before the big day," Vida continues as I laugh.

"And I will. I'm in charge of your bridal shower, remember?"

Vida is quiet for a few moments, and I can almost sense it coming. The dreaded question.

"Are you sure you're okay coming back?" she asks. "I know you left because of… everything. The funeral. What she said in front of everyone." Vida's voice drops. "But I hope this isn't too soon."

"One month, one year. One day. I would have come no matter what for your big day." I do my best to sound cheerful. "Please don't feel bad. I'm okay. I've had three years to grieve… and heal."

More like hiding out in the high desert of New Mexico, far from the whispers and the looks the people gave me— the widow who didn't even know her own husband. But I didn't just cry my eyes out or rage at the moon, screaming out my anger at Josiah and the woman who'd stood at his grave demanding who'd promised her….

"Does that mean you're open to being introduced to someone?" Vida asks.

"Please don't tell me you're introducing me to every single man at your wedding," I groan. "I'm too old for that shit."

"If you believe that, does that mean I'm too old to get married?"

"No," I exclaim, realizing my blunder. "But you know what I mean, right? I don't want what happened three years ago to happen again."

"Not every man is going to be like Josiah," Vida says. "But you'll like this guy. I promise."

"Let me get there first and decide then." As cars speed past me, I realize I've eased my foot off the gas and am doing 80 instead of the 95 miles per hour everyone's doing. "Anyway, I got to go before everyone yells at me for being an old lady driver. I can't believe 80 miles per hour is too slow these days."

Vida chuckles. "You should have flown."

"Shut up or I'll turn around right now," I say before assuring her I'm kidding and saying goodbye.

I've known Vida since I first came to California from the Philippines at thirteen. My mother had married Ananias Soriano, Vida's uncle, after they met through a cousin in Manila. Anaias worked as the vineyard foreman for Hacienda Luz—the family's pride and joy—and suddenly I had a whole new world of cousins, aunts, and uncles. But Vida was special from the start. I can still remember the day we were introduced, how she grabbed my hand and declared us best friends before we'd even finished our first shared plate of lumpia.

After college, we parted ways, with me flying to Europe where I worked as an artist-residence for a few years while she became the chief winemaker at Hacienda Luz.

Yet despite the distance between us, we kept in touch. When I returned to Napa, Vida and I were as close as ever. Thick as thieves, as some people would say. She was there when I met Josiah while I was exhibiting my work at Hacienda Luz. She was there when he and I got married at the courthouse and when we buried him fifteen years later, when an unexpected visitor showed up to prove that you never truly know someone and you're better off being alone, with your heart walled off from the world.

But even though I left Napa three years ago, Vida and I kept in touch. And now it's her turn to find the love of her life and I'm ecstatic for her. Who says you can't find true love in your late 40s?

If I'm lucky, I just might find mine again, too.

The sight of a white car passing a few car lengths behind me forces me to focus on the road. Going dangerously fast, the driver is weaving between lanes. I check my speed, aware that I'm going with the flow of traffic at 90 miles an hour.

Suddenly a flash of white appears in my periphery and the white car cuts in front of me. I curse out loud as the sickening sound of crunching metal and screeching tires fills the air and my car careens off the road. I grip the wheel, doing my best to control the car as it does a full 180-degree turn before coming to an abrupt stop, facing traffic.

Heart pounding, I sit still, momentarily disoriented, my breathing ragged. Dust settles against the hood of my car. The smell of rubber hits my nostrils. I look up, watching cars drive past me like nothing happened except for a black car that drives off the road, stops, and backs up toward my car. A man emerges and hurries toward me.

"Are you okay?" he asks when he reaches the front of my car.

"I think so." My voice is shaking and I've yet to let go of the steering wheel.

"I'm Pascal. I'm a doctor," he continues as he stands outside my door. "What's your name?"

As our eyes meet, I see genuine concern etched on his handsome face.

"I'm Tallie."

"Are you sure you're okay?" he asks, his brow furrowing. "You didn't hit your head or anything because that was a hell of a spin you did there."

I lower my window. "It was?"

"You bet it was," he replies, grinning. "It could have been worse, but as it is, you're okay."

"I'm a bit shaken up, I think." Somehow, his admiration of my impromptu race car driving skills is making me smile.

"I'm glad you're not hurt but your alignment looks messed up. So is your tire."

I open my car door and stand up, wishing my trembling would stop. I take a few steps forward, my heart still racing. As I look at the front of my car, I see what he means. The front left tire is shredded, pieces of rubber littering the highway behind us.

"You must be in shock," he says when I lean against the side of the car. "Are you sure you're okay? Are you experiencing pain anywhere?"

Actually, I'm numb at the moment, or in shock. But as much as I'd want this gorgeous man who looks like he walked off a fashion runway to give me a full physical, all I can think of is getting back on the road.

"I'm fine. I just need to call a tow truck so I can be on my way."

I return to my car and search for my phone which I find on the floor along with the contents of my purse. Grabbing my phone and membership card for Roadside Assistance, I straighten up to find Pascal watching me.

"You don't need to stay," I say. "I can take it from here."

"I'd like to wait with you until the tow truck arrives, if that's okay with you." He looks around. "We're out in the middle of nowhere and I wouldn't be able to live with myself knowing I left you here alone."

I laugh. "We're fifty miles from the next rest stop if that's what you're worried about, so it's not too far. I remember that was the last sign I saw before that idiot cut me off."

Pascal looks unimpressed. "Fifty miles is far."

"Yes, but not in the other direction which is where the tow truck will probably come from." I cock my head in the opposite direction. "Let's say, give or take, the last town I passed is only about ten miles away."

"That would be Baker." Pascal shrugs. "But I'd still prefer to wait with you until the tow truck arrives. I'd hate leaving you here by yourself."

I cross my arms in front of me. "I can take care of myself."

"If it makes you feel better, you can wait for the tow truck in your car and I'll wait in mine."

I roll my eyes. "That's ridiculous."

"Your choice," he says. "I just want to make sure you're safe."

"You're stubborn."

"So are you."

As I study him, trying to gauge if he isn't some serial killer targeting damsels in distress, I have to admit that his determination to make sure I'm okay is cute. And noble. Maybe that's why he's a doctor. It's his job.

As he walks around my car, there's no denying he's much younger than me, probably in his late thirties or very early forties, with a smile that comes with a dimple on his left cheek. He's also got the most beautiful blue eyes I've ever seen, framed by thick dark lashes I have to pay to have for myself.

It's not merely his captivating smile and mesmerizing eyes that have captured my attention. It's the aura he exudes, emanating confidence and grace with every step. But there's the magnetic appeal of his physical features that has my full attention: his broad chest, and slim, sculpted hips form a tantalizing combination that sends a delightful shiver down my spine, leaving me slightly weak in the knees.

"I better call Roadside Assistance," I mutter, suddenly realizing I've been staring at him. "And as long as you're not supposed to be somewhere else, I'm not that paranoid that I'd have you wait in your car. We can wait in mine. Or yours. Your choice."

He tilts his head toward his vehicle. "Definitely mine. It doesn't have that delightful scent of burnt rubber and oil.

More like an 'eau de fresh air and new car' kind of situation."

I chuckle, grateful that he's not only gorgeous and charming, but he's witty as well. "Good point."

Chapter Two

Pascal

As we wait for the tow truck, we settle inside my rental car with the A/C cranked to the max. It's not every day I stop by the side of the road to check on a fellow driver, but today, I'm sure glad I did.

Besides making sure she's going to be safe, there's something about Tallie that makes me want to know more about her, from her smooth dusky skin, bright brown eyes, and her wide smile. And then there are her curves, accentuated by the mauve pleated button-top blouse she wears over her jeans.

But it's more than just her physical appearance. I love the way she carries herself, with an air of confidence and grace that commands respect. And from the way she controlled her car as it spun off the road, there's a toughness to her that's sexy as hell.

"So what are you doing out here?" she asks, her voice snapping me back to the present.

"I had a meeting with my prototype guy."

Tallie's eyes narrow. "Prototype? I thought you said you're a doctor."

"I am, but I also make things."

"Like what?"

I shrug. "The last thing I created is currently being used in surgery."

Her eyebrows shoot up, genuine surprise glimmering in her eyes. "Wow. Do you have to deal with patents and all that?"

"I do, but this last one I ended up selling it."

"Wouldn't you have made more money if you just kept the patent?"

"Let's say their offer was too good to pass up."

Understanding dawns on her face. "That would make sense. What was it?"

"It's a device that provides real-time data on tissue health and other parameters and helps surgeons make informed decisions during the procedure itself."

"That sounds serious."

"Because it is. I could have licensed the invention but selling it allows me to create something new, and so I fly here once every few months to check on the prototypes. Bob—that's my prototype guy—lives out here."

She looks out at the vast expanse of desert along the side of the road. "Why does he live all the way out here?"

"I knew him back in San Francisco, but he grew up here in Baker which is known for its alien jerky and the last chance to get gas before heading to Barstow," I reply. "His parents needed his help around the house a few years ago and so he moved back here where he has a lot more room than he could ever have in San Francisco."

"So that means you've got another invention coming up?"

"You could say that, but that would take this conversation to boring territory real quick," I reply, laughing. "What about you? Where are you headed?"

"To Napa… to visit friends."

"From where?"

"Taos, New Mexico." She pulls out her phone and shows me pictures. "I made a few stops along the way to paint. Yesterday, it was Sedona, and if I weren't in such a hurry, I would have made a detour to the Grand Canyon."

"So you paint?"

"Landscapes, primarily. Sometimes people," Tallie replies, putting away her phone. "But I don't want to bore you with that."

"Taos to Napa," I muse. "That's a long drive."

She groans. "Please don't tell me I could have flown."

"You could have. Although if you did, you wouldn't have been able to stop and paint."

"Even if I didn't plan on painting during my drive, I still wouldn't have flown."

"Why's that?"

She doesn't answer right away but I can tell the question bothers her.

"You don't have to answer–"

"My husband died in a plane crash three years ago," she replies. "He was a private pilot and flew clients over Napa, Sonoma, and Stockton. Executives. Some billionaires."

"I'm sorry about your husband."

"He was doing some video work for a client so he was by himself," she continues as I cover her hand with mine for a few moments before pulling away. What the hell am I doing? She doesn't even know me.

"I'm so sorry. I shouldn't have asked."

"Please don't apologize. I'm glad you did." She gazes absently at the interstate. "Everyone tiptoes around it to where it almost erases the fact that he died doing what he loved." There's an edge to the way she says that last part but I brush my observation aside. She lost her husband, for crying out loud. The last thing I need to do is judge.

"But I can't blame them," she continues. "He was popular with the locals."

"What was his name?"

"Josiah Winters."

I frown. "Cessna?"

She nods. "You knew him?"

I shake my head. "Not personally. I fly, too."

She grimaces. "Oh."

"I'm sorry. I know that's a sensitive topic."

"You have to do what you love."

"I wouldn't be able to do it as a job but I like it," I say. "Maybe one day I could fly you–"

"No." She shakes her head before shrugging her shoulders. "Well, maybe. You can never say never. It would certainly beat driving for hours and hours to this view."

I chuckle. "There is that."

"I left town two months after he died," she adds, her tone turning serious again. "I should have stayed but I couldn't. Everywhere I looked, everyone I talked to reminded me of what I'd lost and so when a friend suggested I visit Taos for a few days, I went for it. He had what you call an Earthship outside of town where it's all sustainable—solar power, wind power, that kind of thing. Off the grid."

"I think I've seen them from the highway, but I've never stopped to investigate further."

"It was so different from what I'd always known about houses with water collection cisterns, thick adobe walls using old tires rammed with earth, and even bottoms of beer bottles taped together and inserted into the walls to create these lovely designs, and so I stayed. A few days turned into a few months and then a few years," she continues. "Some people said I ran away but…"

"People grieve in different ways," I say when she doesn't finish.

"But they're also right." Tallie bites her lip, her gaze distant. "I ran away and I stayed away. Until now."

"Is there a law that says you have to stay in one place in order to grieve? A guidebook that states that if you leave, you must return at a certain time?" I ask as she shakes her head. "You were grieving, Tallie. And I might also say, you were also trying to live the best way you knew how."

She smiles. "I like the way you put that, but you're right. There is no law. But someone needs to tell some people that. I'm sure they'll have a lot to say when they see me again."

"Who are they?"

"My mom and my sister," she replies. "And other people who think they know what's good for me or that I should learn to forgive."

I frown. "Forgive who?"

Before she can answer, the tow truck arrives then, ending all conversation between us as she pushes open the door and steps out. Tallie's all business as I stand a few feet away and let her do her thing. The last thing she needs is for me to take over even as the tow truck driver keeps directing his questions at me until I tell him to deal with the lady.

"It's her car, man," I say as he gets the hint and addresses her.

"Would you like me to drive you to the repair shop or would you prefer to ride with him?" I ask when she finishes signing the paperwork and the driver starts getting her car on the flatbed.

"I don't want to inconvenience you more than I already have."

"You're not inconveniencing me at all," I say.

Her eyes narrow as she studies me, seeming to review her options. She glances at the tow truck driver who spits a wad of tobacco on the ground and then back at me. "Are you sure it's okay?"

"I wouldn't offer if it wasn't."

"That's nice of you to say that." As she smiles, the butterflies in my stomach come to life, dancing with a frenzied energy that I can't ignore. It takes me by surprise, one that I welcome after focusing too much on my work for so long that even dating fell by the wayside.

My last relationship ended a year ago, just before my first invention sold for seven figures. She'd wanted to get married but I wasn't ready. I'd discovered a part of me I'd set aside when I joined the Air Force and later, set up my private practice. Creating things was exciting. Exhilarating. The thrill of crafting something from scratch was incomparable to any other experience I had ever encountered.

Until now.

For as I load Tallie's luggage into the back of my car, nothing feels as good as being around a woman who makes my heart race every time she's near me. And all I want to do is lose myself in her big brown eyes and feel her lips against mine, her curvy body in my arms.

"Ready?"

The sound of her voice snaps me back to reality, at the cars speeding past us on the highway, the tow truck driver who's getting behind the wheel, and the doctor-slash-entrepreneur who suddenly forgot how to act cool.

I close the trunk. "Uh, sure."

Chapter Three

Tallie

Pascal and I meet the tow truck driver at the repair shop where the mechanic promises to check the car as soon as he's finished with the one he's working on. With only one repair shop in town, it means I need to find a hotel to stay for the night while I wait for his call. I just hope he gets the repairs finished by tomorrow so I can be on my way to Napa. With the wedding in three days, I'm cutting it close.

But if I'd flown, I would have missed out on this grand adventure, one that has my body humming with excitement as I gaze at Pascal's hand resting on the gear shift. He has beautiful strong hands.

Even better, he's not wearing a ring.

I also like the way he steals glances at me when he thinks I'm not looking. I just hope he's not some serial killer charming the pants off me but then, even if he were, maybe it's the way to go.

And that's another problem. Why am I so relaxed around him? Giddy even.

Maybe it's the accident. Maybe spinning like an Indianapolis 500 driver on the road knocked a few of my screws loose.

Or maybe I'm still running on adrenaline and it's making me act not quite myself.

But I'm also fooling myself.

I'm in denial.

I was always full of life before Josiah died. It was my personality. I wasn't the life of the party but I wasn't the one to bring the energy down either. I enjoyed being around people. I remembered birthdays and anniversaries, and when you grew up in a Filipino family, that's a lot to keep track of.

But all that disappeared after Josiah died. I retreated into myself and, tired of everyone asking me if I was okay as they looked at me with pity in their eyes, I left town and moved to a place where no one would bother me with their condolences and pity.

No one would know of my failure and shame.

Pascal's changing all that. For the first time since Josiah died, I'm smiling. I'm laughing. Hell, I'm even flirting. Thankfully, he's flirting right back and that makes me feel beautiful… and young. Because heaven knows I'm about to fall off the ledge of cougar-dom and he's probably at least ten years younger than me.

But who cares? I'm stuck in the middle of nowhere and it's not as if anyone is about to judge me.

"I was going to check in at the only motel in town which is down the street," Pascal says as he catches me stifling a yawn.

"Aren't you going to stay with your prototype guy?"

He shakes his head. "Bob has three dogs and two cats who all stay inside because of coyotes. And I'm allergic to cats."

"That wouldn't be fun for you at all." I stifle a yawn again. "Weird, but I feel like I've run out of gas all of a sudden."

"The adrenaline's worn off," he says as I fold the repair shop's estimate and slip it into my purse. "We better get you into a room so you can rest."

Twenty minutes later, we head to the hotel lobby only to find out that all check-one are handled at the gas station across the street.

"Sorry but we've only got one room available," the man behind the counter announces as he peers at his computer screen. "Just rented the second to the last one a minute ago."

"How many beds?" Pascal asks.

"One bed, a queen. If you got here five minutes ago, you'd have gotten the one with two full beds," he replies. "You still want it?"

"We'll take it," Pascal says as a couple enters the gas station. "One night."

I peer at him. "But it only has one bed."

"Your only other option is fifty miles away and with your car being repaired here, this is the best thing," Pascal mutters under his breath as the couple behind us asks about a room for the night. "Unless you have other ideas."

"You taking it or not?" the man asks. "Because I've got other people–"

"We'll take it." I slap my credit card on the counter before Pascal can pull out his wallet. "And I'm paying since you've done enough."

"Nothing like a woman who knows what she wants," the man behind the counter says as he runs my card through the terminal.

"Definitely." Pascal grins, his wide smile making my heart race.

The man takes the lone key hanging behind him and slides it across the counter toward me. "Room 9 is all yours, Miss. There is no Wi-Fi and no coffee maker, but you can get all the coffee and soda you want right here. We're open 24 hours. The cafe next to the hotel has pretty good food but they close at six. Around here, they serve the best chicken fried steak in town. Large servings, too."

"Thank you." Feeling like I just hit the jackpot, I grab the key, clutching it to my chest as we hurry out the door. I don't even care what the room looks like but snagging it means we don't have to drive fifty miles to find a place to stay.

"Let me move the car in front of our room," Pascal says as his phone rings.

As he turns away from me to take the call, I wonder if it's his girlfriend asking him where he is. My chest tightens and for a moment I wonder if it's jealousy that he's taken or regret that nothing will come out of this meeting.

Don't be silly, Tallie. You just met him.

While Pascal gets his rental car, I turn my attention to the motel, a one-story building with mint-green doors for each of their rooms. If my car was in running condition, I'd have made it to Barstow for the night where I'm sure I would have found better accommodations. But beggars can't be choosers when you're stuck in the middle of nowhere.

I'm just glad I'm not alone.

I pull out my phone and text a message to Vida, texting her the phone number of the motel and the room number. Even if I'm not telling her about my accident, at least she'll know where I'll be for the night.

"Texting your boyfriend?" Pascal asks as he gets out of his car that's parked in front of Room 9.

"Just my cousin, letting her know where I am."

"Always a good idea to let someone know where you are." As a smile spreads on his wickedly sensual mouth, I force myself to stop imagining the naughty things that pop up inside my head, like how good it would feel to kiss him or run my fingers down his six-pack abs.

"Why don't we get you settled in the room so you can rest?" Pascal cocks his head toward the door to our room. "You've had a hell of a day, Miss Indie."

I giggle. At least someone finds my stunt driving entertaining. "Maybe NASCAR is more appropriate. They drive regular cars, don't they?"

"You're right." He pulls open the door and gestures for me to step inside. "Miss NASCAR it is then."

~*~*~*~

Chapter Four

Pascal

It doesn't take long for Tallie to get herself ready for a nap after she takes a quick shower.

"It's still three so I hope you don't mind if I take a quick nap." She looks relaxed in a loose t-shirt and matching pajama bottoms as she slips under the covers on her side of the bed, closest to the wall. "Can you wake me up in an hour so we can go get dinner? I can't wait to try out their chicken fried steak but I can't keep my eyes open for some reason."

"The adrenaline's worn off and now your body's exhausted."

Tallie sighs. "I hate being such a party pooper."

"No worries. Just get some rest." I switch off the light next to the bed. "I'll wake you up in an hour."

But when the hour passes, I don't have the heart to wake her, at least, not fully. As soon as she opens her eyes and mumble about dinner, she falls asleep again. So I let her sleep and pick up dinner at the cafe before they close for the day. As basic as the room is, at least it has a microwave and we can warm our food when we're ready.

As she sleeps, I work on my latest project. It's the only thing I can do to distract myself from watching her, checking on her breathing as if she were my actual patient and she needed emergency care.

But who am I kidding? The only one needing emergency care at this point is me.

It's weird but it's been a long time since I've felt like a kid on his first date with the most popular girl at school. Flushed cheeks, sweaty palms, racing heart. I also can't keep my eyes off her.

My phone buzzes with another notification and this time, I glance at it. I've ignored it long enough.

The latest message comes from Bob: I'll have the first iteration ready tomorrow morning, maybe around 10 am so you can come by after that.

I'll be there, I text back. I'm already cutting it close as it is, but since I'm already here, I need to see the prototype for myself.

I scroll down to the next message, this one from my best friend, Rafa Balmaseda, from my Air Force days, who opened his own medical practice in Napa after leaving the military.

Rafa

You going to be here for the bachelor party? Because it will be weird not having the guy who organized the whole thing here.

Pascal

I'll be there.

Rafa

How's the project going?

Pascal

Right on schedule. Seeing the first iteration tomorrow morning, then heading back.

Rafa

I thought you were flying back
today.

> **Pascal**
>
> Something came up.

Rafa

Everything ok?

> **Pascal**
>
> Everything's perfect.

Like the woman asleep on the bed, her thick lashes resting on dusky cheeks.

I look away, needing to focus on my priorities, like this conversation with Rafa, who's getting married in three days. I'm his best man, for crying out loud. I need to be more focused. Instead, here I am acting like a hormonal middle schooler lovestruck in the presence of a goddess.

Rafa

See you when you get back.
BTW, Vida can't wait to introduce
you to one of her friends.

> **Pascal**
>
> Doesn't one of her aunts
> want to introduce me to her
> daughter?

Rafa

That's a different one. You'll
have a full dance card this
weekend, that's for sure.

Oh, great. Can't wait, I text back as Rafa replies with a LOL emoji and says goodbye.

As I set my phone face down on the desk, Tallie sits up, the sheets rustling on the bed. She scans the room, her eyes narrowing as her gaze settles on me, and for a moment, I wonder if she remembers me.

"What time is it?" she asks, her voice heavy with sleep.

"Nine thirty."

She glares at me. "But I asked you to wake me at four."

"You were so out of it so I let you sleep," I reply. "But I ordered dinner before the cafe closed. I think you said something about chicken-fried steak, so I got you one with a baked potato and pie for dessert. You can reheat it in the microwave."

She grins. "What are you having?"

"Ground round steak with a baked potato. And pie."

Tallie walks to the window and peers between the curtains. "It is late, isn't it?"

"Yup. Are you hungry?"

She heads back to the table. "I don't think I had anything else after having breakfast at the hotel."

I pull up a chair for her. "Let's have dinner then. If you want coffee or soda, I can go across to the gas station and get some. But I got some bottled water and iced tea in a can, just in case."

"So you haven't eaten yet?" Her expression falls. "You didn't have to wait for me."

I tilt my head toward the desk, my laptop open next to a yellow pad where I'd been scribbling notes. "I was working."

"Is your girlfriend okay with you sharing a hotel room with another woman?" Tallie asks as she sits down.

"She doesn't know," I reply as her eyes widen, but I hold up my hands, laughing. "I'm kidding, Tallie. I'm kidding. I'm not seeing anyone, so the answer is no. Besides, we're both adults. Even if I did have a girlfriend, I'd like to think she can trust me."

"I'm sorry," she says as she gestures to both of us. "It's been a while since I've been… social with a man. At least, outside of my work or my friends."

"Then think of me as a friend." Even if it's the last thing I want us to be, I almost add. "So tell me about yourself. I know you're headed to Napa so is that where you're from?"

"Originally from the Philippines, but yes, Napa's home. Or it was." She tilts her head. "Terrible luck with the timing, being stuck out here."

I laugh. "You have no idea. My best friend's getting married this weekend and I'm the best man. I'm already cutting it close."

"Where's the wedding?"

"Hacienda Luz. It's a vineyard hotel—"

"I know it." Her fork pauses midway to her mouth. "My stepfather was the vineyard foreman."

I stare at her. "Small world."

"The smallest." She takes another bite, and I wait for her to say more, but she doesn't. What are the odds anyway? Napa's full of weddings, so I let it go.

"Are your parents still in Napa?"

She shakes her head. "My stepfather passed away ten years ago. Heart attack while working."

"I'm sorry."

"He once told me it was the way he'd want to go, doing what he loved and surrounded by the soil he studied all his life," she says, smiling. "My mother moved in with us after she sold the house but after Josiah died, she moved in with my sister who got divorced around the same time. Lindy's got three kids and Mama loves being a lola, a grandmother, especially since I wasn't able to give her grandkids." She quickly rests her hand over mine. "And please don't say, oh, I'm so sorry to hear that."

I frown. "I wasn't going to."

"It's just that people always do and it feels like pity," she adds, pulling her hand away. "Josiah didn't want any kids and that was that."

"Did you?"

She shrugs, not answering.

"How long were you married?"

"Fifteen years." She thinks for a few moments. "Interestingly, I had my eggs frozen before I met him so if I still choose to have kids, I can use those… or not. I may be too old."

"Just how old is too old?"

Tallie groans. "I can't believe I walked right into that."

"You did, but you don't have to answer me."

"I'm forty-nine. And you?"

"Forty."

"You're young."

"So are you," I say, grinning.

"Now you're lying."

"You don't look a day over thirty, and I'm being honest." I pause when she flashes me a withering look. "Okay, thirty-five."

"I'll settle for forty."

"I'm serious. My eyes see thirty-five."

She laughs. "Then you just might need to have your eyes checked, Doctor."

I chuckle. "Oh, they're fine. Twenty-twenty vision."

"In hindsight."

As we laugh, I want to assure her that my eyes aren't lying to me. She's beautiful inside and out and her honesty with its unintended side of vulnerability is refreshing. It hits different. It's deep. She's even more beautiful when she smiles, when all the worries that were written in her eyes when I first met her disappear. And when she laughs, I forget to breathe.

There's still a sense of loss though, one she's not ready to tell me even though she's told me more than she probably expected to. But I'm in no rush to find out anything else about Tallie.

I just want to enjoy the moment and be.

Be present.

Be here.

Chapter Five

Tallie

I remember the moment I stopped worrying.

It was when Pascal gazed at me with a look that stripped me of all my worries, assuring me he didn't care if I was way older than him or if I'm saying the silliest things because I haven't dated in three years.

With him, none of that mattered.

What mattered was that he was seeing me—really seeing me—and liking the view.

There's nothing else to do after dinner but put the leftovers in the fridge and sit on the bed watching TV although we channel-surf more than anything, laughing at infomercials and guessing the ending of trailers and teasers we come across.

"I'm heading to bed," he says when I catch him yawning for the fourth time. "Here, it's your turn to channel surf. I'm going to take a shower."

As Pascal gets up from the bed and heads to the bathroom, I can't help but admire the way his ass looks amazing in his jeans. It's obvious he works out, or at least stays active to have an ass that good. I cover my face as I giggle, feeling like I'm back in high school. I shouldn't look but life's too short to always obey the rules.

And time is speeding past me, leaving me in the dust.

I still remember when Vida told me she'd met the one almost two years ago. He'd shown up at Hacienda Luz asking about a private wine tasting after seeing the sign for the winery, got curious, and stopped in.

It was love at first sight for both of them and they saw each other secretly for a year because he ended up being her grandmother's personal doctor. And there was the age difference. With Vida being ten years older than him, she didn't want people labeling her a cougar.

And as I listen to the water running in the shower and imagine how Pascal must look naked, I wonder if I'd care what people would think if I ended up dating a man like him. Like Vida, I probably would.

Isn't that why I left Napa in the first place, even though the circumstances were different? Because of what people thought?

Besides, daydreaming about Pascal is one thing. Imagining a life with him is another. What if he wanted kids?

Goodness gracious, Tallie. You're getting way ahead of yourself. Slow down.

When Pascal emerges from the bathroom twenty minutes later wearing only a towel wrapped around his slender hips, I catch the scent of fresh soap and shampoo mixed with a scent that's all his own, a unique blend of musk and spice that makes my stomach clench.

"Everything alright?" he asks as he grabs some clothes from his weekend bag.

"Yup." I grab a copy of Machinery Weekly and pretend to read it before realizing I'm holding it upside down.

"Okay then." Chuckling, he disappears into the bathroom. When he returns to the room wearing a t-shirt and pajama bottoms, I don't know whether I should feel relieved or disappointed. I was enjoying the view, maybe a little too much.

But could I be a little too obvious? Whatever happened to that Filipino trait of hiya? Of propriety? Self-respect?

Out the window, obviously.

But that's what happens when it's been three years since I've been alone with a man after the one I loved betrayed me in the worst possible way.

I toss the magazine aside as Pascal slides under the covers next to me.

"You okay?" he asks. "You look like someone just rained on your parade."

I sigh. "I'm afraid I did."

"Now why would you do that?"

I shrug. "Maybe guilt?"

"What for?"

"Doing what I want to do instead of the things I'm supposed to."

"Like what?" Pascal rolls to his side to face me as I rest my head on the pillows.

"Get a regular job, for one. Be the grieving wife and stay in the community."

"Ah, those darn rules again," he says, clucking his tongue. "What else?"

I bite my lip. Should I tell him?

"I can tell it's on the tip of your tongue," he prods. "Spill the beans."

"Not gawking at the sexy young man I'm sharing my room with for the night."

"Sexy young man? Is that what you think he is?"

"I don't just think it. I see it with my own eyes."

A blush creeps on Pascal's cheeks. "Can I tell you something?"

"Sure."

"I gawked at you when you stepped out of the bathroom too. You're hot."

I stare at him. He hadn't even looked up from his laptop from what I recall. But then he'd been focused on something on his darkened screen since he hadn't switched it on yet.

"I am?"

"10/10. Would highly recommend," he says as I laugh. "How do you say beautiful in your language?"

"Guapa."

Pascal frowns. "That's Spanish."

"It's how we say beautiful in Visayan. That's the dialect I speak, unless you want Tagalog so it would be maganda."

"Ah. How do you say handsome?"

"Guapo," I reply. "And if he's really handsome, then it's guapo-guapo."

"That's still in Spanish," he says, unconvinced. "How about sexy?"

"Seksi," I say with an exaggerated accent, giggling.

"What about I love you?"

"Gihigugma ko kanimo."

He pauses. "Wow. That's a mouthful."

"It sure is. Maybe that's why we say I love you instead."

"Can I kiss you?"

"Pwede ko mu-kiss nimo?"

He grins. "Yes, you may."

It takes me a moment before I realize what he's done. "Oh no you didn't!" I hit Pascal's arm playfully but he grabs my wrist and pulls me to him.

He's serious now, his eyes drinking me in, as if memorizing me. "Pwede ko mu-kiss nimo?" he asks, his voice low, his gaze smoldering.

I trace my finger along his jaw. "Yes." If I hesitate, I'll regret not seizing the moment.

Letting go of my wrist, Pascal slides his hand behind my neck and pulls me to him. When his mouth covers mine, I have no idea of time or place. I only know his name, the taste of his lips against mine, and the hunger of his kiss that leaves me aching for more.

My heart hammers inside my chest as his kiss deepens. My whole body sighs under his touch, his tongue flicking into my mouth leaving me breathless.

Suddenly I pull away, my fingers tracing his lower lip.

"Before we keep going, can we agree to have no regrets after tonight? That we just enjoy this night?" I take a deep breath. This is all for self-preservation, a speech to benefit me most of all, to remind me not to expect much other than what this moment offers.

I press my forehead against his. "No promises. No commitments."

Pascal's Adam's apple bobs as he swallows. "If that's what you want."

I nod. "I think it's what I want. I don't know. I'm out of practice."

He smiles. "Why don't we take things slow? One thing at a time?"

"That sounds like a good idea."

"Would you like me to take the lead?"

I nod. "Please."

"If at any time, you don't want to keep going, all you have to do is say stop."

I make a face. "That's the problem. I may not want to."

"Then don't."

As Pascal looks at me with a hunger that I can feel deep in my bones, his eyes dark and intense, I can tell he wants me, needs me, just as much as I need him. I run my finger down his face, tracing the contour of his jaw and neck, the broad slope of his shoulders and down his bicep.

He captures my hand and brings it to his lips before leaning closer to kiss me again. This time there's no turning back, no second thoughts. No doubts or regrets.

His kiss is urgent now, his hands roaming my body as we lay together on the motel bed. My skin is on fire, every nerve ending alive with sensation. I moan into his mouth as our tongues tangle and swirl. He tastes of spearmint, the scent of fresh soap intermingling with an essence that's uniquely all his own, intoxicating and addictive.

My hands move down his chest, feeling the hard planes of his body beneath my fingertips. I can sense his desire growing, pressing against me with a delicious pressure that sets my body ablaze.

With a growl, Pascal rolls on top of me, his weight pressing down on my body in the most primal way as I feel every inch of his body against mine. As his hard length presses against my thigh, I know he wants me just as badly as I want him.

As he leans down to kiss me again, his hands move down to my hips, pulling me closer to him. I gasp as his fingers slip under the waistband of my pajama bottoms, tracing lazy circles on my skin.

"Do you want this?" Pascal asks, his voice low and husky.

I nod, unable to form words as pleasure courses through my body because of his touch, his raw presence.

With my answer, Pascal slides my pajama bottoms and underwear together down my hips, tossing them aside. He moves down my body, kissing and nibbling his way down my stomach until he reaches my core.

My hips buck off the bed as he flicks his tongue over my clit, sending pleasure shooting through me. I moan his name as he continues to tease me with slow, languid strokes of his tongue.

"You taste amazing," he murmurs as he pulls my hips closer, his stubble tickling and scratching my skin.

Finally, I can't take it anymore. I push his head down, urging him to take me completely. He does so eagerly, his tongue moving faster and faster until I'm writhing beneath him, my body on the brink of ecstasy.

With a final lick, Pascal brings me to the edge and over, my whole body convulsing with pleasure.

As I come down from my high, Pascal crawls back up the bed, his own arousal pressing against me. I can feel his need, his desire for me, and I know I want him just as badly.

"My turn." I roll over, pulling him close as his length brushes against my leg. I'm still reeling from the pleasure of my climax, my nerves still tingling, but I want to make him feel as good as I did just now. I want to please him, to show him just how much I want him.

Without another word, I trail my hand down his body, teasing his erection with my fingertips through his pants. I can feel the wetness pooling between my legs at the thought of having him inside me.

"We need to get this off you," I breathe as he agrees, lifting his hips off the bed as I pull his pants and boxer briefs down his legs. He sits up and pulls off his shirt before pulling mine off.

"You're so beautiful," Pascal says against my lips as he kisses me, letting me taste myself on his tongue.

I place my hand on his chest and ease him down. "Lie back. I want to see you."

I wrap my hand around the length of him, feeling him growing harder in my palm. I can feel him pulse under my fingers, his length hardening even more.

As I bring my mouth to his length, his muscles tighten, his desire rising to an almost unbearable level. I trace my tongue over the tip of him, relishing the taste of him, the feel of his silky soft skin in my mouth.

Pascal moans my name, a sound that's like a drug I want more of. His fingers tangle in my hair, guiding my mouth up and down his shaft. I love the taste of him, the feel of him as he thrusts into my mouth, the motion slow and rhythmic. With each thrust, I move my mouth up, then back down again until I feel him at the back of my throat, filling me.

"Fuck, your mouth feels so good," he groans as his thrusts become more urgent, his breathing ragged.

His fingers tighten in my hair as I suck him even harder. I'm lost in his scent, his taste, his ache for me. I've never felt so powerful, so wanted. He trusts me, gives in to me, and despite our short time together, it feels like we've known each other forever.

Pascal's thrusts become more desperate now, his hand guiding my mouth up and down his shaft but just as I think he's about to come, he pulls my mouth off him.

"I want you," he rasps before kissing me lightly on the lips. "Do you want me, Tallie?"

"I do," I murmur as he reaches for his wallet on the bedside table and retrieves a condom.

As he tears open the wrapper and rolls the condom over his cock, the low light in the room makes him look like a Greek god. He's magnificent.

And for tonight, he's mine.

Pascal strokes his cock once, then positions himself between my legs.

"Are you sure?"

I nod as I reach for his thigh. "Yes."

In one quick movement, Pascal thrusts into me. I'm filled to the brim with him, his length throbbing inside me.

He rests his forehead against mine as he stills inside me, his heavy-lidded gaze burning right through me. "Fuck, you feel good."

I wrap my legs around him, pulling him closer. I try to capture the feeling of him inside me, but it's just too much. It's so intense that I can barely control it.

"I want to make you feel good, Tallie," he says, his voice ragged with need as he begins to move against me, leaving me breathless. "I want to make you come."

His mouth slants over mine before I can say anything. Not that I want to say a word for he starts moving inside me, his cock hardening even more. We fit together so perfectly, like a lock and key. There's a rightness to this moment I can't explain. But then now is not the time for such things.

His fingers brush against my cheek and I look up to see Pascal watching me. "Stay with me," he whispers and it's all I need to hear to come back to the moment.

No regrets.

With each thrust, I move closer and closer to falling over the edge. I can sense my body tightening around him, the pressure building until I can't take it anymore.

"I'm coming," I gasp as the heat of my orgasm blossoms through my body, expanding from that part of me no one has touched in a long time. Until Pascal.

He slows down as I climax, his hooded eyes watching my every move, every tremble of my skin, every shudder.

"That's it, Tallie. Give me all of it. Come for me."

I forget myself at that moment. I'm not the older woman hoping to capture her youth in a man so much younger than her. I'm not the widow who gave up on life, believing this was all life offered her. Fifteen years of lies.

No, at this moment, I'm just a woman being made love to by a man who seems to see right through me.

But it can't just be me. I'm not on this journey alone.

"Come with me… come with me, Pascal," I gasp as he sinks in deeper, my name leaving his lips.

With one last thrust, we're both falling over the edge. Pascal stiffens, his face buried against my neck. I can feel him pulsing inside me, his arms like vices as his teeth sink into the skin of my shoulder.

When he utters my name, nothing has ever sounded so perfect, so full of ache and longing now fulfilled.

No regrets.

Minutes later, after Pascal excuses himself to go to the bathroom and discard the condom, I'm draped over his side, loving the warmth of his body. Slowly, I take in the world outside as I return to the present, like the constant rumbling of the trucks parked in a row across the street, their drivers resting for the night, the distant hum of the highway where we'd met hours earlier, and the slow realization that everything is temporary and fleeting, like this moment.

But until then, I'll enjoy it.

Hell, we might even go a second time

Chapter Six

Pascal

"Leaving already?"

Tallie stops in her tracks in front of the door and sighs. "I thought you'd still be asleep."

"I was, but then your side of the bed felt cold and I wondered where you went."

She turns to face me, her expression sad. Dressed in a pink top and jeans, her hair secured in a ponytail, she's packed and ready to go, her luggage propped next to her.

"The mechanic called and said he would have the car ready in an hour," she says. "He said there wasn't much damage, just that my tire needed to be replaced and an alignment, and the fluids topped. His daughter's picking me up in a few minutes."

I sit up, the sheets gathered around my hips. "I want to see you again."

"About that." She bites her lower lip and then exhales. "I think it's best if we don't... you know..."

My jaw clenches. I'd expected this but not so soon. "I get it."

"It's not you, Pascal. It's me," she continues. "I don't do this often. Hell, I've never done this before and so I don't know–"

"It's easy. Either you'd like to keep in touch or you don't," I say. "You don't have to explain."

"I like you, Pascal. I really do, but you've got your whole life ahead of you, and I don't want to cramp your style," she begins. "I'm also way older than you and you'd do better with someone younger."

"Somehow I never thought you'd be the type to tell me what's good for me just because I'm a few years younger than you."

"Not a few, Pascal. Eleven," she says. "You're eleven years younger than me."

"Nine."

"I lied," she says. "I subtracted two years. I'm 51. Too old for you."

"Who cares?" Grabbing my boxer briefs from the foot of the bed, I slip them on and walk toward her. "Tallie, you're headed to Napa which is where I live. It would be nice to see you again."

She chuckles dryly. "Until I leave. And then what?"

"We'll worry about that later."

"I'd love to see you again, too, Pascal, but I know how this story ends. I think it's better this way." She turns away from me and reaches for the doorknob but doesn't pull the door open. "I'll take care of everything as far as reservations go."

"You're scared of moving forward, aren't you?" I say. "You'd rather punish yourself for enjoying something so beautiful between two people, just like you've punished yourself all these years for leaving so soon after your husband died."

"You know nothing," she says accusingly. "Just because I told you that part of the story doesn't mean it's the full story."

"What is the full story then?" I ask. "At least, tell me before you leave."

She thinks for a few moments, shaking her head as she debates whether or not to answer my question.

"I thought I had the perfect marriage," she replies, her expression distant. "He got along well with my mother, better than I ever could, and he was loved by everyone. He even got himself a contract in Stockton flying for a private tour company and he'd come home with these amazing stories about the people he met, the clients he flew to meetings around the area. Then the accident happened, and who shows up at the funeral but his mistress, demanding her share of his estate. In front of everyone."

She pauses, her lower lip quivering. "That son of a bitch left her half of his money. Half. He'd been seeing her for six months but she wasn't the only one."

When I say nothing, she continues, "One day, while I was having lunch with a friend, I overheard his friends talk about how it was my fault that he'd cheated, that a man only cheats if his wife is no good, especially in bed."

"And you believe them?" I exclaim. "They were assholes."

"It got me wondering if they thought that, who else did? Who among my friends secretly believed it was my fault that he'd been having affairs left and right? Because my mother and my sister sure did."

"So what if they did?" I ask. "Would you have corrected them? Would it have mattered?" When she doesn't reply, I continue. "You shouldn't worry about what people think because, at the end of the day, it's your opinion that matters, Tallie, not theirs. Live your life for you, not them."

"I'm just saving myself from any future pain, Pascal, okay?" she snaps. "Is that so wrong?"

"It is when, in saving yourself from this imaginary pain that may never come, you're denying yourself everything else," I say. "Everything else that's good and beautiful. Like us. Last night with you was amazing. It was perfect and it's worth exploring."

Her shoulders sag. "Look, Pascal, it was just one night where we both had fun and I'd like to keep it that way. But if our paths ever cross again, I promise I'll reconsider."

This time, I feel like a child being told next time maybe I can have a cookie if I'm good.

"Reconsider? Why not just save yourself the trouble and don't?" I say, my jaw clenching. "Like you said last night, no promises, no commitments. No regrets."

I can almost hear her gasp but she collects herself as a car honks outside. "I have to go."

"Goodbye, Tallie," I say through gritted teeth.

"Thank you for last night, Pascal," she whispers as the car honks again. "Thank you for everything."

As the door closes behind her, a sense of loss fills me. I shouldn't let her go so easily yet I've already done enough. I've said enough.

I need to take things as they are: we had a great time and now it's over.

Move on, man. Move forward.

Yet I can't deny how much I like Tallie, and how much fun we had last night. It wasn't just 'fun' either. I'd felt a connection and somehow, it felt like she did, too.

But a one-night stand is a one-night stand. End of story.

I should know that. This isn't my first time at the rodeo.

So why am I insisting it could be something more when she clearly isn't interested?

Why can't I let it go?

My phone beeps and I see a message from Bob reminding me that the prototype is ready.

Pascal

I should be there in an hour. Gotta grab some breakfast first.

Bob

I'll be here. BTW you might need to check your messages. One of your investors is in Vegas and wanted to see the prototype if he can. Said he left you a message last night.

Pascal

I'll think about it. Let me make sure the thing works first.

It's a quick change of gears to go right into work mode, but it's the only thing I can do to get my mind off Tallie.

And as the memories of last night's lovemaking come rushing back, from the taste of her to the feel of her body against mine, I'll need all the help I can get.

~*~*~*~

Chapter Seven

Tallie

If I let my emotions get away from me one more time for leaving Pascal the way I did, I'll never make it to Napa without looking like I've been crying for hours. But it's not like I'm crying for him.

Okay, maybe a little bit. No, I'm crying because I'm such a coward.

The things he said hit exactly where they were meant to.

And he's right. I'm too worried about what everyone thinks, and I'm too afraid to move forward.

But what's done is done. I ended it as cleanly as I could, even if it was the last thing I wanted to do.

I need to get to Napa. I didn't drive this far just so I could find myself a boy toy to have fun with in the middle of nowhere.

It was a pleasant distraction, though. And that's the way it's going to be.

It's easier this way.

No complications.

So why can't I stop thinking about him and the things we did last night? Why can't I stop remembering the way he said my name or the way his body felt pressed against mine?

Oh, stop it, Tallie. You're the one who ended it so why the hell are you crying about it now?

I take a deep breath and focus on the road ahead. With Napa only an hour away, it means returning to a world I once knew and loved, a world I left behind because I couldn't stand being the last one to know. I also had to grieve.

Alone.

And oh, did I grieve. I raged. I cried enough tears in my anger and the shame that came from Josiah's betrayal.

But after last night, I think I've moved on.

But some things are easier said than done. For the moment I catch sight of the patchwork of vineyards stretching as far as the eyes can see, I'm struck with panic.

I pull onto the shoulder of the road and cut the engine. The sudden silence seems to amplify every sound around me, from the chirping of the crickets and the rustling of the leaves to the distant hum of traffic on the highway. The earthy scent of dirt and ripe grapes waiting to be harvested fills my nostrils, bringing back memories of Dad helping me find the perfect spot to set up my easel and returning just in time to admire what I created.

How could I have left all this because I was too ashamed to face everyone else for something that I didn't even do? I wasn't the one who cheated. I wasn't the one who promised his lover he'd give her everything.

I didn't have to leave but I did. Sold everything and left, thinking I could start over with a clean slate somewhere else.

But how can one start over when they're too busy blaming themselves for everything that happened?

I close my eyes and listen to the wind whispering through the vines, punctuated by the occasional flap of a bird's wings. When I open my eyes, I see a hawk circling overhead, buffeted by gusts from the valley below.

A sense of peace descends on me then, replacing the panic I'd just felt minutes earlier. A smile tugs at the corners of my mouth.

Pascal was right. I've denied myself everything life has to offer all because I didn't want to be hurt again. It's why I hid myself in Taos thinking I'd be safe from pain, only the pain and the shame followed me there, brought along by no one else but me.

I wore it like armor… until last night when Pascal saw right through me.

Too bad I put it back on this morning when I left him… no, when I ran away from him.

I take a deep breath.

A new beginning is on the horizon and this time I'm ready for it.

I just wish Pascal didn't have to pay for my cowardice. But I can't dwell on that. Not right now.

I have to start somewhere and right about now is as good a time as any.

~*~*~*~

Chapter Eight

Pascal

It's been two days since I returned to Napa and life has gone back to normal… or as normal as life can be when you're the best man at your best friend's wedding. No seeing patients for the week, no working on patents or reviewing prototypes via Zoom. Just me making sure my best friend's bachelor party goes off without a hitch.

It was a simple affair. No strip clubs, no bar hopping. Just a trip to a local resort known for its golf course where the guys from out of town could rent their clubs for the day. We had a blast on the greens but I hate to admit I was distracted.

I'd be lying if I claim not to miss Tallie because I do. She's a woman one can't forget.

Funny, intelligent, and beautiful. And sexy as hell.

How many times did we end up doing it that night? (Two and a half.) And each time we did, watching her open up to me, allowing herself to be vulnerable was the biggest turn-on ever.

I've replayed the way she felt in my arms, the way her mouth tasted, the softness of her skin, the husky sound of her voice when she cried out my name, her body shuddering beneath me.

But then there's our goodbye, one that didn't turn out the way I wish it should have. Maybe a simple no would have worked but I surprised myself when I didn't let her go so easily, not with the excuses she made. But who am I to say that her pain is trivial, that it's easy to move on?

So I turned out to be the dick who pretty much said, fine, do it your way. See if I care. Paraphrased, that is.

But it is what it is. She didn't want any complications and I respect that.

"You didn't hear a word I just said, did you?"

I turn to see Rafa watching me, an amused smile on his lips. "What were you saying?"

He groans. "Please don't tell me you're still working out that damn prototype inside your head. You're supposed to be on vacation, man. It's my wedding weekend."

"I wasn't."

His eyes widen. "I think I've just figured out why you've been so distracted since you came back. I can't believe I didn't figure it out sooner." He grins, a knowing expression on his face. "What's her name?"

"Who?"

"This woman you can't stop thinking about," Rafa says, chuckling. "Come on, man. We've been tight for over two decades now since our Air Force days. You've been distracted since you got back from your trip to the desert."

"What makes you think it's a woman?"

Rafa laughs. "When you missed that tight fairway and when Senator Hizon outdrove you on the long par-five, I knew something was up. You never miss those things yet you did."

I roll my eyes. "I never said I was perfect, man."

My friend's eyes narrow as he studies me. "What's her name and how'd you meet?"

"Don't you have a rehearsal dinner to attend?" I glance at the entourage arriving at the chapel for the wedding rehearsal. "You should be with your bride welcoming everyone."

"She'll be here," Rafa says. "She and Tallie were late coming back from the spa today for their bridal shower. They haven't seen each other in three years and so they've been catching–"

"Wait. Did you just say Tallie?" I know what he said. I also know he said three years but I'll let that go. First things first. "T-A-L-L-I.E. Tallie?"

Rafa nods. "It says Talisa Vicente on the invitations but Vida and just about everyone call her Tallie. Why? Do you know her?" His eyes narrow. "Is she the one?"

"I don't know," I stammer. "There must be more than one Tallie in–"

My voice trails the moment I see her standing next to Vida by the oak double doors at the entryway. Tallie looks stunning in a figure-hugging black lace dress, her dark brown hair falling loose over her shoulders.

"What a coincidence," Rafa says, chuckling as he cocks his head toward the women. "Vida's been wanting to introduce Tallie to you before the aunts try to pair her with someone else. She thinks you two would get along well... although I hope you don't mind if she's a little bit older."

"I don't care," I mutter. "Let's go."

I barely remember weaving through the crowd of guests as we cross the room. All I can think of is how beautiful Tallie is as she laughs at something one guest is saying, the way her eyes sparkle as she listens to them.

Will her eyes sparkle when she sees me again? Will she forgive me for the things I said?

"Mi vida, I finally snagged the best man for you," Rafa says as we reach them.

Tallie's eyes widen when she sees me, her brow furrowing as she looks at Vida, then Rafa, before returning to gaze back at me. "What are you doing here?"

"You know each other?" Vida asks, surprised as she looks at Tallie. "You didn't tell me you–"

"We met a few days ago," Tallie says. "Pascal stopped to help when someone drove me off the road."

"What?!" Vida exclaims as Rafa tactfully guides the four of us out to one side of the portico, out of the way of arriving family members and hacienda staff. "Why didn't you tell me? Is this why you ended up staying somewhere else instead of Barstow?"

"Baker," Tallie replies. "As for the accident, it was minor. A car cut me off the road and it spun me off–"

"It what?!" Vida glares at Tallie. "Why didn't you say anything? You could have been–"

"Tallie handled it like a Nascar driver," I say, clearing my throat. "She was amazing."

"And I was fine," Tallie insists. "And the car was okay. It just needed a new tire and the mechanic topped the oil."

"I stayed with her until the tow truck arrived," I say as Vida and Rafa turn to look at me, clearly trying to understand the new development. "But she said nothing about knowing you two."

"Somehow you missed telling me about this little detail, man," Rafa says as I do my best to act as nonchalant as possible even as my heart is threatening to leap out of my chest.

"He's right," Tallie says, casting a quick glance toward me. "We talked until the tow truck arrived and that was it."

"Are you sure?" Rafa asks.

"Very sure," I blurt out. "I've never been more sure about anything in my life."

Tallie nods. "Me, too."

Silence descends in the tight space we've formed in the corner as more members of the wedding party stream through the doors.

"You two are sounding pretty defensive if you ask me," Vida says slowly. "Don't you think so, Raf?"

"They definitely do," Rafa agrees, grinning as I glare at him.

"I think they need you two over there." Tallie purses her lips toward a group of people beckoning for Vida and Rafa to join them as Roxie, the wedding photographer, adjusts the lens of her camera.

"We'll be right there, Roxie," Vida tells them before turning to face Tallie. "You owe me an explanation."

"You, too." Rafa eyes me with suspicion even as it's canceled out by the knowing smile on his lips. "Now I know why you were distracted yesterday."

"It also explains why you've been avoiding a few of my questions, especially that hickey you kept insisting was a mosquito bite," Vida says as Tallie quickly brings her hand to the side of her neck, her cheeks reddening. "I hope you two are going to be okay."

"Why wouldn't we be?" Tallie says as Vida responds with an arch of her eyebrow before she and Rafa join her aunts and uncles.

For a few moments, Tallie and I don't say anything. Instead, we smile and greet people we know, Tallie more than me for even though she lived elsewhere for the last three years, she's lived here far longer than I have. In fact, now that I know her full name, there's a large painting of Hacienda Luz's vineyards with her signature hanging on the wall a few feet away.

"I'm sorry for what I said that day," I say when we have a quiet moment alone.

"No, I should be the one apologizing, and I'm sorry." She rests her hand on my arm, her touch sending a shiver up my spine. "You were right. I've denied myself so much joy these last three years to protect myself from being hurt again."

"It wasn't my place to tell you, Tallie. What do I know about losing someone I loved?"

"Someone who also cheated on me," she says. "I had every right to be angry and carry that anger with me to where I built a wall around myself all these years… even from my own friends and family." She pauses, looking at the groups of people hugging and laughing around us. "But I can't live that way forever, shut off from the world."

"You didn't wall yourself that night."

A blush creeps on her cheeks. "Not with you."

As I reach for her hand, Vida reappears in front of us. "Everyone's here and we need to start the rehearsal." She cocks her head toward the double doors. "Why don't you two continue catching up during dinner?"

Chapter Nine

Tallie

I was never into weddings—probably because Josiah and I got married at the city hall and he refused to have a church wedding due to the cost—but Vida and Rafa's wedding just might be the one to change my mind.

I love every little detail they've put into the ceremony, from the gold beads on Vida's ivory Filipiniana gown that sparkles with her every step to the rituals included in the ceremony like the presentation of the arrhae, thirteen coins that signify a binding agreement between the couple, the laying of the veil representing being clothed as one, and the ceremonial cord draped over their heads and shoulders in a figure-8 pattern, an eternal bond.

But if the ceremony was divine, the reception is ethereal. With torches and thousands of fairy lights under a breathtaking half-moon, the vineyard is a sight to behold. The air, rich with the scent of grapes ready for harvest, is the perfect complement to the floral arrangements on every table. Violet, the florist, did an amazing job with arrangements of fuchsia snapdragons, pink peonies, and orange tulips gracing every table.

It's actually a miracle I'm picking up on all the details because if I didn't, all I'd think about is Pascal. We're actually doing our best to keep our hands off each other since last night's rehearsal dinner. As Vida's matron of honor and Pascal as Rafa's best man, we still have our responsibilities, and we've agreed on waiting until the wedding is over before doing anything that could get us kicked out of the hotel.

"Have I told you how stunning you look, Miss Vicente?"

I turn around me to see Pascal looking debonair in his tailored tuxedo. How many times have I caught myself staring at him from across the aisle during the ceremony? And now that we're sitting at the main table, my heart is beating so fast that I'm feeling dizzy. It's as if my heart can't pump enough blood to make it up to my head but somewhere else much lower.

"You've probably said it about three times now, but I'm not about to stop you from saying it again."

"Good, because you really do look amazing in that dress. I especially love the bolero with its terno sleeves." He pauses, his brow furrowing. "That's what they're called, right? I want to make sure I get the details right."

"Yes, although some people call them butterfly sleeves, too. But I really do love your attention to detail."

Pulling up a chair for me, he brings his face close. "Wait till I get it off you later tonight. Then we can really dive into… other details."

Color rushes to my cheeks just as a shriek of a microphone pierces the air and Sophie, Vida's cousin welcomes everyone to the reception.

"You need to behave, Dr. Salvatore. Can you do that?" I murmur as Pascal settles in the chair next to me even though he's supposed to sit next to Vida. So much for the meticulously planned-out seating arrangements.

"Only if you promise we can stop behaving when this is all over," he says, his breath warm against my ear as one of the groomsmen stands behind him, confused to find the best man sitting in his chair.

What a coincidence that Pascal turned out to be the best man Vida had been wanting to introduce me to, the very man she believed was the perfect fit for me. It didn't even connect with me when I read the wedding program that Dr. Pascal Salvatore was him.

Sure, he told me he was a doctor and that he lived in Napa but I had other things to worry about the moment I arrived at the hotel, like making sure everything was set for the bridal shower I'd reserved at the spa resort.

There was also the drive to Oakland—the hardest miles I've ever traveled—to visit my mother and sister. Three years of silence broken over lumpia and tears. Mama finally saying the words I'd needed to hear: "It wasn't your fault, hija. We were wrong." Lindy cried. I cried. Even her kids wondered why all the adults were so emotional over fried spring rolls.

Still, all that's in the past because I'm back home, surrounded by friends and family... with Pascal watching me with such unabashed admiration I'm wondering if I should be worried that he's bound to spot the imperfections, like the worry lines that have begun to show between my eyebrows.

But that would be me putting up that wall again and I don't want to do that. Not anymore.

From this moment on, I'm determined to enjoy every minute and be present for Vida and Rafa.

For myself.

"May I have this dance?" Pascal asks as the live band switches gears, playing a slow song that prompts younger guests to leave the dance floor in droves. It's been a few hours since the reception began and although my feet are killing me, there's no way I'm refusing a dance with the hottest man in the room.

As Pascal leads me to the floor, the warmth of his hand enveloping mine sends a delicious tingle down my spine. I don't even care if people are watching us but it feels good to be wanted. To be seen.

"Are you still planning on leaving tomorrow?" he asks as I rest my hand in his and he wraps his other arm around my waist. "Vida mentioned something about your plan to drive home as soon as the wedding is–"

I bring my finger to his lips. "Not if someone's plans for misbehaving go according to plan tonight. If so, it just might delay things a little bit."

Pascal kisses my finger. "How little?"

"A few days."

"A few weeks, perhaps?" There's a hopeful glint in his blue eyes. "Maybe you can paint a few landscapes while you're here. You can even paint me like one of your–"

I kiss him, silencing him with a playful smile. "We can work something out. The idea of painting you like one of my French girls does sound tempting."

Pascal chuckles, his hand tracing soothing circles on my back. "Well, if that's what it takes to keep you here a bit longer, I'm willing to pose for you anytime."

"I like that plan."

Pascal's expression turns serious. "You have no idea how much I've thanked my lucky stars that our paths crossed again. When you left that day, I didn't know what to do other than bury myself in work and bug poor Bob about the prototype."

I pout. "Poor Bob."

"But thanks to our best friends, you were right here."

"If I kicked myself one more time inside that car on my way here, I'd have poked a hole in the floor," I admit. "But I was just scared of the things I was feeling and it was easier to run away than face them."

As his gaze finds mine, my heart stutters. I think about the woman who drove across the desert a week ago, the one who'd built walls so high she'd forgotten what it felt like to be seen. That woman would have fled this dance floor. Would have made excuses about tired feet or helping with the cake. Would have done anything to avoid being this vulnerable, this visible.

But that woman spun out on a highway and landed in the arms of a man who saw right through her.

"Are you still running?" he asks, his voice low.

Around us, couples are dancing to the music, including Vida and Rafa who seem lost in their own world as they gaze at each other's eyes. Distant aunts and uncles, some with enviable ball-dancing skills, sway past us with knowing grins. Vida must have told them about us. Or maybe they felt my walls crumbling.

I shake my head. "I'm dancing… with you."

"I know we've been talking about being bad tonight," he whispers in my ear, "but always know that we can take our time. Walk before we can fly."

The word about flying should scare me but this time it doesn't. With Pascal, I want to soar. "Don't you care about what people will think? You being way younger than me?"

"I've never cared about what people thought and I'm not about to start now," he replies. "You're an amazing woman, Talisa Vicente, and I want to give you everything you deserve from this moment on. My love and adoration, for starters."

His words make every fiber of my being sing even as the music has stopped and we're the only couple left on the dance floor. "I'm going to need more proof to see if you mean every word. In fact, I think we're close to being able to misbehave."

"When would you want me to start?"

I pull him closer by his lapel. "Any day now."

Pascal slants his mouth over mine as teenagers at a nearby table groan and say something about PDAs. In another part of the room, someone gasps, maybe an aunt horrified by the public display of affection. Or maybe not.

But as I wrap my hand at the back of Pascal's neck as his kiss deepens, I realize I don't care.

Let them talk.

Let them say—and think—whatever they want.

The only thing that matters is that I've been given another chance at something good, something amazing.

No, not something.

Someone.

Pascal Salvatore.

And this time, I'm not denying myself the chance to enjoy life again, to love and be loved in return.

Even soar.

As the music swells and Pascal leads me back to the table where Vida and Rafa are cutting the cake, I catch sight of the painting I made years ago—the one of Hacienda Luz's vineyards at sunset—hanging on the wall nearby.

I remember painting it alone, my easel set up on the hill where Dad used to take me. I remember believing that was the happiest I'd ever be.

I was wrong.

"What are you thinking about?" Pascal asks, following my gaze.

I squeeze his hand. "How I'd like to paint a new one. With you in it."

He grins, that dimple appearing on his left cheek. "Like one of your French girls?"

I laugh—really laugh—for the first time in three years without guilt, without holding back.

"Exactly like that."

THE END

About Liz Durano

Although she majored in Journalism, Liz realized she preferred writing angst-filled emotional stories over news and ad copy. These days, Liz writes women's fiction and contemporary romance (sometimes spicy, sometimes not). She lives in Los Angeles with her family and a spoiled rotten rescue dog. You can learn more about Liz by signing up to her newsletter at https://lizdurano.com/subscribe/.

Book List:

https://lizduranobooks.com/links/

Social Media IDs:

Website: lizduranobooks.com

Facebook:@lizduranobooks

Instagram: @lizdurano

Bookbub: liz-durano

The Stand-In

SARAH SMITH

The Stand-In

SARAH SMITH

Blurb:

When florist Violet sees her cheating ex at the wedding she's working, she panics and asks Toby, her ruggedly handsome and tatted up coworker, to pretend to be her boyfriend. Together they make the perfect fake couple, but when Toby accidentally lets it slip that he's been hiding a crush on Violet, it throws their entire friendship for a loop…in the hottest way.

Content Notes: Profanity, Reference to infidelity

Tropes and Subgenres: Good girl/bad boy, fake relationship, secret crush; Workplace Romance

Heat Level: 🔥 🔥 🔥 🔥 (open door love scene, explicit description)

Chapter One

Violet

"Are you sure the flower arrangements don't look too phallic?"

Toby's expression shifts from confusion to amusement before he bursts out laughing. "Um, what?"

"I know that sounds ridiculous, but I'm serious." I gesture to the floral centerpieces adorning the center of each table at the outdoor venue overlooking the vineyards. Fuchsia snapdragons and hot pink peonies burst from the glass vases, like explosions of color against the white table linens.

I take a second to rearrange the blooms. "I thought they looked really good when I was planning the arrangement, but when I looked at them a second ago, I thought the snapdragons kind of looked like penises and the peonies looked a bit like balls."

Toby grips a nearby chair and doubles over as he laughs. One of the vineyard workers on the other side of the property stops and glances over at us.

When he finally stops laughing and straightens up, there are tears in his eyes. "Damn. I haven't laughed that hard in a while." He swipes a tattooed knuckle under each eye before clearing his throat and aiming a steady gaze at me. "Violet, I need you to listen to me. The arrangements don't look phallic. They look beautiful. All of the flowers in this entire place look incredible. I promise. You know I wouldn't lie to you about that."

Toby's words are the reassurance I need. The stress knot between my shoulder blades starts to loosen.

"You're the best," I say to him. "What would I do without you?"

"Just doing my job. That's what assistants are for, right? To be the voice of reason when you need it."

He flashes a smile at me that's one hundred percent warmth. Instantly I'm comforted. It's a whole three seconds before that tell-tale flip in my stomach happens. That's pretty good considering the massive crush I had on Toby when he first started working at my floral shop. A year ago, a smile like that from Toby would have floored me. I would have ended up a literal puddle on the floor. But now I have my crush under control. Yeah, I'm still into Toby, but now I can at least put aside my ridiculous schoolgirl feelings aside and act like a professional.

I think back to the day that he started working at my shop. My one-woman floral shop was finally taking off and I was in desperate need of hiring help. So a florist friend recommended Toby, his nephew who had worked for him for years.

My cheeks are hot when I think about how I stared at him the day he walked into my shop, speechless for a solid five seconds. But I couldn't help it. The guy looked like he had walked straight off the pages of a bad boy romance novel.

He was wearing a white button-up and trousers, a perfectly professional outfit, but that couldn't hide the tattoos on the backs of his hands and all along his throat. Little did he know that was my kryptonite. Straight-laced florist good girl me has a major thing for tatted-up guys.

Well, that *and* guys with dark hair and eyes, thick stubble, a square jawline, and a tall, muscled build—all of which Toby has.

It was like someone had designed my dream guy and dropped him in my shop. But I had to shove aside my feelings. Toby was my new employee and even just letting myself think about how attractive he was felt gross. I was technically his boss. I needed to keep my thoughts as professional as possible. And for the past year, it's worked out. Working together has been a blast and we've become friends.

Besides, I'd bet a thousand dollars I'm nowhere near Toby's type. I glance down at the mint green floral maxi dress I'm wearing. I smooth a hand over the sleek ponytail I'm sporting and tuck a few loose strands behind my ear. I look like a human Pinterest board. Probably the exact opposite of the type of women Toby dates. He's probably into women with tattoos who can shoot hard liquor without wincing, who ride motorcycles, who are fiercely confident and unapologetic…not women who can only handle a couple of glasses of white wine and whose idea of a good time is spending the weekend at the local tulip festival.

I'm a florist named Violet for crying out loud. That's annoyingly cute, and I'm certain Toby doesn't do cute.

I watch as he walks over to a nearby table, leans over, and shifts the glass vase a couple of inches to the left so it's perfectly centered. My eyes go wide as I watch the muscles in his back bulge under the dove gray dress shirt he's wearing.

God, Violet. Quit checking him out. It's creepy.

I blink quickly and shake my head, then survey the reception space. We've just finished setting up all the centerpieces. I take a few moments to soak in the visual.

"This place looks really good," I say as Toby walks over and stands next to me.

He scrubs a hand along the thick stubble of his cheek and frowns at me.

"What?" I ask.

"Good is not the word I'd use to describe this place, Violet. It looks breathtaking."

"You really think so?"

"Absolutely. You transformed this vineyard with your flowers. It looks so romantic and gorgeous. Like a scene out of a movie."

My cheeks heat at Toby's glowing compliment. "Thank you," I say softly.

"Violet!" I spin around at the sound of my name and see my friend Ruby decked out in her white chef's jacket.

She pulls me into a hug. "Oh my gosh, this place looks incredible!" Her rich brown eyes are starry as she does a slow scan of the place. "This looks like something out of a magazine. Wow. Vida is going to freak when she sees it."

"You think so?"

"Absolutely. Amazing job, you two," she says to Toby and me.

"Hey, I just follow orders. Violet is the visionary," he says, nudging me lightly with his elbow.

I smile at him before turning back to Ruby. "I still can't believe I got this job. Thank you again, Ruby. I would have never landed it if you hadn't referred me to your family."

"Recommending you to be the florist for Vida and Rafa's wedding was a no-brainer. There's not a florist in all of northern California that's as good as you. Plus, Vida was blown away at the level of customer service you've given her. You were so great about holding her hand through the entire process."

"It was my pleasure. Flowers are such an important part of a wedding. I want everything to be perfect for couples on their big day."

"I'll never forget how she cried when you gave her the bouquet. She couldn't believe that you were able to get sampaguitas. They're her favorite flower and they're so hard to find here."

"I love it when brides happy cry at the flowers. It's the best feeling."

Ruby gazes around the reception space, she smiles, her eyes misty as she looks between Toby and me. "This is beyond perfect, you two."

I give her another hug. "I can't wait to see what you've cooked up for the big dinner."

She flashes a giddy smile and claps her hands together. "I'm so pumped for you guys to try it. Mason and I have spent the last nine months perfecting this menu."

I smile at the image of Ruby and her chef boyfriend trying out recipes in their kitchen. I lost count the number of times she had me over to her place so they could have me try the different recipes they whipped together.

"I think it's the most delicious meal either of us has ever put together," Ruby says.

She pulls her phone out of her chef jacket pocket and checks the time. "You guys wanna pop in the kitchen for a snack? I think we have enough time before I have to start plating for the reception."

"You sure that would be okay?" I ask.

"Absolutely. Vida and Rafa and the rest of the wedding party are off taking photos. The guests are at the cocktail area having drinks on the other side of the vineyard. You deserve to take a break after all the work you've done."

Toby peers down at me. "Gourmet snacks sound pretty good right about now."

As if on cue, my tummy rumbles. Both Ruby and Toby glance at me. I rest my hand over it and chuckle. "My stomach agrees. Did you make your famous chicken adobo skewers that are a million times better than my own family adobo recipe?"

She chuckles. "Of course, I did."

"Aww come on. Your adobo is amazing," Toby says to me. "I'm always pumped when you bring leftovers to work."

I feel myself start to blush thinking about how Toby raves every time I bring in food to the shop. I know he's probably just being nice, but still. It feels good to know that he likes my crappy cooking.

We follow Ruby across the property. Once we're in the main building, we head down a long hallway and turn a corner. Soft mood music echoes in the distance. That must be from the cocktail hour.

"Kitchen is just up here," Ruby gestures. I spot a bathroom nearby.

"I'm going to make a quick pit stop. I'll meet up with you guys in a sec."

I head to the bathroom and take a minute to touch up my makeup and freshen up. When I walk out the door, I collide with someone.

"Shoot sorry!" I say as I stumble before quickly righting myself.

"It's alright, I…"

I still when I hear that voice. That familiar low and smooth tone. When I look up and see the face of my ex-boyfriend Jeremy, I freeze.

I take in the shocked look on his face, how his expression is conveying the same, "Goddamn it" vibe that I feel right now.

"Violet. I didn't expect to see you here." He frowns as he tugs at his silver tie. A tell-tale sign that he's uncomfortable.

And he should be. The last time we saw each other was when we were dating and I surprised him at his place on Valentine's Day almost two years ago—and caught him in bed with another woman.

All the emotions from that day come flooding back, like a tidal wave leveling me and knocking every last bit of air from my lungs. It feels like a million tiny needles are poking through my skin.

I think back to that day, how I stood in the open doorway of his bedroom, watching as he thrust into her before he noticed me. I think about how as soon as he saw me, he just stood there and stared at me, the expression on his face a mix of confusion and annoyance. I think about how his first words to me at that moment weren't "I'm sorry," but instead, "What are you doing here?"

My stomach churns. I swallow back the urge to gag. I close my eyes and shake my head, willing myself to keep it together.

"You're here for the wedding?" he asks, his tone curt.

"Yeah. I'm the florist."

"Oh. How nice." He frowns before pulling at his tie yet again.

"So, you know the bride and groom then?"

"I work with Rafa. We're at the same practice."

"Oh."

Jeremy yanks his tie for the millionth time and glances off to the side, like he's annoyed and uncomfortable with this conversation. Irritation inside of me surges.

"Uncomfortable?" I say, unable to hide the annoyance in my voice.

He huffs out a breath. "You could say that."

I cross my arms. "I guess that's deserved though, isn't it? I felt pretty uncomfortable when I walked in on my boyfriend screwing another woman."

Jeremy rolls his eyes. "Come on, Violet. It's been more than a year since we ended things. Can we be mature about this?"

"Jeremy, you can't be serious. I walked in on you cheating on me and I'm just supposed to forget that it happened? You didn't even apologize."

It's not till I finish speaking that I realize how loud my voice is. Jeremy glances quickly around us, probably to check and see if anyone heard me.

"Keep your voice down, will you?" he says in a loud whisper. "This is a wedding, not the Jerry Springer show for fuck's sake."

I ball my fists at my sides and open my mouth to scold him when I hear the sound of footsteps. A woman walks up to Jeremy's side and slinks her arm around his. It doesn't take longer than a second for me to recognize her as the woman he cheated on me with.

My stomach drops to my feet as I watch Jeremy give her a quick hug and peck on the lips. For a moment I'm frozen as I watch my ex get all lovey-dovey with the woman I walked in on him screwing.

When the two of them look at me, my entire body tenses. Jeremy is looking at me with a cruel satisfaction in his eyes, like he's enjoying seeing me see the two of them together. And his girlfriend is looking at me with raw pity.

I suddenly wish I could melt into the floor just to escape the humiliation of running them.

"This is Trina," Jeremy says. "Trina, this is Violet."

Trina swipes a perfectly styled blonde barrel curl from her shoulder and aims a pitying smile at me. "Nice to meet you."

Out of habit I almost say it back, but I stop myself. Because it's not true. It's not nice at all to meet Trina, to have to stand here and act civil and dignified when all I want to do is disappear forever.

When I say nothing, Jeremy frowns at me. He shakes his head, like he's disappointed in me.

That churning feeling in my stomach intensifies. I need to get the hell away from these two before I vomit or scream or burst into tears.

I mumble that I have to go and scurry off, but then Trina calls after me. "Violet, wait!"

I ignore her and keep walking toward the kitchen, but she catches up to me easily since she's nearly six feet tall in those stilettos.

"Violet, can I just say something? Please?"

When I spin around, I take in the pained look on her face. I also take in the fact that even in my four-inch heels, I barely clear her shoulder. God, it sucks to be short sometimes. I'd give anything to tower over this blonde glamazon in this moment. It would help me feel slightly less pathetic.

"I just want to say that I'm sorry," Trina says. "For, um, how things started between Jeremy and me. I wish…I just wish that…"

Just then Jeremy walks up to us and gently takes Trina's hand in his. "We should get back to cocktail hour," he says to her before turning back to me. "You've probably got a lot of work to do, don't you?"

I nod, swallowing back the ache in my throat. As I take in Jeremy's neutral expression, I notice that familiar smug look in his eyes. I recognize it from all those times during our year-long relationship when he'd gloat whenever he was right about something and I was wrong.

"Don't worry, Violet," he says. "You'll find someone, I'm sure."

If a passerby had heard Jeremy speak those words, they'd probably think he was trying to be kind and encouraging. But I know Jeremy. Thinly veiled condescension is his specialty. No one can take a well-meaning phrase and turn it into a low-key insult quite like he can. That's exactly what he's doing to me now.

But this time I don't want to give him the satisfaction.

"Actually, I've already found someone," I blurt before I can stop myself.

He raises an eyebrow like he doesn't believe me, which makes me even more pissed. "Really?"

"Yeah. He's here with me now. He's my coworker. We're working this wedding together."

Jeremy's gold-hued eyebrows crash together. "Is that so?" When he tugs at his tie, I have to bite back a smile. It feels really, *really* good to make him uncomfortable.

Trina smiles at me. "That's awesome, Violet."

Jeremy clears his throat. "Yeah. Good for you. Maybe if we run into each other later tonight I'll buy you and the lucky guy a drink. Excuse us."

Jeremy walks off, pulling Trina behind him. And I'm feeling triumphant for a few seconds … until I realize what I've just done.

I just told my ex that Toby and I are dating. And there's a pretty good chance that Jeremy will see us together during the reception and come up to us. And then I'll get caught in my lie.

Sweat beads along the back of my neck as I quietly panic.

Unless…

An idea pops into my head. My nerves go haywire at the thought of pulling this off.

I pause for a moment to work up my nerve. Then I take a breath and head into the kitchen.

~*~*~*~

Chapter Two

Toby

When Violet finally walks into the kitchen, I'm in the middle of devouring a chicken adobo skewer.

I point at the plate as she walks over to me. "You gotta try this."

When she grabs me by the arm, that's when I notice the worried look on her face. "You okay?"

She shakes her head. "Not really. Can I talk to you for a sec?"

"Yeah, sure."

She leads me out of the kitchen and down to the darkened area of the hallway.

"I need a favor," she says as she shakes her hands at her sides.

"Whatever you need, I'm here."

She opens her mouth to speak but says nothing. Only a squeaky sound comes out. She purses her lips, then covers her face with her hands.

Worry rockets through me. I've never, ever seen Violet like this. She's usually cheerful and happy.

"Hey." I wrap my hand gently around her delicate wrist, trying my hardest not to focus on just how silky her skin feels. "What's wrong?"

After a second, she lowers her hands from her face and looks at me. "I did something really, really awful."

"Okay…"

Her shoulders rise and fall with the deep breath she takes. "I told a lie. About you. And me."

"What do you mean? What happened?"

Another deep breath before she speaks. "I just ran into my ex. And the woman he left me for."

"Oh, shit. That sucks, I'm really sorry to hear that."

"Yeah, but here's the thing. So, um, he ended things in a really humiliating way."

I take in the red flush that paints her full cheeks and the way her burnt sienna eyes turn shy before her gaze drops to the floor. That worried feeling inside of me turns into something else. It feels a lot like protectiveness.

Not that I have any right to feel protective of Violet. It's not like we're together.

I'll be the first to admit that Violet is a literal dream girl. I'll never forget the day that I walked into her shop and saw her standing there behind the counter, flanked by a million flowers, her long, black-brown hair pulled up in a messy bun. She looked like an angel.

And the way she smiled at me. Violet has the best smile, hands down. No one even comes close. It's the look in her eyes when she grins that does it for me. When she smiled at me that day we met, her eyes were bright and warm. Not many people can make me feel comfortable and at ease with just a smile. But Violet can.

And that's exactly why it's wrong that I like her. She's just being friendly and kind. After spending so much time working together, we've become pretty good work friends.

We joke and laugh together while we work and even eat lunch together most days. But nothing more. First of all, she's my boss. As sweet as Violet is, I know she'd never cross that line, she's too proper and professional. And second, she's way, way out of my league. She's a hardworking, honest, and successful business owner who's as sweet as she is gorgeous, who's never once gotten in trouble. This woman hasn't even gotten a speeding ticket. And here I am, a tattooed punk who spent my late teens and early twenties in an out of jail for petty crimes, who finally got my life together a handful of years ago when I started working at a relative's florist shop. No way would Violet ever be into someone like me.

I take in the worry etched in her brow as she looks up at me.

That familiar protectiveness surges through me anyway. "What did he do to you?" I don't notice the bite in my voice at first. But I can't help it. Just the thought of some asshole hurting Violet makes me crazy.

She hesitates for a moment. "I went over to his place on Valentine's Day when we were dating a couple of years ago to surprise him. He was in bed with another woman…the woman he's with today."

My chest aches at the pained look on her face.

"Seeing them together just now, I feel like such a loser. For the longest time, I just assumed that they wouldn't last. Because really, what kind of relationship starts as an affair? Certainly not a good, healthy one." Violet glances down at her shoes. "But I guess I was wrong. They're still together. They seem happy too. And I guess seeing that really hurt me. I didn't want to come off as pathetic and single after all this time. So I lied and said I was with someone too. I told him you and I were, um…that we're a…"

"Couple?" I say.

She bites her lip, like she's unsure. "Yeah, that's exactly what I told him."

"Okay, sure. I'll pretend to be your boyfriend."

She stands there, her mouth parted open, quietly staring at me for a solid ten seconds. "You will?"

"Of course."

"So wait, you're not mad that I lied about us being together?"

I let out another chuckle. "Why would I be mad about that?"

"Because I lied. I made you my boyfriend without even asking you if it was okay. Plus, I'm your boss. I don't want you to feel like I'm taking advantage of you."

I almost laugh. "Violet, you're the last person on the planet who would ever take advantage of anyone."

She furrows her brow, looking adorably serious in this moment. "No, you're right. I would never do that."

She still doesn't look convinced.

"On the scale of terrible things that could happen to me, this is pretty low, Violet."

"Really?"

"Really. A beautiful, successful woman just asked me to stand in as her boyfriend. I'm flattered."

I notice her cheeks are flushing pink now. She flashes that gorgeous wide grin. "The way you say it makes things sound a lot better."

"I get it. It sucks running into an ex, especially an ex who cheated on you." I smile down at her. "At least you didn't kick him in the balls."

She giggles. "I could never."

"That's because you're a literal angel, Violet."

Something flashes in her gaze that I can't quite decipher, but then she blinks and it's gone. Her expression turns focused. "You sure you want to be my fake boyfriend for the rest of today?"

I wink at her. "Positive."

That blush on her full cheeks deepens. "We should get back out there. The reception will start soon."

I take her hand gently in mine. She looks surprised as she gazes at our joined hands.

"Practice for when we're out there in front of everyone."

She unleashes a flustered smile that has my heart thumping in my chest. "Right. Good thinking."

"But first, let's get you something to eat."

She shakes her head. "It's okay. I'm not even really that hungry anymore."

Just then her stomach growls. I raise an eyebrow at her.

"Okay, maybe I could use a little something," she admits with a shy smile.

I nod my head in the direction of the kitchen. "What kind of fake boyfriend would I be if I let my girlfriend go hungry?"

She chuckles, and I feel lighter, happier. It feels really, really good to make her smile and laugh after how worried she was just minutes ago.

As we walk back into the kitchen, I relish the feel of Violet's hand in mind. Yeah, it's probably uncool as hell that I'm this happy to be her fake boyfriend. But this will probably be my only chance to get this close, this intimate with Violet. I'm going to enjoy every second of it.

***

I take in Violet's rigid posture as we stand near the bar of the reception while dinner service starts.

"Hey." It takes a second for her to even realize I was speaking to her. She looks dazed, like she's lost deep in thought.

"Sorry, I was distracted there for a bit."

I take in the way she's fidgeting with the material of her dress. "How about a drink?" I ask.

A relieved smile appears on her angelic face. "Great idea."

A minute later we're sipping greyhounds while sitting at the bar. I take in her hunched-over, uneasy posture, how she's fidgeting with the straw in her drink, how she scans the room every minute or so.

I almost ask her what's wrong, but I catch myself. It's clear what's wrong. She's nervous about the fact that her cheating douchebag ex is in the same space with her for the next several hours.

I slide my arm closer to her on the bartop and scoop her hand in mine.

Her saucer-like eyes go wide as she looks at our joined hands. "What are you…"

I lean my mouth close to her ear. "We're supposed to be acting like a couple, right?"

"Oh. Right."

"I figured it was okay to hold your hand since we did it a little bit ago, but if this makes you uncomfortable—"

She shakes her head, cutting me off. "It doesn't. I'm good with it. Sorry, I guess I'm just a little nervous about everything."

"No need to be sorry. I get it, this is a tough situation to be in."

She squeezes my hand and flashes a soft smile. "It's a lot easier now that you're with me."

Something inside my chest tingles. How the hell could her ex have cheated on her? Is he out of his mind? Or just an asshole?

I think about what a gem Violet is. I see how hard she works every day at the shop to make sure that every order is perfect for her customers. I remember how welcoming she was to me when I first started working for her. She brought me cupcakes on my first day as a welcome gift. Whenever she does a coffee run, she always makes sure to ask what I want too. She even surprised me with a cake on my birthday a few months ago. Even when she didn't even know me, she treated me like an old friend, making me feel welcome and asking me about my life as we worked together. And when I opened up to her about my past in and out of jail, she didn't judge me. She never changed the way she treated me. She listened patiently and told me how great it was that I turned my life around.

Even thinking about it now, I can't believe it. She's almost too good to be true.

I'd bet a million dollars she's like that in a relationship too—giving, kind, and thoughtful.

She's also a fucking smoke show. I remember how hard it was for me not to stare at her when we first started working together. I was blown away by her beauty. I'm still blown away by her.

When I look at her now, I take in the rosy blush painting her cheeks and the red stain on her bee-stung lips, how her long, black-brown hair falls in perfect waves down her back in that ponytail she's styled it in.

My gaze dips lower, to the ample swell of her boobs, then even lower to her perfect bubble butt. She starts to turn her head to me, and I quickly aim my gaze back up to her face.

Real smooth, you fucking caveman.

She smiles at me, and I smile back at her before downing more of my drink. Yeah, I'm a creep for checking Violet out just now. But she's beyond stunning and I can't fathom how the hell her ex would ever think to cheat on her. Violet is the whole package. Any guy would be lucky to be with her. If by some miracle I ever landed a woman like her, I'd be on my knees thanking god.

You'd be on your knees for another reason too, you perv...

I instantly evict that thought from my brain. Violet has trusted me to help her through this shitty situation and here I am sitting next to her, entertaining filthy thoughts about her.

I clear my throat before gulping from my water glass.

"Thanks again for agreeing to do this with me," Violet says. "I really appreciate…"

She trails off as she looks past my shoulder. Her eyes go wide. "Crap."

"What's wrong?" I start to turn to see what she's looking at, but she grabs me by the lapels of my suit jacket and jerks me forward. We're nose-to-nose, barely two inches separating our faces. When I inhale, I smell the sugary floral scent of her perfume. Holy shit, that's intoxicating.

"Jeremy is headed this way with his girlfriend," Violet says in a sharp whisper. "He looked right at me and grabbed her hand and kissed her cheek." Pain flashes in her beautiful brown eyes. "It's like he's trying to rub their relationship in my face."

That protectiveness surges through me once more. What a shithead this guy is.

"Give him a taste of his own medicine," I say.

Her eyebrows crash together. "What do you mean?"

"Kiss me."

She lets out a breathy chuckle. "What?"

"This prick sounds like he's trying to make you jealous. Fuck that. Show him that he's the last thing on your mind."

Her expression shifts from surprised to intrigued. "Really? You'd be okay with that?"

"Absolutely."

Not even a second later, Violet's mouth is on me. I make a surprised noise as she presses those impossibly soft lips against mine, her mouth firm and teasing all at once. I let her take the lead as the seconds pass, moving my lips in tandem with hers. I notice she's keeping this a lips-only kiss. Probably because we're technically in a public venue with loads of people around us. But damn, this kiss. I don't know what I expected Violet to kiss like, but it wasn't like this. This urgent, firm, almost desperate rhythm. I guess I thought she'd be a bit gentler and sweeter based on her personality. But I was wrong. Violet kisses like she's in control, like she knows what she wants.

My dick starts to ache as I fantasize about teasing my tongue against the tip of hers. But just then she pulls away, breaking our kiss.

I take in the cloudy look in her eyes, wondering if she feels as dazed as I do. She touches her fingertips to her lips as she glances past my shoulder. She grins wide as she looks at me.

"He looks pissed," she says.

Satisfaction surges inside of me. "Good."

Violet turns to grab her water glass and I hear someone clear their throat behind me. When I turn around I see a guy I assume is her ex based on the fact that he looks like he wants to punch me.

I had no idea what the hell this guy would look like, but it's not a surprise that he looks like a textbook douchebag with his designer suit, diamond cufflinks, and slicked-back haircut. He looks like if Gordon Gekko and that guy from *American Psycho* had a douchey love child.

This isn't the first time I've had someone walk up to me wanting to kick my ass. Given that I was a hellraiser as a teenager and well into my twenties and the fact that I was in and out of jail, getting into fights became a hobby for me.

Because of that, I've developed a pretty good gauge of how to read people. I can tell if someone is serious about wanting to fight, or if they're all bark and no bite, too scared to even throw a punch. I can already tell that this Jeremy guy is the second type. It's obvious in the way he maintains a few feet of space between us and how the scowl on his face dials back in intensity now that he's gotten a close-up look at me. His gaze falls to my neck. I assume he's disgusted by my throat tattoo—a lot of people are. When he glances at the tattoos of roses and crosses on my knuckles, he swallows hard. When he looks back up at me, there's a flash of uncertainty in his eyes that makes me want to laugh. This guy fucking hates me, that's crystal clear, but no way is he going to throw down.

"Jeremy," I hear Violet say behind me. "Where's Trina?"

"Off to the ladies' room," he says, his scowl still fixed on me. "I assume this is the lucky guy?"

"Yup!" Violet hops off her barstool and I do the same. I lace my fingers in hers.

"This is Toby," she says. "Toby, this is Jeremy."

I shake his hand and hold back yet another laugh as this clown attempts a death grip on me.

When I grip him even harder in return, he winces slightly. I flash a grin. "Good to meet you, Jeremy."

I release his hand and he lets out a breath before clearing his throat and tugging at his tie. Dude looks like he's trying to choke himself.

"Likewise. So, Violet tells me that you two work together."

"That's right."

Before I can say more, the bartender stops by and asks Jeremy for his drink order.

"Glass of Macallan," he says.

"I'm sorry, sir, but the closest thing we've got is Redbreast Twelve Year Old Irish Whiskey. I assure you though, it's quite excellent."

Jeremy raises an eyebrow. "Seriously? At a venue like this, I would have expected a bit higher quality."

Violet grumbles quietly next to me.

"I do apologize, sir," the bartender says with patience in his tone. I'm impressed. If I had to deal with pretentious pricks like Jeremy whining about liquor, I'd punch him in the face.

I hold back a smart-ass comment as Jeremy tosses another insult at the kind of alcohol this venue carries.

"On the rocks, then," he says. "It's the only way I can stand to drink that swill."

The bartender makes his drink. I notice Jeremy doesn't even tip the guy, so I pull my wallet out and drop a few dollars in the tip jar. The bartender flashes a grateful smile.

When Jeremy openly grimaces after sipping his drink, I have to fight the urge to punch him.

Easy. You lose your cool and you'll be hauled back to jail.

I take a slow, silent breath and look at him. "Taste good?"

"Hardly," he grumbles. "So you're a florist?" he says, the condescension in his tone barely veiled.

I flash a practiced smile at him. "That's right."

He makes a "huh," sound behind the rim of his glass. "Forgive me for my bluntness, but you don't look the type." He smirks, then gestures with his free hand at my neck and knuckles.

"What exactly does a florist look like, Jeremy?" Violet says, a soft bite to her tone. I give her an easy smile while softly squeezing her hand. I'm heartened at how she defends me, but I don't want her to stress. This prick's opinion of me means less than nothing.

Jeremy shrugs. "I suppose I'm used to a bit more polished appearance. But that's probably my professional background." He chuckles despite the narrow look in his eyes. "My fellow physicians and I are a pretty clean-cut bunch when we're not at the clinic and hospital."

"Good for you," I say.

Violet chuckles at my borderline sarcastic tone. Jeremy purses his lips before taking a long sip from his glass, clearly picking up on the I-don't-give-a-fuck undercurrent of my words.

"Appearance and style don't matter at all in my field," Violet says. "What matters is that Toby has a brilliant and artistic eye. He's an incredibly talented florist."

Hearing Violet sing my praises in front of her ex makes me feel like I could fly. I flash a shit-eating grin at Jeremy, who's glowering at me while he takes another seconds-long pull of that supposedly trash whiskey.

The sound of the emcee of the reception Sophie making an announcement on the stage pulls our attention to the far side of the ballroom.

"It's time for bouquet toss!"

The bride, a stunning older woman in a gold-white Filipiniana terno wedding gown, beams as she holds the bouquet above her head. A massive crowd of women gather behind her, playfully shoving each other as they wait for the toss. When she throws it behind her, a tall blonde woman jumps up in an attempt to catch it, but a dark-haired woman swoops in and grabs it. I think her name is Ava? She shrieks in triumph and the crowd cheers. The blonde pouts before looking over at Jeremy.

"Almost," she mouths with a quirk of her perfectly penciled eyebrow.

I catch Jeremy rolling his eyes as he looks on. "Just great." He moves down to the far side of the bar and flags down the bartender for a refill.

"That's Trina, Jeremy's date," Violet says quietly. That's the woman Jeremy was cheating on her with—Violet walked in on them having sex.

I swallow back that pissed-off feeling and silently remind myself that this isn't about me or how I feel. This is about supporting Violet in a tough moment and making sure she's okay.

I lean down and press a soft kiss to her forehead. When I feel her relax against me, I feel a surge of satisfaction.

Just then Ruby runs up to Violet. "Lola Naty wants to see you," she says.

"Your grandmother wants to see me?" Violet asks.

Ruby grins and nods. "Everything is perfect and she wants to thank you in person. Seriously, she burst into happy tears when she saw the centerpieces on the tables. She loves them."

Beaming, Violet turns to me. "I'll just be a sec."

"Take your time."

She scurries off with Ruby, and I return to my drink. A minute later someone bumps me so hard, I almost fall off my stool. When I turn and see Jeremy next to me, I clench my jaw.

"You need something?"

He glares at me. "You're not good enough for her, you know."

I laugh. "No shit."

My response seems to piss him off even more because he steps into my space. "I'm serious. Violet is a proper, classy woman. She's only with you because she's bored."

I shake my head as I focus on my drink. "Whatever you say, man."

He leans down to me, his breath stinking of alcohol. "I bet you've been to jail, haven't you? You look like a convict. I can't believe she'd hire a low life like you to work for her. I thought she was smarter than that."

That wave of anger I've been shoving down emerges, settling like fire in my gut. Not because of his insult toward me—I've heard way worse than whatever petty criticism this asshole can think to hurl at me in his sorry-ass state. But to insult Violet? No fucking way will I let that slide.

I stand up and face him, planting my hand on his shoulder. When I shove him down to sit on the stool next to me, he lets out an "oof" sound.

I hover over him. "You're drunk. Take a second to get your shit together. And that's the first and last time you ever insult Violet."

I start to walk off when I hear him speak. "I know she still wants me. As soon as she's done with this little fling with you, she'll be crawling back to me. It won't be long before she gets tired of your trashy-ass tattoos and this bad boy bullshit."

That fire in my gut spreads up my chest to my throat and tongue. A half-second later I'm in Jeremy's face and seeing red.

"There's not a chance in hell that will ever happen, you worthless prick," I growl through gritted teeth. "You know why? Because this isn't some fling. I'm crazy about Violet. I have been ever since we started working together a year ago. You're right, I'm a low-life, tatted-up ex-con. But you know what else I am? Her boyfriend. And that's not changing anytime soon."

My heart rattles against my chest when I finish speaking. I notice I'm breathing harder too.

Someone gasps behind me. I turn and see Violet, her expression shocked and something else…something unreadable. I quietly start to panic when I think back to everything I said just now. I sounded like a crazed, jealous freak who just gave away that I've been crushing on her pretty much the entire time I've known her. She probably thinks I'm a psycho.

Jeremy slides off his barstool and walks off. I ignore his drunken grumblings and walk over to Violet.

"I can explain," I say quietly.

"Not here," she says quickly. "We need to talk about this in private."

I nod quietly and follow her out of the reception space and back toward the building venue. We make our way to a quiet area of the property near the gazebo where we set up more floral arrangements earlier. This is where Vida and Rafa took photos with their guests. And now this is where

Violet and I are going to have one hell of an uncomfortable conversation.

My stomach churns.

When she turns and looks up at me, I take in the dazed look on her face. "I need you to be honest with me, Toby. All that stuff you told Jeremy about liking me since you met me…is that true? Or were you just saying that?"

For a second I hesitate.

"At first I thought you were just playing it up for our fake relationship, but…" She blinks quickly, her doe eyes focused. "But you sounded so serious. So passionate. Like you meant every word you said."

She bites her lips as she looks up at me, waiting for my answer. For a brief moment, I think about lying to her. I think about telling her that it was all for show, that I was just trying to sell it hard to Jeremy after the shitty things he said.

But the longer I look at Violet, the guiltier I feel. I can't look her in the eye and lie to her.

"Everything I said was true," I say. "I've liked you since the day I met you, Violet."

And then I hold my breath, look at her, and wait to hear what she'll say.

Chapter Three

Violet

I stare at Toby, stunned. "You like me? This whole time?"

"Yeah," he says in a quiet voice. I notice his broad shoulders are hunched, like he's ashamed to admit this.

I'm quiet as my brain struggles to process everything that just happened in the last couple of minutes. Just the fact that Toby likes me is making my head spin.

"Why?"

He frowns. "Why what?"

"Why do you like me?"

He stares at me like I've sprouted a third arm. "Is that a serious question?"

"Well, yeah. I mean, you're…" I gesture at his muscled form. "And well…I'm…" I gesture vaguely at myself before quickly crossing my arms.

He blinks. "Sorry, I didn't understand any of that."

I take a breath. "I mean this in the least creepy way possible, but you're ridiculously hot, Toby. And not just hot, but, like, bad boy hot. And I'm…well, I definitely don't look like the kind of woman who would date a hot bad boy."

His brow hits his hairline. "Wait, you think I'm hot?"

Awareness hit at what I've said. "Um, yeah." For a second, I go quiet. But then I realize it wouldn't be fair for me to clam up right now. Toby just confessed how he feels about me. I owe him the same honesty.

"I like you too, Toby. A lot. Pretty much ever since you started working with me," I say. "But, um, I tried to keep it to myself because I didn't want to come off like a creepy boss. And I didn't want to make you uncomfortable."

A sly grin pulls at his beautiful, thick lips. "You wouldn't have made me uncomfortable, Violet." He steps forward, closing the space between us. "Hearing you admit that is a fucking dream come true."

A second later his smile drops and he frowns like he's confused. "Wait, why did you say you don't look like the kind of woman who would date me?"

I bite my lip, embarrassed to admit this to him. "Because my vibe is pretty much the exact opposite of yours. You're a tatted-up badass, and I look like a human flower bouquet."

He grins wide. "I happen to really, really like human flower bouquets. I'm a florist, remember?"

I smile back at him. "Good point."

He takes my hand in his. This time when he touches me, my skin tingles. It feels like electricity buzzing between us now that we've both confessed our mutual crushes on each other. Things between us feel more raw but in the best way.

"This whole time we liked each other," he muses before running his tongue along his bottom lip.

My mouth waters with the need to taste him. That kiss we shared earlier was hot, but it wasn't enough, not even close. I want more of Toby. And I want him right now.

The longer I look at him, my heart thuds faster. My face and chest go hot.

"We should make up for lost time," I say.

He quirks an eyebrow. The corner of his mouth tugs up. "I agree."

Even though we're barely a few inches apart, I move closer, pressing my body against Toby. His chestnut stare turns intense as he gazes down at me.

My entire body aches with the need to touch him, to kiss him.

"I want you, Toby. So bad. I always have." My voice is somewhere between a growl and a whisper. I run my palms up his chest, savoring how firm he feels under the thin fabric of his dress shirt.

It's not even a second before I'm unbuttoning his shirt.

"Right here? Right now?" he asks, a smug grin on his face as he does a quick scan of the area. We're the only ones here still.

I nod. "I don't want to waste another minute. I have to have you."

He grins and runs his tongue along his bottom lip. He rests his hands on my hips and pulls me against him. "You know, for a human flower bouquet, that's a pretty risqué thing you've just proposed we do."

"I have a bit of a naughty streak."

A hungry look flashes in his chestnut eyes just before his mouth crashes against mine. He teases open my lips with his tongue and I groan into his mouth. His soft tongue laps gently against mine in an urgent rhythm, like he can't get enough of me. It sends shockwaves through the rest of my body. When he hums against my mouth, I feel a familiar ache between my legs.

I break our kiss to catch my breath. "Your mouth…your tongue…" I trace my index finger softly along his lips.

He blesses me with that smug grin once more. "Just wait."

Those growled words send a thrill through me. I can't wait to see what else his mouth and his tongue can do.

His massive hands firmly grip my waist, pressing into me like he's savoring the feel of my body. He hauls me up and I wrap my legs around his waist. He carries me like I'm nothing, walks the handful of steps to the gazebo, and sets me gently on the wood-panel floor. Then he whips off his suit jacket, lays it down, and moves me so I'm lying on top of it.

"Does that feel okay?" he asks.

I almost swoon at how doting he is in this moment, at how much he cares about my comfort.

I smile up at him. "It's perfect."

I reach up and pull his unbuttoned shirt off his shoulders. He lowers down over me. As his bare torso hovers above me, my eyes go wide at the tunnel of sculpted muscle and ink.

"Whoa…" I stare, mesmerized by the intricate tattoo adorning the top of his chest, shoulders, along both arms, all the way down to his wrists. It's a mix of skulls, roses, and geometric patterns. It stretches all the way up his throat, stopping right below his stubble.

I open my mouth and try to form words, but all that comes out are shallow gasps. "You're unreal," I finally say.

A low chuckle is his response.

"Your body. It's just…" I trail off as I run my hands up and down his chest, savoring the silky feel of his skin. It's the perfect contrast to his firm, cut muscle and the bold black ink of his tattoos.

I lean up and press a kiss to the base of his throat, savoring the hot feel of his skin. The groan he lets slip sends a shiver through me. I wonder how many times I'll be able to get him to make that sound.

Before I can find out, he moves his hands to the hem of my dress. "Can I take this off?"

I nod and bite back a moan as he slowly, gently pulls off my dress. I'm left in a nude lace bra and panties. I watch as Toby's gaze turns dazed. "God, you're gorgeous."

I'm certain the smile I'm flashing is cheesy as hell, but I can't help it. It feels incredible to know that Toby likes my body so much.

He lowers his face down and runs his mouth against my bare stomach.

"Violet," he murmurs against me. The second time he says my name, it's almost a growl.

He gently scrapes his teeth along my skin and the pulse between my legs intensifies. When he starts to kiss down my stomach, my toes curl. He leans up and skims his thumb along the waistband of my panties. My heart rate kicks up in anticipation of where his mouth and tongue are about to be.

I peer down and catch eyes with him. His chestnut gaze boasts a pleasure-drunk sheen. My breath hitches. Eyes still glued to me, he plants a kiss on the inside of my thigh. Something between a tingle and a squeeze works its way up my lower abdomen to my chest. My head falls to the side; my eyes roll to the back of my head. Just the press of his lips to my skin has me on edge. I'm aching, vibrating for more.

With a single swipe of his hand, my panties are at my ankles. When I feel his tongue gently lap at my most sensitive spot, I gasp.

A minute later, I can finally speak.

"Oh, my…whoa," I slur. "God, that's nice."

Toby peeks up from between my legs. "Nice, huh? I can do better than 'nice.'"

He lowers back down and swirls his tongue on my clit, the pressure soft and steady all at once. The pulse between my legs turns to a fiery heat. My jaw drops. Holy crap, I'm already so close.

His low groan gives way to a hum, and my leg muscles start to tremble.

"Oh, my god," I gasp.

He groans in response. I can feel myself winding tighter and tighter as the seconds pass. The pleasure builds and builds inside of me. Heat flashes through my entire body. Before long I'm fisting both hands in his hair. It's not long before I break.

I howl so loud, I make my own ears ring. I'm shaking and thrashing, the pleasure of Toby's tongue almost too much. It's never, ever felt this good. When I finally start to come down, I try to lean up to look at him, but I only manage to prop myself up for a second. I'm so drained from that earth-shattering orgasm that I don't have the strength or energy to hold myself up.

Toby moves up and kisses me, still clad in those charcoal gray trousers that are sporting a massive bulge in the front. Wiping his mouth with the back of his hand, he smirks. I take in how I've completely messed up hair but that's made him look even more handsome.

"That mouth," I mutter as I reach down to thumb his lips. "My god."

I reach down and unzip his pants. He helps me yank them off.

I lick my lips as I take in the bulge in his boxer briefs. "On your back."

He grins wide. "Yes, ma'am."

As I move to straddle him, I take in his massive quads for a moment before I pull down his briefs. The second I do, my jaw plummets to the ground while I gawk at his impressive length. I shouldn't be surprised. He's six feet tall. It's a given he'd be well endowed.

But to see it in person is…an experience.

Under my legs, his thigh muscles tense. He reaches up and rests both hands just above my waist. "Is it okay to take this off?" He runs his fingers along the band of my bra.

I nod my head. In one swift move, he unhooks it. The nude lace fabric slides down my arms and I toss it to the side. Toby's gaze turns starry-eyed as he takes me in.

"Wow," he murmurs. I'm blushing once again, feeling like a freaking goddess.

He cups both his hands over my boobs, gently teasing my nipples with his fingers. Goosebumps sprout up across my skin. When he leans up and takes my nipple in his mouth, my head falls back. I close my eyes, whimpering at how incredible it feels.

Heat and pleasure converge once more in my core.

"Please tell me you have a condom," I whine before leaning down to kiss him. I grind myself against the front of his pelvis, aching to feel him inside me after all this buildup.

"I've got one," he grunts. He reaches for his trousers on the floor next to us. He fishes out his wallet from one of the pockets, pulls out a condom, and tears it open with his teeth.

With his free hand on my hip, he gently scoots me back as he sheaths himself. I plant both of my palms on his chest and lower myself onto him. I move slowly at first, inch by glorious inch. It's an exquisite, intense pressure, stretching myself against him. When I'm fully in place, I take a few seconds just to savor the feeling.

When I look down at Toby, his eyes are closed and he's groaning.

"Fuck, you feel amazing."

"So do you," I gasp.

When I start to move up and down, he digs his fingers into the fleshy part of my hips.

"Go slow," he says, his breath catching at the end. "I don't wanna rush this. You feel so good. I want this to last."

Up and down I move, riding him with an unhurried, easy rhythm. With each thrust I take him deeper, stretching myself from the inside out until I'm howling once more.

When I lean forward to grind my clit against him, he growls.

"Oh, hell yes," he groans. "Just like that."

Pleasure radiates through me. If I keep this up, it won't be long before I come again.

"We should have done this sooner," I say through a ragged breath. "Way, way sooner."

He cups both sides of my face with his hands, kissing me with such ferocity that I'm panting. "You're right. How did we make it this long?"

He leans up and softly bites my shoulder. My eyes roll to the back of my head at how unexpected and divine that felt. "Oh, my god, Toby. Yes."

He bites me again, and I ride him harder and faster. When he moves his mouth to the base of my neck, I'm shouting. It's the perfect contrast. Soft caresses from his hands, the pleasure and pressure of his cock inside of me, the press of his teeth against my skin…it's all divine.

"Tell me to stop and I will," he growls.

He gathers my hair over my shoulder and leans to the right to give the other side of my neck attention. He alternates between kisses and soft bites. His hot, wet breath against my skin makes me shiver.

I shake my head. "No, I love it. Please. More."

My neck is fiery from his bites, and I can't get enough. With my hands on his chest, I push him flat on the ground, rocking back and forth against the front of his pelvis until the sensation is too much.

Climax hits, and I start to scream. Toby reaches up, clamping his hand over my mouth, which turns me on even more. Well, that was an unexpectedly hot move. Underneath me, I feel him tense and tremble. Seconds later there's a long, drawn-out growl as he comes too.

When I finish, I collapse on top of him. He wraps his arms around my bare back and squeezes me tight against him. I sink into him, reveling in the hot, wet feel of his skin. When he nuzzles the top of my head, I close my eyes and snuggle my face into his chest.

For a few minutes, we're quiet as we lie there and hold each other.

"We should probably head back," Toby says after a while. "People are probably wondering where we are." He kisses the top of my head, and I have to close my eyes, it's so sweet.

"You're right."

I don't move to get up though. I'm too content, too comfortable cuddling with Toby. And I'm too blown away at what's just happened between us in the space of an evening.

We went from harboring secret crushes on each other to having sex in a vineyard gazebo during a wedding.

I glance up from where I'm cuddled on top of him, giddy at the happy look on his face. He peers down at me and grins as he smooths my hair, which has come loose from my ponytail, out of my face.

"Maybe we stay like this for just a few more minutes," he says.

I lean up and kiss him. "Sounds perfect."

THE END

About Sarah Smith

Sarah Smith is a copywriter-turned-author who wants to make the world a lovelier place, one kissing story at a time. Her love of romance began when she was eight and she discovered her auntie's stash of romance novels. She's been hooked ever since. When she's not writing, you can find her hiking, eating chocolate, and perfecting her lumpia recipe.

Book List:

Faker

Simmer Down

On Location

The Boy with the Bookstore

If You Never Come Back

The Close-Up

In Love With Lewis Prescott

Dessert Flirt Repeat

Snow, Ice, and Spice

No Freaking Way

Sips & Strokes

Vibes & Feels

Whiskers & Sunshine

Dream Guy

Fake As Puck

Dirty Pucker

Suck My Puck

Of Pucking Course

One Good Puck

Desperate Pucker

So Pucking Good

Nothing On You

Three More Months

What We Remember

Never Ever You

Even If The Sky Is Falling

Pasko Na, My Love

Forevermore

Social Media IDs:

Instagram - @authorsarahs

TikTok - @authorsarahs

Facebook Group - @sarahsmithbooks

Bookbub - sarah-echavarre-smith

Goodreads - Sarah_Smith

Win Your Love

TIF MARCELO

Win Your Love

TIF MARCELO

Blurb:

After being unceremoniously stood up by her fake date to her cousin's wedding, Alexandra Moore's day goes from bad to worse when she has to fight over the last gift of the wedding registry with former neighbor and all-around rival, Jordan Franco. But as the wedding and reception minutes click by, along with their constant bickering and mini-competitions, Alex and Jordan reignite the spark that almost brought them together years ago. Will they let their ambition reign? Or will they finally concede that love wins above all?

Content Notes: Profanity

Tropes and Sub genres: Competition, Second Chance Romance

Heat Level: 🔥 (low heat)

Chapter One

Alex

Things like this didn't happen to Alexandra Moore. While she watched the scene outside the Uber's backseat window switch from highway to town, panic rose within her. "Kyle, the wedding's in less than an hour. I'm picking up our present now. What do you mean you can't go?"

"You know this isn't a good idea. They'll see right through us," Kyle said.

Alex's cheeks burned with the start of desperation, and her eyes watered. Dammit, she *knew* she should have insisted that she and Kyle arrive at Ate Vida's wedding together. But he'd wanted to visit his parents up in Sacramento, and she'd conceded to meeting him instead.

Her instincts had told her that he'd bail, but she'd pushed it down and away. Surely their eight months together would have afforded her one last favor before they fully called it splits.

Apparently not.

She blinked hard and blinked again.

No. She would not cry, not after spending so much time doing her makeup, ensuring her contouring was just right. Not in this dress she spent half a week's paycheck on and shoe-horned herself into.

Instead, she focused on historic downtown Napa passing slowly by. On the quaint facade of the remodeled buildings, the greenery lining Main Street, and the pedestrians walking by with bags in their hands. It was gorgeous today, with a clear blue sky.

It was a perfect day for a wedding.

But thus far, it was slowly crumbling for Alex. She had awakened to her sweet chocolate lab Jupiter getting sick on her white area rug, and her groceries were delivered to the wrong apartment. Then, the hot water in the building ran out. Damn old Victorians. Pretty to look at, and for tourists visiting San Francisco to take pictures of, but on the inside—they're a hot mess.

And now this.

"We agreed to come to this one last event together," she reminded Kyle, shock turning to the anger stage of grief. "You promised."

"That was six months ago."

"You had every moment before today to cancel. We even matched your tie to my dress. We talked about the present last week. This is completely unacceptable. And wrong."

And embarrassing. And humiliating. And mortifying. She was Alex Moore. Sportscaster at the Bay Area Sports Network. She didn't go anywhere alone and surely not at a wedding. To a Moore wedding, at that, and not because she didn't like her extended family—she loved them to bits— but because weddings were the ultimate spectator sport.

Alex only liked competing when she knew she could win. At the moment, she was the epitome of a big L.

"I can't do it, Alex. I can't." Kyle's tone was short of a plea. "Your family is brutal. I won't be able to pretend."

"What do you mean they're brutal? They're the best. Most of the time." Inwardly, she winced at the complication of that statement. There was a fine line between close and overinvolved, and the Moores often overstepped. It was a blessing and a curse, depending on who you were talking to and when.

The Uber driver glanced at Alex through the rearview mirror as if sensing her thoughts, and she lowered her voice. She pressed the phone even harder against her skin, knowing that all the paint on her face would soon be smeared onto the screen. "Kyle, they love you."

"I appreciate you saying that, but you know that's not true. The Moore family puts up with me because they love *you*. Ollie literally gives me the side-eye whenever I see him—"

"He's my brother. What do you expect?"

"And your parents. Not to mention Vida. Do you remember the last time we were together, at Lola Naty's birthday? She asked me, and I quote, 'What have you done to keep up with my niece?'"

Alex groaned. "It's because everyone knows I'm ambitious."

"Well, I tried. And bottom line: we're broken up."

"That's a small detail."

"Huge detail."

The car stopped in front of Joie de Vivre, the specialty home goods store, as the first stop, and she waved at the driver, lifting a finger to signal "one minute."

"Look, do it for me, as a friend." Her voice croaked as she took in the pedestrian traffic that flowed around her. And though downtown was quaint, with the savory scent of food cooking wafting from across the street, from

Moonlight Diner, she couldn't enjoy it. She was being stood up!

She plastered on a smile—any second now, someone would recognize her. Through gritted teeth, she said, "Please."

"No."

Irritation ran up her spine; back to anger she went. "This kind of crap is the reason we were only together for eight months. You do things like calling last minute to cancel when you promise to fake it with me!" Then remorse followed, because he could still make it to the reception if he left right then. "Just ignore what I said and come to the wedding. Drop by? Please?"

"I've got to go, okay? Good luck today. I'm sorry it has to be this way."

"No, Kyle. Dammit. You owe me for your half of this toaster!"

The click of the phone sounded, leaving Alex standing there. Her chest felt heavy, and she pushed a hand against it.

This was it. She was alone, on this sidewalk, and would have to walk into the wedding alone. But as she parsed what was really worrying her, it was the fact she would have to explain her status to the clan. That she, once again, had served and double-faulted. She would become the cautionary tale of the woman who put her career first.

At her Ate Vida's wedding, she would be one of the few women in her upper thirties in line to catch the bouquet.

Numbly, and with a whimper threatening to escape her throat, she stepped back and turned, facing the clear double doors of Joie de Vivre. She pulled on the handle, the soothing sound of the chime drawing her out of her thoughts. All around was the subtle smell of merchandise and a mix of candles and room freshener.

It was going to be okay, right?

Yes, it was.

It depends, the devil on her shoulder said, *on how quickly people find out that you're single.*

She stepped up to the cashier's table to move the moment forward and thumbed on her phone for the gift's confirmation receipt. Finding it and clicking on it, she sighed at the astronomical total cost. The SMEG toaster—champagne color in matte—was supposed to be a combined present. Since the brand was TikTok famous, it had been tough to find, and she swore the prices were jacked up because of it.

Yes, she made good money as a sportscaster, but renting a flat in San Francisco and then keeping up with everything—the clothing, the makeup, the lifestyle—required her to count her pennies.

"Thanks a lot, Kyle," she whispered.

"Alex Moore, as I live and choke on the air I breathe," said a guy next to her. The statement was followed by a chuckle so familiar that whatever self-pity Alex had entertained drained out of her. What was left was her poker face and her pride, and the memory of her and this man sharing a tennis court, and then a bed, which he had then abandoned. But there was more than that—years of childhood angst living next door to him in a quiet neighborhood on the outskirts of Napa.

"Jordan Franco." His name on her tongue left a bitter taste.

Turning now, she faced the man who was, after only seeing him on the screen for many years, the hottest tennis coach in Southern California—not that she'd been keeping track.

Okay, so she had been, but it was her job to know the ins and outs of pro tennis.

Jordan was wearing a perfectly tailored suit, though his face sported a five o' clock shadow, and he was holding a SMEG toaster box. The dichotomy of this tugged at her—Jordan was all levels of complicated—and threatened to unearth the long-buried crush she'd harbored for him.

What was she thinking? Alex shoved that thought far into her subconscious. What was she, twenty-one? Eighteen? Fourteen? This was Jordan, the guy who'd given her shit about everything. The guy who could push every one of her buttons. The guy who'd left Northern California and never looked back.

Which made it curious that he was here, in Napa.

Then clarity descended.

Dammit.

Alex took it back. This was going to be more painful than anything she'd envisioned for today.

Because Jordan wasn't only her childhood next-door neighbor and college arch nemesis. The Franco family had a close relationship with Ate Vida too.

Which meant he was here for the wedding.

462

Chapter Two

Jordan

Jordan had prepared himself to see Alex, but not quite this early, when he hadn't yet donned his imaginary silver armor to prepare himself for battle. His plan had been to walk into the wedding just before it started to avoid her and sit in the back pews. That would have afforded him another hour to steel himself before he ran into her and the rest of the Moores at the reception.

One had to be emotionally prepared to deal with the Moores. And with Alex, one had to always be ready, not only for her attitude and competitiveness, but for how breathtaking she was, even while she was scowling. Years had passed since he'd seen her in person, though she was a mainstay on his television, especially during tennis season. Although, television-Alex couldn't hold a candle to her now, in person, where she was a feast for the senses wearing a mauve dress made of lace that hugged every inch of her curves and exposed her shoulders and miles of her golden-brown skin.

But that was neither here nor there. They weren't on good terms, after all. It had been about five years since they'd been in each other's presence, when his parents had thrown a big party before they retired. Alex's family had attended, and she'd happened to be in town.

And as usual, they'd gotten into it, and that time, it had been during musical chairs. She'd all but punched him for that last chair.

He didn't let her win, of course. Never would if he could help it. It was both of their MOs, this fight for everything.

How had it been to compete against a woman to whom he had been, and still was, attracted to but also wanted to spar with? It was infuriating. Frustrating. And decidedly a turn-on.

If this had been during their undergrad years, he would have been jumping for glee that he was in proximity of this beautiful woman, but now? Not so much.

Not with everything happening with work that he couldn't sort out.

Some things were more important than his libido.

He adjusted the box against his hip and shifted his gaze to the cashier behind him. She'd been stopped by another customer. Guess he had to make small talk with Alex. "Nice day for a wedding."

"It's a gorgeous day." A Cheshire cat smile appeared on her face, as if she was on camera. "How have you been?"

"Good. Flew in about an hour ago."

"And dressed already. That's a miracle."

The insult was like an arrow straight to his pride. Apparently, she was going for the jugular already, reminding him of how he'd always run late.

He refused to fall for it, though. This time, there would be no fighting between them. He was a grown man. "Anything for Vida."

"Didn't know you were on the invite list."

"My parents couldn't make it," he said. "They're on a cruise that had been rescheduled from the quarantine. So, I'm here to represent."

"Joy."

He winced, though he kept a smile on his face. "Surprised you didn't know."

She seemed to flinch.

Bingo. Right to the red dot in the center. Alex hated not knowing everyone's business. She'd been a journalist even before she was hired by Bay Area News Network.

Nosy was more like it.

Two could play the low-blow game.

"I'm surprised your parents didn't ask you to cruise with them," she said, lips curling into a grin. "Then again, you'd probably miss the port call. Though nothing would be as bad as missing your flight to the NCAA championships because you forgot your driver's license."

He bristled. She was good, all right. She hadn't lost her touch. He tucked the gift under his other arm. "Huh. Interesting that you know about that, since it was something I only casually mentioned on my socials. Sounds like someone's been keeping tabs on my whereabouts."

She rolled her eyes, which caused him to roll his eyes. Though inside, he was pumping his fist in triumph.

He'd won this round.

Yes, it was immature, but she'd started it first. Maybe not this interaction, but all the way back to that first challenge on the court when they were in USTA juniors. She'd had such a chip on her shoulder, intent on beating him in tennis, intent on proving to him that she was better. It wasn't enough that by the time they graduated from UC Davis, they'd had their share of wins and losses.

When in truth, even back then, he'd only wanted to be around her.

But a guy had only so much patience.

To his actual joy, the shop person finally slid up to the register. Her smile exuded a kindness that helped somewhat defuse the tension. He took a moment to breathe while Alex was being helped and did a systems check with the rest of his body. It wouldn't be the first time that he'd walked away from sparring with Alex with a bruise or a pulled muscle, literal or figurative.

The weight of both the women's stares dragged him from his thoughts. They were looking at him expectantly. "What is it?"

"That was the item on her list," the shop person said.

"But it was on the shelves."

"It's mine." Alex placed both hands on the box and began to pull.

He tugged back, shocked and yet not shocked by her audacity. He half laughed, because who else would do something as bold as Alex? "Um, no. Unless we're in the Matrix, it's me who's holding it to begin with."

"How does that even have anything to do with the Matrix?"

"That it's a fake reality!"

"Whatever. Look. This toaster belongs to me. I have a receipt that proves it."

Only the box separated their bodies. It was the closest he'd stood next to Alex in a long time, and he detected the scent of her body spray. She never did wear perfume. Instead, bottles of body spray littered the vanity of her college bedroom. It often lingered on the side of the court that she'd just occupied, and it had given him a high whenever he'd walked through it.

If he focused, he could probably pinpoint the scent.

Except she was trying to steal Vida's present from his clutches.

"Alex, let go." He glanced at the cashier, who had a deer-in-the-headlights look. "It's mine. Tell her."

"Um…technically, it can be either?" The cashier's voice was a squeak.

"Yes, but I ordered it a week ago," Alex said. "Which makes it mine."

He tugged back and attempted to cover the images on the box. "It's not the same color you want." He couldn't put it past her that she was fibbing.

A smirk appeared on her lips as her fingers clutched the box. "I can see from here that it's the gold matte. Which is what I ordered."

"I was here first." He pulled the present back, in earnest this time, and stepped away so it was out of her reach. Then he rounded the counter, to the cashier's shock, and handed it to her. "It's my present to give, and I'm ready to pay for it." He reached in his pocket for his wallet, ignoring Alex's glare, and handed the cashier his credit card. "You snooze, you lose."

The transaction went on in utter silence, though Jordan's heart was beating double-time.

Apparently, not enough time had passed to ease the competitive streak between them. Nor had it been enough time for him to squelch the attraction rising inside him. For as much as Alex Moore pushed him to the limits of his patience, this off-the-wall interaction reminded him why he continued to fall for the woman. She was irresistible.

Chapter Three

Alex

It was official. Alex hated Jordan.

Okay, hate was a strong word. But was she pissed at him? Yes.

Jordan just had a way of getting under her skin. She noted his actions down to every smirk or sarcastic tone. For as long as she could remember, everything he did and said had mattered to her.

It was also because Carli, the employee at Joie de Vivre, had picked him over her. The woman had concluded that Jordan deserved the toaster.

It was bullshit.

With every step she took toward the chapel with Alex's present, a gift card in a measly envelope in the smallest gift bag on the planet, hanging off her pointer finger, she sent a curse into the space in front of her.

She was still smiling, of course. People were milling about, some she recognized. This was the same reason why she hadn't contested the toaster, even if she had been a second away from grabbing it from Jordan's arms and making a getaway to the Uber idling outside the shop's doors. People were always watching. The last thing she needed was someone to take video of her making a spectacle.

And to be honest, she had to get out of that store, because it had gotten more claustrophobic by the second.

Seeing Jordan after so many years, in the flesh, had flipped her already topsy-turvy day over itself.

She blew out a steady breath to ease her pounding heart as memories of the two of them cycled through her thoughts. Of them playing game after game, set after set, match after match. Of her adrenaline pumping seeing him across the net. Of that one handshake after a match that felt different and charged, and when it all snowballed to them in bed the night before graduation. Only for him to leave for Southern California two weeks later for his internship.

Jordan had been a mainstay in her life, and their…relationship…had been forged under the sun and across the net. She'd known every nuance of his movements, that a minuscule rotation in his hips meant that his swing would land the ball to her forehand, which was decidedly her weakness.

Even today, after how much they'd bantered, she'd anticipated his every comeback.

It had been why him leaving town had felt like abandonment. She hadn't seen it coming. The biggest L ever because she should have. And the reason why after that, she would never let anyone win if she could help it.

"Alex!"

The sound of her brother's voice swept Alex from her thoughts, and her heart lifted. Oliver Moore was jogging her way, wearing a gray suit.

Her body relaxed, and she smiled genuinely. "Hey, Kuya."

He enveloped her in his arms, and all the little details of her chaotic day fell away. She was back to being five and him ten and brushing the pebbles off her knees when she stumbled over her bright white K-Swiss's. For all the adventures her brother had gotten into, she knew he accepted her, faults and all.

Stepping back, he said, "Where's Kyle?"

Alex's high plummeted. "He's not coming."

He frowned. "Something happened?"

"We actually broke up."

His jaw fell open. "What the f—"

She raised a hand. "It's fine. I mean, it was months ago. It was mutual, though I thought he'd be my plus-one anyway. But then I got to Joie de Vivre and…" She started to explain, but the bells of the chapel rang, snagging their attention. "I'll explain later. Maybe when I have a glass of wine in me."

"I'm sure one of the groomsmen has a flask of something. We can sneak away."

She snorted. "As if Mom and Papa would allow that."

"They're sitting up front. They won't even notice. Without Norah here, I'm plain and boring, and they're definitely not paying attention."

"How is she, by the way?" Ollie and Norah met at Lola Naty's party last year. He'd tried to sneak into the party, and Norah, the hacienda event coordinator, had first stopped him, but then helped him. It had been attraction at first sight.

Alex had bet her cousins that the next wedding would be theirs.

"Norah's having FOMO that she can't be here, but she's where she should be. It's her son's parents' weekend at Cal Poly, and he's in the marching band. It's important."

"Of course, it is. And I like her even more for it. Well, she doesn't have to worry, because I'll keep you company. Like old times."

"You mean you'll be a pain in the ass."

"Hey! I make the best Soul Train partner, and you know it." She slipped her arm through her brother's, momentarily reveling in the moment. This day was supposed to be a celebration, and for once, she'd like to follow all the affirmations she had written on sticky notes plastered on her desk. Even though her date had ditched her, and her ex was here.

No, Jordan wasn't an ex. That had been the issue. They'd never had gotten their relationship off the ground. There was no commitment to speak of, which had been belated salt in the wound.

But anyway…she was going to live in the present. She was going to enjoy the moment. She would look outside of her own issues and be one with the joy of what this day symbolized.

And yet, curiosity nagged at her. As they headed to the chapel, she asked, "Kuya, did you know that Jordan was coming?"

"Um, we all did. We talked about it in the family group chat. Mom was pretty sad that the Francos couldn't make it. They haven't seen them since they moved up to Chico."

"Oh." Their family group chat had grown leaps and bounds, and admittedly, Alex had muted the notifications.

"Is it a problem? I know you guys had a thing, but it's been years. Anyway, he's here for a while, something about making it a two-fer and visiting the Franco rental."

Alex pressed her lips together at the very logical explanation that Jordan's appearance wasn't because he was trying to make the weekend a living hell for her.

Was she being dramatic? Maybe. But that's what Jordan did to her.

"It's not a problem," she said. "It's just that I saw him at the gift shop, and we had a…tiff."

Ollie shut his eyes and shook his head. "You didn't."

"Yeah. Couldn't help it."

"I swear, the two of you were like oil and water from the get-go. Are you going to be able to get along?"

"I mean, yeah. To clarify, though, he started it."

"Uh-huh." He rolled his eyes and wrapped an arm around her, tugging her toward the crowd.

They were funneled across the threshold of the Spanish-style chapel with the flow of people, passing round columns that exuded romance and history. Rounds of air and cheek kisses commenced among the guests. And with the sun streaming through the stained-glass windows and the organ music trilling in the background, the church meticulously decorated in red and gold, for a beat, Alex was swept up into the magic of it all.

Alex *did* love weddings. Yes, what came with it was pressure. Everyone, and she meant everyone, hounded her as to when she'd be ready to settle down. *What have you been waiting for*, they'd asked. *You're almost forty.*

My goodness, she was only thirty-five! And as if it were that easy to find a life partner. As if she hadn't been trying.

Thirty-five meant she was ready for AARP, apparently. In her parents' eyes, her ovaries were past their expiration date.

But this…love in the air, the idea of forever, the feeling of everyone coming together to support the union of a couple? Ate Vida and Kuya Rafa themselves were a testament to this notion of forever love, of love that lasted, of love that came even later in life.

Alex *did* believe in this. It was her hope too.

She'd thought…she'd thought that it would be here by now.

Speaking of her parents—they were surrounded by people. Her father, Ion, was the fourth child of Lola Naty. He and her mother, Paula, were standing near the second row of pews. Following Ollie, Alex continued their customary greetings even as Paula's eyebrows rose. With gritted teeth, her mother leaned in.

"Anak." Paula was almost desperate. "What are you wearing? That dress. We are in church."

Alex laughed, because what else was a grown woman supposed to do when her mother chastised her in public? She said, "But look, I'm wearing your favorite earrings. And did you see my new bag?" She showed off her leather envelope clutch, and then gestured to the black pearls on her earlobe.

Paula sighed. "The bag's nice. And I'm glad you wore the pearls. Next time, wear something more…comfortable, maybe?"

She gave her standard answer "Yes, Mom."

Paula looked over her shoulder. "Where's…"

"He couldn't come," Alex said, not wanting to go down a rabbit hole. "He's under the weather."

"Oh, that's too bad." Except, she said it without feeling. "Who knows, maybe you'll meet someone here."

"Mom!" It was her turn to be shocked, though she giggled nervously. Maybe Kyle had been right about the family not rooting for him after all?

"What? If that boy can't be brave enough to show up to a family function—"

"I said he was sick."

"Mm-hmm." Paula looked up at the change in music, as did everyone else. "Let's take our seats. It's time."

The vibe of the chapel turned to excitement, and Alex pushed down her thoughts of Kyle and followed Ollie to his chosen pew.

Only to find Jordan standing at its entrance, speaking to an unfamiliar man in a suit, their heads bent down. His eyes rose to hers, and against her best efforts, her body shivered.

In *that* way.

In the way that it shouldn't be shivering in a church, stemming from her thighs and her core.

She sucked in a breath, moving one foot in front of the other as she brushed past him to sit, swallowing against the sudden rise in nervousness. While Ollie leaned forward to speak to someone else, to distract herself, Alex fished the wedding program from the bookshelf and skimmed the page, not registering the words at all.

To her relief, Jordan's shadow left her periphery.

Only to have him say from behind, "You're my partner."

She startled, turning. Jordan was seated behind her with a look of exasperation. "What?" she gasped.

"The chapel coordinator needs two people to bring the offering. I guess you and I were on the list."

"I didn't know about being on a list."

"Don't shoot the messenger." He raised both hands, though he looked far from innocent. "I know better than to say no. You can handle the task, right?"

"That's a ridiculous question." Alex harrumphed, facing forward. But even as the ceremony began, what she found more difficult was knowing that Jordan was an arm's length behind her.

Chapter Four

Jordan

Good thing Jordan was sitting behind Alex, because it had rained on his face, and he'd needed a moment before the offering to get himself together. It had been Vida and Rafa's vows that had gotten to him. They'd poked at the soft parts in his heart. That and the combination of the music and seeing all the people he'd grown up with under one roof.

Ollie and Alex's family had been his next-door neighbors, but the Filipino American circles in Northern California were closely intertwined, with the Moores being a large clan with extensive reach. Jordan knew someone in every other row from UC Davis and Napa and Marin County in general, and there was comfort in that familiarity.

To be honest, he missed it up here.

To be honest, he wasn't sure why he had left for Southern California in the first place.

Scratch that—of course he knew. It was tennis. The internship at first, and then assistant coaching. It was getting into the groove of the business of pro sports.

The money too.

But was that everything? Was it ridiculous to think that at the age of thirty-five, he could change course?

Movement in the row in front of him brought him back to the present. Alex had stood, and for a beat, she arranged her dress, which had been bunched at the hips. God strike him down at this moment, because the whole rearrangement of said dress occurred in slow motion over the round curve of her ass.

Butt! He meant butt.

Sorry, God.

He averted his eyes.

By the time Jordan stood, Alex was already marching to the rear of the chapel. Typical of her to not wait for him. When he caught up to her and Mr. Low, the chapel coordinator, he was given a chalice of wine, while Alex was given the bowl of hosts.

Their instructions were simple: after the money collection, they were to head down aisle, then hand their prospective offerings to the priest, who would meet them.

To his surprise, Alex appeared hesitant. She was biting her bottom lip in concentration and staring at the bowl.

"You okay?" he asked.

Her gaze snapped up to him. "Yes. Why?"

"You look like you're about to hurl."

"I'm fine." Then she paused, as if considering. "It's just…there are a lot of hosts in here."

He peeked down at the bowl, and sure enough, round white wafers filled it to the brim, but it surely wasn't a cause for panic. A quiet laugh burst out of him. He'd rarely seen Alex vulnerable. She usually appeared one hundred percent confident. It was both admirable and disconcerting, the latter because he knew that she also faked it to make it. Even on that last day, when he'd left to move to Southern California, she hadn't shown a bit of concern about him, or about them.

Then again, one could wring only so much water from a stone. He'd learned that the hard way with her.

The line between her eyebrows deepened. "This is funny to you?"

"Yeah, because it isn't a big deal."

"Then you take the bowl, and I'll take the chalice."

"I was given the chalice."

"You owe me from the toaster."

"It was my toaster to begin with."

She stepped closer. "It was because you flirted with Carli at Joie de Vivre. You did your little grin, and now I ended up with the gift card."

"Well…being nice works sometimes," he answered distractedly. It was her lips. They were painted red, and whenever she spoke, he could only half hear the words.

"Shhh…" An auntie sitting in the back row glared at them through reading glasses perched on her nose.

He clamped his mouth shut, though Alex apparently wasn't done. She pursed her lips and all but shoved the bowl against his chest.

Dammit. "You're ridiculous," he whispered, and gave her the chalice for the bowl. "After this, we're even."

She grinned, accepting it. Then she stepped up to the starting point.

He stood next to her. "You're welcome."

"Did I say thank you? I don't think I did."

He snorted. "Oh, Alex, how I've missed you."

"Oh really?" She turned and looked up at him. "I've missed you too."

Was that sincerity in her tone? He turned to face her and found that her expression was open and not sarcastic in the least. She resembled the woman he'd woken up to the morning after they'd made love, the person who had known him his whole life.

"Do you know what I miss most?" she asked.

Could it be that they were finally calling a truce with their games, that maybe they could have a peaceful conversation like normal human beings? Enamored and confused, he said, "What?"

"That you're so gullible." Then she bolted from his side, sprint-walking down the aisle.

"What the hell," he whispered.

"You snooze, you lose."

"Mother f—" he began before he caught himself. That whole vulnerable bit? It had been a ploy. A scam so that she could beat him down the aisle.

Which, coming from anyone else, would have been idiotic. From Alex, on the other hand?

It was a strategic move in their perpetual game of chess. A game that apparently had no safe zones, to include a chapel during the biggest wedding of the year.

Jordan lengthened his steps though he trailed behind, so worried was he about dropping a host. Now *that* would have been a bigger disaster than his lost pride if he couldn't keep up.

If he couldn't beat her.

What was the prize? He hadn't had a clue, except that he had the compulsion to continuously show this woman that he was as good as her. That he could keep up. That he was worthy.

Worthy? Where the hell did that come from?

He handed over the bowl to the priest and was now shoulder to shoulder with Alex. Together, they received a blessing before they both headed back up the aisle. For a beat, he thought that the game was over, but the clack of her heels against the floor intensified, and soon they were all but racing back up the aisle.

Whispers followed, but Jordan didn't care. At the rear of the church, he peered at her and whispered, "That wasn't cool."

She gave him the side-eye. "What do you mean?"

"You'll do anything to win."

She shook her head. "Whatever. At least I've always been straightforward. Unlike you." She headed toward her pew, and it took everything Jordan had not to reach out and demand clarification.

He had a feeling that this had everything to do with them, and what could have been.

Chapter Five

Alex

Alex wasn't the type to consider what could have been, but she could certainly harbor a little grudge.

The truth was that if Jordan had told her that he had been considering leaving Northern California for LA, she wouldn't have invested so much of her time—and her emotions—in him. He'd already had her heart, seeing that she'd known him almost all her life in some capacity. The least he could have done was to give it back to her properly.

Instead, he'd waited until the day before graduation, after she'd slept with him, to tell her of his plans. They'd seen each other almost every day on campus, at practice, and he'd hadn't given an indication that he was leaving.

What was it about people simply letting her go without a look back? People had always taken her strength for granted.

Much as Kyle had earlier today. Who else got that kind of treatment?

Strong people need to be looked after too. They need protection and care and gentleness. If Kyle or Jordan or anyone could take a moment to really see her, they would know the second when her facade threatened to crack.

Hence why she wanted the least amount of contact with Jordan at the reception. Despite Ate Vida's gorgeous ceremony, which indeed had made her almost tear up—a feat in itself—she was in her feelings. Even, she, someone who was once called an ice queen, was self-aware enough to know when to go back and lick her wounds.

Seeing Jordan had uncovered the scabs in one fell swoop.

She was holding out her table card to her cousin Eden, standing by the seating chart. "Is there any way I can switch seats?"

Her eyebrows rose. "Um…that won't be possible."

She pointed out her seat on the chart, which was two away from Jordan's, then pointed at the seat of one of their other cousins, who'd arrived without a plus-one. "You can switch me for her. She won't mind."

"Don't you…want to sit next to Ollie?"

Alex's gaze trailed to the party happening behind him. The scene deserved to be in a bridal magazine, with the white tables and chairs against the vineyard background, the gorgeous setting sun behind it, complete with guests in flowing dresses and suits, wearing sunglasses, some in hats.

It was perfect.

Her gaze landed on the backside of a broad-shouldered man with windswept dark hair. His suit was well-tailored, and her eyes trailed down to the tightly fitting slacks, where her gaze lingered.

Until the man turned around.

It was Jordan.

Alex startled at her very serious mistake and smiled belatedly. "Nope. I see him all the time. I'd rather sit closer to the dance floor."

"Well, um." Eden thumbed her iPad on, frowning, zoomed in on the screen, then double-checked the cards left on the table. There were few left, probably a dozen if that. "I'm sorry. I can't switch your place with any of those folks left. Besides, Ate Vida pored over the seating arrangement. I can't switch anything outright without asking her."

"No, never mind," Alex said quickly. "I wouldn't want to bother her. I'll figure it out."

Shit. Alex harrumphed, stalling. She needed a moment before heading to her assigned table. That, and a drink. Liquid courage for this evening that was already destined for the pits. She veered toward one of the servers and plucked a glass generously filled with white wine from the tray he was holding and took a long sip.

To her relief, cousins bombarded her soon after, and she was surrounded by conversation. And while she'd had to deflect questions about Kyle and arriving alone, she began to find the groove of being among her people.

"So, you and Kyle aren't together anymore?" a voice said just behind her. She turned to, who else, but Jordan.

Great. The guy was never without a woman by his side or waiting for him, as shown by his socials. Though he never did update it himself, he was tagged often at events.

Not that she stalked him, of course. But with their slew of mutual friends, somehow, he always made it to her feed.

Okay, so she had checked up on him now and again.

"No," she said with a sigh, veering away from the group, which had gotten a little too rambunctious. "But it's fine."

"You were together what...a year?"

They'd ended up at a framed photo of Ate Vida and Kuya Rafa set up on an easel. It was from their engagement, and it was romantic and ethereal. Next to the easel was a table with an open photo book of the rest of their engagement party. "Send the couple your best relationship advice" was scrolled on a sign. Different colored pens were scattered on the tabletop.

"Almost. But he was supposed to be here anyway, as friends." She sighed. "Apparently, going to this wedding with me would have been too much."

Alex wasn't sure what compelled her to say anything at all, but the wine had loosened her tongue.

She cleared her throat and distracted herself by turning the pages of the photo book. Many were already written on with a myriad of advice including: *don't go to bed angry* and *offer each other the last piece of dessert.*

"Sounds like it's his problem and not yours." He reached around her for a pen, and though he didn't touch her, the space between them sparked, and she inwardly gasped.

He continued, completely oblivious to her traitorous body. "If he doesn't understand how the Moores are when they're together, he certainly doesn't deserve you, or any of this." He gestured to his general surroundings, and she understood that he was referring to the wedding. The family. The total Moore experience.

His words were said in such a matter-of-fact way that all Alex could do was look at him. He changed before her eyes to the kid who'd been a staple at their gatherings. How they had played freeze-dance and Scrabble and sang karaoke, betting lollipops or quarters. He had fit in so well that she hadn't noticed him, truly, until they were in college, away from the clan.

The bottom line was that Jordan *knew.* He understood the dynamics playing within the four walls of Hacienda Luz and the land the family owned. And unlike Kyle, he wasn't fazed by it. He'd enjoyed it; he liked being part of it.

To be honest, she liked that he was a part of it too.

"So…what are you going to write?" She dragged her gaze back down to the photo book.

"What are *you* going to write?" His tone was back to coy.

And just like that, the switch flipped in their conversation. Well, she could play this game. "Hm. I'll probably say something like: *don't be so cocky to jump over the net after a win, or you might find yourself face down on the ground.*" She pressed her lips together to keep herself from giggling.

He groaned at her reference to the one time he'd done just that, and while he had technically won that match, she'd considered herself the winner. "That's messed up, Alex."

She couldn't help it, she burst out into laughter. Then, she hiccupped.

Dammit.

He pointed at her with the pen, eyes flashing. "Aha!"

Placing a hand over mouth, she said, "What?" Then hiccupped once more.

"My advice would be: *don't drink on an empty stomach, else you'll find yourself being carried fireman-style through campus.*" He set a hand on the photo book and dragged it his way.

She winced at the memory, and her cheeks grew hot, because the person who had carried her was him. And that night…that night, he had been a gentleman through and through. No pranks, though the teasing was over the top. "That's not fair. That was my twenty-first birthday. It was my first-time barhopping. I can't be held accountable for those innocent moments."

"You, innocent? Right." He leaned down and began to write in the photo book.

Though said in jest, the words landed between them with more meaning. For all the grudges she felt toward Jordan, one thing was true.

He had been her first. Her first crush, her first dance at her cousin's debutante, and her first kiss, which had been accidental from a hug gone astray.

He had been her first sexual experience.

It was a thought she didn't entertain often, that among those memories of competing and jabbing at one another there were also good, nostalgic ones rolled in that had almost always left her yearning for that same feeling of attachment. She'd continued to chase it for years after Jordan.

Those words said cynically—that she wasn't innocent—made it seem as if it had been she who'd chosen for them to split up. Which was a hundred percent false.

"If there's someone to blame for anything, it's you." She set the pen down on the table.

He looked up from writing. "Alex, I never said…"

She shook her head. She couldn't hear his explanation now, so long after the fact. It was too little, too late. "It's time for a bathroom break. I'll see you at the table." With her heart thrumming, she spun on her heel and walked away.

Being around him was dredging up stuff she couldn't deal with.

No, she'd never been the kind of woman to regret what could have happened, but even now, she wished that things were different.

After all, he was her first love too.

Chapter Six

Jordan

Later, at the table, as the wedding party entered, ushered by applause and tinsel, Jordan tried to catch Alex's eyes, but she refused to look at him.

Jordan couldn't let this silent treatment go on. Alex was angry, more than he'd expected. Competitive and trite? Okay. But there had been some real hurt in what she'd said at the photo table.

If there's someone to blame for anything, it's you.

Her vibe had worn down his entire mood, and all he wanted to do now was fix it. He wanted *his* Alex back. The one who had a grin behind her snark, who pushed him to his limits, yes, but who at the heart of it enjoyed his company.

It was why her dares, her competitiveness, never bothered him. If Alex didn't care about you, if she didn't think you were good enough, she wouldn't push.

He'd been a better person with her around. He'd learned that quickly after reaching Southern California, after meeting so many people in the sport, so many women. He could tell right off the bat when they hadn't expected enough from him—and those experiences had landed like insults.

Jordan had to get Alex alone. Otherwise, the rest of this wedding was going to suck.

More, he was going to regret not fixing things if he left without trying.

The beginning of "Forevermore" was being sung, and Vida and Rafa floated to the dance floor for their first dance. Whistles and clapping followed, changing the vibe from excitement to nostalgia as Vida was swept onto the floor by the hand. Together, Vida and Rafa were a sight to be seen.

He'd grown up with this kind of example, this kind of family. His parents were wonderful. Angela Franco was an interior designer and currently ran an online design business. His dad was a retired banker. His life had been without wants because of their efforts, and being with the Moores replicated the kind of closeness he needed and wanted today.

Oh God, he was tearing up.

What the hell was wrong with him?

He blinked rapidly, turning away from the dancing so he could catch his breath. Lifting his gaze, he caught Alex pressing a napkin against the corner of her eyes.

Something inside him lit. He had felt it earlier when they signed the photo book, and when he'd seen her at the gift shop.

Like the perfect combination of a windless, cloudless day, and the hollow noise of the tennis ball hitting the strings at its sweet spot.

Signs of a win.

And he couldn't ignore it.

He leaned toward Ollie, whose face was dimly lit by the phone on his lap. He was texting. Jordan had never felt the need to explain his relationship with Alex to Ollie. When he and Alex had gotten together, it had been too close to him leaving.

It hadn't mattered anyway, considering how they had left it.

It felt different now. It felt…timely and appropriate.

"Hey, Ollie."

Startled, Ollie flipped the phone over and laughed. "Damn. You scared me. Sorry, was I being a bad guest?"

"You're fine. Everything okay?"

"Yup. Perfect, actually, except that I wished Norah was here. What's up?"

Jordan rearranged his thoughts, biting his cheek.

"Look." Ollie grinned, interrupting Jordan's thoughts. "I can see everything on your face. You're thinking really hard in there, so let me just say this. I might be her older brother, but I've never been her keeper. And I can bet that you being here is the reason Alex is all flustered, and vice versa."

Jordan's jaw hit his lap. He hadn't expected a read-out of their behavior. "That's the thing, I *don't* know what to do about this."

Later, after the formal part of the reception was over, everyone was invited to come to the floor to dance the cha-cha. People stood and shifted, and urgency rose in Jordan's chest.

Ollie nudged Jordan. "Go talk to her, figure this out. Otherwise, neither one of you is going to have a good time at this wedding. And if Alex stays in this mood, then I'm gonna suffer."

As someone brushed Jordan from behind and the lights dimmed, Ollie all but shoved him out of the chair.

He stood. His nervous, shaking hand pulled at his jacket, and he plopped down on the empty chair next to the woman who had served him both aces and heartburn. "Alex."

"That's me." She barely looked at him, though her head continued to bob to the beat.

"Do you want to…dance?"

Her gaze darted to him. An eyebrow rose. "You want to dance?"

"Yeah. I like this song."

"And…you're already listening to it."

"C'mon. For old times' sake."

Something flashed across her face, but to his relief, she stood. She didn't, however, take his hand, and instead stepped out ahead of him to a free area on the dance floor. "Do you even remember how to do the cha-cha?"

He laughed. "Um, yeah. The question is, do you? I seem to remember it was me who figured it out first."

Her face broke out into a smile, and she took the first step. He joined in, and all at once, their surroundings melted away. What was left was him and her at her debut. Those years ago, to her chagrin, he'd been chosen as part of her entourage, which required that they all learn some ballroom dancing.

As a girl, Alex had had two left feet. It had been something he'd teased her about. How could a woman so graceful on the court not know her left and right on the dance floor?

But no longer—not this woman. With the way Alex's body moved and swayed, he couldn't take his eyes off her. He could barely resist taking her into his arms, touching her.

His heart swelled as he watched her enjoy herself, lips in a wide smile, eyes gleaming. He wanted to pull her into an empty room somewhere and relive their one singular sinful night.

But reality came back as quickly as the song changed, to a slow R & B number, and their movements settled. Soon, they were standing a foot away from one another. Eyes on hers, he sensed questions hanging in the air. Should they keep dancing? Where was this going?

What was this?

While other couples left and arrived the dance floor, Jordan contemplated this day. How he'd gone from anticipating her presence, to now hoping he would never have to leave her.

Alex turned to go, but Jordan scooped her hand into his. "Keep dancing with me."

To his surprise, she didn't pull away. Her gaze lingered on their clasped hands, and she stepped toward him. He rested his hands on her hips, hoping this wasn't another one of her tricks, because he was falling for it.

He still had it bad for her.

Then, to his relief, she placed her hands against his chest.

His insides bottomed out at the familiarity. Days, weeks, years of sometimes quirky, sometime contentious friendship had passed, but at that moment, what they'd experienced in that one night of intimacy seemed within reach.

That he could steer them that direction.

That he should.

That is, if she wanted him too. Because Alex wouldn't be steered. She wasn't told. She would need to choose him, and he wouldn't want it any other way.

"Alex," he whispered down to her. "We need to talk about what happened to us."

She gazed up at him, unflinching. "There's nothing to talk about."

"Then why's there this tension between us?"

"Isn't that you and me? Oil and water."

"No." He shook his head. "This is different. This is because of how things ended."

Then he spotted it: a tell. Her lips pressed together, with her right cheek scrunched to one side. "It was good it ended. We went on with our lives. You got that internship, and now look where you are."

"And you went on and got that internship in sportscasting and look where you are."

"Right." Her gaze darted down. Then, her shoulders heaved with a sigh. "But it pissed me off, okay? You knew everything about my plans, and even if we weren't a *thing*, we were friends, right? I thought you would keep me in the loop with your plans."

Her suggestion that they hadn't been a thing, and that he'd abandoned her was an insult. "I applied for the internship at the last-minute, and I did so not thinking I would actually get it. You know that. And you were the first I told about being accepted, hours after I found out. You knew my plans before my parents. But saying that we weren't a thing... It wasn't like you gave me much to go on."

She frowned. "That's not true. I was upset."

"You didn't want to talk about us. You, as usual, shut down. You told me everything was fine. You told me we weren't going to be a couple anyway. That we were too different."

"What was I supposed to do? Tell you I wanted you to stay? We were graduating. We had our whole lives ahead of us. And it was just one night."

He dropped his arms, the blow just low enough that he felt like keeling over. But he couldn't let her see that. "Then why are you mad?"

"Because!" Her voice rose so that heads turned. "Dammit." With a brisk gesture to the side and a tug on his elbow, she led him off the dance floor and to a dark corner. She pressed her fingers against her temples. "Because I was mad. I just was. Not that I regret my life. I love my life. But seeing you at the gift shop and seeing you here made me remember…" She trailed off.

Jordan's heart thumped. His anticipation was more than a match that had gone into sudden death.

She looked up at him. "That maybe we could have had a chance. That we could have one now."

The air left his chest. "What did you say?"

"I miss you. You make me feel…alive."

Jordan had seen Alex's every expression. He had memorized them. This one, lips parted, pupils wide, meant that she was vulnerable. Honest.

That alone was everything for him. She reached halfway; *this* was what he'd wanted from her the day he left.

Resting both hands on her shoulders, he dropped his chin to his chest. "Dammit. I miss you too."

"What do we do now?"

Their foreheads touched, and in that space, they were closer than they'd been in forever.

Still, it was familiar. It was just him and her, as it had been since the moment they'd met.

In cahoots, at odds. With one another.

With a grin, he said, "We can, I don't know, come to a truce. What do you think?"

Chapter Seven

Alex

Alex's cheeks, neck, chest—her whole body—flushed at Jordan's proposition.

A truce.

The truce was as good as a declaration of commitment. It spoke to the part of her competitiveness that she valued in herself. It spoke to Jordan's personality that would always challenge and respect her.

A truce meant that their relationship could be expanded. That there was more to be explored.

But…

"It's going to be a short-lived truce, since you're leaving town soon," she joked, working through the emotions rushing through her. Because they were in the same spot as they'd been years ago. And more, because they had their lives cemented in opposite sides of the state.

But they were grown-ups now, and hopefully more mature, aside from their mini competitions today.

It had been the cha-cha that had given her the bravado to tell Jordan how she felt. The coordination they'd had, the way he'd never once looked away from her. That, and remembering who she had been so long ago, and the reminder that the two of them held so many memories together. Years of friendship, and that one glorious night.

"Who said? We can work on our truce while I'm dealing with my parents' house."

Confused, she shook her head. "What do you mean? I thought you were just checking on renters?"

"I am. They're moving out. And I'm also in a little bit of a transition. I'm...taking a break from coaching."

"Huh. I really need to keep up with the family group chat." She frowned, taking his mood in. "Is...everything okay?"

He half-laughed. "It wasn't something the program has announced yet, or something I've told anyone. If you can imagine the drama that would cause with my parents. I just need a break. I don't know. Sitting there at the church and seeing everyone I care about under one roof...it made me a little homesick. Maybe I'll end up here for good. I have a couple of job prospects in the area."

Alex's brain was still stuck on "end up here."

That this was a possibility.

"Are you...dating anyone?" she asked, her instincts taking over before her brain caught up to stop her.

A grin lifted the corner of his lips. "No, I'm not dating anyone. Are you and Kyle really over?"

"Oh, yes. To make sure that you know without a doubt how I feel..." She stepped toward him, surrendering fully to her instincts. "Because I don't want there to be any confusion between us, ever again." She pulled him down by his suit coat collar.

The press of his lips against hers was the most glorious win. It was like a crowd's applause, the triumph of a perfectly placed corner shot. It was the feeling of finally having won in a way that would matter not just today, but for the rest of her life.

When she stepped away and opened her eyes, she saw Jordan not as someone who'd once left her, but as someone who'd returned. And perhaps it had happened that way because the universe knew, just like Ate Vida and Kuya Rafa did, that the greatest fight, competition, challenge, and joy was to be saved for last.

Her face warmed at the thought, and judging by the way Jordan was looking at her, eyes bright with what she slowly realized was mischievousness, he was feeling it too.

"Something is going on in that head of yours. I can feel it," she said.

"I know I asked for a truce, but it doesn't really mean that we can't compete, does it?"

The anticipation of going head-to-head with the person she most admired caused her to stand straighter, helped by the way his hand pressed against her lower back. "I'm ready for more, if that's what you're asking."

His eyes flashed with desire. "You can't talk like that when we still have at least an hour of this wedding left."

"We can always sneak away. I'm a Moore, I definitely know the inner workings of this place."

He threw his head back with a laugh. "That's right, you *are* a Moore and I know better. Truth, though, I don't want to miss out on the rest of this. I feel like I missed out on so much already."

That was it. Her heart melted. It was mush. She threw her arms around him. Against her eyelids, she felt the start of tears.

Actual tears.

With the thought of those tears, more gathered on her lids. "God, is this really happening?"

"Alex, what's wrong?" He scooped her into his arms.

"It's just…" She began to sob ugly tears. Her makeup was surely over and done with. But she would let it go. With him, she was safe to be who she was.

She'd always been safe to do so. "I'm just glad that you love my family."

He laughed, and with that, she fell into giggles.

"It's been a day," she said between sobs and hiccups.

"Hell, it's been a year."

"It's been since undergrad."

He lifted her chin to him and pressed his lips against the tears on her cheeks. She shut her eyes at the intimacy of it, at the acknowledgment that finally, she'd found a man who was able to handle all parts of her: the feisty, the competitive, and now, the overwhelmed.

"So, are you ready?" he asked.

It brought her back to the question they'd veered from. "For what?"

He gestured to his right, to the dance floor.

Limbo.

Alex cackled.

"That there is a fighting laugh," he said.

"Oh…if you only knew."

"I'm ready if you are."

She linked her fingers in his. "I was born ready, Franco."

Chapter Eight

Jordan

You knew that things were getting dirty in the limbo when people started to take off their shoes.

The limbo stick wasn't an ordinary stick, but a tinikling bamboo log. And at the moment, it was at Jordan's upper chest level.

To his surprise, more than half the contestants were out. The alcohol combined with formal attire had rendered people helpless on the ground. Some didn't even get up, simply shimmying out of the way.

It was a Moore party, all right.

But he and Alex were still in. They were running two contestants at a time, and Jordan counted each person so that he and Alex would be taking their same turn.

When she spotted him, she nodded with a classic *game on* expression. So, he pointed at his eyes with his pointer and middle fingers, then turned them around on her. As in, *I'm watching you.*

He expected another comeback. In fact, he was anticipating it. Much like the kiss earlier, and their previous banter…this was simply part of them.

Foreplay, now that he thought about it.

His body heated at the thought. He'd already loosened his tie, so he shrugged off his jacket.

Eyes widening, she reached up and started to take off her earrings.

His imagination took flight, thinking of what else she could remove, because she didn't have much on, except what she had said was her secret weapon. Her shapewear. She had said that she wasn't afraid to contort herself to win the limbo.

He took off his tie with a flourish, and the people around him egged him on. Apparently, the ballroom had been divided down the middle in loyalty, and now, they looked to Alex for her response.

He gestured at her. "Your turn."

With a poker face, Alex sauntered over to him, looked him up and down, and gave him a kiss.

The ballroom exploded in conversation. People gasped.

So did he.

The Moores ran with news like Olympic sprinters. Jordan had assumed he and Alex would be keeping their newfound relationship a secret. He'd been happy, even ecstatic, that they'd decided to give it all a try.

This must have meant that she was serious. That the thing that was between them wasn't imagined.

If he was dreaming, he didn't want to wake up.

That is, until the bamboo stick was lowered to the level of the upper abdomen of the holders.

"Are you ready now?" she whispered.

"One hundred percent."

They both took their spots, and with the beat of the music, she wiggled, bending backward. In concert, he shimmied under the bamboo.

So far so good. He felt strong.

Halfway under, he glanced over to see that Alex was in the same position. Around them, people chanted, with half the crowd saying "Alex," the other "Jordan."

Alex turned her face to him, her smile so pure and so big, joy overtook him. Like their reunion kiss, it felt like the precursor to more. To forever.

He reached out with a hand, a moment of trust on his end. Joined, one could take down the other. Or one could help the other.

Alex clasped his hand tightly, and as she hopped under the bamboo, she tugged him along.

Or was it the other way around?

Straightening, and to the cheering of the crowd, Jordan brought Alex to his arms and wrapped her into him.

She laughed into his chest, loosening all his hesitation.

Things like this, like falling back in love, usually didn't happen to Jordan Franco, but he sure was glad it did.

THE END

About Tif Marcelo

Tif Marcelo is a veteran US Army nurse and holds a BS in Nursing and a Master's in public administration. She believes and writes about the strength of families, the endurance of friendship, heartfelt romances, and is inspired daily by her own military hero husband and four children. She hosts The Stories to Love Podcast and is the *USA Today* bestselling author of books for adults and young adults.

Book List:

https://tifmarcelo.com/books/

Social Media IDs:

Instagram: @tifmarcelo

TikTok: @tifmarcelo

Facebook: @tifmarcelo

Website: http://tifmarcelo.com

Now That I Have You

MAIDA MALBY

Now That I Have You

MAIDA MALBY

Blurb:

One year after they met, Vida and Rafa are engaged. Soon, plans for a grand Filipino-Cuban American wedding in the fall are underway. As the countdown winds down, things go smoothly ... maybe too smoothly. Will their special day go off without a hitch, or will disaster strike before they can promise to love now and forevermore?

Content Notes: Profanity; Not so strict adherence to some Catholic canon laws

Tropes and Sub genres: Age gap, Later-in-life Love; Multicultural Romance

Heat Level: 🔥 🔥 🔥 (open door intimacies, euphemistic description)

The Proposal

Vida

First Friday of January

Flames danced merrily in the center of the patio fire pit, their brightness making up for the clouds covering the full moon high above. The fire's cozy warmth was much welcomed on this rainy January night in the wine valley. Vida returned to the cushioned seat of the sofa closest to the stone table, sighing dreamily as she draped her cashmere shawl around her shoulders.

"One year," she whispered to herself, marvel in her voice. Tonight, she and Rafa had celebrated their first anniversary with a lovely dinner prepared by two of Napa's young, talented chefs—her cousin Ruby and her cousin's boyfriend, Mason Waller—in Hacienda Luz's tasting room.

Vida and Rafa had split tasks after dinner. He saw to clearing up their table while she came outside to light the fire. The night was still young, and they had the place to themselves. An unusual occurrence on a Friday night that they'd decided to take advantage of.

She grinned at the memory of their first meeting that rainy afternoon. Like now, the grapevines still slept, the mustard blooms that would blanket the Hacienda Luz vineyard grounds in gold all spring had started to sprout, and a steady drizzle cooled the air in the glass-enclosed veranda of their welcome center. As it was now, the flip of

507

the calendar had brought forth promises of exciting changes and new possibilities.

Rafa was both of those things and more. An exciting possibility Vida had never expected but had always hoped for. He'd stood in the middle of the reception area in all his six-foot-two-inch, brown-haired and brown-eyed deliciousness, staring at her with a laser-sharp focus no one had ever directed at her before. She'd been flattered, but more than that, she'd been compelled to go to him, to claim him before the vineyard's younger, more beautiful estate manager could catch his attention.

Warmth rose to Vida's cheeks when she remembered how brazen she'd been. She'd asked if he was interested in an exclusive tour of the property, the property being herself. "In a private tasting," she uttered aloud now like she had then. *Of my body*, was left unsaid. He'd taken her up on her offer again and again. And offered himself in return repeatedly.

One year later, he was a reality she vowed to claim as her own for as long as possible. *Forevermore*. Like the title of one of the Filipino songs on constant play at her Lola Naty's house. Never would she deny his importance in her life like she had the year before. If she had but one new year's resolution, that would be it.

Before Rafa, none of her romantic relationships in the past three decades had lasted longer than six months. After the initial flush of passion had cooled down, at the first sign of adversity or waning interest, they'd called it quits. Some of those breakups had been initiated by her—abandonment issues had fed her insecurities. *Leave them before they leave me*. That had been her mantra.

Until Rafa.

He was the only one she'd felt strongly enough about to keep past the six-month mark. The only man who made her feel desired despite the changes in her body that turning fifty wrought. Even after she'd hurt him by hiding their relationship from her family, he'd never threatened to leave. Rafa had staying power. He was hers. She was his.

Vida leaned her head against the back of the sofa, gazing up at the night sky that was starting to turn reddish as the rain dissipated. Those without romance in their heart would call it light pollution, but she preferred the gentler term, sky glow.

The glass door behind her slid open. Without turning around, she said in a teasing voice, "You didn't have to pre-wash the dirty dishes, you know. The staff will ..." Her voice trailed off when Rafa came into view. She sat up and gaped at the bottle in the ice-filled bucket he carried.

Her boyfriend read the label of the sparkling wine. "La Bella Vida, the beautiful life." He placed it on the round table beside the sofa before sitting down and hugging her close.

It was her first award-winning wine, their most expensive product at the winery. La Bella Vida combined Chardonnay and Pinot Noir grape varieties, the traditional components of champagne. What made this particular sparkling wine highly prized was the inclusion of Pinot Meunier. Hacienda Luz, situated in the cooler region of Napa Valley, was one of only a handful of vineyards outside of Champagne in France that produced the ancient white-wine grape variety.

It was the perfect choice for any celebration, and tonight was certainly that. Vida was surprised because this bottle, with its gold sticker, was vintage. It came from the batch that had won her the prestigious Winemaker of The Year award eight years ago. There were only two cases left—twenty-two bottles after the birth of her cousin Ron's daughter, Kali, and Lola Naty's one-hundredth birthday on Christmas Eve, two weeks ago. Twenty-one bottles now.

"Your grandmother gave me one after I told her about our date tonight," Rafa said against her hair in answer to her unasked question.

Vida shifted to face him. "Wow! Lola is miserly with those bottles. She didn't even give me one for my fiftieth birthday. We just shared hers, remember?" To be fair, her grandmother only had a couple of sips. She and Rafa and her nephew Carlo had finished the rest of it on Christmas Day. "She really loves you."

There was no question about it. Rafa was Lola's favorite physician and an adopted grandson the second they met a year ago—one of the reasons Vida had hidden her relationship with him. She hadn't wanted to sever that precious bond if they broke up.

"And I love her too. But Vee, that isn't why she gave me La Bella Vida." His handsome face soft and earnest, Rafa reached for her hands. "It's because I told her about my plan."

Vida laced her fingers with his. Her heart pounded. Moisture gathered beneath her eyelids.

"I spent half my life searching for something that was missing. I was constantly surrounded by people, but I was still lonely. And then I met you. Fell in love with you right here that very first day." Rafa lifted their joined hands to his lips and pressed a kiss to her knuckles.

Vida smiled through the tears that now flowed down her face. Joy burst through her at his words.

"This past year has been the happiest of my life," he continued. "And now that I know how it feels to have you in my home, I will never be content if you're not there for always." He unclasped his right hand from hers and took a square box from his coat pocket. Flipping the lid, he presented a diamond solitaire ring to her. "Mi Vida, will you make my life beautiful by sharing it with me forever? Will you marry me?"

Vida's breath caught, her emotions overwhelming her for a moment. She'd almost given up on getting married. Had resigned herself to singlehood for the rest of her life. Here, now, was her most cherished dream coming true.

Rafa's grip on her right hand tightened. Who was trembling? Him or her? His eyes were bright, almost beseeching. Did he doubt what her answer would be?

"Yes!" she sobbed. She pressed her lips to his and sealed her acceptance with a kiss.

Only after they were out of breath did they separate. Vida looked down at the ring. The spectacular oval-cut gem glittered at her from its cream velvet bed. Rafa plucked it out of the box and slid it on the ring finger of her left hand.

"Oh, Raf. It's perfect. I can't wait to show it to Lola." She blinked. "Or has she already seen it?"

"Not yet," Rafa assured her. "She only knows I'm proposing tonight."

Vida smiled at her fiancé. *Fiancé!* That sounded so right. "You know she'll want to be involved in planning our wedding, right?"

"Of course," he said, seemingly unconcerned. He popped the cork of the sparkling wine, poured the bubbly liquid into the chilled flutes, and handed her one.

She cuddled close to Rafa's side. "To always," she cheered, clinking her glass to his.

"And forever," he echoed.

Amen.

The Engagement

Rafa

Eight Days Later

Rafa walked up the path leading to Bahay ni Lola, Naty Moore's bungalow at the far end of Hacienda Luz's hotel grounds, counting the cars lined up in the driveway as he passed—an even dozen. Except for Christmas, he'd never seen so many here. Peals of laughter rang out from behind the front door, stopping him in the entryway before he could ring the bell. It sounded like a crowd was in there.

The door was flung open from the inside, making the parol—the Filipino Christmas lantern—that still hung from it fly and slap against the wood. He took a step back. Vida rushed out in her bare feet, a slightly dazed expression on her face. She grabbed his arm and bit out, "Raf! Everyone's here!"

He patted her shoulder to calm her and himself as well. Her sudden dash outside had unnerved him for a second. "What do you mean everyone?"

"All of the Moores who live in Northern California are here. My aunts and uncles, cousins, and nephews and nieces."

All? That was quite a number if he recalled correctly. "How many people are we talking about? A dozen? Twenty?" That many people chose to give up their Saturday afternoon to be here? Wow.

"Something like that. They all want to be a part of your pamamanhikan."

In Rafa's research on Filipino wedding traditions, he'd come across the custom of formally gaining the approval of the bride-to-be's parents to marry their daughter. It was like the Cuban la pedida de mano, the asking of the hand that his brother had told him to do. Rafa was supposed to come with his own parents to iron out the wedding details, but since they passed away a while ago, he was here on his own.

With Vida's parents also gone, he'd thought he was only meeting with her grandmother, whose approval he'd already gained before he proposed last week. He wasn't surprised that some of the elder Moores wanted to get involved, but not twenty.

"That's a good thing, right?" A sudden doubt assailed him. "Is anybody opposed to you marrying me?"

"No! They all love you. Everyone's happy that I'm finally getting married. I just … I can't believe so many of them care."

Rafa smiled fondly at his fiancée. Her humility never failed to astound him. She really didn't realize how loved and cherished she was. "I can. You're kind of a big deal, you know." He kissed Vida's forehead and said, "Your feet must be getting cold out here. Let's go."

They entered the house to a chorus of hellos. Rafa hung his coat in the hall closet and toed his shoes off to the side of the door where several pairs were scattered. He made a beeline for the grand matriarch of the Napa Valley Moores, who sat in a throne-like rocking chair in the living room. He gave her a peck on the baby powder-scented cheek. "You couldn't have given your doctor a heads-up?"

Naty Moore barked a laugh. "You'll be fine. Grab something to eat and we can start planning your nuptials."

She patted his arm. "Rafael, I'm happy I lived long enough to see my Vida get married. Thank you for taking good care of me."

She'd said the same thing to him last week. "I don't deserve half of the credit you attribute to me. You're easily my best patient." Except for the sling he'd put her in after she fell while practicing a dance number, he only kept her on maintenance medicines.

"Flatterer," she said, preening. "Go get some food. There's plenty."

On the way to the kitchen, he exchanged handshakes and hugs with Vida's cousins and nephews and nieces, all of whom he'd met at Naty Moore's one-hundredth birthday party on Christmas Eve.

His fiancée wasn't exaggerating—nearly everyone within two hours' drive of Hacienda Luz was here. Ruby was in the kitchen cooking something intensely aromatic, assisted by her nephew Carlo, Naty Moore's main caregiver now that Vida had moved in with Rafa. Eden and Sophie were talking, along with their respective boyfriends, Nick and Travis. Even the prodigal Ollie was present with his younger sister, Alex. His girlfriend, Norah, was likely at the main hotel where she worked as events supervisor.

Ron and Drew sidled up to Rafa at the large island where a veritable feast of Filipino cuisine was spread out— three kinds of lumpia, four variants of pancit, a mountain of pork barbecue on sticks, white rice, and fried rice, and many other viands he couldn't name but was sure were incredibly delicious.

"Doctor Bal, congrats." Andrew Moore Hizon, the US Senator from California, greeted him with a hearty backslap.

Ron Moore Palacio's handshake was as effusive. "Good luck, Doc."

Rafa frowned at the younger men. "Am I going to need it?"

"Not with Ate Vida. She's the best. I'm talking about the aunties, especially my mom." Ron inclined his head towards the living room where Nancy Hizon and Elizabeth Palacio flanked Vida on the couch with folders in front of them.

Probably sensing his confusion, Ron explained. "Aditi and I frustrated her wedding planning aspirations by getting married in the Bahamas five years ago. Yours will be the first grand wedding in the Moore family here at Hacienda Luz since my parents got married in the late eighties."

"And Gel and I are not ready yet," Drew chimed in. "My mom will get to practice on you and Ate Vida first."

"We'll expect invites to the bachelor party, Doc," Ron said. Drew echoed his agreement before they both left him to contemplate his choices.

Jesus. Rafa grabbed a bottle of beer from a cooler and chugged nearly half of it. He wiped his sweating forehead with the sleeve of his shirt. What the hell had he gotten himself into?

Whatever it was, it didn't turn him off the feast on the table. He piled a plate with as much as it could hold to fortify him for what was to come in this impromptu wedding planning party.

"Raf." He looked up when Vida called out.

He grabbed his plate and beer and walked to where his fiancée now sat alone, her aunts having left her side to sit near their mother. Putting Vida and him in the hot seat, he guessed. Eden and Nick took their places across from them.

An event planner and a former Catholic priest. Made sense they would get involved.

"Rafa, you and Vida have made the entire family happy with your engagement," Nancy began.

"You both waited to enter into a lifelong commitment, and now that you're together, you deserve to have the grandest celebration," Elizabeth continued.

And there it was. Vida's cousins *had* warned him this was coming.

"We know you're both capable of paying for the entire wedding, but will you allow us to contribute?" Nancy asked.

Vida nudged him with her shoulder. How *grand* was grand? Tens of thousands of dollars? A hundred thousand? "Of course. Thank you." What else could he say? He was financially secure and could support Vida and himself, but he wasn't rich. Not Moore-rich rich. If someone brought up the topic of a prenuptial agreement, he wouldn't hesitate to sign. No one could accuse him of being a fortune hunter. Wealth didn't interest him in the least.

"Before we go into details, when is the wedding?" someone chimed in from behind him.

Rafa noticed that everyone had moved closer to the living area. Some had pulled out the chairs from the dining table, others were leaning against the walls or sitting on the rug-covered hardwood floor.

"The weekend of the harvest," Lola Naty said.

"Ooh!"

"Aww."

"Of course."

"That's perfect."

Rafa looked around in bemusement. Harvest? In the fall? He glanced at Vida. She had a hand on her chest, misty-eyed. Turning to him, she explained. "A long time ago, Grandda Robert declared that the day of the harvest at the hacienda would be the second Monday of October. We've observed that every year since."

He vaguely remembered Lola Naty mentioning a crushing-of-the-grapes type of activity last year, but he hadn't participated because Vida was still hiding their relationship from her family at the time.

As if sensing where his thoughts had gone, Vida laced their fingers together and raised their joined hands to her lips. "I'm sorry," she whispered for his ears alone.

He pressed his lips to her temple and murmured, "No apologies necessary. I understand."

She smiled sweetly and leaned her head on his shoulder.

"The second Monday of October is the ninth. Saturday the seventh, then," Eden said as she jotted it down on her tablet. "Before sunset would be gorgeous. Let's say five, five-thirty for the ceremony and seven for the reception? Ten to fifteen minutes in between for photo ops."

Nine months from now? If he had a choice, he'd marry Vida next week. But that wasn't going to happen now. He munched on his food in silence, eating left-handed as he kept the connection with his fiancée with his right hand.

"Rafa, Vida said you're a Roman Catholic," Nancy said.

He nodded and swallowed. "I was baptized and confirmed, yes." He couldn't claim to be devout, but he'd attended mass several times; more often in the past year with Vida than any other time in the thirty-nine years before that, except when he was attending catechism.

"You'll have to do Pre-Cana, the pre-marriage program. That's at least six months before the wedding. Nick, what do we need to do to have the ceremony at the hacienda chapel?" Elizabeth asked.

"You'll need the bishop to approve. It would be tricky because Catholic couples are supposed to get married at the parish church. St. Joseph is only seven miles away," Nick replied.

"The bishop was at Lola's centennial party," Alex piped up.

"We can't use her delicate health as an excuse for staying close to home, then," Carlo added. "He saw her perform a dance number."

Laughter ensued, Rafa included. He'd stationed himself on the side of the stage that night. Ready to jump if Naty Moore showed any sign of frailty. She hadn't, to his and Vida's relief.

"His mother was from the Philippines. We'll use the Filipino card, if necessary," Elizabeth said after the hilarity died down. "Let's talk about the entourage. Rafa, will your family be able to make it?"

"It's only my older brother, Roger, his wife, Mika, and their two kids. I'm sure they'll take the time." They had relatives in Cuba, but their relationship wasn't close enough to warrant an expensive trip to the US.

"Will he be your best man?" Eden asked.

"No. I will ask Pascal, a fellow Air Force doctor. He also lives in this area," Rafa replied, naming his best friend.

"Vids, who will be your maid of honor? I'm guessing Tallie?" Nancy asked.

He recognized the name as Vida's cousin and best friend, so her confirmation was expected.

"She's my first choice. If she's willing to come back to Napa. She's been gone for three years. I'll call her tomorrow."

"Think of who will be your veil, cord, and unity candle sponsors," Eden reminded them. "What's our color scheme?"

"Gold and deep red," Vida said promptly.

"You mean champagne and burgundy," her niece said, a teasing note in her voice. A running joke in the family, it seemed.

"We can't call them those terms unless we're in France," Vida asserted.

"Pshaw. That's only for wines, not colors. What about flowers?"

"Roses and peonies. And sampaguita if they can source it out here in California," Vida said.

"My friend Violet is an amazing florist. If anyone can find sampaguita, it's her," Ruby chimed in from her bar seat in front of the kitchen island. "Mason and I will cook, of course."

Rafa's head spun with all the details being discussed. He flinched when they talked about accommodating two hundred guests at the outdoor venue. Two hundred! A dozen people he could name if asked whom to invite. Perhaps twenty from his private practice and whoever he knew from nearby Travis Air Force Base. They weren't expecting him to provide one hundred names, were they?

This wasn't the wedding he had in mind. His ideal celebration was simple, no fuss. But one look at Vida's glowing face and hearing her quick answers to every question told him the grand celebration the Moores were planning was exactly the wedding of her dreams. The one she'd been envisioning since she was old enough to imagine herself as a bride.

With his thumb, he traced the gold band of the engagement ring he'd placed on her finger over a week ago. There was no way he would deny Vida her dream.

A gentle tap on his side startled him. He raised his head to meet his fiancée's gaze.

"You're not saying much," she said in a low voice. "Are you okay with all of this? I didn't think we would tackle so many details of the wedding this early."

She was sweet, his bride. He kissed her cheek. "I'm perfectly okay with everything that will make you happy to be marrying me."

The becoming flush on her face and the light in her eyes told him his response pleased her. "I love you," she whispered.

"I love you right back."

~*~*~*~

The Planning

Vida

Four Months Before the Wedding

Vida gave a little wiggle from her perch on the couch as she checked off items from the wedding countdown checklist in the hardbound planner she kept at home. At Rafa's home in American Canyon, ten miles away from Hacienda Luz. Her home since Christmas Day last year. "Formal wedding invites sent. Woohoo!"

This afternoon, four months before the wedding, she, her niece Eden, and Eden's assistant, Pinky, had mailed one hundred invitations to friends, relatives, and business contacts all over the US, Canada, and the Philippines. Accounting for plus-ones, entire families, and a few gatecrashers, they could easily have over two hundred guests. Often, Filipinos would not RSVP but still show up.

Rafa handed her a glass of her favorite red blend from the hacienda. "Did you invite your Aquino relatives?"

Vida smiled her thanks and accepted the wine, eyeing his fine form in gray slacks and blue polo shirt that lightened his brown eyes. Her fiancé. Five months since his proposal, and calling him that still gave her a thrill.

"Yes. From Texas and So Cal. As well as the Sorianos, my grand-uncle Danilo's descendants, and the Moore-Sutcliffe-Frasers, my grand-aunt Sylvia's family." She took a gulp before realizing that she hadn't eaten since breakfast.

Ugh. The wine soured in her stomach. Okay, no more of that until after dinner. She leaned forward to set the glass down on the coffee table.

He sat beside her. "Your rival winemakers?"

"Yes, especially those with Filipino connections, like Ava Maldonado and the Russos. Although I wouldn't call Ava a rival. I mentored her when she and her father were just starting out ten years ago." She pushed aside her planner, feeling a pang of guilt at the uneven composition of invitees. "Are you sure you only want to invite twenty?"

"That's the extent of my contact list. It's hard to keep track of people in the military once you're no longer in the same wing. Even more so when you've retired like I have and gone private. I no longer have access to the global address list, unlike those who became civilian employees or government contractors."

Rafa sounded pragmatic, but Vida heard the sadness in his voice. She cuddled close to him. How lucky was she to have him as a groom? He was all in for this wedding. Not only had he gone along with everything her family had planned, but he'd also insisted on paying for things that were normally the responsibility of the bride's family.

Vida's brows knotted. She hoped he wasn't overextending his finances. She looked down at her engagement ring. Her exquisite two-carat oval-cut diamond ring that had cost the same as a brand-new car. She ran her thumb around the thin gold band.

Rafa shouldn't have to spend any more on this wedding. She would take care of everything from now on. It wouldn't even leave a dent in her bank account. Her parents' life insurance proceeds, the generous trust fund from her grandfather, plus her salary and investments from thirty years of working had made her a millionaire many times over.

"What else did you check off?" he asked, breaking into her thoughts.

"I emailed our measurements for my terno and your barong and slacks to my niece Bernadette, Carlo's twin sister, who's a dressmaker in San Antonio. I hadn't realized how many relatives I have in Texas until now. Anyway, she said she'll send me a scrap of material from my gown so I can match my shoes to it."

"Give it to me when it arrives. I'll hand it over to the shoemaker who made your boots. He already has your information and your requirements for a customized insert."

She squeezed his arm in gratitude. Nobody took care of her like he did. His attention to her scoliosis was unmatched. "I've started doing the missalette and reception program. Are there any Cuban wedding traditions you'd like me to include?"

"I think you already have them as Filipino customs. The arras, lazo, and unity candle ceremonies during the mass and the Money Dance at the reception are the same in Cuban culture."

"Aah, yes. From our shared Spanish colonizers." She grinned at him.

"Cheeky. How about your Irish heritage? Will you incorporate anything from your Grandda Robert's ancestry?"

"Of course!" She opened the planner and read from a list. "The bouquet will have a horseshoe charm tied to it, my veil and garter and some of the appliqués on my gown will be made of Irish lace. We'll have a wishing ring in the gazebo where we will take our photos with guests, Irish beers and whiskey will be available at the bar, and my something blue will be a Miraculous Medal of the Blessed Virgin Mary that Bernadette will sew onto my dress when she brings it a week before the wedding."

Her recitation ended with her stomach rumbling.

She started to laugh, but Rafa's frown wiped the mirth off her lips.

"When was the last time you ate a full meal?"

Uh-oh. That was his doctor's voice. Stern-daddy-ish. "Uhm, seven."

Rafa's jaw dropped. "Eleven hours ago? Vida." He hopped out of his seat and tugged her to her feet. "Come on, I'll make us dinner."

She set the plates and cutlery on the island while he grabbed eggs, milk, cheese, butter, and diced pancetta from the fridge for an omelet.

"I didn't mean to forget, but I had to host several tasting tours today because one of my estate ambassadors—Jen, you remember her—had stomach flu." She got up and filled two glasses with water from the dispenser.

Returning to her seat, she continued. "Afterwards, I had a consultation with the Banquet Manager, Gabriella, and Cole, our new Executive Chef. Thanks for recruiting him, by the way." The young former airman and Vida's latest protégée had an obvious but suppressed chemistry. Her matchmaking radar had pinged the entire time she spent with them.

Rafa grunted an acknowledgment and continued cooking while she recounted her busy day.

"And then I had to meet Eden and Pinky for our monthly update. We've accomplished so much in five months, but there are still a million things to do." She drank some water to appease her empty stomach.

Rafa set a plate in front of her and kissed her on the forehead. "I hope losing weight is not one of them. You're perfect the way you are."

She tugged him back to her and rested her head on his chest. *He* was the perfect one. "Thank you."

"You're welcome." He prepared his own plate and sat beside her. "I feel like I'm not doing enough. What can I help you with?"

"Well, we still have to create a playlist. If you leave it up to me, we'll have nothing but eighties and nineties music."

"I have no problem with that. It's the best kind."

"Agree. I will include some Filipino songs, so maybe you can add some Latin flare?"

"I can do that." He pointed a fork at her. "Eat. We'll complete the playlist later."

Back on the couch, Vida read the titles of Rafa's suggestions and laughed. "'Entra En Mi Vida,' 'Vivir Mi Vida,' 'El Amor De Mi Vida,' 'Esto Es Vida' … I'm sensing a theme here." She nudged him with her foot when he sat at the other end. He truly was the most romantic man she knew.

Rafa lifted her feet to his lap and proceeded to massage her instep. "Is it the same theme as 'So It's You,' 'Now That I Have You,' 'Till I Met You,' 'Each Day With You'?" He tickled the bottoms of her feet.

She broke out in giggles, folding her legs up to evade his fingers.

Rafa's hands gentled, became a caress. A gasp escaped her throat. Heat accompanied the path of his hands up her legs to the outside of her thighs under the skirt of her flowy sundress. He rose to his knees on top of her. She widened her legs to give him space in between.

"You know what else we haven't finalized yet?" he whispered against her neck. The evening stubble on his chin sent electric tingles everywhere it touched.

She turned her head to give him better access. "Our honeymoon?" she asked, her voice breathy.

His lips wandered to her collarbone. "What do you think about Boracay?"

Her nipples beaded under her bra, and she arched her back to rub the aching points against his broad chest. "White sand beaches." Not enough. She tugged his shirt up and over his head. Must feel skin to skin. "Glorious sunsets." Her stretchy bodice came down next, baring her small breasts for a nanosecond before she plastered her torso against his. "Sweet mangoes …" She trailed off and just breathed him in. Forest. Sunshine. Man. He smelled divine.

Rafa slid down her body, taking her dress and underthings with him. "There's this resort called Perlas that has it all," he said as he shucked off his pants and boxers.

As far as Vida was concerned, *he* had it all. Brains, beauty, and body. Right now, that body was what she coveted most in the world. She hooked her legs around his hips to bring him back over her. To take him inside her.

Hands braced on either side of her head, her fiancé paused. The tease. She could feel his hardness nudging her entrance. "Vee, should I book it?"

Liquid heat pooled between her legs. She was ready. She'd been ready since the first caress. "Yes!"

He surged into her in one stroke. "Yes?"

Too slow. She needed him to go faster. Harder. "Please, Raf."

He responded with rhythmic thrusts. Each stroke seemingly designed to torture her. "When?"

Not enough. She canted her hips, and on his down stroke, slammed upwards. "Now!"

"Now," he growled, finally losing control.

The Marriage Contract

Rafa

Nine Days Before the Wedding

Rafa quickly affixed his signature above his printed name on the last page of the document and pushed it towards Bert Hizon, the husband of Vida's aunt Nancy, and Rafa's new lawyer. Lifting his coffee mug to his lips, he glanced at the Moonlight Diner's entrance to check for any sign of his often-early fiancée. The corner he'd chosen for their meeting was sectioned off from the rest of the diner for privacy. She might not be able to see him behind the hedge of artificial flowers.

Bert inserted the paperwork into his leather briefcase. "You're a good man, Rafael. My niece has chosen well for a life partner. But you know Vida is going to be very unhappy that you're insisting on signing a prenuptial agreement." He nodded to the other document in front of Rafa. "She trusts you implicitly."

Her uncle had told him that Vida had waved off his suggestion of having Rafa sign one as early as January. "I know that, and I won't ever break that trust. But I don't have any claim to your family's fortune, and should something happen to Vida or me, I want it to go to where it belongs. Back to the Moores."

"It's not mine, either. Who do you think came up with the template to protect the Moore daughters' inheritance?"

"I knew you'd understand; that's why I chose you to retain."

"That contract cannot be fully executed until Vida signs it too. It's a good idea to get another lawyer to go through it with her. It shouldn't be a problem with the family. There's a whole branch of the Moores that's just lawyers."

Rafa knew. The WASPy-sounding Sutcliffe-Frasers. "I'm meeting Vida here at two." In ten minutes. "We're scheduled to get our marriage license this afternoon at three. I'll talk to her about it."

"I'd better go, then. My niece is always prompt. Thanks for the coffee. Unless you and Vida want to meet sooner, I'll see you at the golf course for your bachelor party next Friday."

They both stood and shook hands.

"Tito Bert?" Right on cue, Vida arrived to prove her reputation for promptness true.

Despite his trepidation, Rafa had to smile at the sight of his beautiful fiancée. Fall colors suited her well. Her long russet maxi dress brought out the warm glow in her golden-brown skin.

"Vida. It's great to see you."

Rafa signaled the server to bring Vida's food that he'd ordered earlier while the two hugged.

"The girls are so excited for your wedding," Bert was saying. "Thanks for including them in your entourage and reception program. Laceley has been practicing 'Forevermore' every day since you asked her to sing for your first dance; I already know the words by heart."

"Of course, Tito. Lace is the best singer in the family." Pride and fondness were evident in Vida's voice.

"She took after me. Don't tell your Tita Nancy I said that."

They laughed. "I won't," Vida reassured her uncle.

Bert tapped his leather bag. "Gotta go. I have things to file at the Treasurer's office."

"Oh, okay. See you at the wedding."

"Or sooner."

Bert raised a hand in farewell to Rafa. He nodded in response.

"Or sooner?" Vida gave him a peck on the lips absently before taking the seat he held out for her beside his.

"Thank you," she said to the server who brought her a plate of Caesar salad with grilled chicken slices and a glass of iced café mocha.

"Since when did you start working with Tito Bert?" she asked when they were alone again and Rafa was seated. "Wait." She grabbed his arm, face paling. "Is he your patient? Is something wrong with him?"

He patted her hand. "No. I'm his client. He drew up my last will and testament and health directive."

She relaxed and took a sip of her drink. "I should update mine."

He was so shitty for presenting the prenup in a public place knowing Vida would not create a scene. But this was important to him. She'd been avoiding any conversation about finances for months. It had to be done soon. Giving her nine days' notice before the wedding was cutting it much too close. What would he do if she refused to sign? What if she called off everything? He wouldn't know unless he went on with it.

Rafa cleared his tightening throat. "You should. And add this to your files." He pulled out the sheaf of papers from the manila envelope and handed it to her.

Vida glanced at the cover page and stiffened. Her face lost its glow as she flipped through the first couple of pages. She pushed her untouched food to the side and leaned back in her chair, arms wrapped around her middle.

God! He was such a tool. She looked hurt. Physically.

"A prenuptial agreement? We're not even married yet and you're already thinking of … divorce? Of leaving me?"

The catch in her voice devastated him. He scooted his chair closer and leaned forward to look her in the eyes and impress his sincerity upon her.

"Vee, divorce is the last thing on my mind. The fact that I will never agree to one is the main reason we need to do this. You'll be stuck with me for life. I'm not leaving until I die. The only thing I want from this marriage is you. Not your wealth."

Her eyes filled with tears. "The language in that document is so harsh." She reached out and flipped a page. "'In the event the marriage fails,'" she read aloud. "Why do you even want to put it out there?"

Rafa caught the tears on her cheeks with his fingers. His own eyes burned. "I'm sorry, Vee. I'm not doing this to cause you pain." He ran his tear-dampened hands down her arms. "It's my damnable pride. I am ten years younger than you. With so much less than what you own before our marriage. I just … I don't want to be called a fortune hunter. That's what's motivating me to put this in place."

Vida shook her head vehemently. "I don't think that of you. No one in my family thinks that of you."

"If it were only our families to consider, it would be different. But it's not. We live in a world where every little thing is scrutinized by people we couldn't give two shits about. We both own businesses that depend on customers patronizing our goods and services. Any smear on our reputation could mean losses, not just to us, but to our employees. Vee, this agreement protects them, too."

A series of beeps emanated from his phone. It was the first of two reminders. They had thirty minutes before they had to leave for their appointment. He silenced it quickly and looked at his fiancée, who was patting her cheeks dry with a tissue.

He tucked a strand of hair behind her ear and cupped her shoulder. "Vee, please eat something. I don't know how long we have to wait for our license. We might be there for hours."

She nodded and started to eat her salad. After a few bites, she pulled the document closer to her.

Hope leaped in his chest. She was reading the agreement. Her expression was softening, lightening, was no longer pinched and tense. Once she reached the last page, she traced a finger on the line where her signature was supposed to go and quietly pushed the agreement back towards him.

She still hadn't spoken when his phone beeped its reminder again. He silenced the alarm and dropped a couple of twenties on the table, scooping up the papers as he stood. "We have to go."

Vida was already on her feet with her purse slung over her shoulder.

He held out his hand, an unspoken question in the gesture. *Are we good?*

She took it and squeezed lightly. *We're okay.*

The walk to the Napa County building on 1st Street only took five minutes. They were ten minutes early for their appointment with the clerk handling marriage licenses and civil wedding ceremonies, so he and Vida sat on the hard plastic chairs placed against the wall to await their turn.

A group of three stood in front of the counter. From their appearance, Rafa assumed they were a couple scheduled to get married and their required witness—a muscular guy wearing an ill-fitting suit, a curvaceous young woman in a red bandage dress, and a matronly-looking woman clad in a cream-colored pantsuit. But from the tight expression on their faces and the harsh-sounding whispers coming from all three, he thought they were better suited to an appearance before the divorce court.

Rafa tuned them out. It was none of his business. Vida, on the other hand, was looking on, listening intently, seemingly fascinated by the unfolding drama. She brought her phone out to text somebody. He resisted the urge to peek over her shoulder to see who she was sending a message to.

After five more minutes of awkwardness, the young couple passed by on their way out of the recorder's office. The middle-aged woman locked eyes with Vida for a few seconds before she, too, made her exit.

Rafa frowned. That was uncomfortable. He frowned more deeply when Vida stood and walked to the counter. Fearing she was canceling their appointment, he jumped to his feet to follow, but Vida turned around and held up her palm, asking him to wait.

Heart in his throat, he could only watch while she talked to the clerk. Vida's back covered his view of the other person, so he couldn't make out anything from their conversation.

"What's happening?" he asked when she returned to his side, pen in hand.

"Give me the prenup." She pointed to his messenger bag.

"You're signing?" Surprise and joy mingled in his voice.

Her eyes twinkled. "As soon as Tito Bert gets here. He's still somewhere in the building."

Smiling, he handed the papers to her. "What changed your mind?"

"The group that was just here? The dudebro was supposed to be marrying the mature woman, but he didn't want to sign a prenup. He was a scam artist, and the girl with him was her stepdaughter and his accomplice. They thought the older woman was naïve, but she was only playing along, trying to see how far they would take the con. Apparently, too far."

Whoa. His assumptions were off base. He'd thought the guy was marrying the girl, not the older lady. What a crook.

"I have one request," Vida said.

"Anything." He stepped closer and clasped her free hand.

"Let's get married today." She grinned. "The clerk said we can because the other appointment canceled."

His jaw dropped, but he recovered quickly. "Hell yeah," he all but shouted. "What inspired your change of heart?"

She squeezed their entwined hands. "I realized how silly I'm being. I trust you, Rafa. I thought I would show you that by not requiring a pre-marriage agreement. But you initiating the process when you didn't have to added to the million reasons why you're the only man I ever wanted to marry. I love you, Rafa. I'm in love with you. Our marriage will *not* fail."

"No, it won't. I love you, mi Vida. I love you so much." He enfolded her in his arms and hugged her tight. The kiss would have to wait until later. Until they were married. Officially.

The Rehearsal Dinner

Vida

Night Before the Wedding

"Hm-hm-hm-hm-hm-hmm." Vida elevated her legs to the empty chair on her left and hummed along to the refrain of "Forevermore," their first dance song. Her cousin Laceley was practicing it for the third time since the rehearsal dinner and get-together had started in the vineyard's tasting room. It had been a perfect rendition the first time, two hours ago, and every time since with breaks in between to eat and chat with family and friends. Someone took after their opera-singer great-grandmother, Agnes Moore, and it wasn't Vida.

Beside her, Rafa asked, "Are you tired?" With gentle hands, he rubbed her back, making her moan in sweet relief.

She rested her head against his shoulder. "A little bit." Between practicing her walking, kneeling, standing, and dancing, all her zen from the spa bridal shower this morning had disappeared.

"I'm kinda beat too." Rafa stretched his long legs out under the table.

Vida grinned. "Your round of golf bachelor party this morning wore you out?"

"It did. I'm not as fit as I used to be when I did physical training every day in the Air Force." He dropped a kiss on

537

her temple. "Do you want me to say our thank yous and end the evening now?"

Vida consulted her watch. It was only a few minutes past eight. "Not yet." She looked around the tasting room, at the tables where family and friends sat enjoying themselves with food and wine and convivial company. A more casual, more intimate gathering than tomorrow's grand extravaganza. "I'll be okay. And besides, some of our guests are still eating and dancing."

Several clicks drew her attention to the right. Their photographer, Roxie, had her pretty face almost entirely hidden behind the fancy camera she'd trained on Vida and Rafa.

"Say banana!"

The silly command surprised both her and Rafa into laughter.

"Gorgeous! You two look so wonderful together." She took several more shots before wandering away to take pictures of the other guests.

"You know who would look good with Roxie?" she whispered to Rafa.

"Who?"

"My nephew AJ." AJ was the son of Liza—Vida's first cousin from her father's side—and her Korean husband, Yae-Joon. Vida nodded her head in the direction of the bar where AJ stood staring at Roxie. There was history there. Liza wouldn't have recommended Roxie if she hadn't wanted to reconcile her son with his childhood sweetheart.

"Feeling bold with your matchmaking skills due to your success with Tallie and Pascal, are you?" Rafa teased.

"Your best man and my matron of honor are obviously made for each other." Vida searched the room for her oldest and dearest friend and saw her dancing with Rafa's best friend, who was also a doctor and an inventor of medical gadgets. Tallie's glowing face made Vida ecstatic. Three years was too long to grieve for the death of a philandering former husband. She deserved another chance at love. If Pascal was anything like Rafa, Tallie had a blissful life ahead.

"Just like us," he said, kissing her temple.

"You two are so disgustingly happy, I can't stand it."

Vida drew away from Rafa to peer at her friend Carrie, who stood in front of their table, one hand holding a glass, the other on her hip, eyes narrowed.

"What's wrong with being happy? We're getting married tomorrow," Rafa replied, amusement in his voice.

Despite the smile on her face, Carrie was pale and had a sheen of sweat at her hairline. Vida removed her legs from the chair. "Come, sit beside me. Nausea?" She didn't know much about being pregnant, but that symptom was obvious.

Carrie placed her glass and pack of crackers on the table and flopped down with a grimace. "I don't know why they call it 'morning sickness' when it strikes at all hours of the day."

Rafa moved to stand, but Vida stopped him with a hand clamped on his thigh. *Nuh-uh, buddy. We're in this together.*

"Don't mind me," Carrie said. "This will pass soon. I came here because I've been watching you two all day and I demand to know your secret."

Vida's head swiveled towards Rafa, who looked equally surprised. How did she know? They only had one witness. "Secret to what, exactly?" she probed.

"To your lack of stress. It's unnatural!"

Vida fought to keep from sagging in relief.

"Where's the conflict? The third-act breakup?" Carrie continued.

Vida let out a laugh. "I thought you were a romance author. Isn't the goal happily-ever-after or at least happy-for-now?"

"Yeah, but there must be some angst before that. I swear this is the smoothest wedding I've ever attended."

"Some romance stories are sweet, low-conflict, light on angst," Vida said.

"We had angst," Rafa chimed in. "There were production issues with the limited-edition red blend wine we intended to give away as wedding favors. Some people who were not on our list begged to be invited at the last minute. Our priest took ill, so we had to ask the bishop for a replacement only for him to volunteer to wed us himself. And the missalettes didn't make it to the rehearsal." He gave Vida a nod to continue.

"Oh. Some of the dresses needed to be altered." As soon as she said it, Vida cringed. Carrie was her veil sponsor, one of the four women she'd had dresses made for.

"Right. Blame the woman with the bun in the oven for increasing." Carrie rubbed her barely-there bump and stuck out her tongue.

The comical gesture and light tone assured Vida her friend hadn't taken offense, so she continued. "Early this week, meteorologists forecasted rain for tomorrow."

Carrie finished her drink, which Vida assumed was ginger ale, before asking, "Did you ask your relatives in the Philippines to offer eggs to Saint Clare?"

"Naturally." Many Filipinos believed in approaching the poor nuns from the Monasterio de Santa Clara in Quezon City to help pray for good weather with an offering of a dozen eggs as payment.

"It seemed to have worked because the forecast now calls for a high of eighty-two, low of fifty-one, zero percent chance of rain," Rafa said.

"See? Smoothest wedding ever!" Carrie stood up abruptly. "Gotta go."

Vida rose to accompany her in case she puked again, but her friend pointed a finger at her to sit back down.

"It's just my bladder. Stay and canoodle."

Vida thought she saw a glimmer of tears in her friend's eyes before she fled. Was it because she was missing her baby daddy and seeing Vida and Rafa's happiness made her envious? This wasn't right. She should call Carrie's sister, Robyn, to find that Josh guy. Carrie shouldn't be all alone tomorrow. Everyone should be as happy on her wedding day as Vida and her husband.

She twisted in her seat to look up at Rafa. "I'm glad we got married already. Just the two of us." She gave him a brief kiss on the lips, conscious of the many eyes on them.

Last week's impromptu civil wedding at the city hall had turned out to be a blessing in disguise. The fact that she and Rafa were already legally wed allowed them to keep their cool despite countless stressors, only some of which they'd told Carrie. One of them being the Catholic Church not recognizing their marriage as valid until after the ceremony tomorrow—it had been turned into a convalidation. The consequence of their carpe diem moment was not receiving communion. Which, in the grand scheme of things, wasn't too bad.

"And Tito Bert." Rafa waved to her uncle-by-marriage, their sole witness.

Vida waved as well. "I really appreciate him keeping it a secret from the family."

"That's why we're paying him the big bucks."

She laughed. Last weekend, she'd retained her uncle to help her update her last will and testament. Tito Bert charged favored family members one penny. "I love my family." She clasped Rafa's hand. "And I adore yours. Roger and Mika are relationship goals." Rafa's brother and sister-in-law had been married for twenty-five years but still behaved like newlyweds.

"They're my example. I hope we last twice as long as them."

"I'd be one hundred and you ninety. Are we even still alive by then?"

"It could happen. Exhibit A: Lola Naty."

They both turned to where her one-hundred-year-old grandmother sat in her wheelchair, yawning.

"Oof! That's my signal. Time to say our goodnights." Rafa stood and did just that.

The Wedding Ceremony

Rafa

Rafa's eyes blurred as the stunning vision of his bride glided towards the altar. Towards him. *Ba-bump, ba-bump.* His heartbeat thumped against his chest, pumping double time, it seemed to him. Vida was beautiful every day, but today she was radiant. The thin blusher veil over her face couldn't dim the megawatt smile she directed at him. The stretch on his cheekbones told him he had an answering smile as wide as hers. The gold beads on her ivory Filipiniana gown glittered in the light with her every step, oddly out of sync with the rhythm of the song, "Entra En Mi Vida," that she'd chosen for her entrance. She was hurrying towards him.

He couldn't wait any longer. He stepped down two steps to meet her before she reached the front pews.

With her eyes still locked to his, Vida gave her bouquet to Tallie. They reached for each other's hands at the same time. Rafa guided her up the steps and around the padded bench until they stood facing each other.

Although it wasn't what they rehearsed yesterday, he lifted her veil. "Hi," he greeted his bride for the first time today. Tradition had them not seeing each other until her entrance to the chapel just now. Nearly twenty hours. Much too long.

"Hi," she said, beaming up at him.

Satisfied, they turned to face their officiant, the bishop, who was smiling indulgently at them.

In a booming baritone, he intoned, "My dear family and friends, we are gathered here today to witness the beginning of a new life of togetherness for Rafael and Vida. Let us unite our hearts and minds with them as we pray that joy and peace be theirs and remain with them all the days of their lives."

Rafa kept Vida's right hand in his left as they followed along the rituals of the mass. His mind drifted, silently practicing the words of his upcoming vows. He and Vida had composed them together, but they hadn't printed them in the missalette, preferring to memorize the words rather than read them. He'd rehearsed them many times last night and this morning, but he was still afraid he'd forget everything.

Vida squeezed his hand. He glanced questioningly at her. She nodded in the direction of the dais, to Nick, who was the lector. "This is my favorite reading."

Rafa looked down at the missalette. A reading from the First Letter of Paul to the Corinthians. He followed along as Nick read aloud.

"'If I have not love, I am nothing. Love is patient and kind; love is not jealous, or conceited or proud; love is not ill-mannered, or selfish or irritable. Love does not keep a record of wrongs; love is not happy with evil but it is happy with truth. Love never gives up: its faith, hope and patience never fail. Love is eternal.'"

Beautiful. He raised their joined hands to his lips and kissed her knuckles.

After his thankfully short homily, the bishop addressed the congregation. "May we ask Roger and Mika to light the candles. These burning candles symbolize the life that

Rafael and Vida will live together. Father, you are the light of the world. Bless them, so that they may be light to each other."

Rafa smiled at his brother and sister-in-law. He really appreciated them coming all the way from Florida. To his shame, it had been five years since he'd last visited. He should take Vida to visit them soon. Maybe after Christmas this year.

"Rafael and Vida, since you wish to enter into the contract of Holy Matrimony, please join your right hands and express your intentions before God and His Church," the bishop instructed.

He switched hands as directed.

"Vida, do you take Rafael to be your lawful husband according to the rites of our Holy Mother the Church?"

"I do," his bride's voice rang out clearly.

Rafa blinked. She'd changed the response. It was supposed to be *Yes, Father*. He liked her answer better.

"Do you give yourself to him as his wife?"

"I do."

The bishop turned to him. "Rafael, do you take Vida to be your lawful wife according to the rites of our Holy Mother the Church?"

"I do."

"Do you give yourself to her as her husband?"

"I do."

"You may say your vows."

Rafa felt a fluttering in his stomach. *This is it.*

"Mi Vida, my life. Today, I offer myself to you as your husband. Allow me to stay with you for the rest of my years. As your best friend, your confidant, as your lifelong companion. I will celebrate the wonders of life with you, laughing and loving, and will remain by your side, holding your hand whenever the days seem dark and bleak. I will honor you as my partner and equal in all things." He paused and wet his lips.

"Te amo. I love you. I always have and I always will. I'm looking forward to a life with you, filled with joy and laughter and the occasional tear. I'm ready to love you all the days of my life. Now and forever, I promise to love you to the best of my abilities, to my dying day. Accept me as your husband and partner for life."

Vida beamed at him. Her voice was strong and confident in her own vows. "Rafa, today I offer myself to you as your wife. Accept me as your best friend and partner for all the remaining days of my life. I will rejoice with you in the face of life's glorious blessings and support you in the face of its greatest challenges. Mahal na mahal kita. I love and cherish you for who you are now and who you will be in the future. Together, we will laugh and cry, listen and learn, give and forgive, live and prosper as two hearts and souls united in love. Accept me as your wife and partner for life."

Rafa fought the urge to kiss her right there and then. He settled for pressing his forehead to hers. Their guests awwed and clapped.

"Are we done yet?" he whispered.

"Not yet. Soon," she promised.

He knew it wasn't going to be soon. There were still a lot of rituals—the lighting of the unity candle came next plus more reading from the great prayer book. This was important to Vida, so it was important to him as well.

He perked up when Nick said, "May we now ask the best man and matron of honor to please come forward." Pascal and Tallie brought the rings and arrhae to the altar.

The bishop raised his hands over the items. "Bless O Lord these rings so that your children, Rafael and Vida who wear them, may remain faithful and loyal to each other, abide in your peace and favor, and live together until their lives end. Through Jesus Christ our Lord."

"Amen," the gathering responded.

The bishop held out the jewelries to them. "Now give these rings to each other."

Rafa took the bejeweled gold band that matched her engagement ring and said, "Vida, wear this ring as a sign of my lifelong love and fidelity to you. In the name of the Father, and of the Son, and of the Holy Spirit." His hand shook slightly as he slipped the ring onto her finger.

"Rafa, wear this ring as a sign of my lifelong love and fidelity to you. In the name of the Father, and of the Son, and of the Holy Spirit." Vida's delivery was smoother than his but her voice had gone husky with emotion. She was as affected by the ritual as he was.

He looked down at the plain gold band on his fourth finger with a sense of wonder. *This.* This was one of the things that made this ceremony special. This was what was missing during their impromptu civil wedding. He gazed at his gorgeous bride who was beaming up at him. She deserved all this pomp and pageantry. He was glad he could give her this.

The bishop caught their attention with his next words. "We shall now bless your arrhae, which symbolize the responsibilities of married life. We pray that you will live up to them, in God's will, throughout your journey together. Bless O Lord your children, Rafael and Vida, with sufficiency of material possession which they may use to attain eternal life, through Christ our Lord."

Rafa hadn't attended many weddings, but he knew this part was unique to Filipino and Hispanic ceremonies. "Vida, I give you these arrhae as a pledge of my total dedication to you and constant concern for your welfare. In the name of the Father, and of the Son, and of the Holy Spirit." The thirteen coins inside jiggled as he handed the heart-shaped golden box to Vida.

"Rafa, I accept your pledge. Likewise, I pledge my dedication to you and constant concern for you. In the name of the Father, and of the Son, and of the Holy Spirit." She placed the box on a white pillow that sat atop the wide ledge of their pew.

The bishop opened his arms wide and boomed, "Brothers and sisters in Christ, we have just witnessed the solemn union of Rafael and Vida. Let us now welcome them into their new life as husband and wife." Applause erupted from the congregation.

Rafa jolted. Was that it? Time to kiss the bride? But they were only halfway through the missalette. He leafed through it and groaned inwardly. Prayers of the faithful, laying of the veil and cord, offertory, liturgy of the Eucharist, consecration, communion rite, all before the nuptial rite. They had breezed through these during rehearsals without all the proper words. *Sigh.*

Nick called on Vida's friend and her favorite nephew to come forward. "May we request Carrie and Carlo to lay the veil."

Rafa and Vida lowered to the padded kneeler in unison. He slid his arm behind her and discreetly massaged her left hip. She wore comfortable shoes with customized inserts, but he knew prolonged standing put a strain on her body.

"Thank you," she whispered.

The bishop read from the missalette. "Rafael and Vida, clothe yourselves with love, compassion and kindness, gentleness, and patience. Be tolerant with each other, and forgive each other as the Lord has forgiven you."

Once the veil was draped over Vida's head and Rafa's shoulders, Nick called on the next sponsors. "May we request Cindy and Jake to join you together with the cord which symbolizes the ultimate unity that the love of God has bestowed upon you."

Vida's cousin and Rafa's nephew looped the gold cord over their heads and shoulders.

"May your love grow stronger and bind you closer to each other through the years," the bishop prayed.

When the communion part came, Rafa let out a sigh.

Vida nudged him. "We're almost done."

"You said that two hours ago." He exaggerated. Not by much.

She giggled. "It's true. There's only the removal of the veil and cord, prayer after communion, and then the final blessings. Ten minutes tops."

"You promise?"

Vida's eyes twinkled as she said, "I do."

He wanted to kiss her, but it wasn't time yet.

Finally, the bishop signaled for them to stand. "Rafael and Vida, you have pledged love, fidelity, and welfare to each other and together, offered yourselves to God in marriage. So, before God and His community, I now pronounce you husband and wife. You may kiss the bride."

"Thanks be to God. Been waiting for this since the exchange of the arras," Rafa whispered to his wife before capturing her lips in a long kiss that elicited cheers and applause from their guests and the bishop.

The Wedding Reception

Vida

"Thank you, Santa Clara and Poor Clares." Vida uttered a short prayer of gratitude even as she touched the horseshoe charm on her bouquet. She didn't know who or what was responsible for the phenomenal weather they'd been blessed with, but she was thankful to them, nonetheless.

She leaned her head back against Rafa's shoulder as they stood beneath the floral arch by the entrance of the patio, waiting for the reception to begin. The sun had set ten minutes ago, but the torches and thousands of fairy lights along with the three-quarter moon illuminated the huge patio area overlooking the vineyards as if it were still daytime.

The scent of ripe grapes ready for harvest on Monday combined with the heady perfume of flowers permeated the air that was the best kind of chilly. With the bejeweled, well-dressed guests milling about, looking for their tables and greeting each other, the scene resembled a glossy magazine spread.

"It's spectacular, Vee," Rafa said from behind her, giving voice to the admiration she felt about the setting of their celebration dinner.

"Eden and Violet did a wonderful job. I'll have to send more business their way. Give kudos to Gabriella and the hacienda's staff, too."

He gave her shoulder a light squeeze. "It's you. You created all of this. With incredibly talented support, yes, but it was you who conceptualized and pulled everything together."

A flush of pleasure surged through her. "Thank you, Raf." She turned her head to press a kiss to his lips. She loved that he saw her, that he appreciated everything she did for their relationship.

The microphone on the stand in front of the raised platform gave out a noisy screech as Sophie clicked the on switch.

"Good evening and welcome to the reception in honor of our newlyweds, Vida and Rafa. I am so thrilled to be your emcee for tonight. For those of you who don't know, I'm Sophie Palacio, better known as the first cousin to the gorgeous bride. I also host a little podcast called *She Vibes*, but that's neither here nor there."

Applause and hoots greeted her cousin's introduction. A popular sex podcaster, Sophie was well-known throughout the country.

Sophie continued, "I have the absolute privilege of introducing everyone sharing this momentous day. Yes, I'm talking about all of you! When I call on your family or company, please stand up." Sophie proceeded to name each group of invited guests—the Moores, the Balmasedas, the Sorianos, the Sutcliffe-Frasers, the Aquinos, the winemakers, the medical personnel from Rafa's practice, the military, etcetera.

"If you look at your place setting, you'll see streamers," Sophie said. "Use them to shower the bride and groom with every single ounce of your love, affection, and good vibes. This has been an awesome wedding, and we want to make memories that will last forever … memories we can look back on and cherish. Now, allow me to introduce the hottest couple this side of Napa … Mr. and Mrs. Rafa and Vida Balmaseda!"

"Show time," Rafa said. He clasped her hand tightly and they walked in to the sight of shiny tinsel and the sound of thunderous applause that nearly drowned out the ratatat of drumrolls. They stopped to kiss Lola Naty's cheek and handed Vida's bouquet to Tallie before going to the middle of the floor.

Sophie waited until the noise died down before she read from her cue card again. "The first dance at a wedding reception is truly something special. This moment will be as romantic and memorable as the ceremony and the exchange of vows that preceded it. It is an expression of a new unity—together, the bride and groom circle the floor as one to a song that has a significant meaning to both of them. To serenade the couple with the song 'Forevermore,' please welcome Laceley Hizon."

Vida flowed into Rafa's waiting arms. They swayed slowly to the popular Filipino song her grandmother had played on repeat as a not-so-subtle hint for them to choose it. They barely moved around. While Vida had been able to detach the stiff butterfly sleeves from her gown to free her arms, her mermaid skirt and train did not allow for big steps, despite the long slit on the left side. Bubbles blown into the air by the entourage floated around them as they danced. She mouthed the lyrics, agreeing completely with the words about needing only that one person to be with, their love staying with them forevermore.

Laceley's voice drifted like the bubbles in the air to the end of the romantic song.

Vida and Rafa started the applause. More for Laceley and the band than for themselves.

"We will now proceed with our bridal ceremonies. We would like to ask the couple to slice and taste their wedding cake, which in this instance is the pair's favorite Irish cream cake."

She and Rafa stood in front of the three-tiered cake that was iced with gold buttercream and decorated with burgundy, white, and pink edible paper flowers. Their hands, wrapped around a cutter, posed over the second layer. Roxie fluttered around them, taking pictures. They cut a small wedge and laughingly fed each other tiny bites.

"The center of the wedding feast is the cake. The history of the wedding cake goes back to ancient Rome, whereby the groom would break a thin loaf of bread over the bride's head." Sophie paused. "Sure glad we don't do that anymore," she ad-libbed, making everyone laugh.

"Over time, the wedding cake has become a special food that a bride and groom share, not only with one another to symbolize their love, but also with their guests, representing the closeness they feel to them. The cake will be served as dessert later. Yum. For now, dinner will be served." Sophie ended her spiel with a flourish.

Rafa pulled out Vida's chair behind the table especially set for them on the raised platform. She tucked her skirt beneath her before sitting down.

"Finally," Vida muttered. "I'm starving." The cake was yum, like Sophie said, but she wanted real food. She offered a grateful smile to the server who brought the first course.

"Vee, you've eaten today, right?" Rafa asked in his stern doctor voice.

"I had lunch, but then I put on my makeup early for photos, and friends came in and out of my suite at the hotel for a quick visit." One of them was Holly. Vida hadn't seen Sophie's childhood playmate since she was eleven, nineteen years ago. There was an ethereal quality about the young nurse that intrigued her. Something otherworldly. She kept feeling a sense of déjà vu during that visit.

"Well, eat properly. Ruby and Mason delivered again—these chicken adobo skewers are delicious."

"Yes, Doctor Bal," she teased him.

He leaned closer to whisper, "Wait until tonight when I get you all alone. I will do a thorough physical examination."

Heat rose in her cheeks. "Promises, promises." But seriously, she couldn't wait for her wedding night, to employ some of the racier gifts she'd received from her friends and family yesterday at the bridal shower.

As she ate, Vida looked out at the guests who had joined Rafa and her in tonight's celebration. The majority seemed to be enjoying the sumptuous dinner—a fusion of Filipino, Spanish, and American cuisines—that Ruby, Mason, and Cole had prepared. If they didn't, well, too bad. There was only so much they could do to accommodate all sorts of dietary requests from over two hundred diners.

Lola appeared happy. Rafa was content. And Vida was ecstatic about how everything had turned out so far. She might be selfish, but at the end of the day, that was all that mattered.

After dessert, Sophie went back to the microphone. "We will now ask Ate Vida and Kuya Rafa to toast and drink the ceremonial wine which affirms the bond between the Moore and Balmaseda families, solemnized during the wedding. It also represents the full support and blessings of both families for the couple's new life together."

Both of them sipped. They didn't plan to get intoxicated by anything but each other.

"The Matron of Honor is the person closest to the bride. May we call on Tallie to toast the couple?" Sophie said.

Tallie said nice things about Vida, starting from the time they were children until now. They had met when they were both thirteen. Newly arrived from the Philippines, Tallie was brought over by her stepfather who was Hacienda Luz's vineyard foreman at the time. They'd become best friends, inseparable until Tallie moved away to Taos after the death of her husband. Now she was back, with a burgeoning romance. Maybe she'd stay. Vida would try her hardest to convince her.

She blew kisses Tallie's way when her toast ended.

"Likewise, the best man will give his own toast: Pascal," Sophie called out.

Rafa's best friend was suave and funny. Vida caught admiring glances thrown Pascal's way. She wanted to shout, *Sorry, ladies. He's already taken.* She hoped he and Tallie would make a go of it, just like her and Rafa.

Sophie took to the microphone again when Pascal stepped away. "The bride and groom will have their pictures taken with the guests in the gazebo area."

Vida asked for chairs for her and Rafa in the gazebo. Even though her shoes were flat and custom made to accommodate her imbalance, she wouldn't last fifteen minutes standing.

The picture-taking took more than half an hour. By the time the last group left, Vida was ready to drop facedown onto a bed. But there were more activities—she knew this because she was the one who'd drawn up tonight's program.

And the next of those activities was the bouquet toss. Rafa escorted her back to the dais while Sophie called for the single ladies to gather in the middle. He stood to the side to await his turn.

Vida removed the horseshoe charm from her bouquet and placed it in the pocket of her dress. Pockets! She had hugged her niece Bernadette so tight when she had discovered the hidden gift. It was so clever.

She peeked over her shoulder to wink at the hopefuls before turning her back and letting the bouquet fly. Shrieks filled the air as the women jockeyed for position. After the commotion, Ava Maldonado held the beautiful arrangement of roses, peonies, and sampaguita up in triumph.

Vida raised an eyebrow at her mentee's unbridled joy, as if Ava was fully expecting to be the next one to get married. She didn't know Ava was involved with anyone. Was it her rival winemaker, Sebastian Russo, who she came here with? Hmm.

At Roxie's signal, she stepped off the platform. No need to speculate when she could ask outright during the picture taking. To her delight, Ava was candid about her blossoming romance.

Curiosity satisfied, she returned to Rafa who beckoned her to sit on the chair he'd placed at the front of the platform. Time for the garter toss.

Everyone hooted when her husband made a show of slowly parting the edges of her dress on her left leg to reveal the stretchy lace at the top of her thigh. His eyes held all sorts of naughty promises as he bit down gently on the garter to pull it off her. She shivered in response. Oh, she would take him up on all those promises tonight and every night, all right.

Rafa got to his feet and, without wasting any time, threw the garter back towards the gathered men.

Vida trained her gaze on Ava and saw her joy when Sebastian snatched the white lace out of thin air. "Yes!"

"The couple would like to wish Ava and Sebastian all the best in their relationship and hope to attend their wedding soon," Sophie enthused to the guests' delight.

Taking advantage of the distraction created by the new couple, Vida faced her husband. "You"—standing, she poked Rafa on his barong-clad chest—"are a tease."

Smiling unrepentantly, he encircled her waist with his arms and brought her flush against his body. "And you are so sexy. When can we get out of here? I want to …" He bent to whisper in her ear, "… consummate our marriage soon."

Vida couldn't stop the moan that escaped her throat. Heat flooded her senses. She wanted that too. Wanted to make love to her husband all night long. For them to consummate their ceremonial wedding as passionately as they had their civil one last week. But they couldn't yet. Her voice husky with desire, she whispered back, "After this next dance, we'll make our escape."

"Promise?" Rafa asked.

She nodded. "Promise."

The tinkling of forks against glasses penetrated their cocoon of intimacy. "Kiss! Kiss!"

They gladly obliged, fusing their mouths together in their hunger for closer contact. Conscious of the public nature of their display, Vida cupped Rafa's stubble-laden jaw to cool his ardor. "More later."

He groaned and pressed his forehead to hers. "Last dance," he growled.

Vida turned her head towards Sophie, mouthing, "Money Dance."

Her cousin stepped up to the microphone and announced her prepared spiel. "And now, it is time for the Money Dance, a tradition in both Filipino and Cuban weddings. Here's how we're going to do this: Cindy and Jake will hold out the unity veil that was draped over our bride and groom earlier. Those who wish to contribute to the couple's charity fund will pin their bills or red envelopes to it. There is also a QR code that you can click on to transfer cash electronically. Please give generously, as Kuya Rafa and Ate Vida will match the total amount collected and distribute the proceeds to worthy causes when they go to the Philippines for their honeymoon."

Vida wrapped her arms over Rafa's shoulders as they swayed to the swing ballad classic the band started playing. She had felt his tension ease with every word Sophie said about their unique twist on the tradition.

"This is a lovely song," Rafa said, his lips grazing her temple. He rested his hands lightly on her waist. "Not your typical Money Dance song. I'm glad you chose it instead of a modern one."

"'Moonlight Serenade.' Lola Naty told me she and Grandda Robert danced to this song at their wedding reception. I thought it would be a nice tribute to them and their beautiful love story."

She glanced at her grandmother, who sat in her wheelchair with her eyes closed, a blissful smile on her lined but still striking face. Did the music touch a chord? Was she reminiscing? Vida hoped so.

Rafa was looking in the same direction. "They must have been an exceptional couple."

Vida leaned her cheek against her husband's shoulder, tears pricking her eyelids. "They were amazing. For over sixty years, they loved. Not only endured, but thrived.

Raising their children, raising me, growing this place into what it is today."

She reached for his hand and pressed hers to his, palm to palm. "I pray our love will last as long as theirs."

Rafa held her tighter. "I guarantee you our love will last for as long as we both live and maybe, hopefully, even beyond."

They kissed. Tender yet passionate. An affirmation and a lifelong commitment.

With thoughts of love for always.

Of love forevermore.

THE END

About Maida Malby

Filipino American author Maida Malby crafts foodie, multicultural, and contemporary destination romance stories filled with heat, sizzle, spice, and a whole lot of love.

She is an administrator and member of select writing groups and romance book clubs. Her To-Be-Read Mountain and book reviews are featured on her blog Carpe Diem Chronicles at maidamalby.com. Subscribe to her newsletter (maidamalby.com/newsletter) to receive updates on upcoming releases, book promotions, signing events, and advance review copy opportunities.

Book List:

Boracay Vows - books2read.com/Boracay-Vows

New York Engagement –
books2read.com/NewYorkEngagement

Global City Tryst – books2read.com/GlobalCityTryst

Singapore Fling – books2read.com/SingaporeFling

Island Kisses – newsletter exclusive

Pasko Na, My Love –
books2read.com/PaskoNaMyLove

Forevermore – books2read.com/Forevermore

Social Media IDs:

Facebook - @maidamalbyauthor

Instagram - @maidamalbyauthor

Threads - @maidamalbyauthor

X (Twitter) - @MaidaMalby

LinkedIn – Maida Malby

Bluesky – @maidamalby.bsky.social

BookBub – maida-malby

Goodreads – Maida_Malby

Acknowledgments

Special thanks to Shelley Gonzalez London and Celeste Gonzalez de Bustamante of the Filipino American National Historical Society (FANHS), Central Valley Chapter, for sharing their knowledge and expertise.

~ Mia Hopkins

I would like to extend my everlasting gratitude to Maida Malby - the mastermind and the lead Kwentita behind these amazing anthologies. Thanks to the rest of the Kwentitas - Maan, Tif, Mia, Sarah, June, Aurora, Kaye, and Liz - for their support and for their beautiful, awe-inspiring stories. Also deserving of many thanks is my editor Lyss, who has been one of the most reliable people I have ever worked with. Last but not least, thank you to my loving husband Oliver, and my wonderful kids Sean and Maddie.

~ Elle Cruz

To my dad who now shines on me from above, I miss you. I hope you and Mama are proud of me up there.

To my husband and daughter, I love you both so much.

To my writer and reader friends, thank you for lending me your light during this dark moment in my life.

To the Kwentitas, thank you for your kindness and support. I don't think I have ever felt more inspired and welcomed than I have been with you all. I will forever be your biggest supporter and cheerleader. Thank you for welcoming me with open arms. I am beyond grateful to be in the presence of your greatness.

And lastly, to Chef Clay, I owe you the life I have now. Thank you for saving me in more ways than one.

~ Kaye Rockwell

To Chris and Jack, thank you for every moment – for every hug, and every kiss, for every tear and smile and sorrow. Thank you for the love. Because of you my life is filled with joy. To my mom who let me dream and fly and soar, you are the reason I tell stories. To Maida and all the Kwentitas, thank you for pulling me into your fold. And to you, reading this, you have my heart. I am grateful for you. Always.

~ Maan Gabriel

Thank you to my family and friends for your ongoing support as I go for my dreams. To my Kwentitas, I'm so happy that you all came into my life and I can call you my friends.

~ Aurora Paige

A million thank yous to those who made this story possible, most especially to: Mark, Mia, and Abi, who always put up with me when I go into writer mode. Maida and the Kwentitas, for wrapping an arm around my shoulders and gathering me into the fold. Trish and Mars, for your enthusiasm and feedback. And to the family, who always show support no matter what.

~ June Gray

My gratitude to Maida Malby and the rest of the Kwentitas who inspire me everyday with your friendship and kindness.

~ Liz Durano

Thank you so much to my family, friends, and readers for their support. And huge thanks to the Kwentitas! Love you all to bits!

~ Sarah Smith

My first and greatest thanks to Maida Malby for spearheading this project—I'm so honored to be part of it! All my love to my dearest husband and children who continue to support me despite Qdoba and Chinese food dinners on repeat in order to make my deadlines. Finally, hugs and kisses to readers who make this dream possible! Mahal kita!

~ Tif Marcelo

My biggest thanks go to my husband. If I hadn't married him all those years ago, I wouldn't have been able to write three chapters of my story or be a Romance Author at all.

I'm thankful to my son, whose golf practices get me out of the writing cave to catch some sun and fresh air.

Salamat to my Kwentitas for trusting me with their beautiful stories. They are all a joy to work with and I am grateful I get to call them friends.

Another friend I'm thankful to is Linda Hill, my editor. I would not get anything published without her tremendous clean-up skills.

To Vania Hardy, huge thanks for creating a truly one-of-a-kind artwork for our cover that showcases the beauty of our Filipino culture.

And to my VA Jannie, salamuch for taking care of myriad tasks that would have bogged me down if I had to do them myself.

~ Maida Malby

And you, Dear Readers. We are all immensely grateful for your support of our work. In purchasing, reviewing, and recommending our books. In engaging with us on social media. Maraming salamat!

~ The Kwentitas